# The Hidebehind

Charley Snellings

Copyright © 2005 Charles H. Snellings

Cover art by Jennifer Campbell-Escobedo

All rights reserved. No part of this book may be reproduced or transmitted in any form or by any means, electronic or mechanical, including photocoyping, recording, or by any information storage and retrieval system, without written permission from the author.

This is a work of fiction. Names, characters, places, and incidents either are the product of the author's imagination or are used fictitiously. Any resemblance to actual persons, living or dead, events, or locales is entirely coincidental.

ISBN: 978-1-84728-782-3

Printed by Lulu.com

## ACKNOWLEDGMENTS

It takes a village to write a book; at least it did for my first novel. And the first person in my village, to hear or help with editing, was my son, Jackson. Without his encouragement, I might have thought, "Why am I doing this?" For a boy of 13 (at the time) he had remarkable honesty when it came to telling me what worked or what didn't. Thanks to my daughter, Sara, for her love and unflagging moral support in all my writing efforts. As a child, she spent countless hours listening as I read story after story.

I believe, however, that I wouldn't have finished without the editing and support from my parents: Betty and Don Snellings. Because they have always been there for me, and because they loved the story, I kept striving to make it better.

Other people who were indispensable: Kassia Dellabough, my best friend and captive listener, along with the Hamm House literary group featuring Junee Seegert and numerous other patient listeners. They liked the story, as did my earlier readers: northwest river guides, Greg Pierson and James "Izzy" Whetstine. as well as long-time friend Marshelle Backes. A heartfelt thanks to James Ruch, author and friend, and probably the best class-six river guide in West Virginia…thanks for the inspiration and the editing help. Special thanks go to my whitewater mentor, Skeeter Johnson, River Guru extraordinaire, for sharing his wealth of knowledge with me and for inviting me on some great adventures.

Elizabeth Lyon's Wednesday Night Reading Group and the early incarnation of The Write Guys: John Dewitz, Doug Wise, Bill Lynch, Jerry Wolfe, and numerous others over the years.

The Oregon Writer's Colony is one of the best ideas and most generous gifts I've discovered for writers and quite a few chapters were edited or rewritten there. A huge thank you goes out to my unpaid writing coach and literary writer, Patty Hyatt—thanks for turning me on to the poetry of William Stafford and the *hot word* writing technique.

I want to thank Meredith Bernstein of the Meredith Bernstein Literary Agency in New York for her efforts to sell this story in an earlier incarnation.

Elizabeth Lyon, owner of Lyon's Literary Services has to be the best book doctor west of the Mississippi. She edited the book in its early stages and gave me my first reality check in regards to what it would take to get a raw story into one that could be published. Her encouragement and help over the years was invaluable to my growth, as a writer and a person.

And thanks to Eliza Drummond for her help in formatting this book as well as cover artist, Jennifer Campbell-Escobedo for sharing her talent.

The last edit of this book was probably the most thorough in regards to logic. My fiancée and life partner, Lisan, intuitively found logic problems that I had missed for years. She is a natural writer/editor and her help and enthusiasm for the story has been instrumental in making things finally come together.

If I overlooked anyone, I apologize. Thanks to you all.

# The Hidebehind

Charley Snellings

# 1

## WHITE RIVER, IDAHO

The incessant barking of Harold Brittain's dog woke him from a sound sleep, but it was the agonized yelp that brought him fully conscious. He stumbled to his bedroom window. *Nothing.* It was too dark to see anything except the vague outline of the barn and the quick-moving shadows of his horses.

"What's wrong, Harold?" His wife, Jean, asked from their bed.

"Something's out there."

He pulled on his Levis and made his way to his gun safe in the bedroom closet where he hurriedly worked the combination. The door opened, and he reached for the twelve-gauge shotgun but had second thoughts and grabbed his high-powered rifle instead: a .375 H&H magnum, capable of stopping a charging elephant. *Damn sure stop a bear.*

"Careful now, you don't know what it is," His wife, Jean, said, her voice a pitch higher than usual.

"Don't worry, Hon, I'll stay inside until I see what it is." He held up the rifle. "This'll stop anything on the damn planet."

He shoved several huge bullets into the rifle's open breech, then kissed her on the cheek and stepped into the hallway. It was dark, but not so dark that he couldn't make his way. He heard noises rising from outside that sounded like screams from animals in a burning barn.

"Daddy?"

He glanced to his right and made out the small figure of his daughter, Christa, standing in her doorway. Beyond her, his eldest daughter, Karen, stood rubbing her eyes.

"You girls go get in with your mother. Hurry now!"

They ran down the hall closing the bedroom door behind them. His family was safe. Now he could go downstairs.

He eased his weight onto the top step and looked down on the empty landing below. The smell of last night's trout wafted up from the kitchen.

As he descended he took each step carefully. Watching. Listening. At the bottom of the stairs, he stopped. The recliner chairs appeared as shadows from what little light came through the living-room windows; the pictures hung at the proper angles. Several pairs of shoes sat by the front door. Everything looked normal.

The horses reclaimed his attention as they shrieked wildly; then, one by one the horses' cries were silenced. The hair on the nape of Harold's neck stood like hackles on a Ridgeback.

Quiet set in like a fog. He crept to the front window, peering toward the corral. For a moment the darkness prevented him from seeing past the driveway. Then, the moon shone through a break in the clouds, temporarily painting the barnyard in a silver blue light.

Five horses lay in dark pools, including Sugar, his daughter's mare. In the pen, sheep carcasses were scattered like broken eggs.

A glint of moonlight on metal just beyond the front steps jolted him back from the window, and he shouldered the rifle. He gasped. There on the ground, facing him was the sprawled body of his border collie, Bounder, staring up at him with lifeless eyes.

The moon slipped back into the clouds, and the macabre picture vanished.

Creaking came from the back porch, then—the tinkle of glass—followed by a whisper of cool, night air. Clutching the rifle, he crept to the kitchen door.

"Harold! What is happening down there?" Jean called out from the bedroom.

"Be quiet—I—" He froze.

The outside door stood wide open. Looking to his right he saw the saloon doors still swinging back and forth.

A path of muddy spots across the kitchen floor connected the two open doors.

Suddenly a reek, like a combination of rotten meat, cinnamon, and fish released a taste in the back of his throat as if he were sucking on an old penny. His hands shook.

Behind him, the floor creaked. He spun, frantically searching behind him. Nothing. He faced each direction before running to the base of the stairs and

# CHAPTER ONE

flipping the light-switch. The paintings on the wall still hung at the proper angles. He backed up the stairs, keeping the gun pointed at the space below him.

"Get out of my house, you son-of-a-bitch, or I'm gonna blow your fucking brains out!" He waited for a reaction.

"Jean, Call 911," he shouted over his left shoulder.

*I'll get to the top of the stairs and stand guard.* He knew it would take the sheriff a good half hour to get to the farm.

He reached the landing and turned to climb the remaining stairs. In mid-step a vice tightened on his right ankle. An inhuman force yanked him off his feet and completely through the wooden railing; his body ripping out several of the lathed banisters. He plummeted eight feet and landed flat on his back with a sickening thud. The rifle discharged upon impact, blowing his VCR into hundreds of small plastic chunks.

Barely conscious, Harold's entire body pulsed with a dull flame. The smell of cordite and gunpowder mixed with the other horrid odors.

"Oh God!" He wanted to work the bolt-action and prepare another round, but instead succumbed to raw fear. He looked up and saw what he instinctively recognized as death.

## SOUTHERN OREGON

The yellow lifejacket surged to the top of a huge wave at Old Bushwacker Rapid. Bobby Aldrich hit the same wave seconds later. He could barely see the lifejacket through his tears. Just its bright yellow color, that was all of the kid that was visible.

He figured the boy was probably dead, but still he raced after him. Mile after mile, he ran dangerous rapids with reckless abandon as he chased the young boater whose name he didn't even know.

Although his gut ached, and his arms burned from rowing like a madman, Bobby didn't slow his strokes. He remained focused on the blurry, yellow form ahead.

The river slowed, and he gained on the lifejacket. Finally, he could make out the farmer-john wetsuit as the body meandered into an eddy just above the site for the proposed dam.

Bobby had recently led a group of 300 whitewater enthusiasts in a letter-writing campaign to save the mighty Upper Klamath from a group of profiteers. Now, here at that same spot, he rowed a raft he had commandeered to chase the body of a young rafter he had just killed.

Bobby felt as if an arrow had impaled him as he pushed the oars through the final twenty yards. The water seemed thicker, as if the river had a will of its own and wanted to keep the kid as a prize.

He jumped forward, grabbed the boy and rolled him over. The young man looked about eighteen years old with hair long and brown, and a small silver barbell pierced his left eyebrow. His hazel eyes were open, and his throat had a dark black line across it, the exact same width as Bobby's rescue rope. Blood droplets leaked out along the mark.

Bobby had seen the boy earlier, and watched as the kid spun completely out of control through Caldera Rapids.

"Why were you on this river! You had no business here!" he screamed. Grasping the boy's lifejacket, he pulled him in closer. "You should have hired an outfitter to take you down a river like the Klamath, you stupid fuck! The water moved the boy's hair gently back and forth like wheat in a field. The face remained locked in a grimace.

He'd heard that some people survived underwater for over forty-five minutes, so he hauled the drowned boy into his raft, checked his airway to make sure it was clear, and then began administering CPR.

Bobby's hitched sobbing made the task harder, and the kid's airways were partially blocked from swelling.

*Come on! Breathe damn it!*

An eternity passed before he checked his watch; only three minutes since he'd begun the procedure, only twenty-five minutes since the accident.

A numb feeling crept through his extremities. His face turned into rubber. He stopped and opened the neck of his neoprene paddle-jacket. Pulling his head down inside it like a turtle, he took several long breaths. The jacket was almost airtight and acted like a paper bag. He didn't mind the body odor laced with the spicy scent of fear, it alleviated his hyperventilating.

As his heartbeat slowed, he alternated between giving the young man CPR and breathing the carbon dioxide inside his jacket. He had been performing CPR for over twenty minutes when another raft came down the river.

"Can we help?" A man shouted.

Bobby didn't acknowledge him, he had to keep count of how many breaths he'd administered.

"We'll row down to Copco Store and call 9-1-1," the man shouted as they

# CHAPTER ONE

passed. Bobby knew it would take hours for help to come to such a remote place. He still didn't answer. Come on…please *breathe*!

The last few seconds of the young man's life played over and over in Bobby's mind. Less than an hour ago, another unfortunate whitewater rafter had slammed into a boulder sideways, pinning his boat to the rock. Tons of water pressure held the raft fast, defying rescue. The week before, Bobby had purchased a Z-Drag pulley system for his guide service, designed for accidents just like this. He'd only wanted to help the man pry his raft off the rock.

Z-Drag ropes were pulled taut from the wrapped boat to the shore. Bobby, his customers, and several other guides pulled on a rope attached to the pulleys, in turn anchored to a tree. It was working beautifully, and the boat had been about to peel off the rock when a yellow raft rounded the corner above them.

The kid never saw the rescue-ropes stretched from the tree to the boat in the middle of the river.

*Yeah, but you forgot to send somebody upstream to warn him, didn't you, Bobby?*

Everyone on the bank screamed, but the boy was wearing headphones and had remained oblivious until his raft turned at that last fateful second. The first rope caught him at the throat and lifted him out of the seat. A second line from the raft hung slack across the top of the water. The boy's arm had entangled in it and his weight pulled tight, creating a huge plume of white spray.

"Cut the rope, or he'll drown!" Bobby screamed, but the man in the rock-wrapped boat took many precious seconds to react. The man finally managed to find a knife and cut the boy's body free from the rope entrapment; the kid rolled in the rapid and floated away face down.

Bobby raced along the bank, across rocks and logs. He came upon a large, blue inflatable raft. Bobby ran and leaped off a rock; he landed on the front thwart of the boat, untied the bow rope and bounded into the rowing seat.

He had been close to the boy several times, usually at the pools above each rapid. He had almost reached him just above the potentially deadly Dragon Rapid, but a row of rocks known as The Dragon's Teeth had bitten into the boat, almost ejecting him into the water to join the lifeless young man.

Bobby had made one small mistake of not sending somebody up-river. *But the kid shouldn't have been on a class-five river.* Class-five: "danger to life and limb…experts only using the very best equipment." *You were definitely not an expert.* And the kid's type-three lifejacket, good for benign rivers and lakes, had floated him face down instead of up. He might have lived if he'd had on a type-five with the flap behind the head.

Now, at Salt Caves, Bobby sat and held the boy close, no longer trying to administer mouth-to-mouth. He held the body across his lap like a mother rocking a sleeping child. The dark realization that he had killed a fellow human being with his carelessness sank in.

Several hours passed before the county rescue helicopters finally arrived at Salt Caves. A crowd of boaters swam out into the eddy and pulled them to shore. Still in shock, he clutched the boy tightly, and no one could coax him into releasing his grip. Finally, when the Forest Service representative and two sheriff's deputies arrived, they managed to get him to acknowledge them.

He shook violently from a palsy that invaded his muscles.

"Come on, son—let him go," the first deputy said.

"I killed him." Bobby tried not to cry.

"I already know what happened. You didn't kill him. Now, let him go. It'll be all right."

"No, sir…It won't be all right," Bobby said as he hugged the boy closer.

"We need to take him, son. His parents are going to want him. Let us take him to them, how about it?" The deputy spoke gently. Bobby wanted to comply, but a part of him resisted.

*I'm going to let them take you now. I can't help anymore.* Bobby looked up at the deputy. "I don't know what to do."

The deputy motioned for one of the paramedics and the Forest Service man to help. They lifted the body out of Bobby's arms and carried it down the bank to where the helicopter had landed. Bobby sat alone in the boat, while the deputies took his statement.

The paramedics confirmed the boy was dead. The deputy said, "Your customers are still waiting at Hell's Corner. We could drop you off there if you'd like. The guy whose raft you "borrowed" is coming down right now to reclaim it. The deputy cocked his head and asked, "What'll it be, son?"

Bobby almost didn't care. But he did. "My customers?" He thought for a moment. He had been a whitewater guide in his past life. He stared back at the deputy as he stood and vacated the raft. "I need to take care of my customers."

"If you think you're up to it. We can have the State Police pick them up if you can't."

"No, I can do it." He needed the familiar feeling of doing something normal. Otherwise he might lose his mind.

He followed the deputy to the helicopter and climbed aboard, once again sitting next to the lifeless body. Bobby felt utterly alone.

If his buddy, Jerry, had been along would he have assured him that it wasn't

# CHAPTER ONE

his fault? That the kid wouldn't have been able to gain control of the raft anyway? That he wasn't prepared for what the Upper K offered? Most likely the boy would have spun out of control into the rope just the same. But Jerry wasn't here. Only the deputies, and the dead kid whose name was still a mystery.

Bobby became aware of the smell of the helicopter exhaust, which overpowered all the scents of the desert mountain flowers. He barely recognized the song of a Black-capped Chickadee when it chirped in a nearby tree.

Then the pilot started the rotors spinning, and the chopper drowned out everything as it lifted into the late afternoon sky. He wondered if he was indeed capable of getting his people down to State Line Falls. *What's the worst that could happen?* He began to laugh quietly as fresh tears ran down his cheeks. He knew now.

## PORTLAND, OREGON

The courtroom looked different with the crowd of reporters and T.V. news people all awaiting the verdict, and Abigail Jones didn't doubt what it would be. She had done her job and then some. Even so, in the seconds before the foreman read the verdict, her stomach felt as if she'd left it at the top of an elevator shaft. She focused on her boots and smiled. The D.A. considered her a renegade because she refused to adhere to the dress code. She preferred slacks instead of a skirt, and she never went to trial without her lucky cowboy boots.

"Guilty, your honor," the foreman of the jury said.

*YES!* Her record remained above eighty-five percent in the win column for the State of Oregon. In this instance, she was truly glad she had won. In fact, she would have given up an extra ten percent just to nail this bastard. He had raped and killed a seventeen-year-old girl in Clackamas County. Her county.

Ernie Butters had been arrested three times previously without a conviction. *And that's only the crimes we suspect him of.* When Abigail returned from Idaho, she would do her best to see that Butters received the death penalty.

She glanced up at the clock. *Thank God this ended when it did.* The case had gone four days longer than she'd expected. Only two more hours, until she'd planned to leave on her vacation.

"Sentencing will be set for two weeks from today," the judge said and struck his gavel. Abigail looked at the defendant and smiled. She picked up her portfolio and walked around to the front of the prosecutor's table.

She sensed the action before she actually saw it. One of the bailiffs slammed flat on the marble floor—the other was thrown over the banister into several of the observers' laps. Ernie Butters vaulted over the defense table and lunged toward her.

"YOU'RE DEAD, BITCH!" he screamed, sounding as if it were already a fact.

Shocked, Abigail watched as he closed the gap on her, his hands outstretched to grab her throat. She automatically timed his momentum. Her right foot shot up so fast it caught him completely by surprise. The heel of her boot hit the point of his chin. She had aimed at least a foot behind the target. His head snapped back and a loud crack reverberated through the courtroom.

She knew she'd broken his jaw, but she couldn't stop there—the pictures of young Erica Lynn Ingram's body lying on the floor of the storeroom flashed through her mind. She refocused and spun into a powerful reverse crescent kick. She'd done this series hundreds of times in competition, but this time full, unrestrained contact felt far more satisfying. Her kick impacted with his broken jaw and right temple. She watched his teeth tumble through the air toward the Bench in slow motion, where an astonished Judge Mathews sat, mouth open in an expression of total disbelief.

Butters' look was even more surprised. She would bet he'd never encountered resistance from any of the women he'd raped. They'd probably been too afraid. *I'm not, asshole.* Again her reflexes ruled her actions. She slammed a reverse punch into Butter's solar plexus with his spine as the target.

"Huummmmph!" he groaned as he doubled over.

Still enraged, she brought her knee up flush into his face, knocking him backwards over the prosecutor's table where he landed on his head. Ernie Butters stiffened once then quit moving.

Abigail stood in a Cat Stance waiting to see if he would get up for more. She would be happy to oblige. Walking around the table, she stared down at him. His eyes had rolled back into his head, and blood leaked from his nose, mouth, and ears. She could see small, red bubbles forming in his nostrils. Still alive.

The judge called out, "Order! I'll have order!" She heard the sharp report as his gavel struck several times, but the courtroom broke into chaos. Cameras flashed while reporters stuck microphones into Abigail's face, screaming their questions.

"No comment," she shouted, but they refused to stop harassing her, until she

# CHAPTER ONE

fell into her aggressive stance. There didn't seem to be any doubt what she could do. The reporters gave her plenty of space. Her first priority was to finish the business at hand.

Two paramedics and three deputies transported the battered defendant to the hospital, and after what seemed like an eternity, the courtroom cleared, except for the defense attorney, the judge, a bailiff, and Abigail. She arranged her papers and turned to leave when the other lawyer spoke.

"Ms. Jones, I must say you were quite a surprise. I've never seen anything like that. But now I have an idea why you do so well at your job: sexual frustration. That's why women take up men's sports. I read it in a magazine."

She didn't like him. He belonged to some ancient paradigm. Even his greasy hair and wingtip shoes placed him there.

"Sexual frustration? You read that in *Hustler*, did you?"

The lawyer just smiled and kept putting papers into his briefcase.

The bailiff walked up beside her. "Ms. Jones, I want you to know that you did what each of us, present company excepted," he glared at the defense lawyer and continued, "wanted to do."

"Who said I didn't?" the lawyer said.

A small voice from behind her called out: "Abby?"

Nobody on the district attorney's staff used her nickname. Abigail turned to find a petite, dark-haired woman standing in the doorway at the opposite end of the courtroom.

"Beth, hi. I'll be right there—just finishing up." She walked over to the judge who now wore blue jeans and a T-shirt. Abby hadn't noticed the picture of the large Steelhead. Below it on the shirt numerous hands were raised in prayer. The caption: "Fish Worship—is It Wrong?" stood out in Old English script below it. She smiled and met his eyes. "I'm going on a whitewater trip down the Middle Fork of the Salmon, your Honor. They call the place I'm going *The River of no Return Wilderness*, but I'm definitely planning on coming back."

"Good you'd better come back for sentencing, which I figure will be when Mr. Butters can take solid food again. Have fun, Miss Jones."

She walked toward the door and could see Beth seated in the last row of seats.

"Are you ready?" Beth asked.

"Absolutely, I'm ready and packed...let's get out of here!"

# 2

## EUGENE, OREGON

Bobby thought Jerry Peterson's shop exemplified the old adage: "a place for everything, and everything in its place." Each tool had a neat compartment or peg on the wall. Even his five extra pair of coveralls hung neatly pressed from hangers.

The shop door was opened wide, but all that came in was blistering, late afternoon, summer heat and dust. Jerry lowered the shield on his welder's helmet and tacked something under the fender of a rafting trailer as if nothing were wrong.

Then he lifted the shield to reveal a face remarkable for its anomalies: boyish grin lines around the eyes offset against cheeks deeply creased from a decade of back-breaking labor in a local lumbermill. Bobby was glad Jerry had quit and started his own business. Things were finally looking up.

"You've got to be there," Jerry said as he lit a Camel. "The ranger has to see your driver's license picture." He drew on the cigarette and stared at Bobby as he talked through exhaled smoke. "I realize you're feeling down about the accident, but too many people have taken vacation time, sent in their money; man, they'll sue the shit out of you."

"They can stand in line." He had been ecstatic when he'd received the permit. He'd beaten the odds and won a launch date on the Middle Fork of the Salmon River in central Idaho. Then the accident on the Upper Klamath ruined everything.

"It's like getting thrown off a horse; you have to get back on as soon as you can," Jerry said as he walked to his toolbox to fetch a wrench. The cigarette hung from the corner of his mouth, and the smoke drifted directly into his eyes causing him to squint.

"I'm scared of horses—you should have picked a better example."

"It's the best I could do on the spot."

Jerry continued to work on the trailer as if the trip was still on. Bobby couldn't help but smile. "I appreciate what you're trying to do, but I don't think I have it in me. This may not be as nasty a river as the Upper Klamath, but it's in the middle of nowhere."

"I know where it is." Jerry took a last drag, tossed the cigarette on the ground, and crushed it with his work boot. "Look, you're one of the best guides around. You looked like you were about to give up on life before you started planning this trip. Your divorce really sucked, but you were starting to shine again. Remember, the kid died; you didn't."

"A part of me did die."

Jerry rested a hand on Bobby's shoulder. "Just try to put all this grief shit on hold and see if this trip doesn't change your outlook on life. I've got a feeling it will."

"So do I. A feeling that something bad could happen that far out."

"You've already got your bad out of the way, man. What could be worse than what's already happened?"

"You've got a point," Bobby replied. His palms had begun to sweat. Could he actually go through with the trip, he wondered? Someone could die on that trip too.

"You're the only guy I know who was so terrified of rivers, he had to become a whitewater guide. And you told me when you were a kid, you were afraid to fight. So what did you do? Became a regional kickboxing champion and then joined the fucking Marines. Pardon me, but I think you're full of crap if you tell me you don't have it in you."

"But this time I hurt someone else."

"Everybody makes mistakes…sometimes people get hurt by them. The true test is if you can recover from yours." Jerry grinned at Bobby. "Look, you won't be alone in this. I'm going to help you all the way. Consider this our trip. I'll share the load and the responsibility."

Bobby considered Jerry's offer. Something inside tugged at him. Fear had always been his enemy. It had stalked him in various forms all his life. Once he'd started fighting back, he had never stopped until now. Though it would be easier, he refused to go back to being a coward. Letting fear take away the joy of the trip would be admitting defeat.

Jerry picked up a large wrench from his rollaway. It never ceased to amaze Bobby that Jerry could look at a bolt, walk back to the toolbox, and grab the right-sized tool 95% of the time. "Don't worry, be happy, Mon."

## CHAPTER TWO

"Don't worry...that's it?" He poked his fingers through a slit in the neoprene. "Do you have any Toluol? Guess I better patch the floor in my raft if I'm going."

"A new one in the corner," Jerry said as he pointed with a socket driver. He smiled but didn't acknowledge the comment about going.

Bobby retrieved the can and broke the seal on the toxic Toluol container. The fumes inundated him as he went about patching his old Campways raft. As he worked, he thought about Jerry's earlier statement about overcoming fear. Mainly because he'd been the victim of intense, mind-numbing fear in last night's dream.

*The dream...*

...floating in his life jacket, he tried to swim, but his extremities would not respond to his commands. Helpless, he washed over the brink of Steamboat Falls, and he could see the giant whirlpool below it coming closer. Around and around he went, faster and faster, until he actually could see down the spiraling hole into darkness. Then it sucked him into the netherworld of nightmare madness where he landed on—*ground?*

He looked up to the surface; it appeared to be in a state of flux, changing from water into dark, ominous clouds. A tornado funnel replaced the whirlpool. He tried to run, but his feet felt like cement blocks—his futile efforts in slow motion. Funnels descended all around, closing him in like a prison. Their swirling motion had created a massive dynamo, and lightning struck the ground of the bizarre, mutating landscape. Just when his feet lightened up, he had been catapulted into the swirling darkness where he awakened in his bedroom, soaked in cold sweat.

He set another patch in place, but the memory of the nightmare still gripped him. He had been plagued with two recurring nightmares for most of his life. Probably because when he was a boy, growing up in Texas he had witnessed a killer tornado that had ripped a Dallas suburb apart. Nothing in waking life had ever scared him worse.

From past experience he had learned that when his subconscious needed to warn him, a tornado dream came along to remind him how life can be out of control.

Then, he recalled his other, nightmare—the eyes—and a spasm racked through him.

Jerry's hand on his shoulder brought him back to the present before the fumes from the Toluol overwhelmed him.

"I've got to go outside—I think this shit's starting to get to me," he said. His hands shook, and sweat beaded on his brow.

"Let's take a break," Jerry suggested, and they walked outside into the warm, Oregon evening.

The two men had met through the friendship of their respective ex-wives, and had remained best friends for over ten years, long past the marriages. One reason they were such good friends was they were nothing alike. Jerry was analytic and a perfectionist, while Bobby was one of the Lost Boys. Jerry waxed methodical, while Bobby's eclectic lifestyle made him appear to be disorganized.

Jerry lit a cigarette and leaned against Bobby's pick-up. "Did you call that guy back?" he asked.

"Which guy—Oh, Jacques. Yeah, I called him this afternoon. Sounds like a real character. I couldn't tell him the trip was off, so I set up a pre-trip meeting for the people who live close in to Eugene. Gonna be Monday night at his house. I've never met him, but he sounds like he's on the level, and he's done the river five times before." What Bobby had wanted most was a happy group and a safe trip. Jacques sounded like an asset toward that end.

Jerry said, "Thank God, I'm glad somebody's run it before. I was getting nervous thinking that we would be running this thing completely by the book. I always have trouble trying to figure out which rock is rock 'A,' and which is rock 'B'; they all look so different from the boat."

"Well, I've had enough of those glue fumes: if I smell Toluol again tonight, I'll puke. What say we take off and call it a night?"

The sweet smell of nearby peppermint fields on the cooling night breeze soothed away the remnants of worry. The two men closed up the shop and said goodnight. Bobby waved as Jerry drove away. He left for home as a blood-red moon rose over the nearby hills.

## SALMON, IDAHO

Chief deputy Earl Bohannan looked up from the work on his desk to see Joe Bob Everitt standing at his office door. Holding a copy of the Idaho Statesman, he had a worried expression on his face and blocked out the entire hallway as he ducked to come inside the office.

## CHAPTER TWO

"Come on in Joe Bob, what's the matter?" he asked as he sipped from his coffee.

"Something bad, Earl—real bad. Look at this," the huge deputy said as he handed the paper over the desk. "I saw the first news on our network last night, but it didn't go into this much detail. Rawlins is really going to take heat on this one."

Earl laid out the newspaper and stared at a headline no law-enforcement officer in the country would want to read.

"Does John know about this?" Earl asked. John Bonham was the sheriff of Salmon County.

"Yeah, he wasn't too worried about anything like that happening around here, but he wasn't happy about Ed's prospects for reelection."

Earl Bohannan swallowed hard and was thankful that it involved the neighboring county. He was about to read the grisly article when Joe Bob pointed toward the television behind his desk. "Too late for damage control." Earl spun around and turned up the volume in time to hear anchorman John McPherson deliver the bulletin to those who chose not to read their news.

"Authorities are investigating what many say may be the most savage mass murder in Idaho history. The mutilated remains of Harold and Jean Brittain along with their two children were discovered yesterday, when the family failed to show up for church on Sunday. Their Pastor, Rev. Emmett Vance, drove to the family farm outside White River to check on them and noticed all the horses and other farm animals slaughtered and decomposing in their pens. He called police. They found what was said to be the most gruesome crime scene any of the seasoned officers had ever encountered. The investigation is continuing although there are no suspects at this time. No motive has been established as to why the family was singled out, but anyone with information is asked to contact the State Police Criminal Investigation Unit in Boise, or Sheriff Ed Rawlins in White River County...."

Earl turned down the volume. "Jesus Christ—that poor family; I'm glad Ed's got this and not us. Something like this is bad enough on its own, but in an election year—Christ Almighty. Rawlins had better get this one solved pronto, or he may be looking to get a job with us," Earl said as he handed the unread paper back to the beefy deputy.

Joe Bob gazed at the article and a shiver rolled through his massive frame. He looked up and his voice rumbled as he said, "Let's pray that they get these bastards quick while they're still in White River County. If they come across the line, we could be in deep shit, too." Joe Bob glanced down at the headline again and walked out of Earl's office.

Earl sat back in his chair. He hated crime, especially violent crime. Salmon had an occasional killing, convenience store hold-up, domestic dispute, a fight at the local taverns, but for the most part things stayed peaceful. There were never mass murderers on the loose in Salmon County.

One thought, however, made him feel better. The Sawtooth Range, and the biggest primitive road-less area in the continental United States acted as natural barriers between White River and Salmon. If that weren't enough, The Middle Fork of the Salmon River Canyon—as deep as the Grand Canyon—made it virtually impossible to cross.

There's no reason to worry, he thought.

### INDIAN CREEK, MIDDLE FORK OF THE SALMON

Hank Ridley paused on the hiking trail to remove his Forest Service jacket. The last two days had been wet and cool, but now the sky was blue and the air clean after the rain. He tied his coat around his waist, took the canteen from his daypack and drank deeply. After replacing it, he hoisted the bag and continued toward his destination: a bald eagle's nest. He had noticed it the previous week, but was unable to get close enough to observe. This time he returned with binoculars.

A quarter mile farther up the path, an unnatural quiet descended upon the forest. He stopped and listened. The soft "shrrr" of a gentle breeze passing through the pine needles was all he could hear. *Strange.*

He scanned the trail ahead. Satisfied, he walked on. Another hundred yards brought him to a small meadow. The path wound around one corner of it and vanished back into the pines. He was halfway across that corner when he caught a peculiar scent. The breeze came directly across the field. At its center he sighted a large, brown mound.

For some reason, Hank had a bad feeling about it. He considered passing by

## CHAPTER TWO

without checking it out, but this was Forest Service jurisdiction. His job was to investigate, he reasoned, as he slowly walked toward it.

Within forty feet a sinking feeling overcame him. The mound was covered with bloody, brown fur, and steam rose from its far side. Cautiously, from twenty feet away, he walked around it. His jaw dropped. This was a male grizzly in the 800-pound range. The eyes were still bright—hardly glazed.

*It just died.*

The expression on its face troubled him. Locked in a grimace of pain and *fear?*

The most frightening thing about it he found beyond belief. The bear had been disemboweled, the cavity inside, empty.

*Sweet Jesus! What in the world could you have tangled with?* Hank scratched his head in confusion. "Nothing on this continent—this planet—can match a grizzly in a fight." He knelt beside the dead bear and touched its nose.

*Still warm.*

He looked at the steam coming from the cavity. His mouth suddenly dried as if he had chewed up a dirt clod; his heart raced toward the "red-line." The bear had been alive less than half an hour ago. When he noticed the claws, sweat beaded on his forehead. A liquid that resembled dark syrup dripped into small pools under the bear's paws.

"You fought back, didn't you?" he asked as he stood on wobbly knees.

A gnawing sensation worked its way up Hank's gut. His expression changed from confusion to terror as another odor seemed to arise from the very ground on which he stood. The breeze abated, and total silence smothered the clearing.

He looked to the edge of the meadow and strained his eyes. Nothing moved, but a huge dark shadow seemed to hover between two large pines fifty feet inside the forest.

*To hell with the eagles!* He sprinted to the trail and ran back toward Indian Creek. At the edge of the glade, he stopped and looked back. The shadow was gone. He considered digging out the binoculars until he caught a slight movement. It had been so quick he thought it was his imagination. When he focused on where it had been, it seemed to vanish into the other shadows. He turned to leave when he saw it again. It lurked behind a tree 100 feet closer.

Running with wild abandon, Hank descended the canyon. If anything pursued him, it did so without a sound.

# 3

## THE BOUNDARY CREEK PUT-IN

Everyone complained of being tired after the twenty-hour drive to Boundary Creek. The sky threatened to rain, and Bobby knew setting up tents and tarps would be the first order of business. Tonight's would be an early bedtime, since they would be launching as early as possible in the morning.

The sky loomed dark and ominous at dinner, then the rain set in. It was slow at first but grew in intensity. The rain pelted the trees, but mercifully there wasn't any wind. Bobby sat under a large, blue tarp with several members of his expedition. Jacques sat opposite him with a glass of tea, Jerry sat stoking the fire and nursing a beer, Art Hellstrom, Pat Hilyard, and Gary Graham sat on Jacques' left.

Jacques' real name was Bill Braxton, but everyone called him by his river nickname. Bobby and Jerry had asked about it. He explained that he had been flipped in Caldera, one of the meanest, class-five rapids in the western United States, and a friend had christened him Jacques. "The son-of-a-bitch said he figured I was Jacques Cousteau since I stayed under so long. It stuck."

Jacques looked like he used to wrestle in the light-heavyweight division: five-eight, stocky, a jovial manner. Casual. His bearded face reminded Bobby of Bluto, but his arms looked more like Popeye. Suspecting that underneath the calm exterior was a man he wouldn't want as an enemy.

A big man of about sixty years sat in a lounger drinking a glass of Lavelle's Pinot Noir. His silver hair gave him a certain dignity, but his smile added a hint of mischief. Art Hellstrom, better known as Plato, had received his name from always quoting philosophers and tying their wisdom to bits of everyday life.

"Plato.... *The Allegory of the Cave*," Bobby had said.

"The very same."

"I've read it," Bobby had said when he shook Plato's hand. "I majored in Philosophy. Of course that was before I realized the philosophy industry was beginning a permanent downturn."

"I am painfully aware of the problem," Plato had said smiling. "I'm forced to teach, since it's so hard to make a living as an actual philosopher—the pay being so shitty."

Plato stood about six-four. He had a rich dark tan and laugh-lines around his mouth. Jacques and Plato were relaxed in their friendship, and Bobby wondered how many river adventures the two had been on together. Their friendly manners eased his worry that some of the members might not get along. Both seemed likeable. Like instant buddies—just add water.

On the other hand, Bobby worried over the growing hostility between two members of his party. Pat, one of the two hard-shelled kayakers, had exhibited an almost instant dislike for Jacques at the pre-trip meeting last week. A mutual feeling. It had started when Jacques announced that he planned to bring his dog.

Pat didn't like dogs on the river. He argued that they barked at everything and crapped everywhere. Jacques assured him that if his dog barked, she would have a good reason.

Bobby had sided with Jacques, and as trip leader, that was that. But now a new argument had started during dinner over how the river should be run, and Bobby wondered how things had gone to hell so quickly.

"Gary and I have done rapids on the Upper McKenzie. In the book it says that's where the guides trained for the Middle Fork," Pat said, apparently intending to impress Jacques.

"Son, if you think the Upper McKenzie is going be a preview of the Middle Fork, you better pass on the movie," Jacques warned. "Guides used to train there, but hey—most boxers sparred with unknowns before they got into the ring with Cassius Clay." Bobby observed Jacques' movements as he scratched his beard and glared at the two young kayakers. Bobby spoke up on Pat's behalf.

"I've boated with Pat before. He's plenty capable." Bobby glanced over at Pat. He looked like a testimonial for a health spa: well muscled and a dark tan. Still, Bobby worried about his attitude. He spoke directly to Pat. "But stay with the group…just in case."

Jacques stared at Pat as if lost in thought and hadn't heard Bobby's comment. He continued. "Get one thing straight: The Middle Fork of the Salmon

## CHAPTER THREE

is no small undertaking. Not only is it a class-three/class-four river, but it also cuts through the largest primitive area in the continental United States. The trip starts from here at Boundary Creek, and ends up eight days from now at a place called Corn Creek on the Main Salmon River. There are 300 rapids in this section; forty are major rapids that command a great deal more respect than you're giving them credit for. They're far beyond anything you've encountered on the McKenzie."

Jacques laced his fingers together and leaned forward resting his forearms on his knees. He seemed to calm himself but kept his intensity. "Any accidents here on the Middle Fork could be potentially life-threatening since there aren't any roads for over a hundred miles. There's no way out of here except down the river. Medical help isn't readily available, and some injuries that ordinarily wouldn't be serious can be dead-serious downstream." He handed the Quinn guide to Pat, put his hands behind his head, and sank back in his lawn chair.

In the silence that followed, Bobby listened to the sounds of rain hitting the tarp and the forest floor. Frogs croaked and crickets chirped in the darkness.

Jacques took a deep breath and finished his counsel. "There won't be any turning back. The Middle Fork was originally known in the old west as *The River of No Return* for a reason."

"I thought the Main Salmon was the River of No Return," Gary said, sounding as if he'd caught the older man in a mistake.

"It is now, but before the 1920's it was the Middle Fork."

"I still say we won't have any problem with it—we've done the Rogue twice," Pat replied. "It's got Blossom Bar, Mule Creek Canyon, Rainee Falls, and Tyee Rapids. All those drops are in wilderness. What's the big problem?" Bobby knew the problem and was about to answer when Plato beat him to it.

"The big problem is that they're two rivers with completely different character. We're only trying to set an atmosphere of caution here—that's all. This trip could be the most incredible experience you've ever had, or it can be a nightmare."

Plato paused and sipped wine from his cup and spoke, his voice soft and serious. "Jacques and I were here three years ago last week. We got to be friends with another party on the second day out. Fifth day down-river from here we saw them floating along and approached for our daily water fight. When we pulled up close enough, we could see that most of them were crying."

Plato locked eyes with Jacques before continuing. "One of their members had been careless, unbuttoned his lifejacket to get a tan, and accidentally went over Tappan Falls. He fell out of the raft and was sucked from his loose jacket and drowned before anybody could do anything. Search and Rescue didn't find the body for four days. Needless to say, from that point forward our trip ceased being fun. That's the last time we went down this river."

"That's right," Jacques added as he stood and walked to a camp table where an open cigar box sat next to a plastic goblet filled with small match boxes. Taking one of the cigars and a box of the matches, he turned to Gary and continued, "And we don't want to have a replay. That's why I think we should take every precaution. If you two are good enough to separate from the crowd, the river will tell in the first two days. But I still don't like for people to stray from the group. Not on this river."

Gary hadn't spoken. Bobby saw him grip the handles of his lawn chair. His muscles were long and lean-swimmer's muscles-and could have broken the plastic if he hadn't relaxed. He wore his long, blond hair in a ponytail and when he stood, he reached just over six feet tall. Even though he was only twenty-two years old, he had more rescue experience than anyone else on the trip. Bobby had wanted him along for that reason, but he also liked the kid.

Pat and Gary seemed inseparable. Gary had taught Pat to kayak the previous summer, and here he was already on The Middle Fork. Gary raised his voice and spoke to Jacques. "We came here to experience solitude and that means getting away from the group. Hell, I've done The Cheat and The Gauley rivers back East by myself. They're class-five/six; I shouldn't have a problem on a class-four river."

"Yeah, but Pat only has one season's experience in a kayak…he's not as good as you are," Bobby said. He didn't want Pat to die from underestimating the difficulty. The talk of death made him nervous. He took a deep breath and tried to center himself.

"Whose side are you on anyway?" Pat asked.

"Everybody's. I just don't want anybody to get hurt." No one except Jerry knew of the accident on the Klamath—he wanted to keep it that way.

Jacques' jaw tightened visibly as he glared at Gary. "If you guys split up from the rest of us, and he gets trashed, how the hell are you going to transport him out in a god dam kayak?"

"Look man, we don't need you to tell us how to run a river; I'm ready for whatever this one's got," Pat said.

Bobby watched helplessly as the argument proceeded. He wanted everyone on the trip to get along, but the postures of the men reminded him of two male dogs sizing each other up before a fight. "This is something I hadn't even

## CHAPTER THREE

thought of," he whispered to Jerry who gave a weak, knowing smile behind his cigarette's smoke but didn't speak.

Bobby liked Pat and Gary—they were his friends—but he agreed with Jacques' reasoning: splitting up on this river was foolish.

"Hey! Come on, guys! Everybody take a deep breath and relax for a minute." Bobby studied the kayakers, then the two older men. "Jacques, you and Plato have done the river at low water. Can we get our heavy gear-boats through these upper canyons?"

Jacques paused, then took the cigar, and tore off the cellophane. He licked the big, contraband Havana twice and paused as he thought. "As you know, we'll have to send most of our gear down to Indian Creek by airplane in the morning. The air service in Salmon will pick up whatever gear we leave in the shuttle van and fly it there exactly when we specify. We recover our stuff the morning of the third day. That way our boats are lighter—easier to move across the water for the first two days. From Indian Creek on down, the river gets deeper, and the rocks get fewer. Of course, the rapids get bigger too." Jacques had been boating for thirty years and sounded like he knew what he was talking about. Everyone appeared to listen except Pat. He perused The Quinn Guidebook.

Jacques looked at Gary. "We all need to work out our differences, boys. Honor our diversity. Sorry if it sounded like I was jumping down your throat." Jacques leaned forward and held his hand out to Gary.

Gary appeared to harbor reservations as he reached out for Jacques' hand. Like he suspected it might hide a "Joy Buzzer." The two men shook, and then Pat walked over and did likewise. *Good. That's more like it*, Bobby thought.

He watched as Jacques sat back and scratched his dog behind her ear. She turned her head up toward her master and began panting happily. Bobby loved dogs and had tried to figure out what type she was at the pre-trip meeting, but all he could come up with was a Heinz 57 of noble heritage. She was uniquely beautiful, a mix of white, apricot, and black coloring.

"I never go on a river trip without my good ol' river dog, Fido," Jacques said looking at Bobby as he hugged her neck. "Spelled: P-h-y-d-e-a-u-x. Wonderdog, chaser of bears and beasts."

"I still say a dog will ruin the trip. Dogs shit everywhere, and bark at anything that moves—that's why I want to split up," Pat said.

"Phydeaux here's famous on the Rogue River," Jacques said, defending her. "Why, she's run more bears out of camp than any other dog on record, and considering that she only weighs fifty pounds, it makes her exploits even more remarkable. I think you will find her useful and a good traveling companion."

Bobby smiled at the dog and reached over to pet her. She watched him warily, but allowed herself to be touched. After she sensed no threat to herself, or her master, she wagged her tail and licked his hand.

"She loves rafting more than anything, but she hates getting wet," Jacques added.

"Maybe she needs swimming lessons." Pat's tone leaked sarcasm.

When the meeting finally ended, Bobby noticed that everyone shook hands again except Jacques and Pat.

"See you in the morning," Bobby said.

"Right," Pat replied as he walked toward his tent.

The following morning, at 6,000 feet, the air was damp and chilly, making Polar-fleece jackets the fashion de jour. Bobby figured he would be the first up, but found Jerry already making coffee on the Coleman stove. *God bless him*, he thought, having downed a few beers the night before and feeling slightly hung over. Coffee and aspirin were the only legal, miracle drugs in his opinion, so he downed two aspirin and went to warm his hands at the stove.

After the coffee was ready, Jerry poured them both a cup: "Can you believe this? We're actually here—about to run the Middle Fork of the Salmon! Man, I hope these people appreciate how much work went into making this trip happen."

"Most of them do, but I bet they're glad they didn't get the permit with the responsibility to get all this shit together. As it is, they're all asleep in their bags nice and toasty, while you and I are out here freezing our balls off at six in the morning."

"Well why you don't rouse their lazy asses out of bed to join us," Jerry said zipping up his jacket.

"I guess our brilliant minds think alike." Bobby roamed from tent to tent giving everyone a wake-up call. Since most of the campers disliked getting up so early, Bobby figured his popularity was likely to suffer, at least until everyone had been properly caffeinated.

He went back to the table and poured his second cup of coffee and waited for the aspirins to take effect. The sky hung like a slate-gray ceiling, but at least the rain had temporarily let up as Jerry started breakfast.

Bobby looked across the campground and saw a yellow dome tent that looked vaguely familiar. It belonged to Jim Duncan, one of the two people

# CHAPTER THREE 25

who had found their own way to the put-in. He walked through the trees toward the tent.

Years earlier, he and Jim had gone through guide school together. Their friendship had been forged in the white-hot screaming hell of the Rogue River at flood stage. The Rogue had been running at 13,000 cubic feet-per-second, ten times more volume than the normal summer flow. It resembled a roller coaster out of control, with massive waves smashing everything that floated against its jagged canyon walls. They both passed the final exam—they emerged alive. During that intense experience, a friendship began that spanned 3,000 miles.

Bobby sneaked up from behind. From the back, Jim resembled a poster of Rambo. His long black hair hung down to his shoulders and his well-defined muscles appeared to have been chiseled. "Well, nice to see you finally made it," he said.

Jim, never one to appear un-cool, answered calmly in his Eastern accent. "We've been here since day before yesterday. When did you get here—I didn't hear you pull in."

"We got here late. Who's this lovely creature?" Bobby said facing Linda Duncan. "This lady isn't married to the likes of you, is she?"

"I'm Linda, and yes, this lucky man happened to win me in a poker game. Nice to meet you, Bobby, I've heard quite a bit about yours and Jim's near-death experiences on the Rogue."

"Where is this poker game and are there any more like her?" Linda was slender with dark eyes the color of coal. Her brown hair hung in a braid to her waist and her skin gleamed white even in the gloom of the dismal morning.

"I'm going to be watching you, Aldrich—you pull out any cards on this trip, we're going to have problems," Jim said.

Bobby smiled and turned his attention back to Jim. "Okay, okay. But after you eat breakfast, meet me over by those tents, and I'll introduce you to the rest of the expedition. Guess I'd better wake them up first. Nice to meet you, Linda."

"My pleasure," she replied.

He turned to Jim again. "I'm glad you're along."

"Me, too."

"What the hell do you mean, waking me before the sun?" Suzi Clayton rolled over to face him.

Bobby carried a water gun with him on the second round of wake-up calls. He shot her in the face with a powerful stream of cold water.

"Oh, you're dead now, shit-heel," she warned.

Bobby laughed as he backed out of the tent. "Do you know me? Most people don't—that's why I carry the Super Soaker 200." He shot her again. The cold water brought Suzi to a high state of wakefulness.

"You son-of-a-bitch. You better hope I don't get my hands on that. I'll get you at night—you do know what happens when goose down gets wet, don't you?" She wiped the water from her eyes and grinned a cold smile.

"Wake up, little Suzi. Time for breakfast," he said as he cautiously backed away. She climbed out of her tent and wandered up to the kitchen box in search of a cup. Turning back she said, "I have eight days for revenge, Aldrich...sleep tight."

"Eight days—maybe I was too quick to use force," he said, glimpsing a mental picture of his goose down bag dripping wet and useless. He followed her and poured himself another cup of coffee.

He had received a call from Suzi back in May. She explained a friend of a friend had heard about his trip, and she would do anything reasonable to go. He had liked her right away. She was funny and quite attractive: her ebony hair a pleasing contrast to her blue eyes. She could have been Jim's younger sister. Her muscles flexed as she walked, like a lean, predatory cat that walked on two legs. Bobby discovered she was a gymnast, which explained her intense physical presence.

She had driven up from California a few days early and helped him with the grocery shopping. They bought over a thousand dollar's worth of food. It was fun to see something they wanted and just buy it—a far cry from the usual "scrimp-and-save" coupon shopping Bobby was used to.

"Hell, let's get it; we're spending other people's money," Suzi had said. That was when he realized how much fun she was going to be. He gulped the last bit of coffee.

Wagging her tail, Phydeaux followed Bobby around. She wore her own life jacket. Plato's wife had sewn fifteen small bear patches onto it. Jacques had explained they represented the fifteen bears she had chased out of his campsites. Anytime she chased a new bear out, she earned a new patch; of course, he awarded her with culinary prizes, too.

Bobby noticed that Gary and Pat had already taken down their tents, while Jerry spoke with Jacques and Plato at the camp table. Water gun in hand, he searched the camp for more people to awaken. He greeted the rest of the party: Samuel Baker, better known as "The Judge," his wife Bonnie—an environ-

## CHAPTER THREE

mental lawyer, and two others: Gretta—a close friend of Bobby's, and Scott, a faculty friend of Plato's.

Bobby yelled hoping to get everyone's attention. "There's food…hey everybody, listen up! There's food over by the assembly table. Jerry and I are going to have a safety talk after you eat. Then Jacques is going to tell us all a little about what to expect from day one on the river; then we launch."

After the group had eaten, Bobby stood and addressed them. "Look, some of ya'll know this stuff, but for those who don't, we're going to go over it. Jerry will start off with what to do in the unlikely event of a water landing. All yours, Jerry."

"If you fall out of the raft, put your feet facing downstream," Jerry explained. "It's better to hit rocks with your feet than with your head." He went through a number of safety tips then said, "Remember—If you fall, it's better to fall into the boat."

That was always Bobby's cue to jump in. "Stay aware of the raft in front of you as well as the raft behind you. If someone gets wrapped or has an accident, they'll need all the help they can get."

"What does 'wrapped' mean?" Gretta asked.

"Wrapped is where a boat hits a rock, usually sideways, and is literally pasted to the side of it like a postage stamp," Bobby explained. His voice wavered. "It's bad."

"Real bad," Jerry agreed.

Bobby felt pain at the mention of a wrap but somehow managed to finish the safety talk without revealing visible signals of his feelings to the others. Only Jerry knew.

After Jacques finished his admonitions about the unique dangers of the first twenty miles of The Middle Fork, they began the task of carrying several tons of equipment down the steep ramp.

The boat ramp consisted of vertical logs. Bobby estimated it to be about seventy feet long. Jacques, Plato and Jerry lined up on the left side of Jacques' heavy gear boat. Bobby joined Suzi and Pat on the other.

"God, we're never going to get on the water," Pat complained. "If I could carry my own shit, I'd already be halfway to Elkhorn Camp." Pat glanced down-river and frowned. Bobby figured he would rather be in his kayak, playing in the first wave just downstream from the launch instead of carrying the heavy raft down the ramp.

"If my aunt had balls she'd be my uncle," Jacques returned. "You can't carry your own shit, so shut up and keep lifting."

Bobby could see Pat biting his tongue.

Rigging the rafts took over two hours, and clouds appeared to hang just above their heads as they embarked on the trip of a lifetime.

# 4

## BAD DREAMS

Jacques was the first in the water, followed by a parade of multi-colored rafts and kayaks. Finally, Bobby could settle back and do what he liked best: reading and running whitewater. It filled the hole in his soul as nothing, other than love, had ever done.

During the first few miles, he warmed up on fun class-two rapids. Suzi rode with him. The cold water splashed onto his skin and made him shiver, but the rushing sound of the river soothed him, as it always did. He felt euphoric by the end of the first mile. One look told him that Suzi shared that state.

His feelings for Suzi were not romantic; she was more like his twin sister: definitely attractive but not quite his type. More and more women found their way onto his list of best friends, but none ignited the spark of passion in him.

Bobby saw the other rafts pulled over on river left, the left side of the river looking downstream. He made his move to join them. The book listed the first major class-three rapid as Sulfur Slide, and the group had agreed earlier to scout before running it.

Bobby climbed to the top of the rocks and looked down on the rapids. The river boiled like a cauldron making the air smell clean and fresh. White plumes leapt over rocks, swirled behind them, and whirlpools formed and disappeared at angles to the main current all down the length of the rapid. The constant rumble hinted at the sheer power below him. His batteries recharged as he walked closer. The other side of the river looked like it claimed responsibility for the rapid's name. A landslide had dumped tons of rocks into the river, forming the biggest part of the rapid.

"Damn," Jacques said as he stroked his beard. The rest of the group stood on the rocks looking at the first, real Middle Fork rapid. "I've never seen it this low before. We don't usually run this upper section below 2.5 feet—it makes it too treacherous." He chewed on his cigar and grumbled. "This is 2.26 feet. Bobby and Jerry didn't want to miss all the good rapids in the first two days by flying down to Indian Creek with the gear, so now I guess we'll see if they were right or not."

Bobby grinned. "Let the tourists fly down to Indian Creek."

"But can we get through those narrow openings with the bigger gear boats?" Plato asked.

"Only one way to find out now," Jacques answered.

Bobby had to admit that Sulfur Slide at such a low level looked almost impassable. Boulders littered the channels that at places appeared only as wide as his raft. He could see that the channels would require precision on entering, and skillful maneuvering through each slot.

Jerry walked back from the rocks to his raft. By the time Bobby saw him, he had already begun his descent. The opening at the top was just big enough to allow his thirteen-foot Hyside to squeeze through. Move after move, Bobby and the others watched him slide through incredibly small openings, bouncing from rock to rock until he reached the bottom and caught an eddy.

"Way to go, amigo!" Bobby shouted, but the roar of the rapid drowned his attempt to get Jerry's attention.

The eddy held Jerry's boat from being pulled downstream, which allowed him to relax and watch the rest of them come down. Bobby could see he had pulled out his rescue throw-bag in case anyone fell out of a raft on the way through. *God, I hope he doesn't need that.*

Finally, everyone except Bobby and Suzi had gone through Sulfur Slide. They shared the smallest raft, a narrow, twelve-foot Pioneer, which afforded them greater maneuverability at the cost of stability.

"Okay Suzi, when I need extra power I'll call a right or left draw. You reach out and pull back straight toward the side of the raft I call." Suzi had a guide paddle up front, while Bobby manned the oars.

"Are we going to fit through those rocks?" she asked, sounding mildly concerned as they pulled away from the bank.

"If we don't, you'll be the first to know," he answered.

As always, the pit of his stomach felt as if he'd left it at the top of a roller coaster. Pulling hard on the oars he set up for the chosen slot. They passed by the entry rocks without incident. The current continued to build speed and

## CHAPTER FOUR

force. The roar of the pulsing torrent sounded ten times louder at river level. His sweaty hands gripped the oars tightly, and his arms flexed with each pull. They entered the rapid flawlessly, but as with anything in life, accidents happen. An invisible rock just under the surface bumped them into the wrong channel.

"Dammit! We've got trouble now," he shouted. The channel ended in a row of rocks about thirty feet below them. He couldn't see any room for his raft to sneak between. If they followed the current, they would be plastered to rocks, or worse-flipped. He pulled back hard on the oars and shouted "LEFT DRAW!" Suzi immediately reached out and pulled with all her strength. For a moment they seemed to just stand still against the river's pull. No gain. Bobby stood and braced his feet against the rowing frame and screamed a primal yell as he dug even harder.

The raft finally began moving back upriver. Slowly at first. Suzi's added draw-stroke helped pull the boat sideways without turning them against the current. When Bobby estimated that most of the boat was past the left rock, he tugged on the right oar and shoved forward on the left. "STOP!" he yelled.

Even though the noise of the rapid was equivalent to standing next to a passing train, Suzi heard him and pulled her paddle across her lap. The raft pivoted around the rock into the correct channel. They glided the rest of the way through the rapids, and pulled into the eddy next to Jerry.

"Oh yeah…we bad," Bobby said as he traded high fives with Suzi. "Let's see…that leaves only three more major, life-threatening rapids today. You ready?"

"Ready," she answered with a smile.

• • •

Hank's heart felt as if it would burst, but he kept running. His mouth felt as dry as summer dust; his lungs burned like fire. Just past the halfway point he stopped to catch his breath. He staggered to a fallen log and collapsed on it. After fumbling with the zipper on the pack, he barely managed to pull the canteen out with shaky hands before guzzling over a pint of water without stopping.

Gasping for breath, he eyed the path and felt relieved to find nothing chasing him. For a moment he wondered if he had imagined it all. Things like that happened when you lived alone in the wilderness.

But then he caught sight of a shadow racing along the ridge at the edge of the forest 500 yards above him. It moved in jerky motions that reminded him of Dynamation used in 1960's dinosaur movies. "My God." The speed of it was incredible.

He dropped the pack—mouth agape. The shadow traversed the side of the mountain like a spider on a wall. *It's trying to cut me off.*

Heart pounding, he ran three more hard miles before he came down on the cabin. Jerking the screen open, he ran in and slammed the hardwood door behind him.

"What in hell was that thing?" He leaned against the door trying to catch his breath for almost a minute before he realized that he had forgotten to lock the bolt.

Throwing the half-inch steel bar across the crack, he anchored it into the receiver and jammed his wooden desk-chair under the knob as an added precaution. He reached up to his brow and wiped sweat onto his sleeve.

He finally managed to catch his breath and sat on the floor in the center of the room listening. Only silence and the heat of the day penetrated from outside.

• • •

"Rock-side damn it!" Jacques yelled. Gretta forgot everything she'd been told and did the exact opposite. She jumped on the upstream tube as she, Jacques, and Phydeaux swept into a rock trench just below Ram's Horn Rapid. "DAMNATION!" he shouted. "We've stepped in it now sweetheart—get your pretty, little ass off that tube! Get over here!"

"WOOF!" Phydeaux barked at her. The dog had been on a number of trips and instinctively went to the high side anytime the boat leaned as if it would flip or wrap. Now, they were plastered on a rock in the middle of the river without hope of self-rescue. "WOOF!"

Bobby and Suzi occupied the sweep-boat position. "We go last," he had told her that morning, "we carry all the rescue gear and the first-aid kit. Anybody gets in trouble, we're the 'last chance gas-and-raft repair.'"

He observed Jacques' predicament and pulled over to river left. Jim, Linda, and Scott, already on shore and standing under some pines to avoid the rain, ran to the bank and grabbed his line. He thanked them and climbed out of the raft followed by Suzi. He turned to face Jacques. "How bad?" he shouted over the river's thunder.

"How about a Suck Factor Ten!" Jacques yelled in return. "Gonna need the 'Z drag.'"

# CHAPTER FOUR

"What's a 'Z drag?'" Suzi asked as they climbed out of the raft.

Bobby felt a chill go through him. He hated using the Z-drag unless it was a last resort. It was. He opened his watertight rocket box and began removing different elements from it. A violent spasm riveted his chest as he pulled out the rope…the very same rope.

Realizing he hadn't answered Suzi's question, he spoke quietly, "A pulley system designed to use mechanical advantage. You know, like a come-along or a block and tackle."

He turned toward the boat. "CATCH!" he shouted as he launched a red, throw bag at Jacques. Rope spilled from the bag as it arched through the air. Jacques caught it on the first attempt and climbed down into the cold water. Bobby could see the large raft had partially submerged, and Jacques was already up to his waist in the current.

"OOO-EEE!" he shouted. "This is colder than a well-digger's ass in January!" The water washed into Jacques' shirt as he searched for the opposite D-ring. He clipped a carabineer to the end of the rope and attached it to the metal loop. "Okay," he shouted and signaled with a 'thumbs up.'

Bobby turned and said, "Suzi, run back upstream and make sure nobody's coming. Flag them over if they do, I don't want anybody to get hurt on that line." She looked at him with inquisitive eyes before making her way up the bank.

After she was out of sight, Bobby said a silent prayer, then anchored the 'Z-drag to a tree and began mounting pulleys. "Give me a hand," he asked to those nearby. Jim, Linda, Scott, and Plato helped him pull on the rope. The heavy gear boat didn't budge, even with the added leverage. They tried several more times, to no avail.

"What now?" Plato asked as the rain washed down his face in rivulets.

"We ought to string a line over and unload all that shit," Jim suggested. "He's carrying some of the gear for our two kayakers. Let's get them to earn their keep and set up a shuttle line. Then, we can use my boat, paddle out holding the rope, and bring the gear back to the bank. Once it's empty, the raft will peel off. At least that's the theory."

Pat and Gary strung a rope from the raft to a tree on the right bank.

*You're not such a hot boater, or you wouldn't have wrapped the first day out,* Pat thought with a certain satisfaction. He and Gary, along with Jim and Jerry, shuttled over and back, unloading equipment a few pieces at a time to lessen the weight of Jacques' gear boat. Pat smirked at Jacques on each return trip.

The weight of some of the bags prompted comments like:

"Here's the sack of horseshoes," Jim said

"Here's the anvil box," Jerry replied with a laugh.

"That's the kayak anchor, not the anvil-box," Jacques replied, smiling back at Pat.

"A kayak can't be anchored, they'd sink," Gary said.

"I think that's his point," Pat smiled back but without warmth.

After three hours, they'd remedied the wrap and stood in a line on the bank passing equipment down to riverside where it was reloaded onto Jacques' boat.

Gretta took Bobby aside. "I want to go back," she told him. "I'm getting bad vibes. My inner voice is screaming at me—I don't like this—we could have gotten killed because I don't know what I'm doing out here."

"Well, we most likely would have just gone for a nice, cold swim. I don't think we'd have died, unless it was from embarrassment," Jacques said as he walked by on the way to his raft.

"I'll bet you'll remember to go rock side next time," Bobby said to Gretta with a smile. "Besides, hiking out of here isn't an option, Hon. Look at those canyon walls." They both studied the steep cliffs angling down both sides of the river. Trees, mostly ponderosa pine, grew within 100 yards of the river on the left bank, but none grew on the other side. Only rock escarpments reaching to the gray heavens. "We became bound to the fates once we rounded that first corner."

"I guess I just didn't realize how dangerous this really was when I agreed to come along. This is heavier than I thought it would be," Gretta said. It was obvious to Bobby she was shaken. She also looked as if she might be feeling guilty.

Bobby worried about her. She didn't know anything about rafting and had only come on the trip because he'd assured her safety. *Assured before the Klamath.*

He wondered why he'd even invited her. They were from different worlds. She ate only vegetables and tofu; he was a true carnivore. She liked new-age music, while Bobby couldn't listen to two minutes of it before he wanted to flee. In contrast, he loved the tasteful blues of Stevie Ray Vaughn and Albert Collins. He wondered how he and Gretta had managed to remain such good friends over the years with absolutely nothing in common.

# CHAPTER FOUR

He put his arm around her shoulder and gave her a hug. "Gretta, everyone of us has screwed up on the river at least a dozen times. We all felt exactly what you're feeling now. So forget it, and let's have fun." He looked down and said, "I shouldn't have let Jacques take such a heavy load. It's my fault, not yours."

"It's not a question of fault. It's...it's just that I have this bad feeling I can't shake."

"Hey, I'll watch out for you. Jacques will too."

"But he hit that rock."

"He's a good boater. He was just weighted down with everybody's gear, and it's really hard to see with this rain. We're going to divide it up a little better, and pray for better weather. But trust me; nothing's going to happen to you. I promised your kids, remember?"

Gretta looked up at Bobby with doe-brown eyes and smiled. "All right. I guess I just got a little freaked-out." She walked down to the raft as they strapped the last piece of gear to the frame.

After the three-hour ordeal of the wrap, they shoved off to find their first assigned campsite. They ended up getting to Elkhorn Bar at 7:00 p.m.—a little late to be setting up camp, but a welcome sight to everyone.

"Some of these people don't know each other yet," Bobby said as he handed Jerry a beer.

"Yeah, but this first evening will give everyone the chance to remedy that, *especially* with all the vitamin B going around," Jerry said as he took a sip of beer and held his can up as a salute. "Health food, to go with Jacque's Almost World-Famous Rogue River Chili."

After dinner everyone, including Bobby, retired to the tents except for a few diehards who stayed up until the fire went out.

Bobby listened to the gentle drone of their voices until sleep crept into his tired mind.

Bobby tossed and turned in his sleeping bag. He dreamed he was in a car, driving away from a darkening Texas landscape where black clouds gathered. Eventually, the road changed into a wooded highway that closed in on all sides.

The car suddenly vanished, and he came to a stop on foot; he stood alone in a small clearing, alone except for his second recurring nightmare: eyes in the dark. They glared at him from behind some tall bushes. He had no idea what type of animal these eyes belonged to, but he could feel the familiar aura of malefic intent projected toward him.

They had stalked him since childhood. One of his earliest nightmares had been of these same eyes gazing from behind clothes hanging in his closet. Thirty years later they still terrified him. The smell was always overwhelming, the quiet deafening.

His instinct told him to run, but vines had snared his legs. Each time he tried to raise his feet, he felt thorns biting into his ankles like small needle teeth. Suddenly, the eyes rushed at him—coming faster and faster, closer and closer, until he escaped into wakefulness—sweating profusely in the cool night air. The rain had stopped.

He unzipped the door of his tent and walked out by a fallen pine tree to relieve himself. Night noises comforted him: a nearby whippoorwill and the sound of crickets chirping behind the tent.

In his dream, there had been no sound—only an oppressive silence.

The dream sent cold waves up his spine, so he sought the shelter of his tent. First he walked out to his boat and took the Gerber clip-lock knife off his life jacket. His Bowie Knife already lay next to his sleeping bag, but the laser sharpness of the Gerber—good for close in—gave him extra confidence. Besides, the big K-bar was his throwing knife. In the dark, he knew throwing wasn't so effective. "Just insurance," he said to himself and laughed. He walked back to his tent and snuggled back into his bag, then tried to go back to sleep.

Bobby lay awake remembering his first camping trip into real wilderness. It had been the summer of 1993. He and a group of close friends had driven down to the Devil's River in southwest Texas. They camped in the open without a tent or weapons and smoked marijuana until they were too stoned to talk. They sat listening to a remarkable symphony of frogs, crickets, cicadas, and night birds.

All of a sudden, an unseen conductor gave the signal to stop. It was abrupt—as if someone had pulled the plug on a stereo. The night had become deathly quiet. After a long ten seconds had passed, they heard the roar of a mountain lion. Frighteningly close. Bobby could hear it growling on the other side of the river less than fifty feet away. The river measured barely a foot deep most of the way across, and didn't present a real barrier to a hungry puma, so he had grabbed a nearby butcher knife and held it like a talisman. It was his *magic* to keep a demon away. Being stoned had only heightened his apprehension.

CHAPTER FOUR 37

"My God! Do you think it can cross the river?" he asked his friend who had grown up in the area.

"Only if it wants to," his friend answered, much to Bobby's dismay.

On this night, alone in his tent, he once again clutched a talisman, so many years later and 2000 miles away.

...

Hank had stayed awake all night but nothing more had happened. By noon he was starving, so he opened a can of beans and ate them cold.

Up until now, Hank had been grateful that radios didn't work this deep in the canyon—he had loved the solitude of his job. Now he wished he had a radio, a phone, a fax and every other communication device known to man.

As the resident biologist, if he needed supplies, or to communicate to the outside world, he took a list to one of several pilots who landed daily on the airstrip below, and an air service delivered the goods two days later.

Hank sat in the gloomy shadows of the cabin waiting to hear the drone of an airplane engine. He sipped from a bottle of Early Times and waited.

His thoughts drifted back to Donna. He had chosen the solitude of the mountains fifteen years ago, but it still brought at least one tear every time he thought of her. He missed her now more than he had in all the years since. He longed for the life they had planned together, the dreams of having a farm where they could raise dogs. She had loved animals and adopted every stray that came around. Then, she had gotten sick: cancer of the liver. His dreams had died with her. Although he had considered suicide numerous times, in the end he decided to go on. Now, he desperately wanted to live and that surprised him.

Standing and stretching, he walked to the window facing the airstrip. Three rafts floated slowly around the distant bend below the landing. He had never had a desire to try whitewater rafting—Hank feared the water. But today, he longed to be with the people in those rafts.

It was three o'clock before he heard the plane. He ran back to the window, opened the shutter, and tried to see it through the glass. It circled above the forest canopy out of sight, so he scanned the lengthening shadows of the trees for one particular shadow that didn't belong.

From within the cabin his view was limited. Cautiously, he opened the window and poked his head out. Nothing unusual. Hank began feeling silly. More than likely he had fallen victim to an over-active imagination. *But the bear was real*, a voice in his head reminded him. Repeating his survey from the other two windows, just to be sure it was clear, he decided to make a run for the landing strip. As he watched the plane set down on the grass of the airfield, he realized for the first time how far it was from the cabin.

"There's nothing to worry about," he told himself, "whatever was up there, stayed up there."

*Unless, it's on the roof.*

Shuddering slightly, he walked to the window and observed Charlie, the pilot, unloading someone's equipment on the landing field far above the boat landing. As if transfixed, he stood watching until the job was almost completed. Then, he realized he was running out of time. Charlie would soon be gone, and he would be completely alone again. Opening the small closet by the front door, he grabbed a .22 rifle the ranger had left and worked the action to bolster his bravado. Then Hank reached for the cabin door.

The screen stuck again so he gave it a gentle kick. It flew open with a loud bang. As he walked outside, the quiet again unnerved him. The birds and bugs had quit their usual summer noisemaking, and the effect was eerie. He eased himself off the porch and into the yard, scanning each direction before backing away from the cabin. At a distance of about thirty yards, he turned toward the landing strip and gripped the rifle tighter. *All clear.*

He watched Charlie place a blue tarp over the gear he had just finished stacking before he turned back to the plane. Hank made a run for the airstrip. He feared the engine and the river noise would drown out his cries, but he yelled anyway.

"Charlie! Wait up! Charlie!"

The pilot walked around the plane making sure all was ready for the flight back over the mountains; he checked the wings, the tires, and the engine.

Hank ran toward the plane until something startled him. A large, dark apparition appeared behind a tree some fifty yards ahead and to the right of his intended path. He stopped cold.

*It moved—Oh God—it moved.*

It *had* moved. It moved again.

Though he didn't want to, he sprinted back to the cabin; it was much closer than the airfield. This time the shadow followed. Glancing over his shoulder, Hank caught sight of something huge darting from tree to tree.

Oblivious to his plight, Charlie climbed into the cockpit and began his taxi to the other end of the field just as Hank passed the outhouse forty feet from the cabin. The suspected bear-killer disappeared behind a tree about thirty feet back and twenty feet to his left and closing.

# CHAPTER FOUR

He looked back to the cabin. The screen door had rebounded off the wall and was now shut.

"Fuck!"

He jumped on the porch and literally ripped it off one hinge as he threw it open and rushed in. Hank slammed the cabin door and threw the bolt just as something blocked out all light from the closing crack.

BAM

It struck the heavy door with force. The bolt bent but didn't break. A steady pounding then worked its way around the cabin. Something blocked out each window as it passed.

He gripped the rifle as he prayed: "Thy rod and thy staff they comfort me. Yea though I walk through the valley of the shadow of death, I shall fear no evil. Thy rod and thy staff…thou anointeth my head with oil, my cup runneth over…"

BAM

"Shit! Sorry! God—please—make it stop!"

BAM

The rifle slipped out of his sweaty hands. He couldn't pick it up. Standing horrified in the center of the cabin, he cried like a child.

BAM BAM BAM

Luckily, the bear-killer directed its force against the side of the cabin instead of the door. Still, the cabin shook with each blow.

It was either stupid, or it was trying to scare him. *Please God…let it be stupid.*

The beating stopped abruptly as if his prayer had been answered. Hank strained. He listened for signs of movement from the enemy outside.

His mouth had dried like it usually did after one of his many post-Donna, five-day drunks. It was only a matter of time before he would need water from the pump outside. He already had to visit the outhouse.

Time passed and evening brought darkness. In the gloom, another thought occurred to him. *Brenda won't be here for a week to take over—I might have to wait here that long.*

"No," he said, answering the thought. "When the next plane lands, I'm making a run for it." Running to the airstrip would be dangerous but waiting would be far worse.

Shadows occasionally moved past the cabin's windows until darkness concealed them.

Hank Ridley had never felt more afraid…or alone.

# 5

## POWERHOUSE

The dream had so upset Bobby, that he managed to get only a few hours of what he referred to as "greasy sleep." But the next morning he awoke to the cleanest air and the bluest sky he had ever seen.

He smelled coffee right away and envisioned a cartoon character floating on the aroma of some heavenly scent. If he could have done likewise, he would have. Morning always brought hope, light, *and, thank God, coffee.*

Several of his companions stood in the sunlight with cups in hand as he ambled toward them.

"Well, look who decided to join the living," The Judge chided.

"Better than the alternate," Bobby returned.

"Here, this coffee is the closest thing to illegal I could make," Jerry said as he handed Bobby a cup.

"Thanks, I didn't sleep too well," he said as he gratefully accepted the cup and began nibbling on a cinnamon roll.

"Is that why you look like hammered shit?" Jim asked.

"Thanks for noticing," he said showing a smile full of chewed-up cinnamon roll.

"God, you can be gross," Jerry said, "and I'm truly proud to be your friend."

Bobby looked around the camp. Stragglers who weren't actually up at least appeared to be moving around inside their tents.

Jacques walked up from his tent to the kitchen area reciting lines of a poem he'd composed about day-old chili. After he finished, he took a deep breath and let out a loud belch. Offering a mischievous smile, he addressed the group.

"Bobby has asked if I would bring to your attention the fact that we have a very difficult day today, encompassing eighteen miles of some ass-kicking whitewater. At the culmination of today's festivities will be Pistol Creek Rapids, a true ass-kicker of the first order. The sooner we are underway, the sooner we reach our destination, and the sooner we will be able to relax and enjoy the beauty of God's own favorite campsite—Pistol Creek. But first we have to survive The Powerhouse."

The sun shone through rising vapor creating visible rays that pierced the canopy of leaves. The scent of pine needles mixed with coffee and made Bobby content to just sit all day smelling the intoxicating aromas.

At that point, Bobby looked north and saw a group of buzzards circling far off in the distance. "Some animal has met its end; now carrion cyclone will to Earth descend." Bobby smiled. "What a poet I am."

"A regular mister metaphor," Jim said.

"Okay everybody. Head um up—move um out," Bobby said as he swung his hand in a circle above his head.

When they had broken camp and loaded all the rafts, they shoved off into the current. Like a small parade on water, they departed Elkhorn Camp, and lazily floated down-river.

"See you at lunch," Jim said to Bobby as he and Linda paddled ahead.

Bobby watched the buzzards descend.

• • •

After leaving Elkhorn Camp, Bobby's spirits soared. Continuous whitewater, more technical than anything he had ever attempted, tested his skill. It seemed that one rapid would end, and less than a hundred yards down, another would begin. The sun brought the temperature up into the high eighties, and the cool water splashed him at every wave; it felt more welcome than it had the day before. The warm air dried his skin within minutes, and he actually found himself hunting for more waves to hit.

When the first major series of rapids came upon them, he noticed that Jim and Linda had taken the lead position ahead of Jacques and figured it was because Jim hated following anyone else's line. The pair pulled over and motioned everyone to the left bank. Bobby frowned. He hadn't expected any scouting today, but it soon became apparent why they had pulled over.

Another party had wrapped a boat around a rock in the middle of Powerhouse Rapid. He could see ropes drawn tight to both sides of the river.

## CHAPTER FIVE

If a boat had gone around the turn into Powerhouse, he knew what would have happened. The current would have grabbed the boat like the 'event horizon' of a black hole, making it almost impossible to pull to shore. Then one of his people might have been ejected or clotheslined by the ropes of the Z-drag.

He rowed toward the left bank. "I'm glad Jim had the lead," Bobby said to Suzi. "Being in a paddle boat makes him more maneuverable. A gear boat might not have been able to pull over fast enough; the results could have been disastrous."

"What? Just from those ropes?"

"A kid on the Upper Klamath got killed by a loose Z-drag rope. He wasn't looking—there wasn't anything we could do once he was in the channel. His neck snapped when it pulled him out of the raft." He looked away from her.

*Am I trying to convince her, or me?*

Fighting back a lump in his throat, he continued. "The kid floated unconscious through several miles of class-four whitewater. I was the first to catch up to his body. That was in May; guess I'll get freaked-out any time I see ropes strung out like that."

"Well, you tried to save him—you did all you could," Suzi said.

"It was my Z-drag." He'd done it; he'd actually told someone. But it didn't make the feelings go away like he'd hoped. Bobby fell silent, remembering, as he rowed to the rocky shore. Suzi jumped out and held the boat by the bow rope, but she had the good taste not to pursue the subject further.

The wrap below Ram's Horn and several other minor boating accidents the day before worried him. He wasn't as much worried about the liability as the possible danger to his people.

*But shit happens, Bobby.*

He watched as Pat and Gary paddled downstream to offer assistance. The bright yellow and dark red of their respective kayaks stood out against the blue water as they danced from eddy to eddy on the way down. Bobby figured with Gary's rescue expertise, and Pat's formidable strength, his presence wouldn't be required.

While the rescue continued below, he and Jerry studied the map of the next section. It had gotten wet, taking on the appearance of an ancient mariner's map, like the ones used before Columbus had rewritten history. In olden times, when boats sailed beyond known boundaries, they would see markings on the map, a picture of a sea serpent with the caption: HERE THERE BE DRAGONS. Bobby noticed the water had melted the map's ink into a design, not unlike a sea serpent, just below Pistol Creek Camp.

In a way, these were uncharted waters to all but Jacques and Plato, he thought. He and the rest of the group were experiencing Middle Earth for the first time.

Taking a deep breath of the clean, mountain air, he sat on a large warm rock. Sage, lupine, bluet, and daisy scented the air, mixed with an almost imperceptible odor of fish. He looked up at the scene. Mountains loomed on both sides of the river, and stark cliffs seemed to cut into the water from hundreds of feet above. An eagle cried out from directly above him.

"What a paradise. I've never seen anything like this," he said to no one in particular.

He returned his attention to the raft being pried off a rock several hundred yards downstream. The entire process of rescuing the boat took half an hour from the time Gary and Pat began helping.

Bobby pushed his boat back into the current and pulled hard on the oars. The force of the river grabbed the raft like a feather on a strong wind and pulled them at high speed toward the same rock that had wrapped the other boat. But he knew how to read whitewater. By turning the boat forty-five degrees to the current, he allowed the river to help him push away from it. They missed by over ten feet and he hadn't even broken a sweat. He and Suzi ran Powerhouse flawlessly.

When they reached the bottom, he noticed a woman in a large raft, sitting back, relaxing in the sun as her boat drifted lazily in an eddy. Her long, chestnut brown hair draped in curls over the upper part of a lithe body. She wore only a bikini under her open life jacket. Her lips were full, she was well tanned, as if she lived outside, and the first word that popped into Bobby's mind was healthy. Sexy was a close second.

She turned to him and smiled. Her jade-green eyes reached right inside him. They smiled at each other the entire time his raft passed by, and their eyes never lost contact until he floated around the bend.

*I should have said something*, he thought silently; he hoped for a chance to see her again. Bobby heard the sound of a drum beating nearby. It took a moment before he realized it was his heart pounding in his ears.

He noticed boats pulling over to river right below Powerhouse Rapid. Jim had stopped for lunch on a beach where the chipmunks were so brazen, they sneaked food right off your plate, at least until Phydeaux arrived.

## CHAPTER FIVE

After lunch, Bobby called a meeting to voice a complaint Jerry had brought to his attention: "What the hell happens if one of the last boats has a problem, and everyone else is already downstream?" He paused for effect. "The settlers didn't name this the 'River of No Return' for nothing. I don't want to try to hike out of here. Except for Hell's Canyon of the Snake and the Grand Canyon, this is the deepest trench in the country. Therefore, I for one would certainly appreciate it if each boat would stay within a hundred yards of the boat behind you. That way, we can maintain at least a semblance of communication. If one of the rafts gets into trouble they'll have some help.

Jerry perched on a rock earlier, and Suzi and I were the last boat. We got stuck trying to help him get free. I only bring this up because I'm running sweep and would absolutely *hate* to spend the frigging night in my boat in the middle of the river, understand?" Bobby asked. One-by-one the boat captains all agreed to stay closer.

When the lunch cooler and roll table had been secured, they shoved off. All afternoon the boaters, including Bobby, jammed onto rocks. "Perching," he explained to Suzie. She looked puzzled so he explained the difference between a wrap and a perch to her. "A perch isn't as serious as a wrap. Rocks that don't quite break the surface of the water are usually the ones that perch boats. Like this fucker!" he shouted as he pulled on the oars in anger. Still, the boat didn't move. Suzi smiled at his frustrated antics.

That afternoon, he'd used all types of gyrations to extricate his raft from each close encounter with a rock. Sometimes it was shallow enough that he could get out and push the raft off. But other times required more humiliating actions. "You get into the middle of the boat and gently jump up and down, while I use the paddle to pull us around from the front," he explained to Suzi.

She waited until he reached out with a powerful draw stroke and jumped as hard as she could. With the added force of her bounce he pulled himself completely out of the raft.

When he surfaced, Suzi burst into hysterical laughter. "Revenge—revenge for yesterday morning," she said with a laugh as she helped him back into the boat.

"I left my water gun in the van or you'd have hell to pay," he promised.

"Hey, Bobby, stay in the boat—it's not that hopeless," Jerry shouted from fifty feet downstream. He sat in an eddy apparently waiting for them to get free, enjoying the show too, Bobby suspected.

After ten minutes of effort, they finally managed to free themselves off the "rock from hell," as it would become known at dinner.

Bobby had checked before the trip to make sure all the rafts were of professional quality. Most were Hypalon and neoprene in various mixtures. A good raft could take a pounding against sharp rocks at high speed and emerge none the worse for wear. Even sharp objects didn't usually penetrate them. On this day, however, Jim reported that his boat had received a small puncture just below the 'red line' center point. Luckily, it was a tiny hole. But leaks were bad news on multi-day trips, and Bobby knew they would have to repair it that evening.

At least nothing major had happened. All the potentially bad situations had been resolved without damage or injury. All in all, he felt things were going pretty well.

Just about everyone—even Jacques and Pat—seemed to be getting along for the moment, the equipment was holding up nicely, and the weather had decided to cooperate. *Now, where the hell is Pistol Creek Rapid?*

• • •

Jim wanted to make sure none of the less experienced boaters entered Pistol Creek Rapid the wrong way. To him, they all fit the category of less experienced boaters. He was the only guide on the trip who made a living running rivers that most sane people wouldn't even consider going down, even wearing two lifejackets. This river hadn't presented anything that even made his heart rate go up. But the others would be impressed.

The rivers of the West offered unsurpassed wilderness experiences, but, in his opinion, their whitewater didn't come close to the bone-breaking fury of The Gauley, or the white-knuckled ride The Cheat forced one to endure. They bordered class-six. Still, no reason not to be careful, he thought. His West Virginia Rivers were only hours away from help. Here, help would be days away at best.

As the lead boat, he scouted everything from the river. Late in the afternoon, he heard, then saw Pistol Creek Rapid approaching. He and Linda caught an eddy behind the entry rock and waited.

"Why aren't we going anywhere?" she asked.

"We're in an eddy," he explained. Seeing that she was waiting for a more detailed explanation, he went into his guide-school lecture. "An eddy is usually a relatively calm place where the river current flows back upstream to fill the void behind an object. Since rafts can't effectively be anchored in current, we catch eddies. It's possible to stay in a good one indefinitely, and this is a good

## CHAPTER FIVE

eddy." Jim could scout the entire rapid from his vantage point. From there, he could signal the other boats to enter on river right.

The guidebook had prepared him for Pistol Creek. The rapid began just beyond a blind right-hand turn. He chose the eddy he knew would be behind the biggest mid-stream boulder. Once inside it, he studied the flow of the violent currents. An unwary boater would be into the rapid before he or she knew it. Mother Nature had strategically placed small hatchet-shaped rocks down the left side of the rapid. The current on the first turn would push hard into the left wall. Great effort would be required to stay clear of it, even if an oarsman entered the rapid properly.

If one entered incorrectly, it would take considerable horsepower to break the river's hold. "Like being caught in a tractor beam," he said with a nervous laugh.

Rounding a corner, Bobby saw Jim and Linda behind a rock motioning for him to move to river right. As he came within thirty feet, Jim shouted over the din of the rapid. "Enter right, turn, and ride the cushion around the cliff wall."

Bobby couldn't see what he meant until he rounded the first corner; then it became clear. He reacted second by second, readjusting the ferry angles to keep maximum control over the craft. The cushion of water piling up on the inside cliff wall loomed enormous, and the front of the raft angled up at forty degrees. It was a wild ride. He looked up to see Scott, Jacques and Plato taking pictures point-blank in front of him. They stood less than eight feet away on the rocks above the cushion. He heard their cheers, even over the noise of the torrent.

Adrenalin flowed freely in a class-four rapid like this one. His skin tingled, and his heart raced—an intense rush that Bobby loved. He suspected that most whitewater boaters were adrenalin junkies no different than him. Suzi was certainly no exception—she looked to be in rapture. Glancing back over her shoulder with a big smile she said, "Let's go back—I really liked that one."

"I haven't got enough energy left," he replied. "Besides, the camp is right up here on the left, and my body is telling me that it's time to replace all the calories I burned today." He rowed slowly forward through the calm water below. "Tonight's Plato's night to fix dinner—something called Beef Bourguignonne, and he swears it'll put Jacques' 'Almost World Famous Chili' from last night to shame."

Pistol Creek Camp lay hidden on the left, just downstream of the rapid.

It was the most beautiful camp Bobby had ever seen. Stands of conifers combined with deciduous trees, and a creek rushed noisily through one end of camp; numerous spots offered level places to set up tents. The air smelled clean from the aerated water, and small birds chirped evening sounds from nearby trees. He stood on the beach and watched the rest of the group drift down from the rapid.

Jim was the last, since he had remained in the eddy giving entrance instructions to everyone.

"You can have my Rolex if it gets any better than this," Jacques said as he walked by.

"Why am I not surprised that you'd have a Rolex?" Jim said.

Bobby laughed. Jacques had been right about this place. It was much nicer than Elkhorn. After scouting out the best tent spot, he joined in unloading the boats. They hauled tables, lawn chairs, stoves, kitchen boxes, and personal drybags to make a comfortable home for the night, and everyone worked like ants setting up camp. Bobby and Jim located a suitable kitchen area and started a fire in the fire pan.

The warm evening air brought back memories from forgotten nights of his childhood summers. Pistol Creek's spell seemed filled with the magic of Tolkien's Rivendell. All that was missing were the Hobbits.

A group gathered around the fire and began passing Plato's bottle of Glenlivet. Conversations abounded about the experiences of the day.

"How many river guides does it take to change a light bulb?" Pat asked. His tan skin blended with a large pine tree behind him almost rendering him invisible in the twilight, but for his white shorts.

No one knew.

"Seven," he answered himself. "One to actually do it, and six to say how they could have done it better."

Bobby laughed. It was an accurate anecdote based on most of the guides he knew.

Finding himself in need of privacy, he left the group and walked toward the woods behind the camp. On his way, he passed Gary.

"Hey Bobby, check out this rock over by the trees. There's some cool paintings on it." In the remaining twilight they walked through an opening in the woods. Sure enough, there were drawings.

"The book said petroglyphs—or pictographs—are found all up and down the river," Bobby told him. "Some are thought to be thousands of years old."

"Yeah, but this one is too cool. Check it out." Gary pointed to the drawings

## CHAPTER FIVE

with his flashlight. "These stick figures are people." He moved the beam. "This looks like elk or deer, but look at this, man."

The red streaks had faded, but the intentions of the artist were clear. A huge stick figure dwarfed a stick man. The man's figure appeared to be in a kneeling position.

"I'd hate to meet up with that a bear that big," Bobby said.

"Ditto. Looks more like Godzilla."

"Bobby studied it for a moment. Huge jagged teeth lined its stick mouth. To him it looked like the figure considered the stick man as food. "Thanks for showing this to me, but I need to do my business and get back to help Jim patch a hole in his front tube," Bobby replied. He relieved himself on a dead stump and zipped up his pants.

"I think I'll go get Pat. Shit like this freaks him out, Gary said." The two men walked back to camp.

Evening gradually gave way to night.

• • •

Phydeaux sniffed the camp perimeter. She picked up unusual scents, one of which was completely foreign to her. None of The People noticed her sniffing nervously as she went from tent-site to tent-site. Poised at the edge of camp, she looked out into the gathering gloom and issued a barely audible growl.

"Phydeaux! Come on girl! Get your butt over here, it's chowtime!" Jacques called.

She slowly retreated, not turning her back on the thicket. Once she was within the circle of the main camp, she turned and ran to Jacques.

He scooped out the remains of last night's chili and mixed it with a can of Alpo. Ordinarily, she would have devoured it instantly. Instead, she kept whining, looking at Jacques and turning to stare into the woods. Taking one last sniff of the air, she began eating her dinner. Occasionally, she looked up from her bowl and gave a soft "woof" at the forest behind camp, but no one noticed.

# 6

## APPREHENSIONS

Abigail Jones looked forward to the end of a very long day. First, Charlene had wrapped one of the gear boats at Powerhouse, and it had taken over an hour to extricate. Then, one of the Murphy sisters had fallen out of the raft and cut her leg on a sharp rock, adding an extra hour of wasted time to the day's activities. In fact, it seemed like the other two boats spent as much time perched on rocks as they did moving down the river. Abigail's all-woman crew exuded "positive attitude" but lacked any real whitewater expertise.

She was the only one with any real experience in class-four water, and she worried about the other women. She had believed them when they told her they were experienced boaters. Now she was learning a valuable lesson: people held different definitions of what 'experienced' meant. Next time, if there were a next time, she would give each boater a test on the Upper Clackamas before trying a multi-day trip on a river of this difficulty. In the meantime, she prayed no one would drown on this trip.

Something else bothered her: her group had missed out on camping at the coveted Pistol Creek Camp. The Aldrich party, whoever they were, had gotten the lion's share of desirable campsites by arriving a day early and requesting them from the ranger. Next time, she planned to drive over a day early.

"Oh well, we can't win them all," she said to her friend, Beth Porter, as they surveyed a campsite slightly upstream from Pistol Creek Rapids.

"At least it's level," Beth replied. "Last night I must have slept at a forty-five degree angle; I've been leaning all day."

"I don't think, after a day like today, I'll have trouble sleeping in a tree," Abigail said. After a moment she changed the subject. "By the way, did you happen to catch any of the names of the people in that group ahead of us?"

"A few, why?"

"Nothing."

"Come on Abby, I know you asked for a reason. Spill it."

Abby felt her face flush. "Nothing really, I just wondered if you happened to get the name of the guy in the red raft, since you were talking with him below Powerhouse," Abby said, perhaps a little too cool.

"As a matter of fact, his name was easy to remember. It's the same as my ex-husband's."

"Bobby?"

"Yeah. But that's as far as the resemblance goes. The new one's gorgeous."

"I hope I get to see more of Bobby," Abby said with mischief in her voice. Then she remembered the dark-haired woman who had ridden in the front of his raft. "Do you think that was his wife in the boat with him?"

"I didn't ask him his life story. I just remembered his name, for Christ's sake." Beth laughed as she took Abigail's arm and walked her up to the camp. "I'll tell you what, Abby, tomorrow I'll make a point to find out if he's married. If he isn't, I'll ask him if he's interested in a fiery, green-eyed brunette such as yourself. What do you think?"

"I think you'll die slow and painful," Abby replied as she raised an eyebrow. "Don't even dream about doing that, Beth. I mean it."

Beth smiled, a hint of mischief played across her face.

"Really," Abby said, but she felt a grin edging its way onto her face. Beth smiled back.

She and Beth had been best friends for five years, and loved going on adventures without testosterone overwhelming their fun, the reason they only invited women on their trips. Her friend was petite compared to the other women: only five feet tall, but well proportioned. Beth had short, black hair, brown eyes, and looked to be part Mexican, adding to her sensual, dark appearance, which Abby envied.

She and Beth carried the heavy dry box to its rightful place in camp, while Carol and Cynthia Murphy attempted to set up the kitchen box. Abby knew Carol and Cynthia Murphy were not really twins, though everyone mistook them as such. Both had red hair and freckles; they each stood about five feet-six and had ten or fifteen extra pounds on their hips. Though they looked alike, their personalities varied to the extreme. Carol worked in a veterinary hospital, while Cynthia was a real estate agent. Cynthia had lied, not only to

## CHAPTER SIX

Abby, but to Carol as well, about the true level of her boating skills. Now she was paying the price for her deception.

Abby wanted the discussion about Bobby to end. Allowing Beth to tell Bobby that she was attracted to him meant risking all the protection she had built up over most of her adult life. So to change the subject she said, "Carol isn't speaking to Cynthia at the moment. She told me she's never been as frightened as she has been the last two days. Cynthia's a class-two boater at best. They escaped being trashed in most of the rapids, due to luck for the most part, not skill."

Charlene Blanchet walked by quietly and caught their attention. Abby figured Charlene was almost good enough to be on the Middle Fork. She had made one, critical error at Powerhouse that resulted in forcing the raft sideways into a boulder. One of the unbendable rules of whitewater rafting is to never turn a raft sideways into an obstacle or hole. Abby could tell Charlene was determined not to be the cause of any more delay.

"Beth, could you please help me with my cooler?" Charlene called from her raft.

"Yeah, just a minute." Beth turned and whispered to Abby. "Ten dollars she apologizes again."

"No deal; I know how she feels," Abby said.

"Chicken."

"Give her some slack, okay? She's embarrassed enough. I'll bet you ten dollars she won't wrap a boat again—at least on this trip."

"No bet," Beth replied as she turned to follow Charlene.

"Chicken." Abby walked over to a rock at the river's edge and scanned downstream.

*I wonder what we'll step in tomorrow*, she thought. "Pistol Creek Rapid," she answered silently. She looked up at the other women and sighed. She silently prayed no one would be hurt in the big class-four coming up first thing in the morning.

# 7

### NIGHT VISITOR

After dinner Jim and Bobby took the repair kit out to Jim's boat and began cleaning the punctured area with Toluol. Linda held a flashlight for them as they sipped Jack Daniels and worked at the repair. The entire job took them less than twenty minutes to complete.

Walking back into camp, they noticed everyone drifting to the tents. "What's this? Everybody burned out, are they?" Jim asked with a measure of smart-assed intonation in his voice. "You west-coast boaters are a bunch of pussies."

"Watch it asshole—I'm a west-coast boater," Bobby reminded him.

"Present company excepted. Hey, you want to finish this before somebody else does?" he asked holding up the bottle.

"I'm not tired anymore," Bobby said.

"Well I am," Linda said from behind him. "I'll get the aspirin for you two in the morning. Good night, honey," she said as she kissed Jim on the cheek. "Good night, Bobby." She walked off toward the creek.

Jim and Bobby positioned their lawn chairs close to the fire pan. Reaching over, Jim took a large hardwood log and added it to the fire.

"You'll have to stay up 'til it goes out now," Jacques said from behind him.

"Huh?"

"Now you'll have to stay up with that fire, east-coast super stud. Fires have to be tended until they're out. And don't pour water into my fire pan; it makes too big of a mess. Remember, we have to leave every camp exactly as we found it, if not better. So don't dump it out on the ground and douse it either."

"Go away—please. I'm getting drunk, and I'd like to enjoy it," Jim replied.

"Bobby, watch after this asshole, please. I don't want to wake up to the crackle of pine trees."

"I'll make sure it burns down safely. Go ahead—don't worry about a thing," Bobby promised as he took a hit off the whiskey.

"Why does that not erase my concern?" Jacques said as he turned to go.

"Good night, Mom," Jim said.

"Good night, John-Boy."

They talked and hours went by while the bottle slowly disappeared. Finally, at about two-thirty in the morning, they passed out in their lawn chairs.

Bobby dreamed that he was once again in the woods, alone. He could hear the night birds singing and the sounds of the river somewhere close by. Suddenly, everything became dead silent, just as it had twenty years before on the Devil's River. But this time even the river noise stopped. He found himself sitting in a lawn chair in the middle of a forest. Out in the darkness, two flaming eyes, malignant with hate, opened suddenly and glared at him. The hatred burned like a lighthouse penetrating the darkness. He could hear a dog barking somewhere off in the distance and tried to move; his limbs wouldn't respond. He was frozen solid, like stone. Bobby kept staring back into those horrible basilisk eyes. He knew he was dreaming, but it didn't help. More than anything, he wanted to wake up. *Please!*

He got his wish. Like a veil being lifted, he came to. The landscape in his eyes now matched the one in his dream. The dog barking was Phydeaux, and Bobby could swear he saw the same burning eyes slowly fading back into the thicket.

He attempted to shake off the feeling, but why was Phydeaux going wild? She faced the same bush where he had been looking.

*What the hell is going on here?*

Phydeaux stood between Jacques' tent, and the spot in the woods where she stared. Jacques had awakened to her barking.

"What is it, girl? A bear? Go get it!" he said.

Phydeaux stopped barking and began to growl. The sound terrified Bobby; it was a growl of warning to an unseen enemy.

Bobby reached for a flashlight, as did Jim. They shined them at the spot where Phydeaux directed her aggressive stand. There appeared to be nothing there, but neither of them chose to move away from the perceived safety of the camp.

## CHAPTER SEVEN

After a while, Phydeaux stopped growling, but continued her vigilant watch deep into the woods, her ears tuned for the slightest sound, her eyes watchful for movement, and her body as taut as barbed wire.

"Time for bed," Bobby said, his voice up a pitch and a little shaky. He tried to walk to his tent without staggering.

"Most definitely," Jim answered. "See you tomorrow."

"Incidentally, I have codeine and aspirin if you need it in the morning," Bobby offered.

"Um—Codeine good," Jim said as he looked down two different paths, apparently trying to remember the direction to his tent.

Bobby barely managed to find his own tent. He lay awake for a time listening for any noise of a bear coming into camp, but the Jack Daniels slowly turned out the lights. He awoke a few times to Phydeaux's growls but was blessed by the absence of unwanted dreams, and his mind finally permitted him a few hours of restful sleep.

• • •

While the camp slowly awoke, Phydeaux wandered off into the thicket, pulled by an overpowering odor. The scent was familiar, but never as strong as this. After she had wandered almost a quarter of a mile she found the source. These tents lay at strange angles, as if they had been pulled there and left in a pile. The smell came from within them.

Sniff sniff.

The stench of death didn't bother Phydeaux the way it always seemed to bother The People, so she wandered from tent to tent, smelling the odor of the rotting flesh inside. She also picked out another scent. It was the smell of whatever had been in the thicket last night. It was not still in this place, she could tell that; this was an older smell.

"Woof!"

She took one more run around the area before returning to camp.

On her way back, she heard a twig snap to one side of the path, about half the distance across her back yard, off to her left. Then another. It was moving beside her at an angle toward her intended route. She snarled at whatever it was, and it stopped. The wind blew the wrong direction for her to pick up its scent, so she started moving again. It moved along side her, so Phydeaux ran.

Something pursued her, something big. She felt the uncommon feeling of fear take its frosty hold on her. Whatever was coming through the thicket matched her speed and would intercept her before she made it back to The People. She glanced back to her left and saw small trees and bushes falling flat. Her pursuer, now only the width of her master's patio away, closed fast.

At that same moment, the beast stood and roared a baritone bellow. Phydeaux recognized it at once: a bear. She immediately went into her pursuit mode, and charged. Phydeaux barked furiously around it. Snapping. Barking. Growling.

The bear must have realized that she was neither food, nor a creature that feared it, so it turned and fled into the forest. Phydeaux watched it disappear in the thicket. If her master were here, he'd give her a tasty. She returned to camp as if nothing had happened.

• • •

Bobby smiled as he chewed. Breakfast tasted delicious: French toast with bacon and hash browns. But Jim's coffee was so strong most watered it down by half. Not Bobby, he needed the boost.

Jim looked like he had been in the ring with Mike Tyson. Obviously, the codeine and coffee hadn't taken effect on him. He ambled up to Bobby. "God, what a night! Somebody took a shit in my mouth while I was asleep," he said.

"That's not so bad, I can live with that, but the 'mother of all bears' kept Phydeaux busy all night, which in turn kept me up all night," Scott complained. "I think Pat was right about her being a pain in the ass."

"Well, you may not have slept much, but you will notice that our coolers are still intact," Jacques pointed out.

"I hate bears. One tore up my brand new Gott 172 cooler on the Rogue last summer. I don't mind telling you bears scare the hell out of me. I'm glad Phydeaux's along," The Judge added.

"Aw Judge, bears don't eat people, they just maul 'em every once in a while," Pat said jokingly—Bobby figured to cover his own fear, since he was every bit as afraid of bears as Bobby.

"These are black bears. I've never heard of a black bear mauling anybody without good reason," Jacques said.

"Yeah, but what's a good reason to a fucking bear? Tell me that," Pat challenged as he walked away.

"Well, whatever the hell it was, I'll be glad to get away from it," The Judge replied. Bobby felt the urgent need to get away from "it" also. Last night's dream had confused and frightened him. He recalled the feeling of panic that had attacked him as he awoke in the lawn chair. Remembering the hallucination of the glaring, yellow eyes, he turned and looked at the spot where they had been. In the light of day, there didn't seem to be anything terribly ominous about the bush. Still, he didn't feel like getting too close to it.

Gary added, "I thought I heard something several times last night. Everything got real quiet, and I could hear the slightest of movements until Phydeaux went back to work. Man, whatever it was, it was a master of stealth. Don't bears usually just plod through the woods? Probably a big coon or a mule deer."

*Yeah, a big coon or a mule deer.*

"Right," Pat paused and continued. "This place is nice and all, but I'd like to get on down the road. I like to give bears plenty of room." Bobby was about to suggest the same when Jacques walked up.

"My good fellow, obviously you have never witnessed the actions of the miraculous Phydeaux the Wonder Dog. She holds firm convictions on the bear question," he said.

Bobby took the usual hour to pack everything and load his boat. He made sure he topped off the air in the inflatable tubes of the raft. Then he loaded, and strapped the gear down tight in the event of a flip or a wrap. He knew losing vital things this far away from help could prove more than just an inconvenience.

Before shoving off, he and Jerry made one last sweep through camp to check for litter or items that might have been overlooked. The wind shifted directions, and an unpleasant odor wafted their way. "Something died out there," Bobby said.

"It certainly would knock a buzzard off a shit wagon," Jerry replied.

"I'll bet an elk 'bought the farm' somewhere over that way." Bobby pointed to the west.

"Yeah, I agree, it would have to be that big to stink this bad."

"Boy, I'm glad the wind didn't shift before breakfast," Bobby said.

They returned to the beach and boarded their rafts. Things were coming together. His fears seemed to have been unfounded. Good friends like Jerry always helped him see the positive side of things. Bobby looked up, and once again noticed a vortex of buzzards circling somewhere behind Pistol Creek Camp.

• • •

The sun baked into Bobby's arms and legs as he dodged rocks through a tight rapid, but the cold water shocked his skin temperature back down every time he hit a wave. Below the rapid, calm water stretched into the next bend. Suzi looked up at the blue sky and raised her hands up like a supplicant. Bobby liked Suzi, but he was aware of a growing attraction between her and Jerry. Though he didn't mention it, he hoped it would develop naturally over the rest of the trip. Jerry deserved someone like Suzi.

He tried to think of a way to get her into Jerry's boat without being obvious. On the other hand, he enjoyed her company and wasn't anxious to lose it. Her wit and commentary kept him laughing, and he loved to laugh. It seemed like it had been too long since he had laughed.

His mind then moved to a different subject: the green eyes of the woman in the raft below Powerhouse. She had held his attention for much longer than the usual nod of the head. Totally mesmerizing him as he had rowed by, she had even blushed a little when she smiled at him. At that point, all the blood had left his head and immediately rushed downward. While lost in the daydream, he hadn't paid attention to the river.

"You planning to hit that rock?" Suzi asked, bringing him back to the present.

He pulled hard around the rock. "Sorry." Suzi only smiled. Again he hoped for a chance to actually meet the mystery woman.

At that moment, a plane flew over the river at low altitude a few miles downstream.

"Hey, there's our stuff, right on schedule," Jerry shouted.

"All right!" Gary replied from his kayak, just ahead of Bobby's boat. "It's party time!"

The plane would land at Indian Creek, where Bobby knew they would find their provisions and extra coolers. He had seen to it that most of the beer and wine had been flown in with the heavy coolers, along with the rest of their food.

It wasn't too long before he saw the raised bench on the left. A log stairway led up sixty feet to the top. According to the guidebook the airstrip would be beyond the top of the stairs. He could see their gear sitting at the top to the left. A second stack of coolers and gear set on the other side of the stairs. They were covered with tarps.

"When we get there, just get the stuff labeled Aldrich Party," Bobby said.

The plane took off and turned back over the river. Bobby watched as it got

## CHAPTER SEVEN

smaller and smaller in the distance, finally clearing the huge mountains to the East.

"There goes our last contact with civilization," Plato said as he followed the speck of the plane over the peak with his eyes. "At least until the take-out."

"Yeah, ain't it great?" Pat said from behind him.

They had almost finished loading when Bobby noticed several rafts approaching. *It's her.* He nonchalantly carried a heavy cooler down the stairs to his boat. *Oh shit! It's not cool to be macho anymore,* he thought to himself.

He put the cooler down next to his raft as the green-eyed beauty pulled up.

"Hi," was all he could think of to say.

"Hi," she answered with a warm smile. Her voice was soft, low, and had a throaty quality. It sounded like a musical instrument.

"Enjoying the river so far?" he asked.

"All but the wrap at Powerhouse, the flip at Pistol Creek, and rescuing swimmers every hour or so," she answered still smiling.

"I—I'm Bobby Aldrich from Eugene, Oregon," he said reaching out to her.

"I'm Abigail Jones from Portland, Oregon," she said as she took his hand.

Electricity flowed through the contact points; Bobby didn't want to release. She finally withdrew—her fingers moving slowly until they broke the intimate contact.

"Call me Abby, all my friends do."

"Abby," he said, as if it were the most beautiful word he had ever heard. *Oh God, her name is Abby—YES!*

She could sense his attraction; it was as strong as her own. Her hand still tingled where his hand had touched hers. She wanted to speak, but for the moment felt dumbfounded.

The spell broke when a woman walked up carrying a Rubbermaid Roughneck full of food.

"Is that your wife?" Abby asked, hopeful yet fearful.

"Oh no! She's just a good friend."

Abby smiled as Bobby noticed her unadorned, ring finger. He glanced up and smiled back.

"Hi," the woman said as she loaded the box onto his boat.

"Suzi, this is Abigail Jones, but everyone calls her Abby. She's from Portland."

"I'm Suzi, from San Jose," she said as she and Abby shook hands.

"Well Mister Aldrich, I've been sent to tell you that everyone is ready to go. Maybe you should strap that cooler in so we can join them," she said with a wry smile.

Bobby turned to see everyone in the boats, staring at him and grinning. Dimples appeared on both cheeks and his face turned an incredible shade of red. *God, you're a handsome one, aren't you.*

"I hope I see you later…Abby," he said.

"Me too," she answered softly.

Abby watched as Bobby rounded the corner. He was the type that had always attracted her: well built, with brown hair to his shoulders, and eyes bluer than mountain lakes. But his smile really got to her. It warmed her up inside, and she still felt the vibration where his hand had communicated with hers.

Carol and Cynthia stood next to the unclaimed gear, and Charlene had wandered up to explore, while Abby had been talking to Bobby. But Beth, good ole Beth, had watched the entire exchange from under a nearby tree.

"Well, I guess my services as Cyrano de Bergerac weren't needed after all," she said.

"Naaa, I didn't want to see my best friend die slow and painful for her meddling," Abby said.

Beth lightly slapped her hand on Abby's butt, and then followed her up the log stairs to join the Murphy sisters.

One of them called out to her from the top, "Hey Abby, come here." When Abby made the top step of the stairs, Carol said, "Somebody must have been flown out. This gear has been here at least overnight—the dust had time to settle on their tarps."

Abby looked at the coolers and ammo cans; they were stacked three feet high by five feet long by four feet deep. *Why is that stuff still here?*

"Do you think it's safe to leave it out here?" Cynthia asked.

"It probably belongs to somebody who screwed up on their dates. They told the air service to bring it a couple of days too early, but they'll be along," Abby assured her, but she knew from dealing with the air service before that they double checked the dates so people didn't have the chance to screw up. *Oh well, it's not my problem.*

"Since we don't have to load anything, do you guys want to go exploring?" Beth asked. Their group was small, and they hadn't spent the extra money to

# CHAPTER SEVEN

have their gear flown down. That left plenty of time to take in the sights and sounds of Indian Creek.

The Murphys declined, explaining that they didn't want to take their eyes off the boats since they had personal belongings some river pirate might steal in their absence. But Abby decided to join Beth and explore.

Walking across the airstrip, she noticed the ranger's cabin back up in the woods about 300 yards away. "A ranger lives in that cabin from June until September according to the book," Abby said.

Beth noticed that the screen door hung at an angle, and a wooden chair laid overturned to one side of the porch. "What do you make of that?" she asked.

"Looks deserted," Abby answered.

"You want to go check it out?"

"We're in a hurry, Beth."

"Right! You just don't want that Bobby guy to get so far ahead that we can't catch up to him."

Abby's cheeks flushed, obviously telling Beth she had hit the nail on the head. She was indeed feeling an intense pull to get down river. Then, she stopped walking and realized it wasn't just a pull towards Bobby; she felt repelled by the cabin.

Her analytic mind wondered why. As the top prosecuting attorney on the Clackamas County staff, she trusted logic and reason. She seldom lost a case. Criminal attorneys paled when they found out they had drawn Abigail Jones. Even though the district attorney considered her a rebel, she was still his favorite: good at investigative work, especially good at trial work, and most of all she didn't have political ambitions.

Her intuition now sounded a warning. Logically, she knew there was no reason to be afraid of an empty cabin with a broken screen door. *Probably just budget cuts.*

"Okay, let's take a look," she said.

"All right! Back to the fearless 'wymin' explorers from hell," Beth said as she pushed out her chest and placed hands on her hips in an imitation of Supergirl.

The sight was so ridiculous Abby couldn't help laughing. Her laughter erased the sense of unease, and she continued walking across the landing strip. The cabin stood only 200 yards beyond the airstrip, up in a small break of pines. The buzz of deerflies filled the air, and they constantly needed to be slapped away.

"God, these things are more like vampire bats than flies," Beth said as she slapped an enormous one onto the ground and stepped on it. It made a sickening crunch against the gravelly earth. "Yuccch."

The screen door creaked as a hot gentle breeze blew it back and forth. Abby listened to the river in the distance and the buzz of the flies; the only sounds other than the screen's complaint.

The urge to forget the cabin and run back to the boats reasserted itself. Again she overrode her intuition. Within forty yards of the cabin, she could see the open door behind the screen. Within twenty yards, she could see through the screen.

"What a mess," Abby thought aloud.

"I'll bet the ranger left the door open and a bear had a field day in there," Beth suggested.

"Rangers would know if there were any bear problems around here, wouldn't they?"

"Maybe it was his or her first week on the job," Beth countered as she walked up on the front porch and moved the screen aside.

"Hello anybody—"

Beth froze in the doorway, gagging twice before she erupted. She tried to cover her mouth, but vomit gushed through her fingers as she turned and stumbled past Abby into the small front yard of the cabin. She continued heaving, and rocked herself into a sedate hysteria.

*I'm an investigator*, Abby told herself as she stepped inside.

Darkness shrouded the cabin. She smelled blood a second before her eyes adjusted. The flies hung thick inside the cavity of the human torso on the cabin floor. It reminded her of flyblown meat in the markets of Nogales, Mexico, where she had gone on vacation as a child. Instead of feeling sick, like Beth, Abby felt terror. Whoever, or whatever killed the ranger, had emptied him of his internal organs. She remembered watching her father clean and gut a deer and immediately noted the similarity.

She wanted to sprint back to the rafts and leave. The nearest help was a long two days down-river at the Victor Ranch. They had a radio to contact the air service in Salmon; she could call the sheriff's office from there. Her eyes darted around the room taking in data. *What could have done this?* A renegade bear; a grizzly that wandered down from Canada?

Carefully she walked further into the cabin, completely focused on the mutilated body, while Beth still gagged outside. Abby noticed blood streaked across the floor as if someone had dragged the "gut wad" across it. *Would a bear rip somebody open and only eat the organs?*

There were signs of a struggle. Things were knocked off shelves, and the

# CHAPTER SEVEN

desk chair was shattered as if it had been used as a club. A .22 caliber rifle lay in two pieces beside a bloody jacket. On closer observation she noticed that it looked more like it had been chopped in half instead of broken. There weren't any jagged edges and the all of the ends bent inward.

*Pinched?*

The jacket's brass plate had a name on it. Hank Ridley. Then, the most chilling realization hit her. The blood was still pooled as if it were fresh. That meant it had happened recently, *this morning*, and the thought came to her, that whoever, or whatever had killed the ranger might still be nearby.

Theoretically, she knew a level of fear took over at times of survival. A person either froze up, or took action with a single-minded clarity of purpose. Now it was no theory.

Abby refused to freeze. Her overriding purpose became to get back to the rafts…and to stay alive.

A light, tapping noise stopped her. She turned to locate it. It had been in her ears the entire time she had been in the cabin, but the buzzing flies had masked it.

She could see the entire room except for a closet by the door. The tapping sound came from inside the closet. The idea that the killer might be there turned her emotional thermostat down several more degrees. To get outside she would need to go by it.

The closet door stood slightly ajar, and she didn't recall if it had been when she walked by it before. Abby took the clip-lock knife off her lifejacket. A brown belt in Tang Soo Do, she held the knife the way her instructor had taught: back in a ready-to-punch position. Her other hand shook but rose to a block.

She listened to Beth gasp for air and cough in the front yard. The tapping sound might have slowed slightly, but maintained the same volume. She stood directly in front of the closet, and almost left without looking.

Intuition said, "Don't open the door." She hadn't heeded its warning before; it had been right. Now she wondered if this new intuition was related to her survival instincts, or was she suddenly psychic? Did she, on some level, already know what was in the closet?

*No.*

She heard Beth repeating, "ABBYOHGOD-OHGODABBY!" as if reciting a mantra. She didn't sound capable of saying anything else. *Beth must be in shock.* Abigail Jones turned her attention back to the closet. Giving in to curiosity, she slowly opened the closet door with her left foot. Then, like Beth, she threw up.

# 8

## SOLITUDE

Gary enjoyed floating alone through the wilderness; feeling at one with nature without the distractions other people always presented. He lagged behind in his kayak. As nice a day as anyone could ask for: ninety degrees with an azure blue sky, and little, puffy white clouds playing across the heavens like wild sheep. He floated along feeling the direct power of the river beneath his hull.

*Why would anyone want to hang out with other people today?*

Two hermit thrushes in a nearby pine sang their unusual song. Each phrase started off with a whistle and closed with a mixture of sharp, effusive notes. He looked up and saw a deer on a rock almost within the reach of his paddle. It watched him float by.

*God, I love this.*

He searched for a place to pull over and sun for a while—a serious breach of river etiquette, but he didn't come all this way to rush. The day and the river seemed magical. He had a little weed in his dry bag and planned to add to the day's magic.

Bobby's and Jim's rafts became two dots in the distance before he headed for a quiet eddy that bordered a grassy beach on river-left. He paddled to shore and popped off the kayak's spray skirt. After pulling it up onto the grass, he placed his helmet and paddle inside the cockpit. He walked over to a flat rock that formed a natural bench and sat down with his mini-bag.

His fingers worked expertly, filling the bowl of the small pipe. He lit the bud, pulling the drug deep into his lungs where he held it as long as he could, smoking until the familiar frame of mind descended upon his brain.

*Good shit*, he thought as the second wave kicked in. The river noise was as beautiful as a Brahm's melody. He laid back and listened to it as it meandered by, allowing the heat of the rock to warm his sore back muscles. He looked up at the blue sky, yawned, and drifted off to sleep.

When he awoke, he noticed that the sun had moved a considerable distance across the sky. "How the hell did cowboys ever look at the sky and tell time?" he wondered aloud. The river was the only sound now.

*Where did all the bugs and birds go?*

There wasn't a hint of the breeze that had cooled him earlier in the day, and that made the silence even more noticeable. He thought he heard a rock move somewhere to his right and turned to look. Nothing. He got up and started for his kayak.

He kept his back to the river as he put on his helmet and secured it to his head. Likewise, he stepped into his spray skirt and pulled it up around his waist. Last, he put on his lifejacket, picked up his kayak and paddle, and began making his way to the river's edge.

A twig snapped—this time to his left. He couldn't tell exactly where the sound was coming from, but he had the undeniable feeling that he was being watched.

"Hello," he called. His voice had broken slightly and sounded higher than usual. He cleared his throat and tried to sound lower. "HELLO?!"

No answer. Another rock slipped above and to the right.

"Oh Jesus," he said to himself, *what if it's a mother bear with cubs? She'll attack even if she only perceives a threat.*

He crawled into his kayak slowly though he wanted to get away from there as quickly as possible; he still needed to seal his spray skirt to the kayak first. If he didn't, the first small wave might fill the shell with water and throw him off-balance.

Thirty long seconds later, all was ready. He took his paddle in hand and pushed himself away from shore into the eddy. At that moment, three deer walked out of the bushes and appraised him.

"Shit," he said with relief, as he let out his breath in a long sigh. *Terrified of some deer.* He laughed and felt glad that no one else had been around to witness his moment of panic. He reached out with his paddle and dug into the water.

Something grabbed the end of the paddle and yanked him over upside down. He felt that same something grasp his helmet with inhuman strength, and through the distortion of the water, he looked straight into the eyes from a nightmare.

## CHAPTER EIGHT

∙ ∙ ∙

Bobby didn't consider the third day on the Middle Fork a very exciting day for whitewater boaters. The segment between Pistol Creek and Marble Creek consisted of only two, class-three rapids. It was, however, a stretch where he could relax and take in the sights, with the current slow and almost nonexistent in places.

The lofty mountains stood on both sides of the river—their angles incredibly steep. But he knew it became less hospitable farther downstream. The last two days of the trip would be spent in a place called the Impassable Canyon.

*God, as if this canyon isn't impassable enough.*

The rugged charm of Idaho's canyons was totally different than the soft, rolling beauty of the Cascades. Oregon…green with snow-covered volcanoes, while this stark, jagged land with huge panoramic vistas, seemed to change terrain completely every few hours downstream. The edges to the off-white cliffs looked more like giant props against the rich, deep blue of a surreal sky.

Trees couldn't grow in all the canyons they passed through, and this one in particular. Solid rock angled at more than 45 degrees. Any soil would have lost its grip on the earth and slid into the water. Even steeper palisades guarded the river on both sides farther up the embankment.

He had moved to Oregon at age twenty-five to live the life of an outdoorsman. But river running was something he had become addicted to rather recently, when a few years before, an old friend had practically twisted his arm to get him down the Upper North Umpqua River in southern Oregon. He had been terrified of rivers; he'd nearly drowned on his first rafting trip. Of course, he now knew the reason for his near demise: he'd had no training or knowledge of river running. His friend had promised him that it would be different on that next trip. A professional guide had been hired to take them down the river.

Eventually, Bobby had given in, and it became the most exciting day of his life. Ever since, he had lived and breathed whitewater rafting.

They passed a campground around noon. Bobby noticed tents still standing and boats still unloaded. Five tents, all very bright with various blues, yellows and greens, decorated a raised, sandy bench. Grass grew almost down to the water's edge. A backdrop of sharp mountains and blue sky made the camp "post-card perfect."

"Didn't the ranger tell us we could only take a campsite for one night?" he asked Suzi.

"That she did, why?"

"Well, it's after noon and they're not even up yet."

"Bet they had one hell of a party last night," she said.

"Maybe they're doing a lay-over day and they're off hiking. I think I recall someone saying that you could do that in certain parts of the canyon, if you made arrangements with the Forest Service. But the time limit is still seven nights on the river, period," Bobby concluded. Something troubled him about the quiet scene.

"I guess we'll never know," Suzi said as the camp slowly passed out of their field of vision.

• • •

A short time later Pat sighted Jim and Linda as they pulled over on the right bank. He had tried to lag behind in hopes of Gary catching up, since he carried their weed. Looking up at the sky, he wondered why he had let Gary keep it all with him. His introspection was shattered when Jim shouted.

"Have you seen Gary?"

"No, I thought he was up front somewhere," Pat returned, not wanting to give away his plan.

"Pull over; I'm sure he's behind us," Jim said as he pulled his own raft up on the shore. "All the other boats have gone on ahead except for you and Bobby."

*Crap!* Pat made for the riverbank, as did Bobby who had been following him.

"I'm positive he was behind you a couple of miles back. I think we should at least wait until we see him coming," Jim suggested.

Pat could see his plan dissipating rapidly.

*Great…another day straight.* He listened as the others bitched about Gary.

"I think we should chew him out for falling that far behind," Suzi said as she jumped out and pulled Bobby's raft up onto shore.

"More like kick his ass, if you ask me," Jim said.

"What if he had an accident?" Linda asked.

"Gary? He's an east coast, class-five boater. This stuff is class-one. After the Gauley, he could sleep through this stuff," Bobby assured her.

"I'm still not leaving until we see him coming, then I'm going to kick his pony-tailed ass," Jim said.

# CHAPTER EIGHT

"OK—if you want to, but we don't have the lunch cooler with us—Jacques has it on his boat," Pat pointed out. Always hungry, he took notice of such things.

"No we don't, but we do have some Triscuits and one of the beer coolers," Jim said as he threw Bobby a Budweiser.

"I'm thinking that waiting here wouldn't be all that bad after all," Pat said holding up his hands in a catch position. "Take your time, Gary." He caught a beer and sat down.

*These guys get so uptight when you don't play by their rules.*

"I know Jerry, though," Bobby added. "He goes by the book. He'll pull over and do the same thing we're doing."

"I'm still not leaving until I see him coming," Jim said again. "I can always kick his ass in camp."

"Pat, why don't you go on up ahead and tell everyone else what's happening?" Bobby asked.

"Me? Why me? I want to relax and consume mass quantities of beer." Pat could see Bobby's expression change slightly. His right eyebrow raised as his other one dropped.

"Cause you're in a kayak, and I'm carrying your fucking gear, that's why," Bobby shot back.

He knew about Bobby: easy-going until he got pissed off. Used to be a fighter of some kind. There were pictures and trophies all over his house. Pat decided not to argue. "You've got a point; I'll go after I finish my beer." Sitting back against a rock, he jammed five Triscuits into his mouth all at once, and chased them down with a huge gulp of cold brew. He tried to read Bobby's expression. The brows relaxed, and he settled next to Suzi.

After ten minutes, Pat took two extra beers and went down river to tell the others the reason for the delay as Bobby requested. *You owe me, Gary.*


Bobby sat with Suzi, Jim, and Linda in the shade of a pine tree and talked while they killed the box of crackers and a six-pack. He couldn't say for how long. Measured time was counterproductive to the river experience. On the river, they let time become an unsegmented flow: eating when hungry, drinking when thirsty, and sleeping when tired. The only significant events were sun-up and sundown, and the rapids. He liked it that way.

Bobby glanced upstream-still no sign of Gary. He sat quietly listening to the river. Moments like this almost allowed him to be the old Bobby. Happy.

The new beautiful woman he'd just met was helping him forget too. Abby. *She liked him*—he'd felt it.

He didn't believe anything would happen to Gary, but the nagging tether of responsibility wouldn't let him completely enjoy the peace of the afternoon. Jim and Linda discussed paddling across the river and trying to hike back to search for him, when off in the distance Bobby saw Gary's bright yellow kayak round the bend.

"Son-of-a-bitch," Bobby said, both angry and relieved that Gary was all right.

"Should we wait here or kick his ass in camp?" Jim asked.

"It feels like we've wasted about an hour. It'll take him another fifteen or twenty minutes to get through that 'frog water.' I say let's go and do it later, now that we know he's okay. I'm tired of waiting," Bobby said.

"Yeah, Marble Creek is still about four or five miles, and everyone else will be worried," Linda reminded them.

Bobby agreed. He shoved off, and headed downriver.

• • •

Abigail retched with dry heaves. The thing hanging on the back of the door appeared to be a young woman wearing the same clothes as Charlene. The remains were her size and shape as well. She had realized in the first second, that it was, in fact, Charlene, and the sudden knowledge that she had been brutally killed while Abby had been at the beach talking with Bobby sent a series of cold-steel chills down her spine.

Charlene's death appeared to have been swift and savage. Her face split down the middle. One eye peered in one direction, and the other, an empty hole, faced another. She too had been opened up and partially emptied of her viscera. Blood dripped onto the floor and she recognized it as the source of the tapping sound.

Barely keeping her emotions in check Abby wondered why Charlene was only partially emptied, while the ranger had been totally cleaned out. An answer struck her: they might have interrupted the killer before he was finished.

*Finished what?*

Charlene had gone exploring less than fifteen minutes ago. Whoever or whatever did this, most certainly watched them approaching from somewhere nearby. The killer could even have been hiding behind the cabin…*might still be there.*

# CHAPTER EIGHT

Their only hope was to get back to the boats. She shut the closet door and decided not to tell Beth about Charlene. Not yet. She just might snap, and Abby couldn't risk having to deal with that, along with the fact that a brutal killer lurked close by.

Sticking her head out the cabin door, not knowing what to expect, she saw Beth sitting on the ground a few yards from the door. She wasn't retching any more, but she looked close to catatonic.

"Beth!"

No answer.

"Beth!!"

Louder but still no answer.

"BETH!!!" Abby shouted as she shook her. Beth looked up as Abby glanced around cautiously. "Beth, we've got to get to the boats—now! It's the most important thing you may ever do, so get up NOW!"

"Abby, oh God, that thing on the floor was human," Beth cried.

"Don't think or talk, just do as I say. I mean it, Beth, whatever or whoever did this could still be around. We've got to get to the boats. We might be able to catch Bobby's group. I won't feel safe until we're with more people, so come on," she ordered. Beth stood up trembling.

Abby looked down towards the beach. The Murphy sisters had apparently gone from the top of the landing strip, but she couldn't see anything out of the ordinary. The flies still swarmed, and the day was still hot.

She considered running, but ruled it out. The killer could be waiting behind one of the trees, might even be waiting behind the cabin, in which case the head start in a foot race wasn't enough for her comfort. She took Beth by the arm and slowly began to back away from the cabin. She still had her knife in hand, and Beth stared at it with a puzzled expression.

They covered ground at a crawl, taking care to pass only the smallest trees: the ones too small for a man to hide behind. Abby continued to keep an alert eye. She watched for any movement; she even searched up in the trees for someone, or something, that might drop down on them.

Finally, they came to the edge of the thinly wooded area and had a clear view across the landing strip. Satisfied that they weren't being followed, she shouted "RUN!" and practically pulled Beth all the way across the field to the top of the log stairs.

The first thing she noticed was the absence of their rafts. Looking downriver she spotted them floating around the same corner she had watched Bobby round so long ago. Time slowed to a standstill. Then, a new horror became apparent. Carol and Cynthia floated face down in an eddy some forty feet downstream from where the boats had been tied. The water was dark and billowy around them. They had been killed, and the boats deliberately pushed out into the river.

"Oh God, we're next," Beth cried.

Abby looked wildly around, feeling like a trapped animal.

*Pull yourself together.*

Beth was losing it; she began crying hysterically. "We're gonnnnaa dieeee," she wailed.

Abby almost agreed with her, except that her basic animal instinct told her to *get the hell out now!*

A terrifying calm took charge of her mind. Almost as if a reserve portion of her brain had somehow taken over like mental overdrive; she saw clearly. "Beth, we've got to catch one of our boats. It's our only hope," she said evenly. "Take a deep breath and get up.

"We're going to make it, but you've got to stay with me. You'll need to do everything I say, okay? Beth? Do you understand?" Abby shook her to her senses, and Beth finally showed understanding by nodding her head up and down. Looking up at Abby, tears streaming down both cheeks, she tried to speak but no sound came out. She nodded, and Abby knew she could count on her cooperation.

"Good, now let's get moving downstream," Abby ordered. "Maybe we'll get lucky and find one of the rafts caught in an eddy. Pick up a couple of good-sized rocks, and if we see anybody coming toward us, we'll stone the living crap out of them."

Helping Beth, she carefully, and painfully, began climbing over the huge boulders, ever mindful that the killer could be waiting behind one of them. It was slow going, but at least they made progress.

What she called a Chee Chee bird sang nearby. It lifted Abby's spirit and somehow gave her hope, as did the sun, which still shone bright and hot. Fear didn't belong to days like this, she thought.

She heard the bird again and noticed the return of varied insect noises. The flies had given way to crickets and locusts. She hoped it was a good sign, but intuition again warned her not to let her guard down even for an instant.

Beth whimpered as they made their way down the river but somehow managed to keep up. After half an hour of climbing, jumping, and hiking, Abby saw Charlene's raft caught in a keeper hole.

She knew all about keeper holes having been trapped in one before.

## CHAPTER EIGHT

*Carter Bridge Rapids.*

She had studied this phenomenon: water pours over a submerged rock or ledge, and slams down to the river bottom leaving a void. Then water from downstream rushes back to fill the void so violently that it forms a standing wave. The standing wave at Carter Bridge on the Upper Clackamas had turned her boat sideways and flipped it, as if she and the boat were as insignificant as a straw. She then had experienced what was referred to as being *maytagged* for the first time, where hydraulics trap a swimmer, or in some cases an entire raft, rolling them over and over, eventually spitting them out. It had been one of the most terrifying experiences of her life.

*Just what we need.*

This keeper hole was not a really big one, but it was strong enough to hold the 13-foot SOTAR. The boat bounced and spun violently but hadn't flipped; instead it stayed in the center of the hole without downstream progress.

"Oh shit, Beth! Your lifejacket was in my boat. I'll have to swim out by myself," Abby said, glad she hadn't taken her own lifejacket off when she'd left the raft. She would have lost her knife, and it would have been almost certain death to swim out to this hole without a lifejacket. Even wearing one she knew it wouldn't be easy.

"What if you get sucked under the boat and drowned?" Beth cried.

"Should we go on and try to find one of the other boats?" Abby asked.

She allowed Beth to make the choice. Beth's eyes blinked again and again as they darted from the raft to the trail behind them. If they didn't find one of the other boats, they would be forced to hike without food, and sleep in the wilderness without shelter. With a killer at large, possibly stalking them, that idea didn't sound too pleasant to Abby.

"Let's get this one. I'll swim out too," Beth said.

"No way, lady. You're not that good. You, without a lifejacket in the middle of that hole, that is all I'd need," Abby said

"I'm more scared about ending up like the body on the floor in the cabin," Beth replied. Suddenly, a shocked expression came over her face as she screamed: "CHARLENE! We left Charlene! We've got to go back—"

"Beth! Charlene is dead," Abby said as calmly as she could.

"How do you know?"

Abby told her about the closet. Beth sat down on a warm rock and began shivering.

"You stay here, and I promise I'll be back as soon as I can. If you see anything, or anybody, throw your rocks at them, and then swim out to me," Abby advised.

"Alright, but please hurry. I'm really scared, Abby. Please take care of yourself, 'cause I won't make it if anything happens to you."

"I swear I won't leave you alone out here," she said as she kissed Beth on the cheek and turned to climb down to the river's edge. Abby surveyed the area. A rock wall bordered the river on its far side. Even at the top of the cliff she saw only rocks.

The blue water looked harmless, but she knew it was only a mirage. The undercurrents and eddies under the surface made for hard swimming. She eased herself into the cold water. It took her breath away instantly. From the river level her visibility dropped considerably, making it impossible to see where she was going except when she crested each wave.

She swam at an upstream angle to slow her downstream descent as she traversed across the river. The cold water caused her skin to tingle, then go numb, draining her.

She had entered about twenty-five yards upstream of the hole, but the current was deceptive and pulled her downstream much faster than she had anticipated. She changed her angle to ninety degrees and swam hard. She couldn't believe she was actually swimming out purposefully to a hole, but that was, in fact, what she was doing.

*In ice water, no less.*

She swam onto the reversal wave and almost went over on its far left end. She teetered on the brink of being washed downstream or being pulled back into the hole. The hole won out. It tossed her back into its gaping maw.

Swallowed whole and spit out several times, each time she came up from under the water, she tried to swim for the boat, but the hole kept pulling her down. After what she figured to have been the fifth or sixth trip through the cycle, she managed to grab the perimeter line of the raft. Abby hung for a moment until the force of the current ripped her off the rope. She plunged downward three or four feet, before her life jacket's buoyancy pulled her up under the boat. Trapped against the floor of the raft like a bug on a flypaper ceiling, Abby quickly drained of strength. Her lungs burned for lack of air. She stayed under long enough, that she even considered taking a deep breath of cold water to extinguish the flame in her chest.

*But I promised Beth. I promised.*

# 9

## THE QUIET BEFORE

When Bobby and Suzi finally pulled up to Marble Creek Camp, most of the set-up work had already been done. Completely unloaded, the boats rested on a pebbled beach. He saw Jerry in the middle of camp tarping off the entire kitchen area with some space-age design he had cooked up. All they had to do was show up and enjoy. *Yes!*

Bobby looked around as he pulled in the oars from the locks. The trees grew farther away from each other allowing greater visibility, at least until they reached the log bridge crossing Marble Creek several hundred yards below camp. There the forest reclaimed the path.

A rapid boiled just downstream of the camp. He could see The Judge surfing it in his inflatable kayak, while Bonnie waited for her turn in the pool below. Because inflatable kayaks are unstable, Pat stood down below them with a throw bag. Just in case.

Everyone else sat in lawn chairs drinking beer or coffee, except Plato. He had found the cooler containing one of the boxes of wine, and filled a large mug from its spout.

Jim and Linda pulled up behind Bobby and Suzi.

"Where's Gary? I'd like to talk to him," Jerry said as he tightened one of the ropes on his nearly geodesic creation.

"Well, stand in line. He's a ways back behind us," Bobby said. "We waited until we saw him round the corner above that dead water section. We're going to have a really serious meeting tonight. But coming down on him will only make him defensive." In spite of Gary's mistake, Bobby still thought of him as a younger model of himself, and much like a kid brother.

"Yeah, looks like we need to make everyone aware how far away from help we are—*again*. The only thing resembling civilization between here and the take-out is the Victor Ranch. After that zip," Jerry added.

"The thought of someone getting hurt and having to wait days to get help sure sobers one up," Suzi said.

"Now's not the time to worry about that, my dear," Bobby said.

Jerry grinned at Suzi. "Even when we get to the take-out, there's still a three-hour drive back to the closest thing resembling a town, and that's Salmon," Jerry said. "Shoup doesn't count—it's not even a hamlet."

"What's for dinner?" Pat asked as he walked up, still stuffing the throw-rope back into its bag. "Somebody say an omelet?"

"Bonnie and the Judge fixed up a 'veggie-tofu surprise.' They left Gretta in charge before they went to play in the rapids. She gave me a preview, and I think it's going to be another night of fine river cuisine," Jerry replied.

Bobby grimaced at the mention of a "veggie-tofu surprise." By Pat's sigh he didn't sound thrilled either. On the way to his boat to get his tent and dry bag, Bobby looked upriver; still no sign of Gary. As trip leader he wouldn't be able to relax until everyone arrived safely in camp.

"Damn," he said under his breath as he began unbuckling cam straps on his gear.

After the new arrivals had set up tents and arranged their sleeping gear inside them, they returned to the lawn chairs around the fire pan. The sunny weather had changed so quickly it reminded Bobby of Texas. The temperature dropped to the fifties, and the sky threatened rain—too cool for his wet T-shirt and shorts.

Jerry started a fire before dark, and the heat felt good on Bobby's clammy skin. He welcomed the scent of wood smoke. It always took him back to the memories of his parent's little cabin on Lake Whitney in central Texas, one of his favorite childhood haunts. He hadn't liked the smell then, but it had grown on him over the years. *Wilderness perfume.*

After spirited discussion, they reached a consensus: after dinner, whoever wanted to go would take flashlights and hike the one-and-a-half miles down to the Sunflower Hot Springs. The springs lay on the opposite side of the river, so Bonnie and The Judge offered to take their inflatable kayaks down to use as ferries. The plan was for them to take the hikers across one at a time, bring them back one at a time, and then hide the boats in the bushes to be retrieved

# CHAPTER NINE 79

in the morning when they floated by in one of the rafts.

Sunflower sounded wonderful to Bobby. The Quinn Guide said they would find a hot shower cascading off the rocks above. It also mentioned hot pools at the top of the shower that could be climbed to, and used as wilderness hot tubs. A good idea, if the storm wasn't too violent. The wind already blew at about twenty-five knots. Bobby wanted to go but he didn't feel comfortable leaving before Gary showed up—especially with a storm on the way.

The dinner surprised him; for what he'd always called "rabbit food" it tasted superb, and the wine began to influence the conversation.

Gretta, who had been gazing at the river, turned to Bobby and said, "Shouldn't Gary be here by now? He might be hurt or something."

Pat edged in, "Hey, I don't want to nark on a friend, but…look Gary's got some weed with him…I'm sure he's fine."

Regardless of Pat's assurance, Bobby decided to stay in camp to wait for Gary, and he was growing angry with the young kayaker for making him miss the trip to the hot springs.

Jacques decided to remain in camp to reseal his kitchen box. It had leaked some water, and he said he wanted to make sure it didn't leak any worse in the days to come. Jim and Linda also stayed behind to repair leaks in their dry bags for the same reason. The rest of Bobby's party—Jerry, Suzi, Scott, Pat, Gretta, Bonnie and The Judge—took off toward Sunflower.

At twilight, the bulk of the storm appeared to have barely missed them. It moved by at an angle and disappeared over the mountains as quickly as it had come. Bobby relaxed in his lawn chair and turned to Plato. Remembering that Plato taught philosophy at the university, he decided to test him.

"What's your opinion on the responsibility of Dasein as keepers of Being? You know from Heidegger's *Zein Un Zeit?*" he asked, ready to do battle. When Plato answered in German, he knew he had again bitten off more than he could chew.

A feeling of tranquility descended on him. The wine and the intellectual stimulation allowed him to free himself from worries that had plagued him over the last several weeks. He and Plato discussed Heidegger, Husserl, Sartre, Nietzche, and anyone else they thought of—in English—as the wine slowly unwound their tired rowing muscles.

Off in the distance, Bobby thought he heard a woman's voice shouting, but the noise of the rapid drowned it out. *Most likely Gretta, Bonnie, or Suzi having fun on the way to the hot spring;* he dismissed it and went back to the conversation.

• • •

The turbulent water forced the raft to spin at the instant Abby gave up hope, and she was able to surface. *Oh God!* She gulped a huge breath of air mixed with white, foamy water. She coughed violently but managed to grab the perimeter rope. This time she clutched it with a death-grip.

The boat bucked like a wild bull, but still she hung on. Giving one last effort, with what little strength she had left, she pulled herself up onto the tube of the gyrating raft. Grabbing part of the metal rowing frame, she pulled the rest of her exhausted body onto the floor of the boat where she collapsed.

Abby waved a feeble hand at Beth to let her know she was all right. She tried to get up but couldn't. She wanted desperately to get going but couldn't move, except by the boat tossing her around.

After a few minutes, she sat up and realized the oars were gone. *Time for a plan B.* Motioning for Beth to make her way down to the edge of the river, Abby unclasped the rescue throw bag and mimed her intentions. She would throw the bag of rope to Beth. The other end of the rope would be attached to the D ring on the front of the raft. Then, hopefully, Beth would be able to pull the boat out of the hole from the left bank.

She could see that Beth had gotten into position. Taking the bag the way a quarterback would throw a pass, she hurled it across. *Please God, let her catch it,* she prayed.

She knew it took a long time to re-stuff a throw bag, and she didn't know if they would have that much time.

Its arc took it up to thirty feet. The rope emptied out of the bag as it made its way toward Beth. She missed it. It fell to the rocks below at the edge of the river.

The current grabbed the slack and pulled the bag into the water. Beth remembered how long it took to re-stuff sixty feet of line into a small pouch, too. She jumped into the river, grabbed the bag, and tried to swim back to the rocks, but the current pulled her downstream. When the rope pulled tight, her head formed a huge, "rooster-tail" wave. Water shot up her nose. Fearing she would drown within a few more seconds, unless she released the rope and swam for

## CHAPTER NINE

shore, Beth tried to think. Her chances of making shore in the fast current were not good either.

*What would Abby do?*

At that moment, she accidentally rolled over. The back of her head now formed the plume, leaving her face in an air pocket. In the current, her weight acted like a sail and pulled the raft out of the hole.

Still, Beth was in trouble. She frantically pulled on the rope as the boat released from the hydraulic—pulling until she was beside the raft. Using up her last drop of energy, she attempted to climb in. Abby grabbed her under the arms and helped her over the side tube. *Oh God! Oh thank God.*

Without any way to guide the raft, she and Abby screamed through rapids—bouncing from rock to rock. In one of the calmer stretches, Beth noticed that the lines used to secure the spare oars to the raft appeared to have been severed, and what small amount of calm she had achieved deserted her.

"A bear wouldn't have torn the oars off and left the cooler." She played her thumb across the two ends of the straps. "Whatever killed Charlene and the Murphy sisters must have torn off the oars too. The one on this side was held on with cam straps, not rope. They weren't cut, they've been snapped in two—look, the ends are frayed."

Beth waited for effect, hoping that Abby would grasp the import of what she concluded. Her voice broke, but she managed to squeeze out the words.

"That's impossible for a human being." The water bubbled around rocks making a sound as if a pot of water had been left on a stove to boil. The current raced faster. "Cam straps hold gear in a boat when the river exerts tons of force, like in Charlene's wrap the other day. I don't know anything that could snap one like a rubber band. Do you?"

Abby didn't answer; she stared downstream. "Rockside!" she shouted.

Beth jumped to the downstream side of the raft just as it slammed into a boulder. "Christ!" she yelled. The boat rested against the rock as Abby and Beth leaned toward it. At that moment, a wrap would be about the worst thing that could happen. They would lose the boat, and she would be forced to swim without a lifejacket. She thanked God she had been on numerous trips with Abby. Abby had taught her how to respond to all the emergency commands, and because of that she felt more confidence in their chances for survival.

"If we fall out, try and swim to the right bank," Abby explained. "The killer was on the left bank and swimming across the river will be hard for him. Even if he did manage to swim across, we would see him coming. Don't worry—he won't get in *this* boat," Abby said as she raised her hand to the handle of her clip-lock knife. Regardless, Beth did worry.

Their raft caught in an eddy on the right side of the river, and Abby saw several more rafts ahead on the bank. With luck, she just might grab the perimeter line on one of them, and pull up to shore. "Maybe these people can help us," she said as she used her hands to paddle closer. Reaching the rope with no trouble, she allowed the current to float them next to the rafts. She jumped out and pulled their boat up by the others. She didn't see anyone. Given the day's circumstances, this made her even more apprehensive.

"Hello…anybody here? Please, we need help!" Abby shouted at the camp. *No answer.*

"Oh Jesus, not again," Beth cried.

"Be quiet, Beth!" Something was wrong. Abby's newfound intuition whispered for her to "leave this place," and she listened. But she had to investigate. Had to.

Pulling her knife, she again took a defensive posture as they slowly approached the tents thirty feet away. At the first tent, the overpowering smell told her all she needed to know.

*Oh my God.* She'd been to enough crime scenes where bodies were discovered long after the killer had gone, to recognize the decaying odor of human flesh. They turned and ran back to the raft without saying a word.

Abby looked at the other boats—*oars!* "Thank God!" she said, as she hastily took the spares from the side of a comparably sized raft. She glanced up to find Beth in one of the other boats—tossing things aside until she came up with a suitable lifejacket. *Good thinking.* Then Beth jumped in with her.

Placing the oars into the raft, Abby pushed away from the shore into the gentle eddy. "Come on, God—give us a break!" she shouted as she stomped her foot on the solid rubber floor of the raft.

"What's wrong?" Beth asked.

"These oars won't fit our frame, goddammit, that's what's wrong! These oars were set up for a boat with open oarlocks; this frame has thoele pins. We need oars with clips." Then a thought occurred to her. She could swim back and see if any others were set up for pins, or she could use the stirrups on these pins for a makeshift oarlock. Abby was about to swim back when a noise stopped her.

A sound of some aquatic behemoth splashed from nearby. She could neither see anything, nor tell which direction it had come from. She considered

# CHAPTER NINE

whether what she'd heard had been a reflection off the cliff wall on the other side of the river. The cliff was only about fifty-feet long so she figured it must have been at least that close on either side. Beth had apparently heard it too, so Abby again opted for plan B. She placed the oars through the loop of the stirrups and began rowing away from the morbid place as fast as she could.

She stayed on alert, searching for any movement when they rounded the next bend. On the left bank, she saw three deer watching them, ears cocked. One of them looked across the river, behind to Abby's left; then it spooked. She turned around to see several large rocks that had been doused with water. A wet trail climbed a steep abutment up to a flat, sandy spot above the camp but slightly downstream. The sand also appeared dark. `Wet`. A large thicket sat on top of the small plateau.

Abby felt something. In fact, she would swear they were being watched from inside the thick bushes.

As they passed a big rock bench on the left, they saw a yellow kayak upside down in the eddy. By the time Abby could pull on the oars, they were already past it.

While she watched the kayak upstream, the raft hit a rock and almost launched both of them into the river. Luckily, it was the kind of rock that perched boats instead of wrapping them. They jumped up and down trying to free the raft, but it had stuck firmly on the pour-over rock. They made their way to one end of the boat and jumped up and down, again without moving off the perch. Abby tried to row it off without success. She recognized they were both approaching total exhaustion, so she suggested they sit back and relax as best they could, given their present situation.

She experienced what she'd heard athletes call "cotton-mouth syndrome," where the inside of the mouth felt as if you'd swallowed a large, absorbent cotton ball. Unclasping the water jug, she drained half of it in two equal gulps; her mouth was still dry when she handed the jug to Beth who quickly drained what remained.

Abby estimated by the sun and her internal clock that an hour-and-a-half to two hours had elapsed since they left the cabin. It seemed like much longer; in fact, she couldn't remember what it felt like not to be afraid.

"Abby?"

"Yeah."

"What did you hear back there?"

"A stone slipping and water dripping, but I couldn't tell where it came from," Abby answered. "One thing though," she looked back upstream.

"Judging from the stench, the people inside the tents weren't fresh kills like Charlene and the ranger guy."

"Yeah, that means whoever or whatever it was must have worked its way upriver," Beth pointed out.

At that moment, the yellow kayak passed by, just out of Abby's reach.

# 10

### THE RIVER OF NO RETURN

Bobby thought he heard a woman's voice shouting again. This time it sounded closer.

*They must be coming back, but why?* He wondered.

"HELP!"

This time Bobby heard it distinctly, but he couldn't tell where it came from. He looked at the others; they didn't seem to have heard it. He thought he had just imagined it when he saw Phydeaux's ears perk up. She ran toward the river, heading upstream.

Bobby got up and started walking after her. When she barked at something below, he began running. Out of the corner of his eye, he saw Gary's kayak go by upside down.

*God no. Please.*

He turned and considered chasing the boat on foot, when he again heard a distinct cry for help. He ran towards Phydeaux, who stood on a rock outcropping, barking wildly at something below her. When Bobby arrived at the cornice, he saw a raft approaching with Abigail Jones at the oars, and the small, dark-haired lady named Beth up front yelling for help. No other rafts accompanied them.

Something was dreadfully wrong, and he wondered if Gary lay hurt somewhere upstream. Guilt crept into his soul. *Should have waited until Gary caught up with us.* He could have been hurt when they saw him round the corner, and they would never have heard him if he had been calling for help.

He kept his eyes on the women as he ran back towards the landing. Abby rowed the raft up next to his Campways while Beth jumped out and pulled them out of the current. Then something strange happened. Bobby expected them to run up to the camp trying to enlist help, but instead the two women fell to their knees and held each other, crying. He also noticed that Abby wasn't in the same raft she had been in earlier that day. This raft was blue the other had been red.

He ran to them "What's wrong, Abby?" he asked as Jacques and Plato arrived beside him. Jim and Linda came with towels.

Apparently the women had been storing up their emotions. Now, the dam broke. After a few moments, Abby tried to speak. Incoherent babbling, words out of context, flooded from her lips. However, one word filtered through clearly: *dead*. The word he dreaded. *Gary?*

He knelt beside her."It's all right, come on up to camp and sit by the fire, then you can tell us what happened," Jacques said in a fatherly manner as he gently put his hand on Beth's shoulder.

Bobby watched Abby and Beth as they allowed themselves to be led to camp. Abby seemed embarrassed that she couldn't regain her composure. Every time she tried to speak nothing came out.

Linda ran to grab a couple of sleeping bags to wrap around the shivering women.

From camp, Bobby saw that Gary's kayak had been trapped by the small keeper hole in Marble Creek Falls. The twilight had almost gone, but even in the darkness he could see the bright yellow hull against the foaming, white reversal wave.

The emotional memory of the Klamath surged back. Dead? Bobby felt the weight of the situation. He would get Jim to help retrieve the kayak after he heard what happened from Abby. Not wanting to break down, he tried to focus on helping her. He walked over and sat beside her, wanting to comfort her in some way. He took her hand and squeezed gently, and offered her a drink of water.

"It's all right now, it's all right," he assured her.

She shoved the bottle away. "NO! It's not all right—it'll never be all right again,"

Bobby felt reproached but listened as Abigail Jones tried to recount the horror she and Beth had experienced at Indian Creek. His rational mind had trouble accepting such things that didn't fit into his range of experience. He tried, unsuccessfully, to figure a logical, rational answer to this disturbing turn

## CHAPTER TEN

of events. If the killer wasn't a bear, a wolf, or a puma, all that logically remained was a serial killer loose on the river, a terrifying thought. From the manner of the mutilations, however, it seemed highly unlikely that the killings were perpetrated by anything human. That was even more terrifying—*What then?* Bobby wondered.

He sensed that Abby and Beth were telling the truth, at least as they perceived it. He hadn't known Abby long enough to form a trustworthy opinion, but his gut feeling told him she was definitely credible. More than pretty, she also had an air of integrity. If she were on drugs, it would make things easier to explain away, but she didn't act like someone under the influence. In fact, she didn't seem under the influence of anything other than mortal terror.

Now, he felt fear tingle along his scalp, as his friend's disappearance suddenly took on an even more ominous tone. The same killer, or killers, at Indian Creek, could have dispatched Gary. Bobby's heart sank. He didn't want to believe Gary was dead.

*I should have sent someone upstream.* It seemed like all his problems came from overlooking that one, simple detail. Somebody should always be sent upstream. He felt himself again spiraling down into an emotional whirlpool. He had to do something. He had to focus outside himself.

Taking a bottle of Jack Daniels out of the kitchen box, he poured four fingers into two glasses, and handed one of them to Abby hoping it would calm her nerves. He handed a second to Beth. They both shook visibly and jumped at the slightest noise, but they drank.

The glow on the western rim had all but burned out, and their campfire gave off the only light. Jim added two more logs. The darkness around the camp suddenly became menacing, the silence dreadful. The crackle and pop of the burning logs offered the only comforting sound other than the river.

Bobby watched Jim retrieve a flashlight from his ammo can, then visit one of the rafts, pull an oar off its thoele pin, and return to camp with it. Bobby knew what was coming.

"Bobby, let's go see if we can get Gary's kayak out of the hole before it gets away. We might find a clue as to what happened to him," Jim suggested.

"Right," he said. He couldn't add that he really didn't want to know. Nor did Bobby want to leave the relative safety of the firelight. He felt close to Abby, even though they had just met, and he didn't want anything bad to happen to her. Of course, he didn't want anything bad to happen to himself either. Again, their eyes met, and the horror retreated for a brief interval.

・・・

The group hiked a long time and eventually found Sunflower Hot Springs. Jerry watched as The Judge and Bonnie paddled up the opposite bank. He heard the bubbling sound of a creek, and recognized the familiar, sulfur smell of a hot spring even from all the way across the river.

"Weee'rrreee heeerrreeee," The Judge called. Jerry had watched all the flashlights bobbing up and down on the left-bank trail as they hiked down through darkness toward the river. The Judge and Bonnie paddled their inflatable kayaks across on what looked like a giant black ribbon.

Jerry watched as Bonnie picked up her first passenger: Gretta, the hot springs' junkie. She couldn't wait to get in and had bargained her way into the first ferry ride by taking Bonnie's morning dish patrol.

Trip after trip, the small inflatable kayaks ferried people across one passenger at a time; finally everyone had crossed except Jerry.

He watched the flashlights on the far side of the river. Hearing the 'oooohs and aaaahs' of his companions experiencing the joys of the hot spring, he suddenly felt very alone.

The boat with Suzi was about half way across when he thought he heard something behind him. He turned and shined his flashlight across the wooded scene. There was nothing, except for the reflective eyes of what he guessed might be an owl about thirty yards back into the forest. An owl on the low limb of a tree about eight feet off the ground, he thought. He couldn't actually make out any of its detail—just the eyes. He looked back to the river. The Judge had just started on his way back, when Jerry heard the snap of a twig. *Closer....*

He turned and shined the beam across the scene a second time. The owl did appear closer. He kept the light on it, but it was still too far back to see, hidden by foliage. He continued looking at it anyway.

No movement.

He turned off his flashlight, but continued gazing out into the forest. He wasn't the type that scared easily; he was just extremely cautious. He switched the flashlight back on. The owl hadn't moved. Maybe it wasn't an owl, but since it was up on a limb and had glowing eyes, he couldn't think of what else it could be.

## CHAPTER TEN

"You ready?" came from behind him. His heart leapt into his throat as he jumped forward and swung the flashlight at a surprised Sam Baker.

"Jesus H. Christ, Judge, you scared the shit out of me," Jerry said gasping.

"Sorry. Come on, I want to get wet."

Jerry took a handful of water and splashed the Judge in the face.

"There, now you're wet," he said.

"I meant hot water," the Judge said as he wiped his eyes. Both men laughed as Jerry climbed in.

• • •

Bobby and Jim went to the rafts, and removed the clip-lock knives from their lifejackets. Again, Bobby clutched his knife like a talisman. To ward off evil, and sharp enough to castrate in case the magic wasn't working, he thought. Reaching down to his belt, he felt the hilt of his throwing knife firmly nestled in its sheath. It was too dark to throw accurately, but it added a small measure of security knowing he had it as a backup.

They walked down the same path the others had taken toward the hot springs. The rapid churned 150 feet below the camp. He knew every eye in camp would be locked onto their bouncing flashlight beams and would follow them all the way to the rapid. He wished he were one of them—watching someone else walk into the darkness.

When they reached the keeper hole, the kayak was gone. Somehow it had escaped the reversal's powerful grip. They continued down the path, but Bobby didn't feel comfortable going much further in light of what he had just heard. He saw the flicker of the fire upstream and longed to be back there. The firelight looked warm…ambient…unlike the flashlight's small, blinding circle.

"There it is," Jim said as he shined his flashlight across the yellow hull. It had been washed into a re-circulating eddy about thirty feet below the hole. As luck would have it, the oar appeared long enough. The kayak still floated upside down.

Jim, being taller, stretched out with the oar and, with great effort, managed to herd the kayak to the bank while Bobby anchored him. When it came close enough, the two men each grabbed an end of the craft and pulled it out of the river. They held it upside down to drain the water out, then set it down on the bank. Bobby thanked God Gary wasn't still attached.

It was empty except for the float bags, and Gary's helmet. It must have been wedged in tight judging by the scratches on the plastic floor of the boat. He reached in and tugged on the excess strap, but it wouldn't move. He took rope and looped it through the side ring. Jim grabbed one end and Bobby grasped the other. They braced their feet against the cockpit and pulled. The helmet yielded and Bobby pulled it out. The weight should have warned him. He turned it over and stared into Gary's dead face. It took a second for the realization to set in.

"Aaaaahhh!" Bobby screamed out as he threw the grisly remnant into the river. Jim recoiled several feet.

It only took a few more seconds, and both men began to gag. The specter of Gary's face, contorted in pain burned into Bobby's mind.

When the heaving subsided, they silently stared at the place where the helmet had sunk, imagining the decapitated head bobbing slowly along the bottom of the river. The horrible vision lodged deeply into his mind: everything twisted, from the expression, to the twisted piece of spine that had scratched the floor of the kayak.

*Twisted.*

The chinstrap had even remained tight, making sure its contents rested firmly in place.

"Man, I'm scared shitless," Jim confided.

"Me too." Bobby hadn't felt this type of fear in a long time. Not since his nightmares.

"Let's get back with the others and figure out what the hell we're going to do," Jim said. That sounded like good advice.

They walked back toward camp without speaking. Bobby became aware of every sound around him. Besides fear, he felt an overwhelming sadness. Empty. Unlike the kid on the Klamath, Gary had been his friend, a good spirit with a whole life before him. Bobby would be robbed of all the river trips he and Gary might have made together. Then, Bobby began feeling another emotion plant its seeds in his mind: *anger.* Only a small flame, but it would grow. Oh how it would grow. He vowed, if he got the chance to bring justice, his own justice, to whoever did this to his friend, he would do so…*with extreme prejudice.*

# 11

## HARD DECISIONS

Abby listened as Bobby tried to recount what he and Jim had found in the kayak. He had as much trouble speaking as she'd had earlier. She felt badly for refusing the water.

"Gary's killer was probably the same bastard who killed your friends," he said. He put his head in his hands and rocked back and forth.

Abby realized his comment meant the kayaker had been mutilated too. They had followed the yellow Perception kayak down the river most of the afternoon. Learning that human remains were in it all that time gave her a new batch of the jitters. How close had she and Beth come to joining the body count? A shudder rippled through her like a tremor.

"There could be more than one killer," Plato offered. "As much ground as was apparently covered, leads me to believe one of two things: either one person is inhumanly fast and inhumanly brutal, or there's more than one killer, both inhumanly brutal. Since I choose not to believe that anyone is inhumanly fast, it is logical to assume we're dealing with more than one."

"I didn't mention it, but this morning at Pistol Creek, Jerry and I made a final run through camp. The wind shifted and the smell of what we thought was a dead elk drifted through. In light of this I can only imagine what it was," Bobby said as he put another log in the fire pan. The fire crackled loudly as the new log ignited. Light flared deeper into the dark perimeter of the night, but it didn't make Abby feel safer.

The thought of the silent camp they had visited earlier entered her mind, as did the abandoned gear at Indian Creek. When she considered Gary's death and her own morbid find, the implications made her tremble again.

"God, I wish the others would get back from the hot springs. They don't even know about this," Linda said. "They could be in danger."

"For that matter, we could be in danger," Jacques warned. "Whatever Phydeaux barked at last night could have been the responsible party for all this mayhem." He reached down and scratched her behind the ear. "For all we know, she could have saved our lives," he added softly.

The dog glanced up at Jacques and panted happily. Abby studied Phydeaux. Did her life hang on the ability of a mongrel dog? She wondered. In her world back home, she seldom felt dependent on anyone else. Here, things were suddenly different. She needed these people. She didn't even know them, but they seemed like good enough folks. Especially Bobby. For once she didn't mind dependence. *I'm just glad we're not alone out here.* She looked back to Phydeaux and hoped that whoever stalked the river would be scared away by her warnings.

*Good dog—sure wish you could talk*, Bobby thought. Phydeaux turned and looked at him as if she understood.

He worried about the others at the hot springs. His best friend, Jerry, knew how to take care of himself.

*But against a serial killer?*

Pat and Scott smoked so much pot they might not even realize a murder had happened until they tripped over it. The Judge and Bonnie had more than their share of common sense, as did Suzi. But he really worried about Gretta. She was a city girl, and he'd promised to watch out for her.

*Nothing's going to happen—Jerry's with her.*

"When the others get back, we'll need to set up some defenses other than Phydeaux," Jim suggested. "If she gets too tired to stay awake, whoever or whatever the hell is out there, could come in and waste us while we're asleep."

"I agree," said Bobby. "This guy, or these guys are obviously sociopathic as well as psychopathic. They'll need some real strong discouragement."

"Who said they were guys?" Beth asked. "Who said it was even human?"

A silence fell over the group. Beth's last comment triggered a frightful memory. Bobby frequently visited the library and browsed occult and monster books. At first he hadn't been consciously aware of the reason why, but he'd realized that he was searching for information about the beast in his dreams. A month before the trip, he had perused a hardbound called the *Book of Imaginary Beings*. Somewhere in that book he'd found an article on a Northwood's mon-

## CHAPTER ELEVEN

ster called the "Hidebehind." It was a creature that had never been seen by a living person. Named The Hidebehind because, no matter how many times one turned, it was always behind them. A master of stealth, an old lumberjack legend credited it with killing hundreds of loggers over the last century.

*Who said it was even human?* Beth's question raised the hair on his arms. He wondered if legends had at least some basis in fact. It was a bad enough thought having a serial killer on the loose, so he pushed the Hidebehind out of his mind. A silent shudder passed through him as he remembered the nightmare eyes from his dreams, which he imagined watching him from the darkness just outside the firelight.

He glanced sideways at Abby and wondered how she had been able to cope with the horrible events of her day, especially the discoveries at the cabin. She sat in a lawn chair facing the fire, looking somewhat calmer. He tried to study her out of the corner of his eye without getting caught. That, at least, seemed like a focal point of sanity. But his mind swirled through flashes of memory and painful emotions.

Other voices whispered feverishly as if from close by, but the pounding of his pulse in his ears grew louder drowning out all other sound. Fear seared through his veins, tightening muscles and making him feel hot, announcing its triumphant return. Still he fought to study her—to take his mind away from Gary, and the spell passed.

*So much courage.* He admired her and felt cheated that what could have been the beginning of a river romance, instead had been turned into this bizarre nightmare. Under different circumstances, sitting this close to the fire, next to her, would have been exciting. The attraction had receded to a distant back burner, or maybe it was even hopeless. His mind drifted again.

His thoughts raced too fast with images both real and imagined. He heard the drone of the other's voices, but their words no longer made sense, as if he were listening to a foreign language.

Then, he felt a hand on his shoulder. It was Abby. Warmth flooded his chest. He took a deep breath and sighed. She didn't say anything she just looked at him. Bobby tried to look back at her confidently, but he was sure she could see through the attempt.

"I think we should face outward so we can see what's coming," Beth was saying.

"Honey, Phydeaux will hear anyone coming long before we see them," Jacques assured her. "Try to relax until the others get back, then we'll discuss what we're going to do."

That sounded like a good idea. When the others got back their defenses would be more than doubled. Then a thought occurred to Bobby.

"How many tents were at that camp you passed, Abby?"

"Six, I think, why?"

"You said the tents were zipped up and didn't appear to be torn. If none of those people got away, we can assume that at least six people were killed inside their tents. More than likely, more than one person shared a tent, right?" Bobby postulated as he turned to Jacques and Plato.

"Maybe," Jacques answered, "What's your point?"

"If they were inside their tents, then they were probably killed while they slept," Bobby replied.

"You're assuming," Plato reminded him.

"Humor me," Bobby said. "If that's correct, then they were more than likely killed one or two at a time. The others wouldn't have heard anything, or they would have been killed outside the tents when they went out to investigate. That would have left blood everywhere. Did you see any blood when you walked up, Abby?"

"No. There wasn't anything out of the ordinary except for the smell of death."

"That also means they would have been decomposing for a while," Linda said.

"In those tents, as hot as it's been lately, shit, it wouldn't take long for somebody to get pretty damned ripe," Jacques pointed out.

"What I'm getting at is that they were killed while they were the most vulnerable. While they were asleep," Bobby explained.

"Gary wasn't asleep," Linda reminded him.

"Neither was anyone at Indian Creek," Abby added.

"Then, they were either killed by someone they trusted, or someone who killed silently…real silently," Bobby said.

No one spoke for a while.

"God, I wish we hadn't vetoed the Coleman lanterns," Bobby thought aloud. He and Jerry hadn't wanted the stark brightness of the propane or white gas lanterns, and had opted instead for the ambience of candle and battery lanterns.

"Let's put some of the candle lanterns around the perimeter," Jim suggested.

"Dammit, I wish y'all had listened to me and picked up some firewood above camp," Jacques broke in. "If we plan on keeping a watch tonight, the wood is gonna run out before midnight. I picked up some about a mile up-

## CHAPTER ELEVEN

stream 'cause I knew these campgrounds have been gleaned all the way down to twigs. Now we've got to try to find some in the dark, and I gotta tell you, I don't plan to leave camp before morning. I brought this wood, so somebody else can go find some more."

"Should we go now, or wait until the others get back?" Jim asked Bobby.

Bobby became distracted when the firelight played across Abby's eyes, and they flashed like emeralds in the face of a Hindu goddess statue. However, the darkness behind her looked like black velvet and seemed to swirl. *A trick of the eye.* He turned to answer Jim.

"If we go now, we split a small group even smaller, but if we wait, they might not come back until after midnight, in which case the camp won't have a fire for however long it takes to find more wood. I think we need to go now. I don't want to run out in the middle of the night." He didn't like the thought of keeping watch in the dark.

"I think three of us should go and the rest should stay. Phydeaux should stay in camp. We can't afford to lose her. I'm willing to go," Jim said.

"BULLSHIT!" Linda shot back. "I don't want you out there in the dark with a maniac on the loose."

"You could come with me then—to protect me," he said smiling.

"No way," she answered, "stop it right now!"

"Look, the camp is probably safe as long as someone is awake. You, Jacques, Plato, and Beth should stay. Arm yourselves with knives, rocks or whatever you can think of. Bobby, Abby, and I are the logical ones to go. Abby, because she mentioned that she knew karate, Bobby, because he used to be a tournament kick-boxer, and me, because I'm the meanest son-of-a-bitch in the valley," Jim concluded.

*Damn you and your logic,* Bobby thought to himself. But Jim was right. They would stand a better chance in the dark, though Bobby still didn't want to leave camp. He wondered what kind of strength it had taken to rip Gary's head off. The thought of confronting something, or somebody, with that kind of temperament, in the dark, left him unnerved.

"He's right. We'll use up all our batteries tonight if we don't have a fire. Candles too. We've got to make them last for two more days, until we reach the Victor Ranch. We might be able to get there sooner, but I think we'd be pushing ourselves too hard if we try. It's thirty-six miles from here to the ranch, and we face some nasty rapids on the way—Tappan Falls for one."

Bobby looked at the other's faces reflected in the firelight, then continued. "I'd like to get there tomorrow if it was possible, but if we push that hard, we might be too tired to stay awake tomorrow night. I don't like that idea." He tossed a twig into the fire and said, "I think we should go get the wood now and stay in camp the rest of the night. We'll need to keep the fire burning bright so we can use it as our primary light source. We'll also need to set up sentry duty."

Jacques, who had been silent, spoke:

"I think we should stay on the same schedule that we were on. We should stay at the same campsites too, and I'll tell you why. We're going to be burned out after fifteen to twenty miles a day on the river. If we pass our camp, and try for one further on, we might just find it already occupied with dead campers. I don't know about you, but I damn sure don't want to get caught near sundown with that as my only option." Jacques lit a cigar and scanned the darkness beyond the firelight.

"Will you put on some coffee-the way I like it?" Jim asked Linda, "I'm staying up all night." She nodded her head and hugged him tightly. Watching, Bobby felt a lump in his throat. He wanted someone to feel that way about him. His eyes found Abby, but he knew not to hope for her. She was way out of his league.

The three wood-gatherers changed into warm clothes, and put on hiking boots. Each carried a flashlight and a knife. Bobby took along his K-Bar Bowie as an extra, in case he had an opportunity to draw and peg something from a short distance. He could throw the big knife with incredible power and accuracy.

"We're going to stay together so don't worry," Jim assured Linda.

Bobby could see it was obvious that Beth didn't want Abby to go either, but she didn't say anything. She merely sat as close to her as she could. Abby must have been her only hold on sanity during their entire hellish afternoon, and he figured the fear of being separated among strangers must be a frightening prospect for her as well.

"Godspeed," Plato said as he offered Bobby a bottle of Stolichnaya. The glass bottle clouded with condensation, chilled from the dry ice in the cooler.

"My favorite, but I'll have to pass. I should stay sober," Bobby told him. Plato smiled that he understood, and then took a sip of the cold vodka.

"Keep your asses covered," Jacques said, "I mean it, watch each other's backs."

"You don't have to tell me," Bobby said.

The three looked at each other nervously, turned on their flashlights, and left the fire-lit area of the camp. They headed up the trail leading back upriver-

## CHAPTER ELEVEN

away from the hot springs, with Jim in the lead, Abby in the middle, and Bobby in the sweep position—again.

*I'm always last, on water or land*, he thought as he looked over his shoulder to make sure he wasn't being followed. Walking in silence, he listened to the sounds of the night.

• • •

Back in camp, Beth watched the beams of their flashlights fade into the darkness. The camp fell silent except for the crackle of the campfire. She suddenly felt completely alone. *If anything happens to Abby….*

"Let's do what we can to make this camp more secure," Jacques said as he stood up and walked to the kitchen box. He removed a wood-handled hatchet from its contents along with some matches and a small silver canister.

"I'll keep this white gas and these matches handy in case I have to bar-b-que some ape-shit psycho this evening," Jacques said.

Beth watched Plato open up his ammo can and remove a survival knife. The razor sharp blade gleamed, brightly reflecting the firelight along its edge. Unscrewing one of the legs off of a camp table, he took a roll of duct tape from the kitchen box and taped the knife to the end of the leg, rolling the tape around behind the handle so it wouldn't slip backwards if it were thrust into something. Within ten minutes he had fashioned a deadly looking spear.

"That should give me a little extra reach," he said smiling at Beth. "Would you like a knife?" he asked her.

Was this man talking to her? A knife? Violence is never a solution. How many times had she said that or thought it. "I wouldn't know how to use one…that way," she said, and even to her, her voice sounded very small. All she wanted to do was hide, but the only places to hide were either outside the firelight or in her mind. She wanted to retreat inside, but people kept talking to her.

"You just cut like you're cutting a steak or a prime rib. Go for the stomach, slash across from right-to-left if you're right handed. It's hard for someone to fight effectively when they have to hold their intestines in," he told her.

The thought that she could actually consider killing someone brought her to nausea. She was afraid of everything: afraid of being killed, afraid that Abby or someone else around her would be killed, afraid that she might actually have to fight for her life and kill some one, or thing.

The whole idea of the trip had been based on their woman's group philosophy: to celebrate life. *All life is sacred.* The other thing they had agreed to practice was facing their fears. Beth figured that she had faced enough fear to last her lifetime plus a few others, and that someone, or something, on this river believed in the antithesis of her group's ideals. Life didn't appear to mean much to them. *I just want everything to be okay again.*

Beth began centering. First and foremost, she knew that she wanted to live. She thought of her friends. She thought of her dog, Sadie. After taking inventory, Beth decided unequivocally, that she very much wanted to live, even if it meant defending herself…even if it meant killing. She looked at Plato and tried to smile.

"I will take that knife after all," she said.

Plato took an "Old Forge" butcher knife from the kitchen box and handed it to her handle first. Grasping the handle, she looked at the sturdy blade and realized the power she held in her hand. *The power of life and death*, she thought.

• • •

Jerry's back finally got its first real relief on the trip. The hot spring sent wet heat into his muscles. He'd been having spasms since the previous week, but now his back felt considerably better.

The storm had passed them by, leaving a sky filled with more stars than he had ever seen, and no lights to interfere with the pleasure of contemplating them.

He liked Sunflower Hot Springs. He had showered in the hot waterfall and then climbed up to join the others in the pools above. Lying on his back next to Suzi and watching an early meteor shower added to the romantic appeal of the place. It was even nicer since they were both nude. He realized an unspoken physical attraction sparked between them, but neither of them seemed willing to make the first move. For the moment, he felt comfortable just being with her.

The moon rose over the mountains, putting an end to stellar observation, so they decided to head back to camp. It was getting late, and he figured if he didn't leave soon, he might be too relaxed to hike back. Everyone appeared to have had enough soaking for the evening, with the exception of Scott and Pat. Being stoned, and claiming the hot water to be nirvana, destroyed any motivation they had to leave. Jerry got dressed and ambled down to the river's edge.

The Judge paddled him over first. Recalling the ominous feeling he had experienced before, he waited down by the rocks while Bonnie brought Suzi across. After Suzi had been dropped off, they waved goodbye to The Judge and Bonnie and headed back towards Marble Creek.

# CHAPTER ELEVEN

Bonnie watched their flashlight beams bouncing down the trail as she turned the small craft and began paddling back for another passenger. Nearly halfway across, she could barely see her husband's shadowy shape shoving off with Gretta, when a sound of something breaking the surface splashed off to her left. She turned, but couldn't see anything. The moon hadn't quite reached the river, and the shadows hid the cause of the disturbance. She approached within twenty-five feet of Sam's inflatable kayak when she heard a second, louder splash. The Judge's boat looked submerged for a second, then it folded in half in the center, as if someone had crossed a cable at its mid point and winched it under.

Panic spread through her chest. She heard a loud bang as one of the tubes exploded. Both the Judge and Gretta spilled into the water.

"SAM! SAM, ANSWER ME!" Bonnie screamed. There was something dreadfully wrong with what she had just seen, but she couldn't take time to sort it out. She had to save Sam. At that moment, Gretta broke the surface and let loose a skull-piercing scream that echoed through the entire canyon. She slapped the water with whirlwind speed, as she shrieked unintelligibly, and coughed up water.

What was left of the inflatable kayak broke the surface, and floated downstream as Gretta reached the shore. Bonnie watched her scramble up onto the rocks, and back away from the river...*as if she's afraid to turn her back to it*. In the moonlight, she could see Gretta's blouse had been ripped, and that she was bleeding from two deep slash marks across her chest. Her face appeared to be an artist's study of fear.

Bonnie paddled to the spot where the boat had done its bizarre dance and looked through the darkness for any sign of her husband. Two hands plunged out of the water and grasped the left tube of her inflatable. She gasped as The Judge's head cleared the surface. He coughed something dark onto her tube; his face projected intense pain. Bonnie also noticed something dark on his neck in the second that he remained visible.

"Sam! What's wrong?" she cried as she reached for his arm.

"GO! NOW!" was all he could say, and it had bubbled with a terrible sound, as if he were gargling something thick and sticky.

Ripped from the kayak with incredible force, he released the tube when he felt the powerful tug from below. His last thought had been to let go so Bonnie wouldn't capsize. He knew his wounds were mortal.

The powerful enemy grabbed his lifejacket and pulled him down deeper into the dark water. First, he felt something warm in his throat spread to his navel in less than a second; then, he felt the flood of cold water fill the cavity inside him, as the water around him seemed to grow warmer at the same time. He sank deeper and deeper into the darkness.

Bonnie screamed. Hysterical, her only thought was to get away. Sam had even told her to go, but she sat motionless, hoping he would reappear and everything would be all right again. She looked for him in the black water.

*He was wearing his lifejacket. He should come up, unless he's caught on something*, she reasoned. Five feet in front of her, his bloody lifejacket broke the surface and floated downstream.

For what seemed like an eternity, she just watched it drift away. Then a cold flowed down her spine, like the mercury in a thermometer falling in a blizzard. She went into frenzy, paddling wildly for shore.

A shadow appeared in front of her, and she felt the boat rising up out of the water. She swung her paddle at the shadow and hit it solidly…without effect. Actually, she did notice one result: the most noxious odor she had ever smelled suddenly overcame her. The front of the boat flew up, causing her to tumble backwards out into the river as the shadow submerged. Her life jacket brought her back to the surface almost at once. She looked up to see Pat and Scott standing on top of the small cliff above her and about twenty feet away. They were naked, staring down at her with blank looks on their faces.

"SOMETHINGSINTHEWATER!" She screamed. "ITGOTSAM! ITSIN THEWA—she went under before she could finish.

"What the hell's going on?" Pat screamed at Gretta below. Gretta couldn't answer. She was having convulsions.

Bonnie came back to the surface, gasped for air and tried to scream again, but her lungs sounded full of water. She reached up at Pat, but he was too far away to help her. Then Bonnie stiffened as if an electric shock had hit her. Her body lifted slightly out of the water, only to disappear into the indigo current. All Pat and Scott could see was her shadow melting into the dark water. A few seconds later, her yellow lifejacket broke the surface and floated away.

"Jesus, Bonnie! Oh shit! Oh God!" Scott shouted.

"She said something was in the water. What the hell does that mean?" Pat asked near panic. "Gretta, what happened?"

She climbed up the rocks, and wandered cautiously around the hot springs,

## CHAPTER ELEVEN

obviously afraid to get too close to any water. She didn't respond to him. Apparently she had checked out.

• • •

"Who screamed?" Jerry yelled from across the river. He and Suzi had heard the terrified shriek from up the trail and returned.

"Jesus, Jerry, something happened to Bonnie and the Judge, I—I think they drowned," Pat shouted.

"Drowned? Oh God, no!" Suzi cried out.

"How?" Jerry shouted.

"I couldn't see. I just heard splashing, screaming, and Bonnie yelling that something was in the water, and it had gotten Sam," Pat replied.

"Something in the water? She said that?" Jerry asked, not sure that he was hearing correctly.

"I swear that's what she said. Gretta was in the Judge's boat, but she made it to shore. She's all fucked up though. Maybe she can tell us something if she snaps out of it," Pat replied.

"We're stuck over here. The boats are gone, and we can't get back up to camp from this side. The terrain down river gets too steep, and there are several big creeks to cross," Scott shouted.

"And I ain't crossing no creek!" Pat yelled.

"Ditto!" Scott said.

"I'm not going across this fucking river either, Jerry. I don't like the idea of a goddam shark-thing waiting to sink another raft just to get my goodies," Pat shouted.

"Pat, you and Scott hang on. You're going to have to keep your shit together. But until we know what's going on, don't go near the water," Jerry instructed.

"Duh," Pat returned.

"We're going back to get help. We'll figure some way to get you out of this, so hang on and wait there," Jerry instructed them.

"Where the hell are we gonna go?" Pat asked.

"Hurry man, this place gives me the creeps," Scott pleaded.

Jerry and Suzi turned and ran back towards Marble Creek.

The moonlight filtered through the trees, making the path into a patchwork of gray and black. In the darker parts of the forest they used their flashlights to dispel the night's shadows. Running at top speed, he still found himself slightly behind Suzi. They didn't speak while they ran. It took most of their breath to feed oxygen to the needy muscle cells in their legs. Occasionally, they stopped for a breather.

"I can't believe this is happening," Suzi said as she gasped.

"Maybe they didn't drown. They both had on type-five life jackets. Type-five should float them on their backs even if they're unconscious. Pat could have misunderstood what she said, about there being something in the water that got Sam. There's an explanation," Jerry assured her.

"I think we should come back with more lights, and first-aid stuff in case they're hurt. They could even be stuck on a rock in the middle of the river suffering from hypothermia," she said.

"I agree. We'll get the others and bring along some sleeping bags to bring up their body heat in case it's necessary. Don't worry my first-aid kit has everything. You could practically do brain surgery with the stuff in it." His breath returned. "You ready to go?" he asked.

"After you," she replied.

• • •

Pat tried to coax Gretta out of her hiding place. She had crawled behind a natural rock cairn and squatted down looking off into space. He focused on helping her, and it pushed back his own fears. If he didn't concentrate on helping her, the fact that Gretta had seen something that fried her brain might really freak him.

After a while the night chill made him look for his clothes. He dressed while keeping a watchful eye on the river. Scott stood about twenty feet away to his rear and above the pools.

"Jesus, this is really happening," Pat said.

"What did you say?" Scott asked.

"I said Jesus, this is really happening." He paused for a minute. "We're fucked, Scott. We can't go back across. If a goddamn shark is in there, it could chew up a raft like bubble gum. I sure as hell don't want to be the soft, chewy center for no fucking shark."

"There's no such thing as a fresh-water shark outside Lake Nicaragua," Scott replied.

"Okay, Mr. Wizard, how about a great, big, fucking alligator?" Pat asked.

"Too cold—the water's too cold for an alligator. They like warm climates and warm water," Scott informed him.

## CHAPTER ELEVEN

Pat kept searching his mental inventory for other underwater predators, but came up empty.

Scott led Gretta out of her hiding place and over to where Pat stood. She followed him the way an awestruck child follows a parent through a large crowd.

"What happened to her?" Scott asked.

"I don't know. Maybe you should ask her."

"Gretta…GRETTA!" Scott slapped her, but she didn't even blink. "Man, she's gone! What could have turned her off like this?" he asked.

"Fear—fear is all I know that could do it," Pat replied.

Gretta stared into nowhere, as if watching a movie with her inner eye.

"Man, I hope they hurry. I'm creeped." Pat gripped his head in his hands and shook his head. "I just don't want to end up like her," he confided.

Scott looked into Gretta's eyes. "I think she's a step up from Bonnie and The Judge. At least she's somewhere. They're probably dead.

"It's going to take at least two hours for Jerry and Suzi to make it back down here, so try to relax," Scott told him.

"Two hours! Fuck! I can't handle two hours alone in the dark with whatever the hell is in the water down there. What the hell are we gonna do if it can come out of the water, huh? Piss at it?"

To Pat two hours sounded like a lifetime. Sixty seconds was all it had taken to end the lifetimes for Sam and Bonnie Baker, he thought with a shudder.

"Relax, he says," Pat thought aloud. The night was silent and getting cold. It was to be the longest night of their lives.

# 12

## PATROLS

Bobby watched the rear, while Abby and Jim dragged several tree limbs back towards the camp. He carried an armful of large, odd-shaped, wood chunks and estimated that what they had between them should last until morning. If it didn't, they agreed not to be the ones to go back for more.

Every noise caused them to drop their loads, and form a three-sided wedge—a back-to-back triangle of knife-wielding paranoids.

It had taken about half an hour for them to get far enough upriver to find any sizeable firewood. The area near the camp had been stripped of deadfall by previous river travelers, but they finally located a cache of several downed trees in a small side canyon.

The moon had risen over a cleft in the mountains, adding an eerie blue glow to the landscape. Bobby peered out through the woods for any sign of movement. None caught his eye, except once when a nighthawk flew at him from a nearby tree. He jumped five feet, and again they dropped everything, took defensive postures, until they realized they weren't being attacked.

The image of Gary's face staring out of the helmet popped back into his mind. He wasn't ready to confront such a savage killer. With the rhythmic sound of his boots crunching leaves and twigs his mind drifted back ten years...

...He had been the floor manager for the largest nightclub in Arizona; a euphemism for head bouncer. He had worked for Vito Scalise. Of all the people

Bobby knew, Vito was the toughest. He didn't need a bouncer, but Bobby was just glad Vito had liked and hired him.

One night, a group of boot camp Marines had come into the club to raise hell. Normally, Bobby let Marines get away with a lot, not because he was afraid of them, but because he knew from experience what they had been through.

When the profanity had reached the level where it was bothering other customers, Bobby picked out the leader and walked up behind him. "If you don't change your attitude you'll be asked to leave," he said very business-like.

The Marine made the mistake of turning and grabbing Bobby's shirt. Without a second to prepare, Bobby jammed his thumb into the backside of the leader's hand. He twisted the Marine's wrist effortlessly and took him to his knees. He bent low to whisper something to the unlucky grunt, when he realized the guy was trying to reach back and hit him. He brought his knee up lightning fast, flush into the face of the troublemaker, sending him flat on his back onto the hardwood floor.

One of his buddies stood up to join in and was immediately kicked in the testicles hard enough to lift him off the ground. Bobby then hit him in the chin, with such power, that his jaw broke on both sides. Another attacked Bobby from his right. A side, snap kick caught the attacker in the solar plexus, penetrating a foot deep. Without thinking, Bobby finished his *kata*: a front kick slammed into the face, a crescent kick found his temple, and a raking heal kick to the opposite side of the man's head gave the unfortunate boot camper a serious brain concussion. All of it had happened before any of the other bouncers could respond. The rest of the party sat where they were…awestruck and silent.

"Anybody else want to show me how much you learned in six weeks?" Bobby asked them. No one spoke. They gathered their wounded comrades and went off in search of a trauma center. Bobby felt bad for the men he had beaten, but he was like Israel. If you start something, you better be prepared to go the distance, because you would get back tenfold what you gave. He had been at his best that night, reacting with instinct.

An extra dry branch snapping under foot brought him to full alert. He breathed hard with each stride. Tonight, he hoped he wouldn't be put to the test again. At least the Marines had been sane people. Out here, somebody wasn't so sane.

## CHAPTER TWELVE

After a while, he saw the glow from the campfire as it lit the underside of Jerry's tarp, and the small group huddled around it. They rejoined the others and Bobby felt such relief to be back, sitting around the blazing fire in his lawn chair, that he almost laughed, but it would have been inappropriate. Instead he leaned forward and placed a new log on the dwindling fire.

"Nothing's happened since you left," Jacques informed them. "Phydeaux didn't growl once." Bobby felt doubly grateful that he had sided with Jacques, and the dog had come with them.

• • •

After what seemed like hours, Jerry and Suzi crossed the log bridge that spanned Marble Creek, ran the final 200 yards, and entered the campsite. Out of breath and unable to speak, they both stood—bent with hands on knees—gasping. What Jerry saw made him wonder if he'd returned to the wrong camp. Most of the group looked the same, but everyone held knives and spears. Two women from another rafting party he had seen earlier in the day were there too. He recognized Abby right away, but he was still too winded to acknowledge her. After a moment his breath returned, but Suzi spoke first.

"Terrible…drowned…Bonnie…shit!" She tried to spit but her mouth was apparently too dry. Then Jerry tried.

"Bonnie…Judge…fell out…something was in the water…had to leave Pat, Scott, and Gretta on the other side." A gasp filled each space between his phrases.

"We've got to go back and see if they're downstream—hurt or something," Suzi said, finally finding her breath.

"What happened Jerry? Start at the beginning," Jacques said quietly. Jerry sensed a reason existed for the two new members in camp, as well as for everyone gripping weapons. He decided to wait to ask, until he and Suzi finished telling them about the terrible news from Sunflower.

Bobby listened intently as Jerry and Suzi exhausted all the details they knew. The line: "something got Sam; there's something in the water," sent chills into Bobby. Up until now, he had suspected a human element in the murders. That at least was a starting point—human. Humans could speak, could relate on some level, and could be defended against. How do you defend yourself against something in the water? He wondered.

It could kill on land or in water. It had hung Charlene Blanchet, Abby's friend, on a coat hook for effect, killed the ranger, maybe killed a bunch of campers, and possibly killed three of his friends, all in one day. More than likely, it had been close to them last night. It may have even considered killing them too, but backed off when Phydeaux barked.

*What the hell are we dealing with?*

Bobby told Jerry and Suzi what he and Jim had found in the yellow kayak. Then he relayed Abby's story. It became clear to Jerry that Bonnie and The Judge were beyond the need of his first-aid kit. The decision still had to be made, however, concerning what to do about their companions across the river.

Bobby said, "Okay, we've got to get Scott, Pat, and Gretta; how are we going to do it?"

"We'd have to take a raft to get across the river, but there are some big problems," Jacques said. "If we risk going to get them tonight, we deplete our numbers and become vulnerable to attack in the dark by 'something in the water,'" Jacques paused, then said, "Plus, we would be in the rafts, running Marble Creek Falls by flashlight. Even if we didn't have an unseen adversary in the water, the prospect of trying that sure as hell don't turn me on. Plato and I have seen seasoned boaters flipped in both holes at Marble."

"We can't just leave them there all night with whatever is down there," Suzi challenged.

"It may not still *be* down there. I think we'd better worry about us," Jim said.

"How can you say that?" Beth demanded.

Plato laid a hand on her shoulder and said, "Look, you heard what Jacques said, there's no way we can do it tonight. But I think those kids have a good chance."

"One other consideration is that we don't know if they will be there…alive, even if we do set out to rescue them," Jim added.

Bobby stood up. "It pains me to say this, but bottom line, we can't go, and we can't split the group. We'll just have to get them in the morning." He still felt guilty when he saw Suzi's expression of disbelief.

"It's time we formulated some kind of plan for the defense of this camp," Plato said.

"No shit, I second that," Jim said as he poured himself a cup of thick, black coffee. "Any ideas?"

"I think we should sleep in the middle of camp, without tents, and with a posted guard of at least three people on each of three, separate shifts."

## CHAPTER TWELVE

"I'm on all three watches then," Jim said. "No offense, but I'm sure as hell not going to trust anybody else not to fall asleep."

No one seemed offended.

"I've got some ten-pound fishing line," Jerry said, "We could run a perimeter line around camp with empty beer cans and lures on it to make noise if anybody or anything trips over it. It would be almost invisible. Other than that, posted sentries, and Phydeaux, I can't think of any other warning system," he said as he looked through his tackle box and found the line.

"At first light, we get the hell out of here," Jacques said in a serious tone. "Whitey Cox camp is sixteen miles downriver. As tired as we'll be after tonight, we'll be lucky to make it and still have enough energy to unload the boats tomorrow evening. Let's try to get as much rest as we can tonight. We'll pick up Pat, Scott, and Gretta in the morning when we pass Sunflower…if they're still alive."

Hearing Jacques' comments made Bobby anxious. "From now on, we've got to stay close together. Don't even go to the bathroom by yourself," he advised.

"We should keep a watch on the boats somehow. Ours were purposefully pushed or pulled out into the river," Abby warned.

"Good point…thanks, Abby." Bobby walked to the edge of the firelight and stared into the darkness towards the boat landing. "We've either got to pull the boats up into camp, or post a second watch on them. Choice number one makes more sense to me."

"Well, nothing's getting done just talking about it," Jim said. "Let's go get the rafts up here so at least somebody can get some sleep tonight."

As a group they walked down to the riverside. Bobby wondered if the others felt as reluctant to step into the water as he did. They cautiously surrounded the heavy gear boat and lifted on the count of three. Even with nine people carrying the boats, it was still an arduous task. They would carry each boat a while and rest. This went on, time after time, until they'd brought all the rafts within the firelight. Jacques' was still the heaviest, so it had to be unloaded before it could be carried up.

With all the boats inside the visible campsite, Jerry and Suzi began laying the early-warning perimeter line around the camp. Jim and Linda put on their Polar-fleece jackets to fend off the cold and began packing up the tents and gear, so it would be easier to load quickly at dawn the next morning. Jacques sat back in his lawn chair and listened to night noises, as he lit a cigar and laid his hatchet across his lap. Plato sharpened more knives. Tomorrow they would become spears.

Bobby had drawn the first watch along with Abby and Beth; Jim began his all-night vigil as he had promised; Phydeaux slept at her master's feet. It was just after midnight and all was far from well.

• • •

Pat shivered, not only from the cold but also from fear. He watched Scott huddle with Gretta trying to keep warm on the rocks nearest the hot springs. It hadn't been cool enough for them to be concerned, once the storm had passed, so none of them had brought jackets.

Pat's eyes returned again and again to the spot where Bonnie had last gone under. He kept expecting her to surface and swim to shore, where she would float up next to him and tell him how great it was down in the river.

"You should try it, Pat," she would say. "It's fun to be dead."

*ENOUGH!* I've been reading too many Dean Koontz novels. He had to quit thinking these thoughts—it was spooky enough already.

His teeth started to chatter, and he began shivering uncontrollably, when it dawned on him that he could build a fire. He had matches in the bag with the marijuana. *If I hadn't been so stoned when the heavy shit came down, I would have thought of it sooner.* "I'm going to get some wood," he told Scott through typewriter teeth.

"Be careful, man, Gretta's not too much company tonight," Scott replied.

"Don't worry, I'm not getting anywhere close to that friggin' river," Pat assured him.

"Okay, but call out if you need me."

Pat stayed as close to the hot springs as possible at first, but the immediate area around Sunflower offered only small branches and twigs. To get real firewood, he would have to leave the clearing and go into the forest by moonlight.

He was on his second trip for wood, thinking of what he had seen earlier. Something had registered in his subconscious mind, and it troubled him. He couldn't quite put his finger on it. A dark shadow had broken the surface of the water just in front of Bonnie's boat an instant before she flipped over backwards. The speed and the jerky motion of the shadow had seemed somewhat unworldly…and terrifying.

It was at that moment Pat got a feeling of being watched. He looked in all

## CHAPTER TWELVE

directions. Moving around, looking for firewood had warmed him up for a while, but now he felt truly cold again, cold from the feeling, not from the air temperature. He was only about thirty yards away from the hot springs and could see that Scott had a small fire already going.

Pat found a good-sized limb that he figured would last at least two hours. Then Jerry and Bobby would be back. Then, he would be forced to summon enough courage to get into a raft and cross the river. He would have to cross the spot where something had killed Bonnie and The Judge. For now, he occupied himself with getting the wood back to the fire, and shaking off the feeling that he was being stalked.

He didn't hear a sound behind him but kept expecting to turn around and find Bonnie, dripping wet, telling him to come down to the river and meet her new friend. He fought the image until it shattered like a broken mirror. *Seven years of bad luck, man.*

A trace of a strange odor wafted past his nose. It was unlike anything he recognized. Instinctively, it caused him to run back. *What the hell is that? Battery acid? Rotten cinnamon rolls maybe? Fuck this.* He sprinted out of the woods.

Back next to the small fire, its warmth immediately made him feel more hopeful. Assuming that his fear had been caused by an over-active imagination, he dropped the wood and sat down next to Gretta. In the firelight, he could see her injuries more clearly.

"Something really gashed her good. I didn't notice that before, did you?" Pat asked.

"Yeah, I saw them when she first came up here," Scott replied.

"Why didn't you say something?"

"What difference would it have made? She doesn't appear to be feeling any pain, and she doesn't look like she's ready to tell us what did it, so fuck off," Scott warned.

"You fuck off, asshole!" Pat shot back.

For a moment they hung on the edge of fighting.

Pat watched Scott lean back and take a deep breath. He did the same and returned to building the fire. After five minutes of silence, he spoke: "I'm uptight man. I don't mean to be pushy, I'm just real scared, so try to bear with me." Pat put a small branch on the fire and looked out into the woods. He watched the light from the campfire shine into the edge of the forest. It illuminated the clearing but danced on the trees and the knoll above them, casting macabre shadows that moved in a hellish rhythm.

Pat still struggled with the feeling he was being watched. A breeze again blew the stench of whatever was out in the woods into his nostrils. The branch he had just added flared brightly, illuminating farther into the forest behind the hot springs. He noticed the source of his disquiet in the reflection of a pair of glowing, amber eyes, staring from the exact spot where he had exited the woods only minutes before.

"Probably a friggin' bear." he said.

He picked up a baseball-sized rock, stood, and threw it directly at the eyes. For once in his life he was right on the mark. Maybe not a Nolan Ryan pitch, but he had really put some heat into the throw. It sizzled through the air and struck the target just above, and directly between the eyes. They blinked out. Pat likened the sound of the rock striking its shadowy target as similar to hitting a watermelon wrapped in newspaper with a baseball bat.

"Holy shit! I nailed it!" he shouted.

He wanted to go investigate, but knew if it had indeed been a bear, it might just be a little pissed off. It might have a bad headache and decide to take it out on his body. *No, I'll stay next to the fire; animals are afraid of fire.*

The wood he had collected would easily last the two hours until Jerry and Bobby returned with the others. *They'll be along anytime now. Nope, it won't be long now,* Pat thought to himself as he nervously watched the spot where the eyes had been.

He watched in silence. Scott held Gretta's head against his breast, and gently stroked her hair. He also kept glancing to the wooded area where the animal had been, as he silently prayed for deliverance from evil—*amen.*

# 13

## FRIGHT NIGHT

No one could sleep at Marble Creek. At the fire pan, Bobby and Abby sat in lawn chairs and kept watch on the wooded side of camp. Any other night, they would have been getting acquainted and looking forward to the possibilities that a new relationship offered. Instead, the day they met would always be remembered as one of the worst days in their lives. The "trip of a lifetime" was certainly living up to its title, but not the way he had hoped.

The new evidence that "something in the water" had, in all probability, killed The Judge and Bonnie, added new problems. They still had sixteen miles to descend to Whitey Cox Camp, and another eighteen miles to Sheep Creek Camp beyond that. All that way, they could be in danger from that same "something in the water."

According to the guidebook, The Victor Ranch was less than two miles beyond Sheep Creek. If they arrived early enough, it would be possible to hike to the ranch by sundown, day after tomorrow.

Bobby imagined a hideous and deadly enemy, lurking just under the surface of the water, waiting for them to run a deadly gauntlet.

He felt alone, even in the middle of so many people, even in the presence of such a compelling lady. He'd always been shy when it came to breaking the ice with women. They usually had to make the first move. If his ex-wife, Karen, hadn't planted a two-minute kiss on him the night they met, he would never have gotten married to her. For some reason, Bobby found the courage to break the ice with Abigail Jones. Maybe it was because she seemed so virtuous. Maybe it was because she was so pretty, but he found himself speaking to her, without even knowing what he was going to say, until he heard the words coming out of his own mouth.

"Abby?" he asked.

"Yes."

"I know you don't know me from Adam, but I hope we get out of this. I'd like to know you better." Abby looked stunned. She didn't answer for a moment, and Bobby feared he had been too bold.

"Abby?"

"I'm sorry, it's just that I was thinking the same exact thought when you spoke. You startled me."

"Mom always said our family had a touch of clairvoyance."

Bobby stood, as did Abby, and he wrapped his arms around her waist. He pulled her close. Her head nestled just under his chin. He could feel her squeeze him tightly and the electricity that had pulsed through them earlier, returned. The current ran the full length of their bodies. He hadn't intended anything sexual, but he felt it.

Abby realized Bobby was becoming aroused. For that matter, she was, too. They stood holding each other for a few minutes without saying a word. While in his arms she managed to block out the terrible danger they faced.

*It's strange that I could feel this way with all that's going on*, she thought. She wished that things were different. She would have enjoyed exploring the sensual side with Bobby.

She pulled back from him slowly, and looked into his deep, blue eyes. He certainly was attracted to her; she could see it in his expression, as well as feeling it through her body. After a few moments, they both realized nothing was going to happen between them that night, so they parted reluctantly and sat back down.

Abby scanned the woods, realizing that they hadn't paid attention while they had been locked in the embrace. But at least nothing seemed out of place.

She wished in her heart that time could revert to the moment she and Bobby had met, and they could relive the day differently.

• • •

Just before the shift change at 2:00 a.m., Phydeaux awoke. She sniffed the air for a moment and stood. Alerted that something approached from the

## CHAPTER THIRTEEN

downstream side of the camp, she began growling and suddenly raced out of the firelight into the shadows.

Bobby immediately awakened and held the blade of his Bowie Knife in hand—ready to throw. Everyone else jumped up around him holding spears.

"Oh God, I should have tied her up," Jacques said, obviously worried that she was about to come to harm. Anyone could see he loved her a great deal. She was his river companion of many years, and the thought of her being hurt or killed visibly sickened him.

"PHYDEAUX!!! COME HERE, GIRL!!! COME HERE, PHYDEAUX!!!" Jacques cried out. He turned to Bobby. "She doesn't know what's going on, she doesn't know that she's in danger, damn!"

Bobby heard her barking from somewhere about a hundred yards out beyond the edge of camp. The moon passed behind a cloud and complete darkness enveloped the world outside their fire's light.

"PHYDEAUX!!!"

The barking stopped.

"Phydeaux, Oh God—PHYDEAUX!"

The deep perimeter line that Jerry had placed across the wooded path began rattling cans and lures as Phydeaux yelped in pain.

Jacques grabbed a flashlight and sprinted toward the sound.

"Shit!" Bobby exclaimed as he grabbed a spear from Plato and ran after him.

Within a few seconds, Bobby and Jacques had covered the distance, and located Phydeaux. Alive. Bobby shined his flashlight on her. She had been snagged by one of the lures on the perimeter line. Whatever she'd been chasing was gone, and apparently she had been obeying her master's command to return to camp, when the hook sank into her shoulder.

"Somebody bring some needle-nose pliers," Jacques commanded from out in the night.

At first, not knowing what had spooked Phydeaux, the group in camp had not seemed eager to comply. However, after the reason had been explained, Jim brought them a pair out of his repair kit.

There had been some extremely nervous moments when the dog's scream of pain echoed through the canyon. They had all assumed the worst. Jim walked back to camp and left Bobby and Jacques alone with Phydeaux.

Bobby didn't feel safe outside the firelight. The clouds and the trees overhead, blocked out any light the moon would have provided. He felt vulnerable. The beams of their flashlights failed to give comfort. In fact, they impaired night vision and made the darkness outside their small circle seem somehow even darker.

Removing a treble hook from the dog by flashlight proved to be no easy task. Bobby had to perform the surgery, while Jacques held Phydeaux. She would never have bitten Jacques for any reason, but Bobby wasn't so sure she knew him that well. Jacques held her tight, while Bobby used the pliers to push the barbed hook through the skin and snap it off.

All throughout the process, the fear of the dark, and what might be lurking just a few yards away, kept him intensely alert. *Even though she's being held, I'm sure Phydeaux will give us a warning*, Bobby assured himself.

After they finished, they headed back to camp with Jacques carrying his wounded, canine companion. Bobby felt relieved to know the dog was all right, but he didn't want to have her run off into the dark again chasing God knows what. They needed her.

If he had the whole process to do over again, he would have simply cut the line, and brought her into camp to remove the hook. Then he and Jerry could have gone back to repair the line later.

*Why didn't I think of that?* He wondered. He knew the answer. He was dead tired, and dead-tired people couldn't make good decisions. In fact, if people didn't make good decisions in situations like this, *they just might end up losing their heads*, he thought, feeling miserable.

The first few hours of fear started to level off. He wondered if things would still be as high-strung tomorrow. Without adequate sleep, judgment could be impaired causing them all to make "bad" decisions.

He and Jacques tended Phydeaux's wounds in the firelight. After they were through, Jacques took some flat hoopi rope and tethered her to a tree with approximately thirty feet of slack. She could make it to the edge of the darkness, but no further. It didn't matter. For the rest of the night she slept like a puppy at Jacques' feet.

No one else got more than two hours of rest at Marble Creek, and everyone became familiar with Bobby's term: "greasy sleep." Mercifully, the rest of the night passed without incident.

• • •

The fire at Sunflower Hot Springs went out about 4:00 a.m. After the incident of the alleged bear, Pat didn't feel like another excursion to find more firewood. He and Scott had kept their hopes up until the last branch burned down. Shortly after it faded to coals, he realized no help would be coming

## CHAPTER THIRTEEN

before morning. He even wondered if Suzi and Jerry had made it back to Marble Creek. They could have had an accident, or...*something might have gotten them*, he thought.

Pat had no trouble staying awake. At the moment, he couldn't conceive of ever sleeping again. The night noises spoke ominous messages to him; he wondered how Scott could be so calm. He just sat next to the dying fire, poking the coals as if he were merely on a camp-out. Maybe from Scott's perspective, he appeared calm too. Inside, in his mind, hundreds of terrible scenarios played themselves out on his mental screen. He leaned back against a rock and tried to relax, but his muscles spasmed even worse. He sat up straight.

Pat felt cold again. The fire wasn't putting out heat, since it had waned to a few glowing embers. He considered taking off his clothes and getting back into the hot springs, but somehow being naked, under the circumstances, seemed much too vulnerable. He huddled with Scott and Gretta instead. Gretta still stared off into some unseen place as Pat appraised her condition.

"Shit—I hate this," he said under his breath as he drifted off into more dreadful scenarios.

• • •

Bobby's heart lifted with the first glow in the eastern sky. The night had relinquished its gloomy grip on the world, and the sun brought light to dispel his fears. Even the faint glow at the horizon gave the promise of sunrise, and a warming of the spirit as well as of the body.

This morning, he was glad to be alive, but he still felt pangs of guilt. The sharp realization stabbed him deeply, that people he had known alive yesterday, were dead today. Where were the sparks that fueled his friend's bodies? In fact, where the hell were their bodies?

He considered the loss. It would be felt publicly as well as personally. With Sam's death, Oregon had lost one of the best jurists its Supreme Court had possessed in over thirty years. And Bonnie had been one of the state's leading environmental lawyers. Their deaths would profoundly influence Oregon's future. He wondered if the day's events were part of an assassination plot by the timber industry or Korean fishing fleets.

*Why kill all the others then? A diversion?* Gary hadn't been close to where they were killed. The Forest Service ranger and Charlene—both killed at Indian Creek. Bobby watched the sky glow brighter as he continued contemplating.

The memory of Jerry saying: what's the worst that can happen? replayed in his brain. He almost laughed, but instead choked on the golf ball lump in his throat when he recalled his vow to get everyone down the river safely. *Great job so far.*

These had been people he knew. Friends. It hurt worse than the kid on the Klamath. A pinecone falling to the ground directly in front of him brought him out of his somber trance. He stared at it lying on the ground, knowing he couldn't quit. That option no longer existed. The murders of his companions demanded a fight, a fight between himself and an unknown adversary. At stake were the lives of his friends—and his own.

Jim had a fresh pot of coffee on the propane stove; he looks like "hell warmed over," Bobby thought. Jim hadn't slept since the night before at Pistol Creek. No sleep and river-running go together like taking sleeping pills and flying an airplane—not a good idea.

Everyone else rose shortly after dawn, and even those who didn't drink coffee appeared ready to start. They still faced a lot of work to strike camp and get on the river, so they exchanged few words during the morning chores. Most busied themselves in action or thought.

Bobby stood by his boat drinking coffee in the cool morning air. The sun was already touching the tops of the mountains behind camp, but it would be over an hour before it reached the river.

Just seeing the sunshine gave him more confidence. No one whistled for joy, but the air felt considerably more optimistic than the previous night. Last night had seemed like some "bottomless-pit" nightmare. But even bottomless pits had bottoms in reality; you just didn't know how deep they were until you fell into one, he thought.

Bobby heard Jacques calling everyone to the kitchen area.

"Y'all eat as much as you can for breakfast. I don't think there'll be a lunch stop today. Load up now so you won't find yourself in a calorie deficit later," he suggested.

"I'm about to float away, and I have a definite, calorie-residue surplus. Do any of the other women-type people need relief?" Suzi asked.

Beth and Abby both held up their hands like second-grade kids seeking permission to go to the rest room. Suzi laughed at their childishness. It was the first laughter Bobby had heard since the day before, and it was a welcome sound. That seemed like a lifetime ago, but he understood, somehow, it was important for them all to laugh.

## CHAPTER THIRTEEN

Three by three, everyone went to the outhouse. It faced away from camp to give some privacy. All the sites that had been assigned to Bobby's group had outhouses hidden somewhere just outside of camp like the ranger had told them, just far enough away to cause uneasiness.

For some reason, Bobby had them do everything in threes. Three felt safer than two. The Murphy sisters had been dispatched together, Charlene was found with the ranger—two again—and Bonnie and Sam Baker had been taken practically at the same time. *Two is not a lucky number.*

They finished breaking camp and topped the rafts with economy of motion. They carried the boats back down to the water one by one and loaded them. Suzi, Beth, and Linda packed up the camping equipment, Bobby, Abby, and Jim carried gear to the boats, while Jacques, Jerry, and Plato loaded and secured the gear.

Bobby bet that he wasn't the only one feeling apprehensions about what grisly discoveries they might find on their way down river. The thought of the helmet, and the possibility of finding Gary, headless, floating in an eddy, brought Bobby's gorge to his throat; he fought it back down. He also fought the thoughts of what else might be waiting downstream and focused on the moment.

He knew the rapids would be taking on a different character the rest of the way down river. Before, they had been fun roller coasters to be enjoyed; now they would be perceived as sinister traps that could flip a boater in the river with… "something in the water."

Ahead lay at least a dozen more possible traps by his reckoning. Today, every rapid would be considered a class five—extreme danger, with high likelihood of injury or death in case of a swim.

Sitting down to breakfast before pushing off, they discussed their options.

"I don't think hiking out of here will be as safe as floating out," Jerry said.

"If there's something in the water, we should hike out," Beth pleaded.

"The ranger wasn't killed in the water," Bobby said. "We at least know where the river ends up. We could get lost in the wilderness and die of thirst. And we couldn't carry the coolers up those canyon walls—there goes the food."

"Something about an underwater thing terrifies me," Beth said looking out at the river.

"It scares us all, honey," Jacques said. "If it weren't for that ranger, your friends, and the campground full of dead people, I'd be right with you. I'd rather take my chances with dying of thirst than ending up like them. But they were killed on land. That means we're not safe either way; but that being the case, I vote to at least be comfortable and full of food while I'm in peril. Let's stay with the boats."

"One other thing," Bobby added. "According to the maps, once we crossed the mountain, we'd be walking down one of a hundred some-odd wooded paths, single file, and we wouldn't know if there are any defensible campsites. Besides, if all those other arguments aren't enough to overcome any objections, look at those steep canyon walls down river."

One look at the angle of the canyon discouraged any remaining proponent of the hiking plan. After some grumbling, the vote was unanimous.

As soon as they loaded the remaining gear, they shoved off and immediately began setting up for Marble Creek Falls. As a guide, Bobby immediately began his analysis of what lay ahead. Many rapids are called "falls," when they actually don't resemble a true waterfall at all. Marble Creek was one of these. It consisted of a rock island, which divided the river into two channels. The hydraulics of the powerful current forced boats into the left bank. This was due to the rapid being situated in the middle of a right "dogleg" in the river. There were two large "holes" capable of flipping any of their boats; they would have to avoid them.

No thrill-seeking today, he thought. Their main goal had become getting to the Victor Ranch alive. That meant reaching Whitey Cox tonight, and Sheep Creek by the following night. Any boating accident would set them off their schedule, so safety took on a new level of importance.

As Jacques set up for Marble Creek Falls, the others took their places behind him in the pool above the rapid. Bobby passed the yellow kayak on the left bank and felt his throat close. It was not a good time to get emotional, so he refocused on the drop. Still, he couldn't help trying to see under the surface of the water. The feeling that Gary's head might be facing up from under the blue cover filled his stomach with a swarm of butterflies. But worse, whatever killed him might be under there too.

Apprehensive about a class-three rapid for the first time in years, he gripped the oars tighter. He'd swum through class-five rapids without too much damage, but Marble Creek seemed more intimidating than any of them today.

Suzi had moved into Jerry's boat, not only because of her attraction to him, but to make space for Pat in case he refused to paddle his kayak. Bobby agreed to take him if that became the case. However, Suzi's absence left him feeling alone… incredibly alone. Abby and Beth followed him closely, but it wasn't the same as having human company, especially Suzi with her welcome sense of humor.

Bobby watched the rafts in front of him. Jacques and Phydeaux came close to hitting the second large suck-hole, but some heavy pulling on the oars had taken them by within one foot of its grasp. One by one, they made it successfully through the rapid, but he knew no one enjoyed the ride. They were all too busy trying to watch for anything out of the ordinary, and looking for ordinary things that might be capable of doing extraordinary mischief. The unknown always creates the worst fears, he thought.

Another class-three rapid lay in wait less than a mile below Marble Creek Falls. "Sneaks Up on You" was the only name listed in the book, and true to form it was on him before he had time to prepare. This time the river turned to the left and was almost completely blocked by huge boulders. One boat at a time, they came around the corner and faced the obstructed rapid.

It was sometimes hard to see an entire rapid from upstream, but a seasoned whitewater boater learned to look for certain things when scouting from the river. One of these phenomena was called a downstream "V". It usually meant that a clean, safe passage was available if the boater headed through the open part of the V, and centered on the tip. Another rule was to take the first, viable drop you could see. In this case, Bobby determined that the first and only viable drop was a slot on the far left side of the river. On a dogleg left, all the current forced a boat to the right side of the river. If that happened in this rapid, Bobby would encounter several large boulders and a probable "wrap."

Bobby rounded the corner, as he rounded most corners, in the center of the river. This gave him the option of reaching either side much faster. He sighted Jacques below the boulders. Apparently, he had made it without incident.

In this case, setting the proper angle, and administering three hard pulls on the oars, set him up for the narrow slot. His boat slid through with over a foot to spare on both sides of the raft. He pulled up next to Jacques and waited for the others. On his orders, class-five safety procedures had to be applied in all rapids of class-three or greater. No one seemed eager to stray from the group anyway.

After all the boats had maneuvered through "Sneaks Up on You Rapid," they caught the first sign of Sunflower Hot Springs on river right. The hot waterfall sent steam up into the cool, morning air. At first, Bobby didn't see any sign of life. Then Pat emerged from the woods just above the pools and saw them. He began shouting and waving his arms as if they might pass him by otherwise.

*At least Pat made it*, Bobby thought. The boats pulled over to the rocky shore as Scott and Gretta appeared on the rocks above. Something was terribly wrong with Gretta. She looked vacant, as if she had been lobotomized. The reunion was, at least for a moment, joyful to all but her. Even Phydeaux wagged her tail.

"Hey Pat, are you going to paddle your kayak, or do you want to ride with me?" Bobby asked.

"What the hell do you think? There's no fucking way I'm getting back in a kayak," he replied.

"Is Gary still kayaking? Where's Gary?" he asked, as he searched the water for Gary's yellow Dancer.

Pat and Gary had been best friends, and Bobby couldn't bring himself to say the words. Especially to Gary's best friend. Pat, quick to figure out what Bobby's sudden silence implied, lowered his head as tears rushed from his eyes. It took him several minutes to regain his composure.

As he climbed into the raft, his tears subsided into an angry silence. Bobby knew what he was feeling. He felt the same rage every time he thought of the helmet and its mangled passenger.

They waited and watched as Scott tried to get Gretta into Jacques' boat, but she had frozen like a stubborn donkey. Her expression changed slightly as they tried to coax her into the raft. She obviously didn't want to get close to the water.

Finally, Scott and Jim lifted her up and placed her in the boat. She began trembling, even though her expression hadn't changed. Jacques draped a jacket over her shoulders. She seemed to be vibrating with a force powered by her fear of the water.

Sliding down into the front floor compartment of the raft, she stared blankly up at the sky. It was as if she were safe as long as she couldn't see the river. After a time, she settled back into her state of non-awareness, and the boats once again prepared to shove off towards a new destination.

*She blew a fuse*, Bobby thought. Jacques administered first-aid to the two slash marks across her chest before they left Sunflower. She didn't even flinch at the alcohol burning into the raw cuts. What crushed Bobby most were her eyes; they were devoid of expression. Gretta, who almost always smiled, was gone, and in her place was a zombie. Her feet had shuffled down across the rocks, and she had stared right through whatever, or whoever she looked at. Seeing her like that fueled Bobby's anger even more, but worse was the knowledge that he had promised to take care of her, and failed.

Pat watched the steaming hot falls disappear over his right shoulder, as he and Bobby slowly drifted down the river. He kept his eyes glued to the spot where Bonnie had last gone under. He felt hot tears stream silently down both

## CHAPTER THIRTEEN

of his cheeks.

Glancing forward, he saw his kayak strapped to the back of Jerry's raft. He looked at it and realized he wouldn't ever be kayaking again. *Nope...too unstable...I might hit something and roll over.*

An Eskimo roll would bring him back upright, but the very thought of being that close to the water, or being in the water, caused his bowels to loosen slightly.

Kayaking was a sport he used to enjoy but no more.

Throughout the next six miles, they rafted class ones. Then, a nasty class-three came upon them. By the guidebook, Bobby figured it to be Jackass Rapids. It looked like a major drop from above. It was choked with boulders all down the left, and a narrow opening on the right revealed a horizon line, which was indicative of a waterfall, or a steep vertical drop.

Just for a moment, Bobby fought back a panic attack at the thought of going over a waterfall. Abby drifted into the opening, and disappeared over the tongue of the drop; he was relieved to see her reappear below, still upright and in her boat. It looked to be about a six-foot drop. Usually, he wouldn't even take a deep breath for that, but today he gave it three times the respect he normally would have. He followed Abby's line without difficulty. Even with Pat's extra 180 pounds, the boat still responded perfectly. He and Pat went over the brink.

Bobby felt the brief sensation of free-fall, followed by impact, as the boat flattened out. As before, all the other boats had pulled over just below the rapid in case of an accident. He was glad they hadn't been needed.

They spent the afternoon pushing the oars without a break into class-one and class-two rapids. The current had slowed dramatically. The big drops were getting bigger, but they were also getting farther and farther apart. Somehow Pat managed to sleep in the front of the raft

Miles passed by without anything unusual taking place. Occasionally, Bobby pulled up next to Abby's raft and talked to her. It took his mind off of the events of the last twenty-four hours. In the process, they learned a great deal about each other. He told Abby that he had been a kick boxer, a musician, and a river guide. He told her that he owned his own small outfitting business on the McKenzie River called MAD, for McKenzie Adventures Downstream and that his life marked him a "jack of all trades."

With Abby's encouragement he talked about himself like he hadn't in years.

In the growing warmth of the day, and in the growing closeness he felt for Abby, he became more comfortable sharing his personal history.

As the day progressed, Bobby grew more tired, and the constant rowing took its toll on him. The only thing that made him feel better was that he wasn't as bad off as Jim or Pat. Neither of them had slept since Pistol Creek.

He drifted back to the sweep boat position for the rest of the float. After a while, he saw the welcome sight of boats grounded on the right shore of the river. That meant he was approaching Whitey Cox Camp. It was 3:30 in the afternoon when they arrived, considerably earlier than anticipated. But Bobby knew night would come in less than six hours, and with it the darkness. Then things would be different.

The actual camp spread out above the beach. A flat, second level, situated inside a grove of trees, provided them fifty yards in the center to camp. It made an excellent place for Jerry's new, improved perimeter line.

Bobby helped dig holes for pongee sticks. That had been Pat's idea. Together they had studied the lay of the land and positioned them in places where the terrain and the trees would funnel a would-be intruder, at least if it approached from above. He alerted everyone in camp as to the pit's locations, and Pat vowed to remove them in the morning. It was a long shot that anything would step on one, but they were willing to try anything after last night.

# 14

## PERIMETERS

Hot springs located inside the camp would normally have made this campsite particularly attractive. Abby took in the surroundings. Two large pines shaded the area from upstream, and a beautiful sand beach, with a wall of conifers on the downstream end, spread out below a large clearing with ribbons of trails up to the hot springs high above. Whitey Cox's grave marker stood at the center of the clearing.

Abby eased herself into the hot pool next to Bobby as he dozed. She was careful not to awaken him. She knew how badly he needed sleep, as they all did, and watched to make sure he didn't slip under the surface.

She wanted the chance to get to know this man. His ruggedly handsome mystique intrigued her. She felt as if she were connected to him somehow. Interesting men didn't come along that often. When they did, she usually had to grade them on a curve for physical appearance. With Bobby, she didn't have to use the curve. Although Beth, Jacques, and Plato sat across from them, she took an occasional opportunity to be a voyeur. She studied Bobby's body, his face, his lips, and came to the conclusion that she wanted him for a lover.

She gently rubbed her leg against his, and the excitement of touching him sent a jolt through her. No one else could see due to the angle of the sun reflecting off the pool's surface, and the fact that she touched him in such close proximity to the others aroused her immensely. She felt the same excitement she had experienced when she kissed her first boy at age twelve.

*Stop it Abigail*, she scolded herself. *You're ready to jump this guy's bones and you hardly know him. We could practice safe sex,* she thought, before realizing the irony of her concern. She chuckled inside. *Here I am worrying about AIDS, when I'll be lucky to make it off the river alive.* Pulling her leg away from Bobby, she let her sexual tension die a natural death. She rolled up her towel and used it as a pillow. Lying back, she took a deep cleansing breath, while still caressing his body with her eyes.

Actually, she was happy to share the hot pool with Beth, Jacques, and Plato. Pat and Scott occupied lawn chairs on opposite sides of the pool and held spears while scanning the surrounding landscape for any sign of an intruder. Though strangers, she already felt connected to them all.

After a while, Jerry, Suzi, Pat, and Scott traded places with their group. As it worked out, everyone except Jim and Linda soaked in the spring. They had been busy making dinner close by, and weren't too crazy about being naked in the event something came for a visit. Abby didn't blame them; she had felt vulnerable while soaking, even with Bobby and the others all around her.

Sunset came early in the western river valleys. The sky remained light until about 9:00 p.m., but the sun sank behind the 7000-foot ridges hours earlier. It had just slipped behind a jagged peak, when the second group climbed out of the hot spring. Most of them stood around the camp table under a nearby tree.

"We should set up watch before dark. That's when it hit last night," Pat suggested.

"You've got to quit that linear thinking, son," Jacques countered. "This son-of-a-bitch hits anytime it wants to, in case you haven't noticed. Abby's friend got it at the cabin around lunchtime, Gary probably got it shortly thereafter, and who knows when the campers above Marble Creek got it? Because of the fact that Abby said they were ripe, I'd guess the night before at least."

"You don't know shit," Pat growled. "Anything I say, you say the opposite."

"I don't mean for it to sound that way; I just think you'd better not start thinking in one way about this…thing. If you do, you're likely to let your guard down at the wrong moment. For now, let's all just try to think clearly. We need each other."

Bobby watched as Pat's tense shoulders relaxed slightly. He exhaled a long breath. He was glad Jacques had taken the initiative to cool down the conflict. Pat hadn't been quite the same since learning of Gary's death. He seemed more on the edge. Evidently, Jacques had clued in on Pat's state and given him more room. At least one problem looked to be working itself out.

"We can also figure that whatever it is seems to be equally dangerous on land as it is in the water," Plato added. "If there are more than one of these

## CHAPTER FOURTEEN

predators, one could be land-based, and the other water-based." He thought for a moment. "But logically, since there hasn't been a phenomena like this reported on the Middle Fork before, it would seem coincidental that two separate entities, of apparently different species, would show up at almost the same instant. The odds are stacking up in favor of one, highly mobile, extremely, efficient killer, whether it's an it, or a he. Excuse me—he or she," he said looking at Abby. She smiled and nodded back.

"We'll all be up until around ten tonight," Bobby said as a yawn forced itself on him. "At least I hope I can make it until ten. Let's make the first shift from ten to one, the second from one to four, and the last from four to seven in the morning. The sky will start getting light around six, but everybody except the sentries should sleep until seven. I think we're all going to need the extra rest.

They drew paper strips for the different watch shifts. Bobby, Jerry, and Linda drew the first shift, Abby, Plato, Scott, and Beth drew the second, and Pat, Jacques, and Jim drew graveyard.

They set up a tent for Gretta. Scott spoon-fed some yogurt to her before they zipped her into a sleeping bag for the night. They didn't want her wandering off into the woods, and she seemed content to lay face up and stare at the top of the tent.

Bobby built up the fire an hour before dark. He needed coals to prepare his specialty: baked spaghetti. Linda and Jim had made the sauce, which he mixed with the pasta and poured into Jerry's Dutch oven. Suzi grated mozzarella cheese on top, and they set it on the coals to bake.

Bobby needed to clear his mind, so he took a few moments to unwind by throwing his Bowie knife. He found a dead tree and stood back the intuitive distance for one spin. He had practiced drawing his knife, and throwing it at targets for years. It relaxed him, and he had become quite proficient. He had seen "The Magnificent Seven" as a child. The scene where James Coburn drew a knife and threw it into the heart of a gunfighter had sparked the hobby of knife throwing in a young Bobby. There had been something exotic about throwing a knife that appealed to him then and still did twenty-five years later.

Bobby drew the knife and threw it at a knothole on the old snag. It sank in solidly. *Pegged.* He pried the knife from the wood and backed away to the distance he perceived to be two turns. He drew the big knife with lightning speed and launched it in a slow tumble; one turn, two turns…SHUNK!

It sank in three inches deep. He walked over to the tree and rocked the knife up and down until the wood loosened its grip on the blade.

Walking back to the point where he felt three spins to be, he put the knife back into its sheath. This was the tricky one. Three spins was as much luck as it was skill. He concentrated on the target. Everything else faded out to an obscure circle around the periphery of the knothole. He took a deep breath and exhaled. Drawing the heavy knife, he hurled it at the target.

Its arc took it slightly higher than the knothole and to the left. It struck just short of the third spin, causing it to hit in much the same way a hatchet would have. The blade bounced off of the tree into the dirt.

*Close but no cigar*, Bobby thought as he walked to the tree and picked up the knife. He cleaned the blade on his T-shirt and placed it back in the sheath he wore on his belt. It made him feel a little safer having the reach of two spins between him and an attacker. Remembering the Dutch oven, he returned to the fire pan.

A few minutes later, a delectable treat known as "pizza-getti" came out of the big cast iron pan and disappeared within minutes. They seemed to draw more than sustenance from the communal meal. After a dessert of apple pie, Bobby suggested everyone change into warm clothes since the sun had retreated to a mere glow in the western sky. He rubbed goose bumps on his arms from the cooler air, and as likely from the encroaching gloom.

They all prepared for another night of silent siege.

• • •

Pat searched for more rocks of the same caliber as the one he had used to hit the bear at Sunflower. Still, he thought of it as a bear, but something about its eyes hadn't been quite right for a bear's eyes. His subconscious mind kept sending him subliminal pictures—quick flashes of memory, but he couldn't quite focus on them. He only knew they were troubling.

He had seen something wrong…very wrong and couldn't put his finger on what it was-the same thing he had experienced when Bonnie had flipped out of her kayak. Glued to the edge of his memory, like something he could see out of the corner of his eye, but when he turned to catch it, it was gone.

He decided to go to bed early and hopefully shake the unsettling feeling. Stopping at the edge of Gretta's tent, he scanned the woods above camp. Once again he experienced the feeling of being watched.

## CHAPTER FOURTEEN

Phydeaux was not happy. She was stuck on the end of a long rope, her freedom gone. It had happened last night when she heard the deer wander up the path. She had never been tied up for chasing an animal before. It confused her.

She caught a faint smell on the wind from upriver. It was distant, but familiar. She laid her head at Bobby's feet and stared off into the night. Once again they had tied her up for reasons she couldn't comprehend, and something was coming.

Linda drew the first watch at ten. Everyone in camp except her, Bobby, and Jerry had already crawled into sleeping bags. Jim had complained of being too tired to fall asleep, but she heard his breathing finally slow into an even, rhythmic meter. She was glad. He'd been their strength, especially hers, and rest was long overdue.

They sat quietly as three sentinels and listened to the river's soft melody. By agreement any night noise drew close scrutiny, no matter how familiar. Once, around midnight, a mule deer wandered into camp. It bumped the perimeter line causing the cans and lures to rattle. The startled deer jumped into a nearby bush and became momentarily ensnared in the branches.

The noise awakened Phydeaux, and pandemonium spread quickly. Phydeaux's barking awakened everyone in camp except Jim and Pat. Linda figured both men too exhausted to be awakened by anything short of a nine on the Richter scale. She stayed put while Bobby and Jerry frantically played the beams of their flashlights across the entire upper end of camp, until they located the unfortunate deer.

The deer freed itself and ran away. Now Bobby and Jerry faced the unpleasant task of checking the perimeter line. It had worked twice, and they had to make sure it hadn't been broken by the deer's intrusion.

She didn't like the idea of being left to guard camp alone, but she liked the idea of leaving the firelight even less. She watched as they slowly walked the entire circumference of the fishing line boundary surrounding the camp. Their lights bounced along the ground as they checked for breaks and signs of wear.

They walked up to the natural funnel between the trees where Pat and Scott had dug the pongee pits. Linda felt a rising sense of panic when, for a few brief moments, they disappeared into the trees.

She wished they would hurry it up a little. The night had become so still she could hear their footfalls as they went through the darkness of the trees. More than once, she thought she heard a slight echo, a little heavier, and further away. *My imagination. Please, be my imagination!*

After what seemed like an hour, Bobby and Jerry's lights pointed toward her. She was relieved that the "echo" had abated. More than likely, it had been caused by the way the trees reflected sound waves back toward camp. She meant to mention it, but the probability that it had been her imagination caused her to forget the incident.

With Bobby and Jerry back safely, they once again arranged their chairs in a triangle facing away from each other and scanned the darkness as the moon glowed on the horizon. Time passed at a snail's pace, but one o'clock finally arrived: it was time for shift number two.

The previous night they had been unable to accurately measure the time for each shift. Linda had been lucky to find the watch in The Judge's ammo can, as keeping time had once again become a necessary evil.

Several times during his shift, Pat noticed a deathly quiet descend on the night. No insect noises, no night bird songs, nothing but the perpetual lullaby of the river. Once, he thought he heard something walking quietly out in the darkness. He had looked at the others, but they apparently hadn't heard it. It was in fact so quiet that he wasn't sure if it had been a footstep, or just leaves blown by a phantom wind.

The night passed without another event. As the last shift ended, Jacques and Jim awakened those who still slept. It was 7:00 am and all seemed well. They even talked about the possibility that they may have come far enough downriver to evade whatever stalked them through the last two days and nights. Optimism spread quickly.

They voted to have the Elk Bar breakfast, intended for the last day, this morning instead. More than likely they would be flown out from the Victor Ranch and wouldn't get the chance to have their best breakfast, unless they ate it here at Whitey Cox Camp.

"Pass the biscuits and gravy," Bobby said as he took two more sausage patties from the platter.

"Slow down, boy, you're gonna founder," Jacques chided, but with good nature.

"I don't want to end up in that-what did you call it—calorie deficit? Yeah,

## CHAPTER FOURTEEN 131

it would be terrible to get down to Tappan Falls and experience calorie deficit. Pass the scrambled eggs while you're at it," Bobby asked of Pat.

Pat accepted the challenge with Bobby to see who would be the least likely to experience calorie deficit, and filled his own plate with eggs before passing them to Bobby. "I experienced that cee dee once," he joked. "I ran out of juice above 'Boateater' on the Illinois River…it ate my boat with me in it. I don't intend for that to happen again. Pass the orange juice, por favor."

After breakfast, everyone went to the outhouse in shifts of three. Then the packing and cleaning began in earnest. Breakfast had lifted spirits even higher, and everyone felt more rested than they had for several days. After the cleanup was completed, Jerry reeled in his perimeter line.

Seeing Jerry reminded Pat of his duty to remove the pongee sticks. He called Scott over to help him with the chore.

"Bring the small shovel," Pat called.

Scott brought it, and they walked up to the three traps together. Pat removed the spikes from the first hole and Scott filled it in with the shovel. They repeated the action at the second stop. The last trap, had been caved in, and two of the sticks were gone. They stared at each other for a moment before Pat called out to Bobby and Jerry.

"Hey, come take a look at this," Pat shouted.

Jerry and Bobby rushed over.

Pat and the other three stared at a black stain in the bottom of the pit, with small pools every few feet leading back into the woods.

"Let's all go take a look," Jerry suggested. "This shit might be blood. If something stepped on a couple of these, it might just be pissed off too, so let's be careful."

"Durrr," Pat said.

They headed off into the woods. Pat didn't have far to go before he spotted the two pongee sticks in a small clearing above the traps. They were covered with slick, black ichor.

He stared, horrified at the dripping spikes. "What could have stepped on one of those, walked up here, and then pulled them out without making a fucking sound? Huh? Tell me, man, what?" He rubbed his temples. "This is really creepy; it was here watching us," he said as they turned and walked swiftly back to camp.

Pat sat on a rock, alone, holding his head in his hands. He imagined some ungodly creature sitting, smiling as it pulled the sharp, wooden spike out of its foot, grinning a devil's grin and staring at him with eyes *that glowed in the dark.*

The sinking feeling again hit him that just maybe the bear at Sunflower hadn't been a bear after all. Maybe, it had gotten hit between the eyes by a rock. Maybe it was severely upset about the whole thing, too. He shook the thought from his mind as Bobby walked up.

"Hey man, you didn't tell anybody about this did you?" Bobby asked quietly.

"Not yet, why?"

"I think it's better if we keep everybody's morale up right now. I talked it over with Scott and Jerry and they both agreed."

Pat looked across the camp at Scott who nodded affirmatively.

"Okay, I'll say it was the ubiquitous, fucking bear that stepped on the spike if anybody asks, how's that?" he said, not able to keep the hysteria out of his voice. From the contortion in Bobby's face, he too struggled to maintain sanity.

"Pat…we've got to keep it together, or everyone will think something's wrong," Bobby said.

"Something is wrong, God damn it!" Pat exclaimed. "Something is hunting us like fucking, game animals, man. Something I've hurt twice is out there right now, somewhere, probably thinking of a way to kick my ass. I'd say I have a right to think something is wrong."

"Hey, just try, all right? We're leaving soon. There's a chance that we'll be out of here by tonight," Bobby said and forced a smile.

Pat looked back at him for a moment, and then went about packing his dry bag as if the entire exchange had never taken place.

# 15

## MATTERS OF LIFE AND DEATH

Just after noon, they came to the upper section of the Tappan Series. The first part was class-two plus, but below it awaited the infamous Tappan Falls. The guidebook suggested that it be scouted from the right bank, just below a rock point at the end of the class-two entry rapid. All the boats pulled over.

"My God!" Bobby whispered, in awe of the hydraulic monster confronting his group.

The book warned readers that Tappan Falls had claimed more boats than any other rapid on the entire Middle Fork. Bobby could see why. This was a waterfall—*a raging waterfall* with a huge reversal about twenty feet off the right bank. The only route through was about five feet beyond it. His fears turned away from the unknown and centered back on this known. This rapid appeared to be capable of killing someone.

*In fact, wasn't this the one that killed Jacques' and Plato's friend?* He knew it was. Taking a deep breath he centered himself.

Fear like this he understood well. Back in guide school, he had felt it take control of his entire body. He and Jim had paddled his small twelve-foot Campways Pioneer down the Rogue River at flood stage.

Blossom Bar Rapid was the worst he had ever seen. All the giant boulders shown in the Quinn Guide were buried, creating huge holes. Several reversals looked big enough to engulf motor homes.

Bobby's mouth had gone so dry he couldn't spit or swallow. His knees had become shaky and weak. Somehow, he had fought the feeling and climbed into the boat. He'd survived. The funny thing about that day was that once the boat left shore, he calmed down, and focused on what needed to be done.

From that point on, he had looked at fear with the attitude of "just move through it and do it right." That was what he intended to do with his current fear as well as the rapid that induced it.

The deafening noise vibrated through his body. Tappan rated a solid class-four and demanded extra respect. He would definitely give it that.

He watched Jim and Linda paddle through first. Jim set up and executed his descent in a manner that made it look easy. An excellent paddler, with a great deal of class-five experience, his run wouldn't be the rule—it would be the exception.

Jacques had bested Tappan several times, and even though his boat was extremely heavy, he made the slot and disappeared over the falls to emerge again above the horizon line—safe.

Both Jerry and Plato went over the main falls and caught the edge of the giant reversal. The adrenalin level in both men soared so high they actually rowed over the standing wave.

Bobby witnessed Jerry's color drain a shade or two lighter from fifty yards away. He knew he didn't want to get caught in the hole in his small craft. He might not be as lucky as Jerry and Plato had been.

Abby went next, and Bobby's heart sank as she vanished over the rim of the falls. It seemed to take her longer to appear over the horizon line than it had Jacques. Maybe his feelings for her made it seem longer. At last, she appeared safe, in full control of the raft, and he began breathing again. Until his turn came.

Bobby had watched the entry of all the boats and decided to run the slot Jacques and Jim had chosen. What had looked fearfully difficult was actually easy. He set up perfectly, then: BOOM! He and Pat went over an eight-foot drop. The impact would have thrown him over Pat's head and out the front end of the boat if pushing the oars so hard hadn't braced him.

Three more sections of Tappan remained. The entire series extended over a mile long; most of it was class three whitewater. Only the falls rated class four. The rest of the rapid shouldn't pose any problems for anyone. He felt his confidence growing, mixing with a sense of greater optimism about their chances of actually getting through to the ranch.

Bobby watched each oarsman from the sweep position and was relieved not to have beginners in his party. That would have compounded problems. However, the thing that really caught his eye was not the skill of a particular oarsman, but

## CHAPTER FIFTEEN

of an oarswoman. Abby somehow made rowing a boat look graceful. She was lithe and tall, and her long legs flexed with each pull on the oars. He watched her every movement between glances at upcoming rocks, while Pat sat in silence in the front section of his raft. *We just might make it after all.*

Bobby realized they hadn't encountered any other boaters or campers on the river since the day before.

*Is it because someone warned them off of the river, or is it because they're busy decomposing?*

He couldn't shake the feeling that something terrible still followed them, and followed them on purpose, not by chance; he could feel it. *Why would it keep following us?* He wondered…*doesn't want any witnesses?* Or worse—maybe it held a grudge. That would imply intelligence as well as savagery. He didn't like the direction his thoughts were headed.

"Pat. You awake?" He asked. He gently shook him from behind.

"Huh?" Pat had been dozing, and startled to his intrusion.

"I said, are you awake?"

"I am now, what do you want?" Pat asked.

"I'm trying to figure something out; tell me again, everything you saw when Bonnie was taken at Sunflower."

"Taken? You make it sound like she got screwed or went for a ride. She got fucking killed! Something took her all right-something took her straight to the Twilight Zone."

Bobby felt his face flush and his temperature rise.

"I'm sorry," Pat said, as he took a bale-bucket of water from the river and poured it on his head to cool off. "Something big that looked like a shadow came out of the water in front of her boat. The moon hadn't quite reached the river, so I couldn't see anything but shadows anyway. It flipped her over backwards, then it kinda melted back into the water. After that, Bonnie came up yelling 'something was in the water that had gotten Sam.' Looked like she got hit in the stomach by something that lifted her out of the water. Then she went under; her life jacket popped up a few seconds later and floated away. That's it," Pat concluded.

"You never mentioned the lifejacket part before," Bobby said.

"I didn't think it was that important."

"Think! What else happened that might have been considered out of the ordinary."

Pat shrugged his shoulders and seemed about to answer 'nothing else,' when a look of revelation came over his face. "A bear, or something, came out of the woods just beyond the firelight at Sunflower later that night," he said.

"What made you think it was a bear if it was outside the firelight?" Bobby asked.

"I could see its eyes reflected by the fire."

"Why a bear though? Why not a deer?"

"The eyes were too far apart. It was too big to be small game. It must have been a bear…a big bear," Pat continued, as if trying to convince himself.

"The eyes were about eight feet off the ground. The only thing that could have been that big would be a bear standing on its hind legs." Pat scooped another bucket of water from the river and poured it on his head, then continued. "I nailed that bastard right between the eyes, too."

"What do you mean?"

"I mean I threw the hardest fastball I've ever thrown and hit the son-of-a-bitch dead center. Of course, I threw a rock instead of a ball."

"You're sure you hit it?" Bobby asked.

"Hell yeah, I'm sure. I saw it. The rock stayed right on course until it went into the shadows. Then I heard it impact with something that definitely wasn't a tree."

"Did it make any noise?"

"No. In fact that was what spooked me about it. Maybe I knocked it out," Pat said hopefully. He paused as if recalling then paled.

"I thought I saw eyes in the dark at Pistol Creek the other night," Bobby said. "Remember when Phydeaux woke everyone up by barking at something in the thicket? "

"Yeah, I remember."

"Well, I was having a nightmare. When I woke up, I swear I saw two eyes, glowing like coals, out in that thicket where she was facing. There's one thing that's strange about it though," Bobby continued. "The fire was down to just a few embers so it couldn't reflect, but the eyes were glowing bright yellow. Then, they just faded back into the night."

"Shit, man, I don't want to hear that," Pat said. "I want it to be a bear, cause the thought of some 'thing' out there pissed off at me doesn't make me feel better."

Bobby knew how he felt. He too wished it had been a bear. But he sensed that Pat knew it wasn't a bear. He didn't have any idea what it was, but it wasn't a bear. He tried to make Pat feel a little better. "Today is hopefully the last day

## CHAPTER FIFTEEN

we'll be on the river. God, I never thought I'd say that about any river, let alone the most beautiful river I've ever seen, but I'm ready to get out of here as fast as I can," Bobby said.

"Ditto. I want to go to the Victor Ranch today, and I ain't never coming back. I'll pay someone to bring my shit out. But after today, I'm through. In fact, I'm never going in a fucking river again—period."

Aparejo Point Rapid came up suddenly and they turned their attention to running it. Bobby saw a sharp bend to the left, and a downstream V formed about twenty-five feet off the left bank. Below the boulders that formed the V, was a rather large drop, followed by standing waves of two to three feet in height.

All the boats had already gone through except for Bobby's. Lining up for the V, he went over the drop perfectly…or so he thought. The boat rammed into an unseen object with a heavy impact. The boat stopped, and then spun a full circle. The wave had appeared clean; in fact he had seen Abby go over the exact spot only a moment before.

Looking down at his feet, Pat turned with an expression of true horror, his face a ghoulish white. Water splashed through the front section of the small raft, as Pat sank through a hole in the floor descending down to his waist. He screamed: "OH GOD! NO!"

Bobby watched in shock, as Pat clung to the front thwart for dear life. Bobby dropped the oars and grabbed his wrists. He pulled as hard as he could, but Pat continued being pulled under by an irresistible force. To make matters worse, the floor began ripping down the seams. The bulk of Pat's body hitting the current added exponential force to whatever had snagged him, and the floor ripped all the way back to the cargo area behind Bobby.

As Pat went under the thwart, Bobby's arm hit the frame, forcing him to release Pat's wrists or face a broken arm himself. But in that instant, he saw something move: a huge shadow directly under him. Then, Pat disappeared beneath the cargo.

*God, don't let this happen! Please!*

Liquid fear surged throughout his body triggering fight or flight mechanisms. He could feel his blood pressure rise instantly. His heart rate accelerated. Blood redirected to muscles. His heart climbed into his throat.

The shadow vanished. *And Pat gone. Dead.* Bobby looked down and saw rocks under the water's surface flying by under his feet. He wasn't worried about the raft sinking; the tubes would keep him afloat. Grabbing the oars, he began a hard pull against the current in hopes of slowing the raft.

*What happened?*

Something grabbed Pat through the bottom of his boat-something incredibly powerful. Whatever had done the grabbing would have been directly under his seat while doing so. Bobby lifted his feet up from the crossbar foot brace and positioned them higher on the frame.

The rocks flying under his feet gave him vertigo. Knowing what was probably happening to Pat brought the taste of bile to his throat.

At that moment, Pat broke the surface. Alive! He clung desperately to the trailing material that had, until recently, been the floor of Bobby's boat. Less than a foot of glued rubber connected it now. Bobby rowed harder to slow the raft's descent, making it possible for Pat to grab the rear tube.

He was coughing water and bleeding badly from wounds in his shoulder, but he was alive. Bobby shipped the oars and jumped to his rescue. He had pulled him up enough to balance his body on the rear, side tube, when the same unseen power arrested his progress and pulled Pat back into the water. Pat's eyes glazed with fear, madness, and insanity as he screamed:

"B-B-BOB-BEEEEEEEEEEEE!"

"Hold On!"

"OH GOD-IT HUUURTS!"

"I'm not letting go, Pat! Try to help me! Kick! Come on! FIGHT!"

Bobby locked into a grotesque tug-of-war with something just under the surface of the water. Pat kicked and squirmed as he had instructed and almost made it into the boat.

"That's it! Just another foot!" Bobby shouted as he grasped Pat's lifejacket and leaned back across the seat with all his weight. His foot braced against the frame for extra leverage.

Suddenly, an ungodly sound came from Pat. Pain shone from his eyes. Still, Bobby held on to him. Again he saw the dark shadow just beneath the surface. A large, black shape with one exception: the eyes from his dreams had taken shape in reality and burned like underwater flares from just under the water's skin. They projected the same evil, the same malice, and the same intent that the eyes in his dreams always had. It looked so intensely black and sleek that light seemed to vanish into it—as if a black hole had taken shape in the water.

Bobby wanted to let go of Pat, but he was frozen. Just like in his dreams he wanted to run, but couldn't. Something warm had splashed over his arms when Pat screamed. The coppery smell brought awareness.

Then Pat wasn't screaming anymore. He wasn't doing anything but looking at Bobby with dead eyes. He rolled over as if he were on a giant rotisserie,

## CHAPTER FIFTEEN

revealing the source of the blood, and his demise. *Evisceration.*

Bobby couldn't move. Even knowing that if he didn't let go of Pat soon, he would most likely end up like him, couldn't bring him to budge. Pat was obviously quite dead, but still Bobby argued internally:

*Let him go.*

*But I promised.*

*He's gone now it won't matter. Let him go.*

*But—*

An interruption made his decision easy.

Something shot out of the water—the shadow of an arm. At its end, something vaguely resembling a hand, reached out with its three, finger-like appendages. Dark, black claws that looked sharp—very sharp and hard, elongated, reached for him.

*A perfect killing tool,* Bobby noted: *Black gutting knives.* They looked like three-bladed dikes that could easily clip off a head.

Awakened from his trance just as the shadow claw sliced toward him, he released Pat at the last possible instant, and the claws clacked together inches in front of his face.

The shadow thing had been holding Pat with its other claw and had probably released the moving boat to attack. Bobby turned and watched Pat's body in the middle of a boiling, feeding frenzy. The predator shook his remains the way a pit bulldog would shake a cat, splashing blood and foam everywhere.

Bobby couldn't quite make out the dark shape at the center of the turbulence, but he could tell by the way it thrashed Pat's corpse around that it was big, and more powerful than any animal he had ever seen.

More than anything, he wanted to wake up in a cold sweat and find out this was only a bad dream, but that wasn't going to happen. His dream had somehow become real, and he thought he might be on the verge of joining Gretta in never-never land. He forgot about rafting. He forgot about everything except the fury upriver from his raft, slowly getting farther and farther away.

He heard someone shouting at him.

"Look out!"

Abby?

He turned just in time to see his raft hit a boulder. The impact knocked him out of his rowing seat, and into the front, section sans floor.

It was dark, and cold bubbles tickled his arms and legs. Then his shoulder impacted a rock, and sent a white-hot jet of pain down his right arm. He didn't know which way was up or down. From past experience, he tucked into a ball and broke the surface fifteen feet downstream. Taking a big gulp of air, he surveyed down river. Abby was about seventy-five yards away, pulling hard on the oars in order to slow her descent. That would make it easier for him to catch up to her.

*I'm in the water with it!* Bobby suddenly realized, and his fear radiated like a homing beacon. Somehow he knew that the shadow-thing was aware of his presence in the water. Someone watching from the cliffs above would have seen the feeding frenzy stop abruptly. Then, a large, dark shape headed downstream at frightening speed. He knew it.

Bobby swam for his life. In guide school, and from all his books on whitewater, he had been taught to swim a rapid in the classic position: lying on his back with feet downstream. All of that stuff was irrelevant now.

For a moment, he was back in Denton, Texas at the AAU state finals. On his stomach, face down in a freestyle position, he swam faster than he had in all the years since that day. In that race, he had won a bronze medal for his efforts; today he could win his life.

He saw Abby's raft approaching rapidly. The current had helped him. *Of course, it'll help it too*, he thought.

"Hurry Bobby! Faster!" Abby shouted.

"Don't look back-just swim!" Beth screamed.

He closed the last twenty feet and grabbed the perimeter rope as he went by; it jerked him back like a disobedient dog on a leash. Beth grabbed his lifejacket and tried to pull him into the raft, but she was small, and Bobby too exhausted to be any help.

Abby dropped the oars and offered a hand. They pulled his limp body up onto the side tube, but his legs still languished in the water. The look on Abby's face when she glanced upstream gave him the incentive to call on his last drop of energy. Her look said: "The shadow is closing fast, Bobby; better get in the boat. You might end up like Pat."

That was all it took. He kicked while Beth and Abby pulled together and fell onto the floor of the raft just as a large, dark shadow passed under them.

Bobby lay on the floor of the boat in total exhaustion. His hand rubbed the floor: a solid floor encased in the Lexitron material. Thank God for SOTAR. It gave him hope. If it had been a standard floor boat made of traditional neoprene, they would all surely end up like Pat. Now he hoped the material would hold up to its advertised claims.

A jolt hit the raft and he bounced two feet into the air.

"It's under the boat!" he yelled. "Get down and hold on!"

## CHAPTER FIFTEEN

The next bounce felt even harder. It continued trying to penetrate the floor. The SOTAR had been designed to take the punishment of sharp rocks and logs. It was the only reason the floor hadn't yielded like Bobby's older boat. But why didn't it come over the side tubes, he wondered.

*Is it playing with us?*

The water slowed and became much deeper, making it harder for the creature to push the boat over. Still, all three held onto the rowing frame with a vengeance. The buffeting continued for close to a minute. Earthquake tremors bounced the raft as if it were in a class-five caldera. Bobby feared it would somehow lock onto a tube and flip them. Then it would be all over.

# 16

## THE UNSEEN ENEMY

"It's underneath them!" Suzi shouted at Jerry.

He and Suzi were just downstream of Abby's boat. Jerry turned to see her raft acting as if it were being plagued by a poltergeist. He saw the dark shape under them, but it moved too fast to actually focus on.

*Why isn't Bobby in his raft? In fact, where the hell is his raft? Where's Pat?*

Jerry wanted to row downstream as fast as he could to get away from the thing under the boat—the thing that had most certainly been at Sunflower two nights ago.

Internal survival mechanisms screamed for him to get away, but Bobby was his best friend. He cursed under his breath and began slowing his descent.

"Suzi, I've got to hold until they catch up—maybe you should get into Jacques' boat."

"Bullshit!" Suzi replied, even though she too had apparently reached her limit on the terror meter. "You're on the oars, so how are you going to help anybody and keep control of the boat at the same time?" The look in her eyes told him that her mind was made up. He began pulling on the oars harder.

The oars bent as if they might break from the stress they were under; somehow they stayed just below that point as Jerry held against the power of the Middle Fork.

Every bump from below sent Bobby into the air. Abby's boat bucked in the grip of the earthquake assault from below, when Jerry and Suzi closed the last twenty yards. As they came within ten, the attack stopped as abruptly as it had begun. Bobby, Beth, and Abby huddled in the floor of the raft, afraid to get back up in case the onslaught resumed. Bobby and Beth had wedged into the front compartment holding onto the "chicken strap" surrounding the front cross-tube. Bobby lay across Beth from behind.

He had jammed Beth down and wedged his feet under the front tubes using his body to keep her from bouncing out of the raft. Abby lay spread-eagle on the floor in the middle compartment; she had used the rowing frame to hold herself in place.

"Is it g-g-gone?" she asked.

"I wouldn't count on it, but I sure as hell hope so," Bobby answered his voice shaking.

"Why won't it leave us alone?" Beth cried out from under him. "I want to go home now. I can't. I can't, I've got to go home."

Bobby watched Jerry spin his boat around to a position facing upstream as he and Suzi cleared the last few feet between the two rafts.

Just as they were about to make contact with the other boat, a loud splash sounded, accompanied by a large black shape that shot out of the water. A split second later a second appendage manifested on the opposite side of the boat, and two three-fingered claws came down on the opposing side-tubes of the SOTAR.

"God almighty," Bobby said in a low, awe-struck tone. He was so shocked, he could only watch. One of the claws had scarcely missed his nose, and he now studied it from close up. The claws resembled some insectile, digging tool, while the texture of the limb looked smooth and cold, like the jet-black hide of a snake or lizard. What he would remember most about the thing—next to the eyes—was the appearance of its skin texture. He'd seen a king cobra in a zoo, and it had this same slick, black hide.

*Now it's going to flip the boat.* He came out of his haze and reached for his clip-lock knife, but Suzi was the only one in a position to take action. She cocked the six-foot guide paddle, and swung it like a logger falling a tree, hitting the shape at the same spot corresponding with a human forearm. Black ichors splashed back onto her T-shirt as well as the side of both boats. She began to gag. Her action had achieved results, however, the dark limbs vanished below the surface, and large bubbles rose up under the boat.

A massive shadow under the surface shot toward the left bank where a willow grew out into the river. Bobby heard a splash as it broke the surface. He also heard something sucking air like the bellows of a giant accordion. All but

# CHAPTER SIXTEEN

Beth, stared at the fallen tree. It hid within the foliage, and it was watching them. Bobby knew.

He watched the willow, as they drifted slowly away from the bank, fighting the urge to panic and jump for the opposite shore. Soon the raft drifted around the bend, out of sight of the tree.

*The Dream Watcher got away when female food hurts Itself. After darkness. Itself will find them. Must eat female that hurts, and the Dream Watcher inside… then the small food that barks.*

"Jesus, I just want to be off of this river," Jerry said with a shudder. "Anywhere." Suzi didn't reply. Bobby, Beth, and Abby sat silent, too shocked to speak.

Beth remained quiet and held tenaciously to the strap; she lay on the floor of the raft prepared for the next assault.

"What in the hell was that?" Jerry asked, his hands shaking visibly on the oar handles.

"I don't know, but I think you're right about where it came from," Bobby replied as he scanned the river looking for an incoming shadow under the surface.

Suzi still choked on the noxious fumes emanating from the black ooze that had peppered her T-shirt. Under different circumstances, she usually would have jumped into the river to wash off the terrible smell, but instead took the bale-bucket, and filled it with water. She poured bucket after bucket on her head, letting the cascades of cold water wash most of the ooze away.

"That shit stinks like dried, buzzard puke. Are you okay? Suzi?" Jerry asked.

No reply.

"Thanks, Suzi," Bobby said as Abby pulled next to them.

"That goes double for me," Abby affirmed. "I—we owe you."

Suzi still hadn't spoken; she sat staring at the paddle lying next to her as if it were the instrument of her doom.

Jerry turned to Bobby and asked a grave one-word question to which he seemed to already know the answer.

"Pat?"

Bobby hung his head, as much from the shame of being powerless, as from the sadness he felt from the loss of his friend to such a horrible death.

He raised his head and realized Jerry still looked to him for more explanation. "Pat's gone. It pulled him right through the floor of the raft," Bobby said looking up first at Jerry, then Abby. "It went after him," he continued. Seeing they didn't grasp the meaning of his last statement, he explained: "He hurt it, and it went after HIM—on purpose! This godamned thing holds a grudge," he said without thinking.

"OH GOD!" Suzi cried as she finally came out of her self-imposed silence. "I'm dead! Oh Jesus!" Distraught at having been the one to injure the creature, she cried out, "I want out of here—can we please go faster now?"

"I'm sorry, Suzi," Bobby said as he tried to undo the damage. "I'm probably wrong about it. It's just that it seemed to pick him out. Pat mentioned that he saw some eyes in the woods at Sunflower, and he slammed them with a rock." He realized he wasn't undoing the damage; Suzi cried out again, then she whimpered.

As they rowed frantically downstream, Jerry interrupted with a revelation of his own. "Eyes in the woods?" he said. "I saw them too! It must have been there the entire time we were in the hot springs." Jerry was filled with awareness that he had come very close to death.

The Judge had been killed just after dropping him off on shore, which meant that it had most likely lurked under the surface when he'd ferried across. His survival had been a matter of luck. He felt his arms and legs weaken at the sudden understanding.

"I stood there on the bank and heard something behind me," Jerry continued. "Saw the eyes. They were there before I went across, but gone when I returned."

"I saw them too," Bobby said, "At Pistol Creek. I woke up when Phydeaux barked at that bear. I don't think it was a bear anymore, Toto. I think Phydeaux saved us from ending up like that other group above Marble Creek."

"Why didn't it attack anyway?" Abby wondered aloud. "It didn't mind attacking the Judge, Bonnie, or Pat while others were around. Hell, it just killed Pat in broad daylight."

Beth spoke for the first time since the most recent assault: "Maybe it's afraid of Phydeaux," she said, sounding more confident.

"It could rip Phydeaux apart. I felt it tear Pat out of my hands. He was

## CHAPTER SIXTEEN

strong as a gorilla, but between the two of us we hardly offered it any resistance. Unfortunately, I don't think it's afraid of Phydeaux," Bobby concluded. But he, too, wondered why it hadn't attacked them.

All eyes nervously scanned the banks to see if it was moving along beside them on land. They also kept watching for the sudden, aquatic approach of a large shadow from upstream. Nothing moved, and no shadow sped beneath the surface. They floated in silence.

• • •

Sheep Creek Camp was located less than a mile below them. The book told them to watch for a cable crossing the river. The camp lay on the left bank directly below it. They were tired, scared, and definitely ready to get off the river.

The rest of the party had gotten word of Pat's demise by shouting from raft to raft. As a result, a life and death debate began on the beach at Sheep Creek Camp.

"I say we leave the boats here and head to the ranch right now," Jim said. His motion was seconded by Suzi, Beth, Linda, and Scott. "We can be there in less than an hour, even if the terrain is bad. We've still got over two hours before the sun will set."

"I agree. I think we should leave the fucking boats and just get the hell out now while we still can—not by river either," Scott added as he looked at the green waters flowing past. "I'm not spending another night on this river, wondering if that thing is going to get tired of staying in the shadows."

"Yeah, another night, and I'm going to either be weaving baskets or pushing daisies," Suzi said. "I think I made its shit list back there, and I vote to go now before it gets even. And I don't give a damn about my camping gear—it can stay and rot for all I care."

"Somehow, I wonder if we shouldn't set up camp first, just in case," Jerry said. "Our systems have been working; let's stay with them. What if the people at the ranch have already found out about this thing and left the area. It wouldn't hurt to cover our bases." Jerry didn't know why he felt so strongly. Logically, they should have just floated to the ranch and camped there, but he trusted his instincts, and they told him to set up camp at Sheep Creek.

"I agree," Bobby added. "I can't explain it, but I'm getting the feeling that covering our asses seems like the smart thing to do."

"No way," Linda said.

"You guys are crazy if you think I'm waiting, when the ranch is just two miles from here," Jim stated.

"Why don't those who want to go, go, and those who want to stay, stay," Jacques suggested. "I, for one, agree with Jerry. We would be getting to the ranch at dusk, and who knows what to expect once we're there?"

"If we go there and don't come back, you'll never know if we made it or not," Linda pointed out.

"We should go together," Scott said. "If only those of us go who want to go, that leaves us split up into two smaller, more vulnerable groups. Whatever we do, we should do it in force."

Abby's intuition refused to be ignored. It told her to stay put. Something was wrong at the ranch, just like it had been wrong inside the cabin. However, she couldn't use feelings to argue someone else out of doing what logically sounded right to them. She had ignored her instincts before and had ended up wrong.

At the same time the actual argument was taking place at Sheep Creek, an internal argument was taking place between the left-brain and the right brain of Abigail Jones. The argument at Sheep Creek—in reality a debate between those who trusted reason versus those who trusted intuition—heated up, and for once Abby overrode the familiar, comfort zone of logic, in favor of her newly acquired, primitive, survival system. She would stay.

Bobby called for a vote. Beth, Linda, Suzi, Scott, and Jim voted to go to the ranch immediately. Beth stared at Abby.

*She's wondering why I haven't raised my hand.*

"I'm staying," Abby said softly, turning her eyes to Beth, who appeared to be ready to leave even if it meant hanging on a rope under a logging balloon.

"No, Abby, we've got to get out of here, right NOW! Please come with us. I have to go, and I need for you to come, too. Please Abby," Beth pleaded. Abby saw tears well up in her friend's eyes.

"I can't come with you. You wouldn't understand if I told you why, but I can't," Abby said as she took Beth's hand. They were like sisters, and it was a hard moment for her. She considered turning on her persuasive courtroom powers to try to convince Beth to stay but knew it wouldn't be fair. Beth's fate was different than her own. Convincing her to change course could alter her destiny, one way or the other.

## CHAPTER SIXTEEN

Abby hugged Beth tightly. Tears filled her eyes. They cried in each other's arms; Abby didn't allow the embrace to end until the weeping subsided.

The final outcome of the debate: twenty-five minutes of sunlight had slipped away, and no one had argued convincingly enough to change anyone else's mind.

The group going to the ranch would get help. As soon as it was light, they would return with the Forest Service, sheriff's deputies, or whoever in authority arrived first. The group staying behind would set up camp and remain on guard duty all night, unless someone came for them sooner. If any of the departing group shared the others' premonition, they chose to ignore it.

• • •

Jim took his spear and led the others toward the Victor Ranch. The goodbyes had been kept relatively short due to the ever-increasing angle of the sun. Sheep Creek was less than two miles from the ranch; so they headed north at a good, steady pace, hoping to leave the river, and all but bad memories behind them.

The hike took about thirty minutes since the trail to the ranch was well worn and easy to follow. On the last rise, Jim had been able to see the ranch house. They reached it just as the sun lowered below what he guessed to be Gray's Peak. He had overestimated how much time they had until sundown because of the huge mountain towering into the western sky. It had effectively caused sundown half an hour earlier than it would have at other locations along the river, and he was glad they'd arrived before dark.

Approaching the yard, he noticed nothing out of the ordinary. A cat even walked up to Beth and purred against her leg, as if it were starved for affection, before it turned and ran toward the barn.

Jim walked up on the porch and knocked on the door. There was no answer, so he knocked harder.

BAM—BAM—BAM

The front door creaked inward.

"Anybody here? We need help!" he shouted at the silent ranch house. He cautiously pushed the door open and walked into the concession area. Holding his spear out in front of him, he let his gaze sweep over the room. Several chairs, a table, and a counter where ice, cold drinks, cigarettes, and beer were sold to the river travelers during summer looked to be the only furnishings.

"Spread out and let's find the radio," Jim ordered.

"To hell with spreading out," Linda shot back.

"Yeah, I don't think so," Suzi agreed.

"Where are the people who run this place? Why aren't they here?" Beth asked.

"I don't like this," Scott said.

"Look, even if the people have already left, what we need is the radio. Now, if you don't want to spread out, we'll just have to look together," Jim said.

They began searching the first room en masse. After looking for five minutes they gave up and proceeded to the next room. Finally, their hunt led them to the dining room and kitchen. To the left of the doorway a closet without a door contained several shelves holding adhesive, tools, and a stack of heavy-duty PVC pipe. Jim wondered if someone had been in the middle of a project when they were rudely interrupted. He walked in first.

The dining room was the largest room in the place, capable of seating over seventy people. From the description in his guidebook, Jim knew it had been made to accommodate companies who used to have "getaway" business meetings prior to the river receiving its wild and scenic designation back in the late nineteen-sixties.

The rest followed him in single file into the large open-beamed room. The place was practically destroyed: tables overturned, chairs shattered and strewn about; broken glass littered the floor.

*The radio.*

They fanned out across the room with spears and knives at the ready. Jim walked five steps ahead of the rest. As they came to the other end of the room, their hopes were raised by his discovery of the radio behind a small counter. Slowly and warily he rounded the corner and looked behind it. The others stood where they were. Frozen. Broken glass lay all around.

A spiral cord from the radio hung down from the unit and disappeared into a partially closed cabinet.

"I wonder if anyone managed to get out a call for help," Scott said. Jim figured he didn't realize his comment sounded as if he'd assumed the people at the ranch were dead.

"No way to tell," Jim answered as he carefully stepped through the broken glass. He opened the cabinet, half expecting some ungodly tentacle to grab his wrist and pull him under the counter. He tugged gently on the cord, and the microphone came out. It had been used after all. The remainder of a hand still clutched it firmly. The skin and muscle on top had been sliced, but the bone had been broken jaggedly. Gristle and skin underneath had been torn like the

## CHAPTER SIXTEEN

ragged edge of a tree felled by a hasty logging crew.

The sight jolted him, and he sat on broken glass. He turned his head. For a moment he thought he might vomit, but even that was a luxury he didn't have time for. Luckily, he was the only one who saw it. He took a paper towel from above the counter and removed the grisly remains from the microphone, then dumped it into a wastebasket under the counter.

Locating an on/off switch, he discovered the unit was already on but not functioning. He checked the power cord and realized the radio was unplugged. Within seconds he found a nearby wall socket and plugged the male end into the receptacle. Static immediately filled the room, causing a small cheer of relief from everyone.

*At least something is going right,* Jim thought.

Trying to figure out how to make the transmitter work, he soon learned that the microphone had a send button on the side. He pushed it and called out:

"MAYDAY! MAYDAY!"

No reply.

Having made several more attempts without getting a response, he was about to change channels on the C.B., when all the lights went out. A distant hum slowly died to total quiet. The electricity in the ranch house had been shut off, and the radio's light faded to darkness.

The twilight from outside was the only light in the entire structure, and it dawned on Jim, that in their hurry to leave, they had forgotten to bring flashlights. "Somebody cut the generator off," he said as he tried to focus his eyes in the gloom of the dining hall.

"IT'S HERE—OH GOD!" Beth cried out.

Jim looked up at the window to the kitchen just above his head, and his heart climbed into his throat. *She's right.*

# 17

### SOMETHING COMING

Sheep Creek Camp surrounded them with small Jack Pines and moderately tall aspens. The camp felt more closed in than any other place they had been, making Jerry second-guess if they were wrong in not joining the others. The camp space, about thirty-five feet across one way and thirty feet across the other, made him claustrophobic.

He set the perimeter line in close since the trees encroached on the camp so tightly. The idea of not getting a signal until the enemy was right on top of them concerned him, so he set up a second line deeper in the woods—to give a little more warning if the visitor approached. The fire blazed as Bobby helped him cook dinner in the Dutch oven.

A sudden storm blew over the ridge and looked like it would hit any minute.

"Just what we need," Bobby said. "A God-damned storm." He turned to Abby. "With thunder and wind we won't be able to hear anything coming."

Bobby, Abby, Jerry, Jacques, and Plato made a circle and faced outward in different directions, hoping they could see movement from any angle of approach. The flames blew in the wind making a sound like a sheet on a clothesline flapping in a strong breeze.

"I hope they got through to the sheriff," Abby said, breaking the silence.

"I guess we won't know anything until tomorrow morning," Bobby replied feeling he owed her a response.

"Dinner's done," Jerry called from behind them. "We'll have plenty if anybody feels like eating."

"What did you prepare for us, Mr. Peterson?" Plato asked.

"Mexican food casserole-trust me, it's edible."

"Well, we might as well try it; we don't have anything else to do but wait," Jacques said.

Jerry filled his plate and went through the motions of eating. Nobody else seemed to have an appetite either. Privately he wondered if the others were all experiencing doubts that maybe they should have gone to the ranch after all.

The sky continued to get darker, and the storm's arrival appeared imminent. Bobby tarped off the camp area, but Jerry knew a bad storm could render his efforts useless. The wind picked up, adding considerably to his uneasiness.

Lightning struck, illuminating the entire canyon and created a bizarre flash across their camp. This time only ten seconds elapsed before he heard the explosion of thunder. A light rain began blowing under the tarp, and they were forced to move their lawn chairs closer to the edge of the clearing.

Just as they finished dinner, the storm hit with all its power. Lightning struck every few seconds and wind gusted at what felt like gale force. The noise was constant, but even through the cacophony, Phydeaux must have heard something coming. Jerry saw her ears stand up as she stiffened and faced the northern path. Whining and pulling to the end of her rope, she began barking wildly as she looked into the nightmarish landscape caused by the intermittent lightning bolts.

Everyone grabbed their weapons and listened. They tried to hear whatever the dog's ears had detected, but the only audible noises were the wind and rain, punctuated by thunder rolls and lightning cracks every few seconds.

"It's coming! This is it!" Abby said as she brandished her knife. She said it with such authority they all believed her. In fact Jerry knew that the bad feeling of Sheep Creek combined with the storm's sudden rage created a perfect setting for an attack.

"It's coming! I can hear it!" he shouted. He grasped his spear even tighter and faced the direction of the noise.

It was completely dark now that the thick black clouds filled the evening sky. Lightning flashed again. The scene lit up, and through the trees Jerry saw movement.

• • •

"Beth, be quiet!" Scott whispered.

"What now? Any ideas? Anybody?" Linda asked.

## CHAPTER SEVENTEEN

"Wait! Everyone be quiet," Jim said as he held up his hand. "Something's in here. I just heard glass get crushed."

"OOOOH NOOO! OOOOOOH GOD!" Beth moaned.

Scott put his hand over her mouth.

"Sssssshh," he whispered in her ear.

They heard another glass break in the dishwashing area behind the serving window that joined the two rooms. The sound came from directly above the radio, so Jim quietly backed out and away from the counter. He smelled something he had never before encountered. The scent wafted through the serving window, and, in him, the reek generated pure, unadulterated fear.

Realizing the only way out was the way they had come in, he motioned for them to back slowly away. The only sound he registered was the machine-gun heartbeats inside his ears. Eventually, they all reached the entry door of the dining area.

Jim had a feeling that something dreadful leered at them from within the dark cover of the serving window. He was about to shut the hallway door when the double doors to the kitchen swung open.

Only darkness.

He heard Linda gasp and suddenly he saw that two lights had turned on near the top of the kitchen door. Except he knew they weren't lights. They were eyes, glowing with the same evil glee of a twisted, front-porch jack-o-lantern. The eyes moved down. Then he saw the darker shadow in the pitch-black kitchen. It bent to get under the door.

*It's coming!* To see it, he wanted to wait until it walked in front of the dining-hall windows before he made his getaway, but he remembered curiosity killed the cat.

He stood directly in the doorway, when out of the corner of his eye he noticed the lengths of PVC pipe stacked in the corner beside the closet in the hall. A plan formulated in his mind. He moved slowly.

The teratoid creature still hid in the shadows-the burning eyes the only evidence of its presence. Its amorphous outline seemed to be even darker than the blackness, which surrounded it. The floating eyes were clearly aware of his presence. The shadow stopped for a moment at the kitchen's double doors then moved forward, slowly, the way a cat advances on unsuspecting birds: rigid, and poised to spring. The sweat of fear dripped in his eyes, and Jim felt frozen by the amber glow of the two, hellish portholes. His limbs felt sluggish, and unresponsive to his wishes.

In another few seconds, if he didn't make them obey, he would most probably die a horrible and painful death. *Then Linda.* He wouldn't let it kill her without a fight. His will reasserted itself.

He grasped the door handle intending to slam it shut, but the door was equipped with an air pressure release which braked its closing for several very long seconds. As he pulled on the door with all his strength, the beast made its move, sprinting across the hardwood floor. He saw the huge shape closing across the dining hall just as he managed to seat the stubborn door into its frame.

He heard the creature's approach through the closed door, clacking its claws as it scuttled across the room and slid on the waxed hardwood. Panting and grunting, he grabbed a piece of the pipe, fumbled, then slid it through the loop of the door handle. It came to rest on a shelf that bordered the door, effectively acting as a lock-bar. He thanked God for the outside loop on the door: ornamental but heavy duty.

He had just managed to slide a second pipe into place, when an incredible pull was exerted on the door. The pipes bent but didn't break. At the current level of stress being applied, the PVC wouldn't last long, however, and Jim added two more five-foot lengths. That was all the door handle would hold. He heard one of the women sob and turned around in the narrow hallway to see everyone staring in terror, knowing that the murderous enemy stood only a few feet away doing its best to remove the only protective barrier between them.

"That won't hold long, we've got to get out of here quick and quiet," Jim said taking the lead position. They silently retreated back the way they had come. The raging noise of the unseen aggressor could be heard as if they still stood just beyond its reach in the hallway. There wasn't any sound like a growl, or a roar, only the sound issuing from its assault on the door.

They reached the entry room where Jim noticed a familiar golden helmet sitting on the bar. *That wasn't there when we came in.* It faced away from them as they continued their withdrawal. He knew that had it been placed facing towards them, Gary would be staring at them with empty eye sockets where fish had feasted. His face would still be locked into that last horrified expression. Jim swallowed hard and silently pushed open the door.

They could hear the creature still attempting to rip the oak door in. As soon as they were all outside, they began backing away from the ranch house. They were almost out of the front yard, when the attack on the door suddenly stopped. The silence grew more oppressive than the racket had been. They turned as one and ran for their lives. When they reached the first rise,

## CHAPTER SEVENTEEN

some seventy-five yards from the house, they heard breaking glass. It was now outside, too.

The sky still glowed in the West, but clouds had appeared over the eastern rim, and the wind rose rapidly. Lightning flashed somewhere in the canyon, washing the mountain across the river with a stroboscopic effect. It took ten seconds before they heard the rumble of thunder.

They ran as fast as pure adrenalin would carry them, but the effects from fatigue began to take their toll. Jim had to stop and wait for all but Linda. She was a long-distance runner and slightly faster than him.

When the rest caught up to them, they took off again trying to maintain a steady pace that would keep them together. After they had covered half the distance to Sheep Creek, they stopped for a momentary breather. Jim searched the gloom behind them for evidence of pursuit but detected no sign of movement.

Lightning flashed closer, announcing the advent of a violent thunderstorm and once again they ran. He waited until the others had gotten slightly ahead and was about to turn his back on the path when he saw movement 100 feet off the trail and eighty yards behind.

"RUN! RUN LIKE HELL! IT'S GOING TO CUT US OFF!" he shouted as he sprinted up the trail behind them.

Fear spread like a contagious disease. Every time a fever point had been reached, some unseen control would turn the thermometer up another degree. Beth and Suzi ran side-by-side, twenty feet behind Linda when Jim passed them, followed by Scott.

Lightning struck several times, illuminating the canyon, but he couldn't see it by looking back over his shoulder. He did, however, see Beth and Scott. They ran side by side, trying to stay out of last place.

His side ached as if someone twisted a hot spear into it, but he managed to run a little faster.

Another flash, and he could see their pursuer by the river. *Closer.* It ran impossibly fast as it traversed the rocky terrain next to the bank. *It's faster on the rocks than we are on the trail.* Onward he ran as night enshrouded them.

Finally, Jim could see the trees in the distance. They were less than 400 yards from camp. *Four hundred yards…a par four on a golf course*, he thought as lightning seared the sky, adding a surreal quality to the canyon. He could see in its sudden light, that something very large and fast ran even with him. But it moved only in jerky frames, and he could only spot it whenever the lightning struck the mountaintops.

The wind gusted directly into them slowing their progress. A cold rain mixed with hail started, and it stung like tiny darts sinking into his flesh as they closed the remaining 200 yards. Jim saw a pinpoint of light through the woods ahead. He knew this was the campfire where his friends sat, waiting for rescue…*that won't be coming.*

The path ahead shone like luminous, light-colored sand scratching its way across the dark, dry flora. It appeared to glow and was easy to follow, as long as their eyes weren't recovering from the flashbulb assault of the lightning.

At 150 yards, Jim heard Phydeaux barking. He wanted to shout, but he needed all of his breath.

Only 100 yards from camp, he slowed down. Muscles rebelled. The others had spread out over sixty yards. Linda had fallen back even with him, while Suzi stumbled thirty yards behind. Scott and Beth were both still fighting for second to last place yet farther behind Suzi.

The ground seemed to go under Jim in slow motion. The longest part of his entire run was the last. He and Linda both gasped for air as they put on the final push.

At that moment, lightning flashed, and they saw the shadow jump into the path ahead of them.

"HOLY SHIT!" Jim yelled with his last breath.

"AAAAAAAAGGGGHHHH!" Linda screamed.

A flashlight beam came on blinding them momentarily.

"It's okay. What's going on?" Jerry's voice called to them anxiously.

For a second, Jim's relief was so total, he forgot about what was wrong. Gasping in as much air as he could hold, he forced himself to speak: "It's here," was all he could say as he passed Jerry making for the welcome light of the fire.

"Watch out! One of the perimeter lines is right there. The other one is about ten feet into the shadows outside of camp." Jerry waited as the others staggered in, one by one.

He led them over the warning line and back to the fire. They were too out of breath to speak, but Jim communicated the fact that it had been chasing them.

"Close," Scott said, sucking wind. "Saw it."

"Tried to cut us off—back there," Jim added as he gasped air.

Phydeaux, who had temporarily stopped barking, began to growl. She

## CHAPTER SEVENTEEN

turned in several directions, not certain where the noise came from. She bared her teeth like an angry wolf, and her growl changed into a threatening, guttural warning. She pulled on her rope towards a spot in the darkness.

Lightning flashed, and it didn't give his eyes enough time to focus, but Jim thought he saw movement thirty feet out into the woods, then only darkness.

The outside perimeter line began its warning that an intruder had breached the camp.

"IT'S HERE!" Jacques yelled.

"EVERYBODY GET IN CLOSE!" Bobby screamed over the wind.

Phydeaux snarled and growled at the unseen intruder. Her hackles raised, and it gave her the appearance of a miniature Rhodesian Ridgeback. She pulled to the end of her tether, three feet from the edge of the clearing, stood on her back legs, and literally dragged the heavy dry box she was attached to across the campsite.

Jacques tugged on her rope, but she suddenly changed her direction of focus by ninety degrees to the right. It had moved. She looked confused for a moment, and then it was behind her. The last move put it upwind from her, and she sniffed its unique scent.

She rushed at the other side of the clearing while Jacques took the opportunity to shorten her rope. His hands burned from the friction when her weight hit his applied resistance; he managed to pull her back only six feet.

Lightning pulsed in the night sky, but still Bobby and the others could see no sign of the intruder. He wondered if it were toying with them. Phydeaux seemed to be the only one who was able to see, or hear it. She continued running from one side of the camp to the other in a circular motion forcing everybody to jump over her rope as Jacques tried to reel her in.

Voices shot from every direction.

"Over there!"

"No, It's over here!"

"It's circling!"

"Nothing can be that fast!"

"It's looking for an opening!"

Bobby felt almost dizzy with the confusion. Then the gale began to lose strength rapidly. In fact, it was uncanny how quickly it passed. Within five minutes, it faded from a raging storm to distant flashes, a gentle breeze, and a light shower. Five more minutes passed, and the night sank into a deathly quiet. Even Phydeaux had become silent.

The level of exhaustion varied from person to person, but no one relaxed. Nothing moved, but he felt it. *It's still out there.* The only sound was the river meandering by, and the pounding of his heartbeat in his ears. Phydeaux peered into the woods and growled deep in her throat.

The inside perimeter line began its warning.

"It's inside!" Bobby shouted.

"SHIT! Where?" Jerry asked as he shined his flashlight on the line. It clearly moved, but for no apparent reason. Bobby shined his light one direction, while Jerry shined his the other. They followed the line all the way around the clearing, 360 degrees; still no evidence why it was moving, yet the cans never stopped rattling during the search.

Phydeaux went crazy again. She couldn't see it, but the smell of fear on The People reached such a pitch, that she wanted to tear the intruder to pieces. And besides, its heavy, putrid stench irritated her nose.

She came back close to Jacques, not from fear, but because she would protect her master with her own life if need be.

# 18

## SCREAMS

Gretta sat in a lawn chair facing the river, never batting an eye during the entire onslaught. She was soaking wet and all but forgotten to the others. No one paid any attention to her, since they were all too busy worrying about their own survival.

If anyone had been paying attention to her, they would have noticed a slight change in her expression. From blank, it became mildly concerned, like a mother finding her child making a mess on the floor.

From concern, her expression changed to worry, as if waiting for a daughter out on a date well past her curfew.

From worry, it changed to fear. Fear, like the fear one might experience being followed by sinister footsteps down a dark street, in a bad part of town.

From fear, her countenance changed to terrified, like the terror in knowing someone is chasing you, intent on murder.

From terrified, her expression changed to truly horrified, like when one looks into the face of something as lethal as what she now saw.

No one else saw. Nobody noticed that her mouth opened as if she were trying to speak…or scream. Her fear, bottled up like vintage champagne had been shaken, and the cork was about to pop. Again, she stared directly into the eyes of the basilisk. Medusa herself couldn't have frozen Gretta more solidly. She alone could see it. She understood why it had come.

A shadow raced through the corner of the camp where Gretta sat. It moved so fast, no one saw it. It grabbed her and carried her into the darkness so fast, that nobody even realized she was gone until they heard her scream.

The scream wasn't one of pain, but of release, like a lifetime of fear focused into one ten-second burst.

Bobby was the first to realize what had happened.

"It got Gretta! *Oh God No!* "GRETTA!" he wailed.

Then they all called out, but she did not answer.

Somewhere in the darkness, another scream rang out. This scream sounded different than the last one—this scream was one of agonizing pain. Gretta continued to whimper from somewhere just beyond the reach of their flashlights. Every minute or so, terrible cries shattered the silence.

Bobby continued to scan the darkness with his flashlight, but he saw nothing. All quiet for a while and then another bone-break scream. After each outcry, Bobby heard her sobbing from somewhere in the nearby woods but was unable to locate her. Another yelp, then silence. It slowly tortured her in order to frighten them, and it worked—at least on him.

Crying out in empathy, Phydeaux raged to get free of her rope every time Gretta screamed. The dog hated the reek of this enemy. Vile and rancid, and while dogs have a high, stink tolerance this one sickened even her. It also angered her more than anything she had ever smelled. The stink prowled close by, and if she could free herself from the unwanted rope, she would attack it.

Bobby picked up an odor of something he couldn't identify, something foul, and for a moment he thought he had smelled it before. It was reminiscent of childhood fears, and monsters in the closet, but most of all it brought back memories of his worst nightmares.

In between the times she screamed, the group endured dreadful silences. During one of these silences, Gretta stumbled into the edge of the firelight holding her abdomen and whimpering. She looked directly at Beth and tried to raise one of her hands for help. Then, as if she were a puppet on a string, she flew backwards into the shadows and screamed again.

"We've got to do something," Beth cried.

"What can we do?" Abby shouted.

## CHAPTER EIGHTEEN

"Let's all go together and rescue her," Beth pleaded. "She's alive, and we've got to help her—we can't leave her out there."

"It wants us to do that," Bobby replied, "If we go out there, we're playing into its court."

"In case you hadn't noticed, I'd say we are already in its court by the way it just came in and took her," Plato pointed out.

Gretta screamed again. The timbre of this scream penetrated all their souls. It was the pain of someone who has mortal injuries, but is not allowed to die. This scream made even Beth realize the hopelessness of rescuing her. Gretta was beyond help now. A scream from that deep was a cry from someone who already stood at the entrance to the tunnel; The Reaper's scythe already swung its deadly stroke; loved ones approached to lead the way to the other side.

Gretta still moaned and groaned between the terrible cries. Her screams sounded as if her deepest, most sensitive nerves were being seared by white-hot metal.

Their helpless witness to her torture continued for close to an hour, when one final scream rang through the night. The cry built in both volume and pitch, until abruptly cut off. It had apparently tired of torturing Gretta and finally killed her. The sudden cessation of her scream made her death a foregone conclusion. Who would be next?

Phydeaux watched the shadows, while everyone else watched Phydeaux. She sniffed the air, and occasionally her ears stood up-straining to hear the slightest noise.

No one spoke after Gretta's last scream. There were quiet sobs, not only for her, but also for all their friends that had been lost in the last three days. Her death made everything real. It had been close, and heard by them all.

Bobby experienced more than fear and guilt. He had been forced, by fear, to abandon a friend, one he had promised to watch out for, and twice he had failed…the responsibility weighed on his soul.

Lately death followed him around like a skeletal dog. He even cursed the day he'd gone on his first whitewater trip. He'd seen death in the marines, but he expected it in warfare. *Not here.* Whatever stalked them from the shadows killed with far more efficiency than the best assassin.

He felt totally empty, much the same way he had on the Klamath. Pat and Gretta had been his friends. He hadn't known Sam and Bonnie Baker very well, but he felt their loss as if they were his friends too. He almost felt like running into the forest with his knife drawn, blasting a primal scream, hoping to confront whatever monster awaited. Offer himself as its sacrifice.

He wanted to, but couldn't. *Coward. Give it up, Bobby.* He held himself and gritted his teeth. Fear gave way to pain. And pain faded into anger, which burned red hot. When anyone hurt his family or friends, they became the object of an incredible drive for revenge. Something had just killed five of his friends. "I'll get you," he whispered behind clenched teeth. "Whatever you are, you'll pay, mother-fucker…I swear you'll pay." Tears welled in his eyes.

They all returned to the fire facing outward. A cool night breeze rustled the tarp; Jerry and Suzi stood closest to it and jumped. Second by second, minute-by-minute, time etched its way into an uneasy future. After a while, Jacques spoke:

"I take it something went wrong at the ranch."

"You could say that," Jim replied. He told the story of their terrifying experience at the Victor Ranch as the others listened.

As Abby heard their story, she realized their ordeal wasn't nearly over. Forty miles remained to the take-out point on the main Salmon River-forty miles, most of which wound through the Impassible Canyon. The most treacherous rapids on the entire river lay in that section.

With everyone on the brink of total exhaustion, it wouldn't be easy. The Impassible Canyon got its name for a reason. She knew once you entered, you had no chance of climbing or hiking out. The cliffs angled steep enough to require technical climbing gear, and the mountains reached 7,000 feet into the Idaho sky. Climbing out, even with technical gear, would be an astounding feat.

She also realized the improbability of making it in one day to the take-out by floating the river. They'd scheduled three more days, and two more nights with the Forest Service. After the last three days, she figured everyone would push to get out sooner. No one wanted another night on the river. However, with forty miles left at this low of a water level, she figured it would take them at least two days. Two days meant one more night. *Of course, that's only if we live through this one first,* she thought and shuddered.

"Bobby?" Abby called.

"Yes."

"Are you all right?" she asked, having seen him remain static for over half an hour. At first she knew that he had been in some deep, inner turmoil, but then he had mellowed into a peace she hadn't wished to disturb.

Bobby seemed to consider her question for a moment before answering.

"No. Like you said, I may never be all right again," He looked at her and took a last, deep breath as he continued: "But don't worry about me. I'm just scared, and I hate the feeling."

They watched the fire in silence. The return of normal night noises, and the crackle of the fire offered comforting sounds. He felt more at ease in Abby's presence. The sound of her breathing helped him maintain his own. Out from the darkness came a bird song without discernable melody. Five notes walked through a scale. It repeated the same notes in different orders. A series of single notes followed. Each rose to a crescendo, and then faded away. Crickets and frogs added their instruments from up and down the river. Bobby waited. After a time, Suzi spoke:

"What are we going to do? We can't just wait for that—whatever the hell that was—to come back."

"What are our chances of getting in the boats and leaving right now?" Beth asked. Her voice shook.

"Very slim to none," Bobby replied. "There are quite a few major rapids between here and the take-out, one of which is just below where we are now called Haystack. It's quite capable of wrapping, or flipping one of our boats, and it's one of the easier ones. The book says that Redside and Weber Rapids have killed people during daylight hours. Imagine running them by moonlight."

"Yeah, but those people were killed at high water. This is low water. Those rapids might not even be there at this level," Jim suggested.

The scent of pine drifted on a gentle breeze. Then the smell of wood smoke settled back into Bobby's face. His eyes watered, but he didn't care. He didn't feel like moving. The breeze returned and redirected the smoke into Jim's face, but he didn't act bothered by it either.

"Ladies, gentlemen, I am about to collapse, as I suspect you are," Jacques said, his voice heavy and slow. "To try to run the remaining section of water at night is almost certainly suicidal. If the murderous thing in the river doesn't kill us, the rapids will. Earlier, I trusted my instincts, and I plan to now. I think we need to post our watch shifts again while the rest of us try to get some sleep. Running the Impassable Canyon in an exhausted state is begging for disaster. I've seen it, and I won't do it." Jacques, the voice of reason, had spoken. "Besides, now that the ranch isn't an option, we'll have to—"

"Hold on a minute." Bobby interrupted. He looked at Jim. "You said the generator went off, but the radio worked. We could go back, restart the generator, and try the radio again. I want to get out of here as bad as anyone else, and if we can get a plane to take us out tomorrow, that would be a hell of a lot better than the alternative, don't you think?"

"I can't go back there," Beth stated flatly. "It was there. It could be waiting for us to come back."

"I don't think it matters," Abby contended. "It seems to find us any time it wants to, whether we're here, on the water, or at the ranch. We won't be safe anywhere, until we kill it, or get off the river."

"Hard to kill something we can't even see." Jerry said. "This thing is smart, but so far it's exhibited more of an animal-like cunning. It stepped on the pongee sticks but appeared to play with the perimeter line once it figured out what it was. I think the way to get this fucker is to build some kind of trap for it."

"Yeah—right," Suzi snapped. "We don't even know if we have the means to kill 'this thing.' What the hell are we going to do if we do catch it? What then? The only weapons we have are knives and spears, and I damn sure don't want to try to stab something that moves faster than my eyes can focus," she said looking at Jerry.

"I don't think stabbing it is the answer, but I don't know what is," Jerry admitted. "I'll work on an idea though." When Jerry worked on an idea, Bobby knew it was well thought out, though Jerry worked slow and methodical, and he didn't know if they had enough time. It did make him feel a little more hopeful, however.

"We don't have any idea what this thing is, so how do you propose to catch it?" Scott asked. "I mean, what would you use for bait?"

"I think we're the bait," Jerry said grimly.

"I'll try anything reasonable," Jim said. "But I agree with Bobby: before we do anything else, I want to give the radio one more try."

"Reasonable right now would be choosing shifts and getting some sleep. I'm passing out on my feet," Bobby said.

After they drew shifts, they arranged the sleeping area. The first shift fell to Jacques, Beth, and Scott; the second shift consisted of Jerry, Linda, and Suzi; the final shift would be comprised of Bobby, Plato, Abby, and Jim.

Bobby zipped up his goose-down sleeping bag to ward off the night chill that invaded his bones. Abby lay next to him; gazing at her he began drinking in her image. She snuggled close and put her arms across him.

He kissed her gently on the cheek and once tenderly on the lips. She slid her hand into the hair behind his neck and kissed him passionately. Then she

## CHAPTER EIGHTEEN 167

smiled at him and said goodnight as she turned facing away. He "spooned" up behind her, and the thought entered his mind that he would like to sleep this way sometime in the future, only nude.

He thought he was too tired to sleep, but within two minutes he entered the delta state of deep sleep.

Bobby awoke in his childhood bedroom. His closet swung open.

Gretta rocked in a nearby rocking chair with an expression of maniacal glee. A hand grasped the doorframe of the closet. It belonged to a very dead-looking Pat. He walked out through the closet door and stopped just inside the bedroom. Water dripped from a long slit in his torso.

The cadaver held none of Pat's warmth and humor as it beckoned for Bobby to come into the closet. He had no intention of going into the closet, but his dream director had other ideas. Against his will he climbed out of his bed and walked seemed to float towards it, unable to alter course. Pat smiled a lifeless smile, devoid of emotion, and walked into the darkness inside the door. Bobby followed.

The closet took on new dimensions as he crossed the threshold. Pat vanished, and the Gretta-thing laughed insanely from somewhere behind him. Her laugh faded away as the closet door slowly closed.

He found himself standing inside a tunnel. A light shined at its far end.

The light drew closer. It became the headlights of an approaching car. Its speed increased as the tunnel narrowed. *The car's trying to run me down, but why?* When the headlights were nearly on him, Bobby saw that it wasn't a car. Instead, it was a pair of hideous, burning, yellow eyes. He fought to ascend towards wakefulness, but instead took another detour through time and space.

He now sat in the front seat of an old Buick Riviera—the scene outside the car, a hamburger stand on Irving Boulevard. His mother sat beside him watching people as they ran wildly about. Dozens rounded the corner looking up into the sky as if Godzilla had come to Dallas, Texas.

*Of course, in a way, Godzilla has come to Dallas*, Bobby thought. He remembered the day well. April second, he couldn't quite remember which year. But it had been the day he had experienced his greatest fear, and he knew why the people were running.

"A plane's going to crash," his mother said as she reached for the car's radio dial. But it wasn't a plane crash. Bobby knew everything that would happen. It was an exact replay of the events from his childhood. The nuances of his mother's movements, and the actual expressions on the same people's faces were precise duplications of that dreaded day. His mother backed the car up so they could get a look at whatever was causing all the commotion.

There it was: a tall, black shadow sucking parts of Dallas into its "vacuum-cleaner" funnel. It destroyed property and lives in much the same way Godzilla always did to hapless Tokyo. But two of the people passing by weren't part of the replay—they were new additions. The Judge and Bonnie walked up to the side of the car as the radio announcer's voice faded to a distant mumble. Bobby's mother didn't see them, but Bobby did. They were dripping wet, and they smiled through sightless eyes.

"It's coming," The Judge told Bobby. "It's coming here."

"You know, if it looks like it's standing still, it's moving towards you," Bonnie warned.

"If it's moving sideways, stay where you are," The Judge added. He grinned as he spoke. "It knows you're afraid, Bobby. The more you fear it, the more it wants you."

"Judge, what can I do?" he asked. "I don't want to die." The Judge didn't answer…he just looked up.

The tornado stood still and mutated. Bobby knew what it would become if he waited around. He opened the car door, took one look at his mother—she was so young and beautiful—opened the door and said, "Come on, Mom, we've got to get out of here!"

He exited the car and began running with the crowd, looking frantically for his mom. His heart pounded in his chest as he ran. Then, something grabbed him from behind and shook him…

…He awoke to find Abby shaking his shoulders. He panted as if he really had been running. Sweat poured from his brow, and he wondered if he burned with a fever. Holding Abby close to him, as though she had saved his life, he wept openly like a small child.

# 19

### ECHOES

Abby cradled him in her arms. She didn't ask about the dream. In fact, she didn't say anything. She rubbed the back of his neck softly. He took a few deep breaths, and began to relax again. The comforting sound of normal night noises and the drone of quiet conversation told him that things were safe for the moment. Hearing Jacques' deep voice, told him that it was still only the first shift, hours before he had to get up for guard duty. He looked up at the firelight dancing on the canopy of trees and slipped back into sleep.

Bobby awakened to the smell of coffee, and the sight of Jerry holding a cup under his nose.

"Already?" Bobby asked, trying to shake off the narcotic of sleep.

"You've been sawing logs," Jerry told him.

"Man, it feels like I just closed my eyes," he said as he took the first sip of coffee.

"It's your turn all right," Jerry told him. "I'm about ready to crash and burn." He took a deep drag from his cigarette and said, "Thank God it hasn't come back."

Bobby climbed out of the warm sleeping bag and stretched. Jim was already up tending the fire, and Plato looked to be awake in his bag, yawning and stretching. Since they had an extra person on the final shift, Bobby decided to let Abby sleep a while longer.

Jim and Bobby watched as the moon set on the western mountains. Some of the light would be gone, so they put more logs on the fire to compensate.

"I wonder why this thing strikes at random. It's out there somewhere right now. It knows where we are, yet it seems to have other purposes most of the time," Plato observed.

"I'd hate to be its full-time focus. Geez, what do you think could have caused something like this thing to evolve?" Bobby asked Plato.

"Can't say. Strange creatures have inhabited this planet before. Dinosaurs. Mammoths. It's possible that most legends come from at least a semblance of truth," Plato replied.

"Hell, it could even be from another planet for all we know," Jim said as he lit a cigarette.

As they discussed the beast, a number of sharp reports rang through the still night air, distant, but clearly audible.

"Gunshots!" Bobby shouted jumping up from his seat. "From down river."

"I counted six; sounded like a fairly heavy caliber," Jim said. "Five rapid shots, and then a pause followed by one final one."

"Get the book," Plato said with excitement. "We'll see which campgrounds are below us."

Jim leapt to the kitchen box and retrieved the Quinn Guide. He returned to the fire and flipped through the pages. "Here we are, page 115—we're at mile number 64.6. Then, the next camp down from here is the Airport Ranch Camp at mile 66.8. How far would you say sound could carry in this canyon at night?" he asked.

"I wouldn't know. With the echoes in the canyon it could be up to ten miles I'd guess," Plato replied. "Could I see the book?" Jim handed it to him still open.

He studied the page in the firelight. "There's another small camp at Bernard and another at Cold Springs, mile 70. There are a number of other camps below them; I'd guess one of these." He pointed to the map.

Four camps represented by small tee-pees marked the spots. "The last one within ten miles is Woolard Creek. That's where we're supposed to stay tomorrow night, but I have a feeling we'll want to make it a lot further than that," Plato said.

"Well I don't see that this makes any difference," Jim added. "We're not going anywhere before daybreak. Nothing has changed, and if you're thinking that somebody killed it, well, that would be great, but I don't think it should change our plans. That thing out there is like a gun: you treat it like

## CHAPTER NINETEEN

it's always cocked and loaded, and you're better off. I still think we should try the radio again, then make a run for it if nobody answers." He took a sip from his coffee and said, "We'll be safer if we don't assume anything and just stick to the format." He looked to Bobby.

Bobby thought it over for a moment. "We should try the radio. If we can get the generator started, we could be out of here tomorrow. If we can't get it started, that means we have to spend at least one more night on the river. It also means that we'll have to make for Elk Bar tomorrow instead of camping at Woolard Creek, and that makes for one hell of a long day." Bobby looked at the guidebook and calculated the mileage. "That also means we have to make twenty-four miles the last day, all in the Impassable Canyon. Let's just pray the radio works."

"What if Plato's first thought was right? What if there's more than one of them?" Jim inquired as he poured another cup of coffee.

"I can't answer," Bobby replied. "I just hope he's wrong." A loud splash in the river brought his and Jim's spears to attack position. They faced the river as still as statues. Bobby broke the silence. "I still hear the bugs and birds—maybe it was only a fish."

"Yeah, besides that shot we just heard probably wasn't a spot-lighter hunting by moonlight," Jim replied. "They were shooting at that shadow fucker."

"If there's only one shadow fucker," Plato said.

Bobby continued to scan the river. Then an idea occurred to him. "How often do you think the Victor Ranch contacted the air service for re-supply?"

"I don't know," Plato answered. "Cessna like the one we saw at Indian Creek might bring in over 1000 pounds. That's a lot of beer and cigarettes. Possible for them to go for a week without ordering more supplies. If they called yesterday, I don't think the air service will be worried for at least a few days."

Bobby turned to Jim. "You were there yesterday—how many employees would you say worked and lived there?"

"I'd guess about five or six based on the size of the place," Jim answered.

"You didn't see any bodies. Where do you suppose those employees are?" Bobby continued.

"I don't know; the place was a mess. They might have seen it coming and ran like hell, or maybe it's got them stashed somewhere," Jim replied.

Abby listened to the conversation from her sleeping bag. Jim's last comment made her shudder. She had heard the shots, and she too prayed that the bullets had found their mark.

*God please let this be over.*

She had only known Charlene just over a week, and the Murphy sisters she had met at Boundary Creek, but she felt a tremendous sense of loss from their deaths.

She crawled out of her bag and went to the table for her cup. Jim poured her some much-needed coffee, and she joined the group on sentry duty. The entire area looked much darker without the moon, but the sound of a nearby nightingale made her feel less apprehensive than she'd felt earlier.

"I heard those gunshots; what do you think they mean?" she asked Bobby.

"I know what I hope they mean," he answered. "That somebody put this thing out of our misery. Whether they were shooting at the same thing and whether or not they hit it, we may never know."

"At least we know there's someone on this river with a gun," Abby said. For a moment, she tried to think of a name for their enemy, other than "It," or "The Thing." A number of names shot through her mind but none of them fit, since they hadn't seen what they were up against yet. "Anybody want to suggest a name for this thing?"

Bobby spoke. "I read about an old lumberjack legend at the library back home. A monster called The Hidebehind supposedly killed ninety-four loggers over ten years along the Santiam River in Central Oregon back in the 1890s."

"Maybe it was an early environmentalist," Plato joked. "But this is the 21st Century, and we're hundreds of miles from there. What legends come from here?" Abby watched him put the book aside. He turned toward her. "No, Ms. Jones, I think it would be a mistake to give it a name. A name won't change anything it's going to do. It won't protect anyone from it. You're searching for talismanic protection by giving it a name, but in doing so, you'll be putting our learned characteristics on it. The chosen language may be prejudiced, or cause prejudice in someone else's mind. It could even cause a misperception on a subliminal level that could have a consequence in our microcosmic, dialectical outcome. My suggestion is to 'empty your cups,' and take from it—don't give anything back to it, or you might overlook data that could be useful to our collective survival."

"What did he just say?" Jim asked, turning to Bobby.

"He says to be a phenomenologist…in other words, don't put it in a box—

# CHAPTER NINETEEN

think WAY outside the box." Bobby explained.

"Thank you, Bobby, for the Cliff Notes," Plato said as he nodded his head and smiled.

"It's just strange calling some creature by "It," or "Thing." It reminds me of all the old horror movies I saw when I was a kid," Abby said.

"Well in case you hadn't noticed, we have a hell of a horror story going ourselves," Jim pointed out. He paused for comic effect and said, "I think we should call it Frank. I like that a hell of a lot more than calling it The Hidebehind. That scares the shit out of me."

Abby had seen the results of adverse circumstances, usually at a crime scene or in police photos, and humanity's dark side had hardened her. She had been forced to develop a twisted sense of humor, since her job constantly put her in contact with the Ernie Butters of the world.

It was easy to forget that most people are good, and that her job as deputy D.A. was to keep society's predators away from those good people. *Predators.* If she could only take care of this one as easily as she'd dispatched Butters.

Now that would be the trial of the century. Put this thing on trial for murder. She envisioned a black reptilian creature wearing a business suit sitting with a defense attorney.

*Not fair, your honor. The defense attorney has cleaned up the defendant.*

Of course she'd be overruled. She figured the judge would have to be especially careful during lunch breaks.

To have gone through the horror of the last several days and still be able to make light of the situation seemed impossible, but they were doing it. She would have bet most of them would still brush their teeth after breakfast. *We may all be killed any time, but humor and good dental hygiene are important up until that point*, she mused.


The sky began a slow change of hue in the east. The river's noise faded in with day sounds: clinking pans, soft conversations, and the haunting whistle of a breeze in one of two lone pines above her head.

Abby sat silently watching the horizon and thinking how lucky they were to still be alive. Considering her growing feelings for Bobby, she was having the worst experience of her life, but for some odd reason, it only added to the attraction instead of diminishing it.

She watched him as morning crept over the mountain ridges across the river and formed a backdrop for him. He was handsome and intelligent.

"Bobby," she called quietly so that he was the only one to hear. He turned to her. "We don't know much about each other, but I want you to know that I hope we get the chance to rectify that. I really like you." She smiled. A warm feeling in the pit of her stomach buzzed awake.

*Those eyes.*

She could feel his presence like a soft envelope pressing against her body—even at a distance—making her tremble slightly. The song of the lark replaced the nightingale, and it sounded like someone had changed channels to a romantic music station. He walked toward her.

"I like you too, Abby," he replied. "I've been thinking about all the things I'd like to do with you, and how I hope we get the chance. I never thought I'd feel this kind of excitement, but here I am."

"I'll tell you what, if we make it through this, you can come up to Portland, and I'll show you the town—my treat."

"It's not the town that I want to see," Bobby said grinning mischievously.

Abby put on what she considered her sexiest smile, leaned close to him, and whispered her warm breath into his ear: "Well, I guess that gives us something to look forward to," she said as she bit his earlobe gently and pulled away.

She and Bobby flirted casually back and forth until 7:00 a.m., while Jim and Plato kept a vigil on the surrounding woods. Another night ended. The time had come to awaken the others and continue their flight down the river.

Jerry cooked pancakes, which disappeared as soon as they came off the griddle. After breakfast, Bobby noticed several people standing at the camp table to brush their teeth and saw Abby laughing to herself for some reason.

He waited until everyone had returned to the center of camp, then he called for their attention and explained about the gunfire they had heard, and speculation over its meaning. He introduced his idea of returning to the ranch to radio for help, and then called for a vote.

"Vote or no vote, I'm not going back to that friggin' ranch," Suzi said.

"I second that," Linda agreed.

"It's our best chance to get out of here today," Jim said. "I don't want to go back in there either, that's for damn sure, but I know it's the best chance we have."

"It was there yesterday. It might not be there today. At least it seems to be dividing its time between us, and somebody down river. Besides, we don't all have to go inside. Three of us could go in, while the rest wait at the boats."

# CHAPTER NINETEEN

Bobby knew the quickest way to get to the ranch was by boat, but after what happened to Pat on the river, Jim's group had opted to walk instead. After last night it didn't matter; they would float down in the rafts.

"Makes sense to me," Jacques added. "That way we try the radio, and if it won't work, we'll just push harder to catch our shooter downstream."

"Let's vote," Jerry suggested. "Daylight's wasting. How many for going back to the ranch?"

All but Linda, Beth, and Suzi held up their hands. Even Scott, who had heard the footsteps on his heels, voted to go back.

"I'll go, but I'm definitely staying in the boat," Linda said.

"The ranch it is," Jacques said as he walked toward his raft. "If the radio don't work, we get the fuck outta' Dodge—pronto…pardon my French, ladies."

After they completed the loading, Abby suggested they look for Gretta's body. That brought reality crashing in on Bobby. The thought of finding her body scared him. Actually, the thought of finding a part of her was what scared him most. He vividly remembered the discovery of Gary's head and still feared finding the headless corpse sitting on a rock, or floating up to the raft in hopes of a lift.

They searched but found no trace of her. Not even a bloody spot where it might have killed her. It was as if she had never existed. At least Bobby didn't have to confront her in death. He wanted to remember her the way she had been. Now he could.

The group left Sheep Creek in silence. The sun warmed the air, and the sky turned a brilliant blue, but there was no warmth in the people. The fear of being attacked in the water cooled everyone's enthusiasm for leaving Sheep Creek.

In the slow current, it took about half an hour before Bobby saw the beach below the ranch house. They could see the huge log structure from the sandy beach. A few large oaks grew in the front yard, and a rose garden decorated the path up from the river. The ranch itself was a quarter-mile hike past the airstrip. He jumped out, and pulled the boat onto the sand. Beth and Abby both remained in it.

"I'll go in," Bobby said.

"Me too," Jim said as he climbed out of his raft.

"Do either one of you know how to operate a ham radio?" Jacques asked.

"No," they answered simultaneously.

"Well, I guess I'd better go along too, since I was a radio operator in Vietnam; at least maybe I can figure out what they have."

"Anybody else want to come?" Bobby asked.

"No volunteers?" Jim chided mildly. He waited for an answer. "Don't all volunteer at once."

"That's OK, three's enough," Bobby said. "But if you guys see us come running, go ahead and shove off; we'll dive for the boats," he said half laughing, but in fact being serious.

Each of the three took their personal spear, and an extra knife with them. Bobby had the big K-Bar on his belt in case he had the opportunity for a "draw and peg."

Bobby and Jim stood aside while Jacques allowed Phydeaux to sniff the front of the ranch house. She didn't act upset by anything she smelled, so they entered through the front door.

"Gary's helmet was right there yesterday," Jim said as he pointed to the bar. "It's been back since last night."

Jesus—God! "How do you know that?" Bobby asked.

"We had it trapped in the dining room, and it broke a window to get out. We heard the glass break right before we made a run for it. The helmet was the last thing I saw when we left, so it must have come back later and moved it."

"This thing is being creepy on purpose and it's pissing me off," Bobby said. "How the hell did it recover Gary's hel—head from the river? And why the fuck is it carrying it around?"

"I don't know, but let's proceed as if it's still here, cause it damn well might be," Jacques advised.

They slowly moved into the adjoining room, then into the hallway. The pipes still barred the door. Jim carefully pulled them out one by one while Bobby held his spear at the door, ready to impale anything that came through the opening. Several of the pipes were crushed where the force had pulled them against the doorframe, but they hadn't broken. Looking at the crushed pipe gave him an idea of the strength this creature possessed.

"Thank God it didn't have any leverage on that hardwood floor," Jim said with a shiver. He rubbed his finger in the indented pipe and put it aside.

After he removed the last pipe, Jim and Bobby looked at each other, then at Phydeaux. She cocked her head and sniffed under the door but didn't seem agitated by what she smelled. They slowly pushed it.

## CHAPTER NINETEEN

The door opened along the back wall of the room. The opposite wall had windows reminiscent of a grade school classroom running the entire length of the dining hall. One of the windows was shattered. The kitchen lay at the far end of the room, directly behind the counter where the radio was located.

"That's where it came from yesterday," Jim said as he looked toward the broken window.

"I heard the noise just after the lights went out. It came from back in the kitchen area. For it to cut off the generator and come after us so fast would mean it would have to have been back in there somewhere."

They walked across the dining hall to the double doors where Jim said he had seen the eyes burning from the shadows. They opened the doors slowly. The drone of flies was the first noticeable sound caused by anything other than themselves.

The only light in the kitchen filtered in from the serving window and the double door. This time they had brought flashlights. At first, nothing looked out of the ordinary except for some dots on the floor.

The beams playing across the darkness of the kitchen resembled a pair of searchlights advertising the opening of a new shopping center. A faint coppery smell mixing with the odor of rotting meat assaulted Bobby's olfactory senses as they entered the kitchen.

Walking further into the room, he spotted blood and his skin prickled with gooseflesh. It looked as if gallons had been spilled from a prop blood-bucket in a Hollywood, horror movie. Dark puddles covered the back portion of the kitchen and lying in its midst was new evidence of carnage that froze them in their tracks.

He thought he might vomit for a moment, but the feeling passed. They inched forward holding shaky flashlights that added a macabre effect to the grisly scene.

A body lay balanced on its side with a large gaping hole in the front of its torso. It looked as if the skin might actually be a flesh-colored neoprene wet-suit, where someone left the zipper down.

*My God.*

The face on the corpse was frozen in a mask of terror. Phydeaux sniffed the blood, the body, and went off to investigate other parts of the kitchen.

The body on the floor resembled a man, about average size, and in his mid-thirties. From the look on his face, there was no doubt that he had seen his killer from point-blank range.

"Jesus H. Christ! I've had enough of this shit!" Jim exclaimed. "Let's find the generator, and get out of here."

"Look behind that cabinet, and then check that closet over in the back corner," Jacques ordered.

"Hey, who died and made you God?" Bobby said. "Let's go together. I don't mind telling you I'm scared shitless." He clutched his spear as he gazed at the closet. "If Phydeaux smells that door, and doesn't growl, I'll open it, but you cover my ass."

"Okay, I'm right behind you," Jacques said.

Walking to the cabinet, Bobby glanced behind it only to find a mop and bucket. They worked their way past the lake of blood, and the cadaverous remains, to stand nervously in front of the closet door.

"Hey! Look at this!" Jim called from behind them.

They both jumped as if they had been goosed by an electric cattle prod. Even Phydeaux barked at him for giving her a start.

"Sorry," Jim said. "Look at this."

There was a knife on the floor, and it was covered with black ooze. Bobby could see that it was the same stuff that had been on the pongee sticks at Whitey Cox Camp.

"The guy over there must have stuck it with that," Bobby said.

"Oh shit—this guy stuck it pretty good. By the way he smells, I'd bet he was here when we were here yesterday. The blood's mostly dried, and as ripe as he is, he would have had to have died before we got here—do you know what that means?" Jim asked.

Bobby and Jacques both shrugged in the flashlight's reflection.

"It means that it did all that shit to us last night, after it had taken that knife to the hilt. I don't like the implications of that. For one thing, it could mean there really are more than one of these things, or it could mean that sticking it with a butcher knife doesn't even slow it down." He looked at the knife on the end of his spear. "Not good news."

The dead man had been lying on his side when Phydeaux accidently bumped him over with her nose. Jacques shined his light on the corpse, and noticed that the right hand had been torn off.

"Jesus," he said under his breath.

"The hand's in the dining room-in the garbage," Jim told him. "It was still hooked to the microphone yesterday."

"Nice touch," Bobby said, "but why was it in there, and the body in here?"

## CHAPTER NINETEEN

"I don't know, and I don't give a shit right now, I just want to find the generator and get out of here," Jim said as he looked back toward the double door as if expecting a dark visitor to appear at any moment, trapping them in.

Jacques called Phydeaux to the closet door. She sniffed around, cocked her head, and began digging at the crack under the door as if to gain entry.

Jacques held her back, while Bobby cautiously opened it. The closet was a large storage room that had been added to the back of the ranch house. The generator was there, and Jim had been right in his postulation—the enemy had most definitely been back since last night.

Leaning against the back wall, straddling the generator was what was left of Gretta. Her expression couldn't be read through the slaughtered mass that had been her head, but the remains wore her long, tie-dyed T-shirt and her blue jean shorts. Her innards had been removed, like the body on the floor. Jacques threw up his breakfast.

Jim jumped back. "Holy shit—Motherfucker!"

Bobby had hoped he wouldn't have to see her in death but here she was, displayed for his benefit. Tears filled his eyes between heaves as he turned away from her mangled corpse.

He remembered his promise to watch out for her. He had invited her along. If not for him, she would be spending the summer at home with her kids. Alive. *I'm sorry, Gretta…so sorry.*

"I can't go in there," Bobby said.

Jim steeled himself. "I'll do it," he said. He studied the generator. He didn't want to touch Gretta's body, so he moved slowly and carefully. He checked the tank and found it one-quarter full of gasoline, and then made sure the spark plug was still in the on position before pulling the crank cord.

It turned over once and coughed. He tried again, but it still didn't start. On the third try, it coughed, rattled, and hummed to life.

"All right!" Jim shouted. "It's about time something started going our way."

"Why didn't the lights come on?" Jacques asked.

"Shit!" Bobby shouted as he punched his fist into the nearest wall. The sheet rock caved in making a deep hole.

Jim followed the powerline out of the generator. It was a big one with over 10,000 watts of output and ran the entire ranch. Usually, a generator had a built-in outlet where things could be plugged into it, but this one had been wired directly into the electrical system that ran throughout the ranch. It served as a mini power plant.

He followed the line around the storage closet and out into the kitchen. The bare wires were clearly visible behind the cabinet as were the white sparks shooting from them.

"Turn it off!" Jim shouted.

Bobby jumped into the closet and closed the switch—careful to avoid touching Gretta.

"Hey, radio expert. Do you know how to splice heavy-duty electrical wires?" Jim asked.

Jacques walked over to where he stood and examined the severed wires. "I can damn sure give it a school-boy try," he answered, as he pulled out his Leatherman's Tool.

Jacques cut the cables back and stripped them down at two separate places on the positive and negative wires. With no electrician's tape handy, in its place he used band-aids from Jim's pocket first-aid kit. He signaled that he was finished. Jim went back into the closet and again pulled the crank-cord. It started up the first time.

The lights came on, but Bobby heard a noise out in the dining hall and looked out the serving window to see what it was.

"Turn it off—quick!" he yelled.

Jim turned it off immediately.

"What's wrong this time?" Jacques asked with an air of frustration.

"Something's shorting out the radio," Bobby answered.

They joined him in the dining hall and saw smoke wafting from one of the radio components.

"It's a linear amplifier for this base station," Jacques informed them. "It must hit a relay on the eastern mountain that shoots the signal into the valley on the other side. They have a big antennae outside, and I'll bet this cable goes to it." He scrutinized the amplifier. "There's a puddle of that black "oozy" shit that's leaked into the cooling access on the amp." He checked the other unit. "You didn't see any smoke or hear any noise coming from this unit, did you?" he asked Bobby.

"No. Just that one there," he said pointing to the linear amplifier.

"Well, I'm going to unhook the booster amp and try to send a message just using the C.B. It's only five watts, and it probably won't have enough power to

## CHAPTER NINETEEN                                    181

reach Salmon, but we're here, and we might as well give it a try," Jacques said. "I just hope it's on the right channel—there's probably not a lot of traffic on the air waves out this far." He turned the knob on the front of the unit and said, "What the hell, we've got forty channels to choose from."

He unhooked the amplifier and had Jim go back to re-start the generator one last time. It turned over once again, and this time the radio filled the room with static. Jacques turned the squelch all the way down so he could hear any response, no matter how faint. Only ghostly white noise whispered from the speaker.

The C.B. was set on channel 39. Jacques took the microphone and depressed the send button.

"Mayday! Mayday! There is a killer loose on the Middle Fork. Please come back, over. Repeat, Mayday!"

No response.

"We believe over one dozen killed in the past few days. Mayday! Mayday!"

Nothing.

"We are at the Victor Ranch, please acknowledge. Mayday goddammit!"

Nothing but distant static answered from the radio.

"I'll try another channel," he said as he switched to channel 19, the trucker's channel.

He repeated his distress call on every channel without a response. Finally, he turned to them and said: "I think we gave it our best shot; I'm ready to go." Jacques took a deep breath and turned off the radio.

"Why don't we leave the generator on in case there's someone behind us? Maybe they'll be luckier than we were," Jim suggested as he went to the door of the kitchen and turned off the light.

Bobby felt a little more of his hope slipping away. The radio had worked, but nobody had been listening. *Bad luck*, he thought to himself. *Can't stand too much more of that.*

Gretta's remains were in the storage closet, but he couldn't make himself go back in and carry her out for a burial. *There might not be time anyway. If we make it off the river, I'll send someone back for her—for all of them. If there's anything left to be found.*

Phydeaux's ears perked up as if she had heard something move somewhere in the ranch house.

"Time to go now," Bobby said, even if it had been only a mouse scurrying through the wall, he felt they had stayed too long. Phydeaux sniffed the air, and "woofed" softly.

"Well, nothing more we can do here," Jim said.

Bobby wanted to scream, but managed to stop his emotional descent before it reached that level.

The three men headed for the entrance. Slowly, and carefully, they followed Phydeaux to the front porch of the ranch house.

Standing outside in the sunlight did little for Bobby's hopes. They now had to descend through the Impassable Canyon, and in the process spend another night on the river. The radio was not the way out.

# 20

## A CRY FOR HELP

Tommy Barnes lay in his bed, listening to the morning sounds around the farmhouse. Everything had been quiet all morning. Mom and Dad had gone into town and left him alone. He liked being alone.

As a ten-year-old, he enjoyed the feeling of being independent. His parents showed their trust in him by giving him the option of staying home when they went to town.

He was about to get up and get dressed when he heard the base station come to life in the den. The voice sounded distant, and static almost drowned the signal, but the message came through as clear as if it had been broadcast directly into Tommy's mind.

"Mayday! Mayday! There's a killer loose on the Middle Fork. Please come back, over. Repeat—Mayday!"

Tommy's heart raced. He tried to get himself positioned for entry into his wheelchair. It usually wasn't very difficult for him—he'd done it every day of his life since he was four years old, but at this moment he was frantic.

As he tried to ease himself into the seat, the chair rolled. In his hurry he had forgotten to check the brake and almost went sprawling onto the floor. Barely managing to catch it before it rolled away, he pulled himself into it.

"We believe over one dozen killed in the past few days—Mayday! Mayday!"

Tommy couldn't believe what he was hearing. Nothing like this had ever happened before. For a second, he sat motionless wondering if he were dreaming or awake.

"We are at the Victor Ranch—Please acknowledge! Mayday, goddammit!"

Tommy wheeled his chair at top speed, out of his bedroom, into the hall, and finally into the den. He raced across the room, grabbed the microphone, and called back: "Victor Ranch, this is "Mr. T"—I acknowledge," he said, not sure how to answer so serious a message. "Hello, Victor Ranch, come in—I hear you, over."

No answer came back, except the static of the open channel.

Tommy envisioned the sender of the terrible message being garroted like the guy in "Marathon Man." He had seen it on a movie channel the satellite dish picked up the previous week. The man's eyes had bugged out as he kicked helplessly, while his head turned a dark purple. It had impressed him as a truly horrible way to die.

*What should I do?* He wondered. He had no experience in matters like this. *Don't panic.* Dad would know what to do. He could wait until his dad got home and ask him. But if people were in danger now, he reasoned he should act now.

Turning the dial until the red, digital readout showed Channel nine, he then depressed the send button. His parents had told him Channel nine was monitored by the emergency dispatcher in Salmon, but to never use it unless it was a real emergency.

"Mayday! Mayday!" Tommy called out. "Emergency! Please come back, over." There was a moment of silence, then a woman's voice came out of the small speaker, filled the den, rendering Tommy momentarily speechless.

"This is Salmon emergency dispatch—please identify yourself, over."

"This is "Mr. T"—uh—Tommy Barnes. I just got a Mayday call from the Victor Ranch. They said that somebody killed a bunch of people on the Middle Fork."

For a moment only static returned to the speaker. Then the woman spoke again. "How old are you, Tommy?" she asked.

He hadn't expected that question. Puzzled for a few seconds, he answered the woman.

"Ten years old."

"Where are your parents?"

"They're in town getting supplies, over."

"Tommy, it's a very serious matter, playing on the C.B."

"PLEASE! I swear I'm not playing. The guy on the radio didn't sound like he was playing either. Please, do something," he pleaded. Having heard the man's voice, he knew it wasn't a joke.

## CHAPTER TWENTY

"Tommy, where are you now? Over."

"I'm at our farm, just east of Taylor Mountain." He waited for her to respond. After what felt like several moments she came back on.

"Are you Fred and Marcia Barnes' son?"

"Yes ma'am."

"You're sure the man said that people had been killed?"

"Yes ma'am, he said a dozen people had gotten killed in the last few days at the Victor Ranch, over."

"Did you ask him his name?"

"No ma'am, he was gone by the time I got to the microphone."

"What channel did the call come in over Tommy?"

"Channel thirty-nine, over."

"Tommy, try to think. Did he say anything else?"

"No ma'am, that was it." *Except he said 'god dammit' at the end.*

"Okay, Tommy, I'll tell Sheriff Bonham what you told me. Stay there and keep monitoring your radio on the same channel in case he calls again. The sheriff might want to talk with you so stay close. Over and out."

After the lady signed off, he sat listening to radio static. He turned the dial back to channel thirty-nine and awaited another distress call, wishing his parents were home, since he suddenly felt very alone.

. . .

Jerry felt glad that Bobby wasn't running when he came over the horizon. However, he could see by his expression, they hadn't been successful in reaching anyone on the radio.

He listened as Jacques explained what had happened from the moment they left until now, telling only essentials since time was of the essence.

Jerry cringed at hearing about the discovery of Gretta's body. He had known she was dead, but hearing it from Jacques made it real…a fact. The creepy manner in which she had been displayed gave added evidence of the cunning the creature possessed. Again, it had flaunted that cunning to unnerve them, and again it had worked as intended, on Jerry.

"We have no other logical choice; we have to go from here to Elk Bar," Jacques said. "It means another night with this monster stalking us, but if we wait here, we could be waiting for days before anyone decides to check on why these folks don't respond to their radio. I don't want to take that chance. Let's get out of this God forsaken place and see if we can find that shooter." Jacques walked to his raft. He looked haggard, and his pace seemed slower. *As if he's given up*, Jerry thought.

No one argued to stay at the ranch anyway. In fact, no one spoke. Instead they all silently boarded the rafts.

Suzi chose to ride with Jerry in his Hyside. He glanced back at the others. Jim and Linda paddled Jim's small Campways; Jacques rowed in the big gear boat with Phydeaux; Plato and Scott rode in the self bailing Maravia, and Abby and Bobby took turns rowing the SOTAR, while Beth sat as a passenger up front.

The first campsite was about half a mile down from the ranch. Nobody was there. A mile below he found Haystack Rapids, a solid, class-three rock garden but had no problems with it.

He and Suzi drifted on in silence, listening for unusual sounds and scanning the banks. After about half an hour, he saw rafts pulled up on a beach at river right. Jim and Linda had already pulled ashore. Jerry looked for movement in the camp and saw none, but he heard the drone of flies.

"That sure is becoming a familiar sound," Jacques said from shore.

This time, no effort had been made to conceal the bodies. They had been killed in the open and left to rot in plain sight. Jerry was unnerved by the creature's sudden lack of caution.

He pulled to shore, climbed out of the boat and looked around. About fifteen people had been killed. Savagely. His knees began shaking.

*Jesus, this is too much.*

This was the first carnage he'd actually seen. The others had described what they had seen, but it wasn't the same. For a moment he thought he would throw up but managed to close his eyes and calm his stomach.

*My God—help us.* He suddenly felt like the odds for their survival had gone down considerably.

There were obvious signs of struggle. Knives lay in the sand; mutilated corpses still clutched clubs, and blood seemed to paint the entire landscape. These people had been prepared and it still got them all.

While he and Jim joined Bobby in searching the gruesome camp, he noticed Phydeaux had jumped off Jacques' raft and had begun her own investigation. She didn't seem agitated, so he figured the enemy was gone.

Following Bobby's gaze upward, he saw dozens of buzzards circling overhead. When he looked back down, a reflection off metal caught his attention. He blinked and looked again.

## CHAPTER TWENTY

*Could it be...?* He left the others to investigate. *Thank you, God!* "Hey, look! Over here!" he shouted.

Bobby and Jim ran toward him. Jerry finished prying a stainless steel revolver out of a dead man's hands.

"He shot himself," Jerry stated. "That explains why the entire back of his head is all over that tent behind him." Once again, Jerry felt like he was about to lose his breakfast. If he did, he figured Jim and Bobby would probably lose theirs too.

This had been a slaughter, except for the man in front of him, the man without a back to his head. The tent behind the corpse presented a veritable smorgasbord for the flies. To keep from gagging, he concentrated on the revolver.

Jerry emptied the spent shell casings out of the cylinder, and admired the find: a .357 magnum.

"He killed himself before it could get him," Jim said.

"I wonder how many rounds hit it," Bobby thought aloud. "A .357 magnum could blow an elk's head half off if the load's hot enough. A 158-grain bullet, hot loaded, could even stop a charging bear. If he hit it, it might be dying out there somewhere right now," he said.

"Yeah? Well why did this guy kill himself then?" Jim asked.

"Maybe it's hurt," Jerry suggested.

"It was hurt before it hit us at Sheep Creek. That knife in the kitchen was covered by that black blood, but it took that lickin' and kept on tickin'," Jim observed.

"Well, we're wasting our time—let's look for ammunition before this thing decides to come back for lunch," Bobby advised.

Trying to hold his breath as often as possible, Jerry searched the camp and looked for more clues. He passed several bodies but saw one that stopped him in mid-step. He locked eyes with what until last night had been someone as alive as himself.

The corpse sat, leaning against a cooler in a casual fashion. The face had been scraped away to leave a grinning skull; its hand pointed down river. It looked as if the Grim Reaper were warning them of impending doom downstream. The portents and omens were as clear as the smell of blood was nauseating. More than anything he didn't want to come to the same end as this man.

His knees shook uncontrollably as he sat back on a fallen tree. Acid climbed the back of his throat, and it was all he could do to swallow it back down.

He held his T-shirt over his nose and mouth. The odor had gotten worse just since they arrived. The temperature climbed rapidly: *it must be ninety degrees already. Going to be a scorcher,* he thought.

After searching the campsite and coming up empty, they returned to the unfortunate party's boats. Several ammo cans were still strapped to the rafts, and it was a logical place to start before digging into their coolers.

In the first two cans, they found nothing but personal items: cameras, extra batteries, prescription drugs, and a map. But in the third box they hit pay dirt.

"Bingo," Bobby called out as he held up a small ziplock bag containing three bullets. They searched the other rafts, which yielded nothing. Bobby emptied the three cartridges into the palm of Jerry's hand.

"Aw shit! These are .38 special, not .357 magnums. They'll work for target rounds, but they don't pack much of a wallop."

"Yeah, well it's better than nothing," Bobby replied.

"A little." Jerry carefully inserted the shells into the cylinder, and turned it so they lined up into the chamber. He had the holster they had found lying in the dirt next to the body of the gun's owner, but needed the corpse's belt for a strap. He somehow felt like he was violating the body, so he apologized to the man silently as he pulled it through the loops and backed away.

Glancing back at the reaper-man he shuddered. He would choose the same exit his benefactor had. Save one bullet for himself. If he witnessed his friends being turned into shredded meat in front of him, he would do it for sure—after he put the first two into the son-of-a-bitch.

Walking back to the boats, he put on the belt, and strapped the holster to it. It fit perfectly, and the gun felt good on his side.

"How good a shot are you?" Jim inquired from nearby.

Jerry figured he knew a good question when he heard it. If someone else had the gun, he would be just as concerned about his or her ability. He turned to Jim and forced a smile. "I've got a gun exactly like this, and I can hit six out of six cans at twenty-five yards," he answered, remembering the day he had shown off for Bobby. "If anybody can do better, they can be my guest."

"With a handgun, Jerry can shoot as good as anybody I know," Bobby said, "I can vouch for him." Bobby put his hand to his chin and rubbed with his thumb and forefinger. Bobby looked at him and dropped his arms; then he spoke: "Tonight we're going to have three shifts, and we need to find out who else has experience with a pistol. We don't have enough bullets to have a shoot-off, so we'll have to stress the importance of being real truthful about our marksmanship. I know Jerry's good. As far as I'm concerned, he's the gunman

## CHAPTER TWENTY

on his shift. That leaves two more slots, but we can discuss that later. Right now I just want to get the hell out of here."

Jim hoped Bobby was right about Jerry's prowess with a gun, but he wondered if it mattered, as he looked at the man who had owned the gun until a few moments ago. It hadn't helped him any, *unless you count suicide.*

They checked the camp one last time, when he saw something familiar. *What the hell?* Strange, but unique, indentations dotted the sand. He recognized their configuration from the kitchen area at the ranch. The same quarter-sized marks had been everywhere. These looked as if tent stakes had been pulled out of the ground, whereas the ones in the kitchen had been two-dimensional dots painted with blood.

"Hey, come here," he called. "Ever see these before?"

Phydeaux was the first to arrive. She smelled the holes and growled as Jim watched her closely. She looked out into the meadow behind the camp and "woofed." This time everyone noticed. She didn't seem too excited, but the picture started to form in Jim's mind. He looked at the holes in the sand for a moment before Bobby answered.

"Those were all over the kitchen floor this morning."

"What do you think they are?" Jerry asked.

"Footprints?" Bobby answered.

"Maybe it's the equivalent of a footprint, but it ain't from any foot I've ever seen," Jim replied.

The configuration was not only strange, it was huge. He wondered if the noise he had heard scraping across the dining room at the Victor Ranch had been made by whatever claws made these holes. If he were a gambling man he would have placed a bet on it.

He made his way to the waiting boats. After boarding, he and Linda shoved off without comment to the others.

Bobby rowed on past lunch, and arrived at Elk Bar by three-thirty in the afternoon, far ahead of schedule. This was another of the *paradise* campsites.

A large sand beach stretched out 150 yards down the left side of the river. All white sand, and it reached back up into the Ponderosas and Douglas Firs that bordered the camp.

At the rear of Elk Bar stood a high cliff, maybe sixty feet tall. The river in front meandered by at a slow, easy pace and was bordered by another cliff along the opposite bank. The rock face came down into the water and formed the backdrop for a deep, green pool.

"Just one more night," Bobby prayed quietly as he pulled the boat up onto the sand. "Please God, let us all make it—one more night."

They only unloaded essential items from the boats, and the camp went up within a matter of minutes. Bobby looked at Elk Bar and considered how best to protect it. It was defendable, but it had weak points. The cliff loomed above them. Both ends of the beach consisted of boulders tapering into firs and pines, making the best location for the camp in the very center of the beach.

The perimeter line lost practicality at Elk Bar, since there weren't any trees on the riverside of camp to string it around. So he and Jerry decided on a crescent configuration that would hopefully warn them if the beast approached from the wooded ends of camp, or the cliff side in the rear. He wasn't sure it would be effective again anyway. The creature had discovered the line last night and toyed with it. He was thankful for Phydeaux; she was still their best warning system.

Jerry drew the revolver and examined it closely. It was a Smith and Wesson model 686, stainless steel, and it was a carbon copy of his own pistol right down to the six-inch barrel. It gave him a little boost of confidence, but he hoped he wouldn't be put to the test with it. He hated tests.

In school he had always been able to do the work. No problem turning in the assignments or projects on time. But he always blew the tests.

He had never been able to concentrate unless he had time to think things through, slow and methodically. Every question he answered had always been right, but he had never been able to finish more than a few before the period ended.

Being in business for himself gave him the luxury to take all the time he wanted. No one could match the quality of his work—he knew it. So did all his customers. But shooting the gun at a moving target—one that wanted to kill him and his friends—that was a real test: a final exam to end all finals. Everyone would be counting on him to make an A-plus. *Not too much pressure, huh?* He wished he'd let someone else pick up the gun.

"Hey, Jerry," Bobby said as he walked up. "I'm going to have everybody arrange their sleeping bags on a large tarp, directly in the center of the beach. Then sentries can walk around the inner circumference of the camp, what do you think?"

Jerry thought for a moment. "Good idea, but let's expand the watch to four

## CHAPTER TWENTY

guards per shift for extra security. So each side will always be covered, and each sentry will be within twenty-five feet of another at all times."

"I knew there was a reason I asked you to come on this trip." Bobby smiled at him and turned to leave when Jerry grabbed his arm.

"Remember back in the shop when I told you the worse was over for you and what else could happen?"

"Yeah."

"Well kick me in the ass the next time I get philosophical, will you?"

Bobby put his hand on Jerry's shoulder. "I'll be glad to. Should I start now?"

"You don't have to give in so easy." Jerry looked up at the cliff and back at Bobby. "You want the gun? You're a pretty good shot."

"Not in your league. Are you okay with it?"

"Oh yeah——no problem," he lied.

"Well, when you get settled, help me set up the kitchen. I'm so tired, I'm about to pass out."

"Yeah…I'll be right along." He watched Bobby walk away.

The Cold Spring's group had obviously been alerted to the beast's presence, but it murdered fourteen of them with what appeared to be relative ease, Jerry thought as he remembered the grisly remains of the fifteenth man. He had chosen to end his own life after seeing what had happened to his friends.

*What could look so bad that it would cause someone to do that?*

He didn't want to find out. Hoping that the beast had taken them by surprise, and that was why it had easily defeated so many, he still felt a lingering doubt nagging at him. He was starting to think that it might be playing with their group, saving them for something.


Nobody had much of an appetite, but they went through the motions. The final cooler, opened an hour earlier, revealed that the dry ice had worked too well. The still frozen steaks forced them to opt for a different dinner.

After the fire had burned down to coals, Bobby added a liberal batch of charcoal. When the black cubes were rimmed with white ash, Jerry placed baked potatoes, wrapped in aluminum foil, strategically inside the fire pan. Jerry put a metal grate over them and all the chicken breasts on top of it.

An hour later, Bobby filled his plate, and went to his lawn chair. The food tasted good, but he couldn't eat much. He was exhausted and could hardly keep his eyes open.

Having only eaten half of his dinner before he could no longer keep his eyes open, he laid his plate in the sand next to his chair where Phydeaux made sure none went to waste. He put his head back and listened to the sounds of the late afternoon: the clinks of forks and knives, the drone of insects flying through the warm air, the soft lullaby of the river, and the quiet voices of his friends talking nearby. The warmth of the sun sank into his skin causing him to drowse....

...When he awoke the sun had gone down. It was cold, and there weren't any sounds. The scene resembled a Salvador Dali painting: heads and hands were carefully laid around the campsite. Some set on tables; some on the cooler; one hand even held a fork up to the mouth of a head setting on a roll table.

Phydeaux licked blood off one of the hands. Taking it in her mouth, she jumped over a cooler and carried it off toward the river. The old phrase, "She's biting the hand that feeds her," strolled through Bobby's mind, but it carried no humor.

Looking over to the other row of lawn chairs, he saw the dark enemy sitting with Abby in its lap. She sucked her thumb and looked off into space in the same manner as Gretta.

The eyes of the creature shined hateful, killing beams onto Bobby's chest, like laser sights on a sniper rifle. The beast stood up without making a sound, held Abby by the throat, and turned its malevolent gaze on her. Her thumb fell out of her mouth and hung limply at her side as she stared into the bright yellow coals that were its eyes. She wasn't struggling; she just hung flaccidly as it gripped her throat even tighter.

It turned its glare back upon Bobby as he stood...helpless...immobile. With a savage thrust, it stabbed its claws into her solar plexus reaching deep. It grabbed her beating heart, and ripped it out of her chest.

Bobby woke up screaming in the late afternoon sunshine. Gasping for air, and fending off the horrible sight, his arms slashed through the fading dreamscape.

Leaping up, he frantically searched the camp until he located Abby. She stared back as did everyone else within earshot. Suzi stood nearest to him.

"Are you all right?" she asked.

It took a moment for him to recognize her and respond. "No...I don't

## CHAPTER TWENTY

think I am," he replied in a voice that revealed the degree of terror he had just experienced.

Suzi put her hands on his shoulders and rubbed gently. It felt soothing, and he began to relax.

Abby walked over and took his head in her hands and studied his face. She shared a worried look with Suzi, who squeezed one last time and went to sit down.

"What was it, Bobby?" she asked as she led him back to his chair. She took his hand and they sat down.

"I had a really terrible nightmare. I dreamed you got hurt. I felt helpless. My worst fears always seem to come true in dreams. Sometimes I'm not even aware of what it is I'm afraid of until a dream rubs my nose in it."

He looked deep in her eyes. "I know you can take care of yourself, and I don't want this to sound macho, but stay close to me tonight, and let's protect each other, okay?"

"We're already doing that," she answered.

Bobby sat with Abby and surveyed the afternoon scenery. It was beautiful, but he knew somewhere in that landscape, hidden from view, was their enemy. *It could be on the cliff above us right now, or maybe in the river.*

At that moment he heard a sound from upstream. It was the distant drone of a single engine aircraft, miles away but definitely in the canyon. It was the first airplane he had heard since Indian Creek.

"Listen!" he shouted as he ran to the edge of the river.

Jerry, Jim, and Abby all ran to join him. They too heard the hum of its engine, though it was too far away for any to see.

"Someone's flying to the ranch—I'd bet money on it," Jim said.

"That means someone will be looking for us. Once they see the carnage at the ranch, they'll come looking for survivors," Jerry said.

"Or suspects," Jim added.

# 21

## SUNDAY, COMING DOWN

Jake Ellison's phone rang at 10:00 am Sunday morning just as he finished shaving the last stroke with his trusty Gillette single edge. He quickly toweled his face and ran into his living area to catch it on the third ring. He always caught it by the third ring. That way, he reasoned, whoever called had to figure he was busy.

He was surprised to find Claire Mitchell, the emergency dispatcher in Salmon, on the other end of the line. He had expected Brenda, or someone else at the ranger station, calling with a question. Claire sounded dead serious.

"Jake, Sheriff Bonham told me to call you since the Middle Fork is under Forest Service jurisdiction."

"What's up, Claire?"

"Maybe nothing, but a call came in from a ten-year-old boy on channel nine. He reported picking up a Mayday call from the Victor Ranch. Jake, whoever broadcast that call said over a dozen people had been killed."

Jake swallowed hard. After a few seconds of silence, he asked: "Do you know the boy?"

"No, I don't, but I know his folks, they're good people, and something in his manner, and the tone of his voice, told me that he wasn't foolin' around. Now the guy that he heard could be a different story."

"How did the guy say the people were killed?" asked Jake.

"According to the kid, the sender was off the air by the time he got to the unit to respond."

"Did you try to reach the ranch by radio?"

"Yeah, there was no answer. The air service usually gets at least one call a day from them, but they haven't gotten a call since Friday afternoon. That's two days and on a weekend. It could be a coincidence, but if what the kid says is true, you may have a killer on the loose."

"A killer? You said people had been killed, but you didn't say anything about a killer," he said, beginning to feel uneasy.

"Well I am now. That's what the kid heard."

"Can you remember anything else he heard?" he asked with growing concern.

"No, that was everything. The sheriff said that when you fly out there to check it out, if there's anything to it, he'll bring some deputies and come himself. He'll even call in the State Criminal Investigation Unit from Boise, but he can't act until you request help for a specific violation. So call on the plane's radio as soon as you find out, and I'll be listening for you."

"I suppose the plane is already waiting to take off, courtesy of the sheriff," he said hoping to convey more than a trace of resentment in his voice.

"You guessed it. He also suggested that you take your cannon with you. He said you'd know what he meant."

"I know what he means," Jake replied. "I'll call you from the ranch, oh and Claire?"

"Yes?"

"Thanks for ruining what could have been a nice Sunday at home."

"Goodbye Jake, be careful."

"Goodbye."

He was already dressed. He'd had no intentions of staying home; he had planned to drive to Salmon to see a woman he'd met the previous week.

*Now my day's shot to hell for sure.* "This has got to be a mistake." He walked to his dresser, and opened the top, middle drawer. His *cannon* rested on several pairs of underwear: a single-action Super Ruger Blackhawk .44 magnum.

He strapped the holster onto his belt and tied the rawhide strap around his leg to prevent it from bouncing up and down against his thigh. He hoped it would discourage any would-be lawbreaker just from its size and from the intimidation factor of its "Dirty Harry" reputation as the biggest handgun in the world. Of course, he knew the .454 Casell Magnum was now the biggest, but not many lawbreakers knew, nor cared that much about the difference. It was still a cannon. He locked the cabin and jumped into his Jeep.

The valley of the Middle Fork looked as beautiful and peaceful as it always

## CHAPTER TWENTY ONE

did. A shiny ribbon of river ran through the twisting canyons. Jake could see the mountains below and tried to imagine how anything bad could happen in such a Garden of Eden.

He hadn't told the pilot much—just that nobody had responded to several radio calls to the ranch. He didn't like to engage Frank in conversation too often, since the man was illiterate and opinionated on just about every topic. Jake preferred to stay quiet for most of the flight.

From appearances, Frank didn't come across as possessing enough intelligence to actually fly an airplane. Instead, Jake thought he would look more at home with a double-barrel shotgun in hand, a grin on his grisly face, forcing some river traveler to squeal like a pig.

As they approached the ranch, Jake told Frank to make a low pass and circle once around the entire area to see if anything was out of the ordinary. The engine roared as the plane banked to a fifty-degree angle.

Everything appeared normal except for a broken window. Even so, the shattered glass and the lack of activity below struck him as foreboding elements. A part of Jake Ellison wanted to tell Frank that everything seemed okay; let's go back—false alarm, but he tried to bury his fear, and remained silent while Frank lined up on the airfield. Just before Frank cut his speed, Jake said, "Before you land, fly upriver for a few miles."

"Would you make up yer damn mind?"

Jake felt slightly perturbed at Frank's attitude but he explained anyway. "I didn't see any boats on the river, did you?"

"Come to think of it, not a damn one."

"Let's check out as far as Tappan Falls—see if we can find some floaters. Then we'll come back."

Frank pulled the plane back up and flew upstream. After ten minutes they hadn't seen a single raft. Usually, people were spaced a day apart. Six launches, three commercial, and three private were allowed per day.

Jake didn't know what the reason for the lack of boaters might be, but he didn't like it. He told Frank to go back to the ranch, unable to put it off any longer.

Landing the plane with only a few minor bounces, Frank jammed both feet to the floor on the plane's brakes; they stopped well inside the boundaries of the small airstrip. The Cessna taxied to the end of the field nearest the ranch house where Frank killed the engine.

"Well, let's go," Jake said as he climbed out of the aircraft.

"I notice you're wearing your "hog leg." Now I don't know what you heard happened here, but I don't think I want to be part of it if it involves carryin' guns. It just ain't me," Frank confessed.

"All right, be a chicken shit. I'm just wearing my gun to be on the safe side," Jake answered.

"Well, let's just say I don't want to lose my damn hearing in case you have to fire that thing—just to stay on the safe side."

Jake couldn't figure out how to change Frank's closed mind—a mind that earned him the reputation of being as stubborn as a mule. His cold gray eyes hadn't blinked, and his expression looked as if he considered requests for more than flying beyond what his job description stated. *If he could even read it.* Jake thought for a moment and became dead serious.

"Okay Frank. You stay here, but if you hear a gunshot, call Claire and tell her to get the sheriff here as fast as possible. That'll mean there's trouble—big trouble," Jake advised. "All kidding aside, someone called from here on the radio saying that a bunch of people had been murdered."

Frank recoiled, and his eyes widened, one of the few times Jake had seen him speechless.

Jake continued. "Did you notice that nobody came out to greet us? And we should have seen at least half a dozen boats upriver from here. Something's weird about this. Anyway, like I said, I'm not kidding. If you hear a shot, call for help."

Frank found his voice. "Shheeeeit Jake!" I ain't about to go in there, and you shouldn't go in by yerself."

"If you'll just call like I asked, I'll be happy. All right, Frank?"

"You sure we shouldn't just call now?" Frank asked looking around nervously.

"I'd never hear the last of it if I called in and nothing was wrong," Jake pointed out. "Just stay put, keep your eyes open and listen for a shot. I'll be back as soon as I find out what's going on."

"Awright, but chew be careful."

"I plan to do just that," Jake said as he turned and made his way toward the lifeless ranch house.

He walked slowly. The silence of the afternoon seemed strange. Ordinarily, Scout, the owner's German Shepherd would have been all over him, licking and jumping.

The wind in the pines bordering the airstrip was the only noise he could hear except for the popping sound of the plane's engine cooling. He took a

## CHAPTER TWENTY ONE

deep breath of the pine-scented air. He loved that smell, a main reason he had joined the Forest Service years ago.

He loved being outdoors, especially in the mountains, in the pines. Today it reassured him. Things couldn't be bad when they smell this good, he thought as he approached the side of the house.

He really didn't want to go inside unless it became absolutely necessary, so he walked around to the rear where he had noticed the broken window. The glass sprinkled all over the ground as if it had exploded out from the dining hall.

He picked up an unpleasant odor within ten feet of the broken window. Jake drew his gun as he neared it. He peered into the dining hall and saw what looked to be the end result of a barroom brawl.

The stench almost knocked him down. He ran twenty feet back to get a fresh breath of air. He had a weak stomach, especially when it came to bad smells, and this was a very bad smell.

Walking around the building, he cautiously looked into each window as he passed. He saw nothing but had a sinking feeling the call had been real. That meant he was going to have to go inside the ranch house to continue his investigation. Needing real proof before he called in John Bonham and ordered the SCI-Unit, he walked around to the front porch. Real proof meant a dead body, nothing more—nothing less.

The front door had been left open—*as if someone departed in a hurry*. He stuck his head in and called, "Hello?" His voice sounded shaky and higher than normal.

No answer.

He crept into the front room where nothing seemed out of the ordinary, except that no one stood behind the counter to sell beer and cigarettes.

He moved through the room and into the hall. As he walked its length, he followed the big magnum into each room, until he finally came to the dining hall where again the smell of something terrible assaulted his nostrils.

The odor was intolerable; he turned and walked quickly back up the hall to the restroom where he pulled several paper towels out of the dispenser. He wet them slightly and poured some of the fragrant soap onto them. He walked back to the door and held the towels over his nose with his left hand. Jake clutched the gun in his right hand, and walked into the dining hall. The smell got stronger even through the wet towels, but they at least made it bearable.

He really wanted to find some proof and get back to the plane to call it in. At that moment, his main desire in life became getting far away from the

Victor Ranch, and the sooner he was finished here, the sooner he would be gone.

He heard buzzing in the kitchen and the hum of a generator. Otherwise, total quiet. *Flies?* He opened the double doors and looked into the dusky twilight of the kitchen. He could barely see in the dimness, and the flies were so thick he had to constantly swat them out of his face.

Nervously searching for a switch just inside the door, he found it and turned on the light. He discovered an abattoir—a blood bath. The bright light intensified the evidence of butchery and made everything vivid but unreal. *Still, no body.*

Jake tasted bile rise in his throat. This was not what he had expected to find. A Forest Ranger was supposed to catch rule violators, administer policy of the Forest Service, and answer questions about the wilderness areas.

*This—this was definitely not in the job description.*

Although horrified, he continued deeper into the kitchen. Rounding the cabinet, he found his evidence: a body lying on the floor. He noticed blood splattered all around the room, and, much to his dismay, vomit.

It was all his poor stomach could stand. He heaved in great spasms, spewing his lunch into the miasma. He gagged and coughed for several minutes, while holding his gun out of the spray. Each time he thought he had finished, he would gasp in a large breath of the effluvium and start again. It might have gone on indefinitely, but Jake ran out of bile.

He began backing slowly out of the kitchen. Once in the dining hall, he broke into a dead run for the front door. As he entered the concession area, he stopped, and bent at the waist trying to catch his breath.

Something had caught in his throat. Choking, with eyes watering, he decided to grab a soda behind the bar. He figured that would also remedy the terrible, puke after-taste. Keeping his gun in front of him, he stumbled behind the bar to get the drink and kicked something heavy. When it came to rest he could see that it was a helmet. He could also see that it was not empty. A head was still strapped tightly into it, and the very dead face of its inhabitant stared with eyeless sockets directly at Jake's feet.

Suddenly, he wasn't concerned with the taste in his mouth, or the chunk caught in his throat. Jake shook all over, terrified more than he had been since he had confronted an angry grizzly bear on The Yellowstone River five years before.

It began to dawn on him how far someone had gone across the line to commit a crime like this. Then, an icy feeling danced in his empty gut. A tingling

## CHAPTER TWENTY ONE

fear that maybe, just maybe, whoever did this might still be inside the ranch house. A chill crept across the back of his neck like the unwanted caress of a centipede.

He bolted for the exit and ran as fast as his shaky legs would carry him. Rocketing through the door, he sprinted toward the landing strip. From 200 yards, he could see that the door of the plane was open.

*Where's Frank?* He continued running at top speed, closing the distance between himself and the empty plane.

When he arrived, he glanced inside. No evidence of blood, or struggle. He felt surprised that he wasn't even out of breath.

"FRANK!" He shouted. "FRANK!"

No answer.

Jake reached into the cockpit and grabbed the microphone.

"MAYDAY! MAYDAY!" he screamed into it.

No answer.

"OHJESUSOHJESUSOHJESUS," he said to himself. The prospect of being alone right now was not one to his liking. He couldn't fly the plane, he couldn't get the radio to work, and somebody might have killed his pilot.

He saw movement in the bushes on the western side of the airstrip, closest to the plane. Leveling his .44 magnum, he cocked the hammer back, aimed it at the center of the movement, and began to squeeze on the trigger.

He saw Frank's hands go up over his head a second after he emerged from the bushes. A roll of toilet paper unfurled on the ground toward Jake.

"Man, I'm glad I already shit, cause I'da just messed my britches if I hadn't," Frank said, his hands still in the air.

Jake looked at Frank, at the gun in his hand, and carefully released the hammer as he slowly lowered it into his holster. His whole body trembled; he leaned back against the side of the plane. "I almost blew you into the next world," he said as he finally exhaled.

"Well thanks for changing your damn mind. What the hell is going on Jake? This ain't like you pointing guns at people."

"Can you get that radio working?" Jake asked, still shaking.

"Of course, I just need to turn it on."

"Well do it! I need to call emergency dispatch, and I can only go through this once." Sweat poured off his face.

Frank reached into the cockpit, switched on the radio, and gave the microphone to Jake.

"This is Jake Ellison—come in Claire."

After five seconds came the faint acknowledgement:

"Roger Jake, this is Claire, over."

"Claire, call the SCI-Unit and the sheriff. Tell them to get here as soon as possible. It's real bad—your kid wasn't fooling, over."

"Oh my God," Claire said. "Jake, I'm going to call Sheriff Bonham. He said that he'd wait at home until I heard from you. He's got Earl Bohannan, and Joe Bob Everett on standby to meet him at the airstrip. He said they'd be there within an hour-and-a-half from the time you call, so hang in there. I'll call the SCI-Unit too, but they probably won't be there before dark, over."

*Before dark?* Jake thought. He hadn't realized that his position required him to stay.

"Jake? Are you still there?"

A moment of silence, then: "Claire, I don't really feel like waiting around here. The ranch looks like a slaughterhouse. I can't believe what I just saw, it's inconceivable." He tried to catch his breath.

"JAKE! Don't say any more on the air. We don't know who's listening," she ordered.

He realized she was right, but he didn't like for her to order him around, especially on the airwaves. In the present circumstance however, he let it slide.

"Okay Claire, but I got to tell you, I don't like it here, so you get John, and you tell him to make it fast."

"I will Jake, just sit tight. He'll be there before you know it, over."

"Claire, tell him to bring a bigger cannon, over and out."

Jake looked at Frank, some of his own fear showed in the pilot's eyes.

"What the hell did you see in there, Jake? I've never seen you like this before. Hell, I didn't think you could even get scared," Frank stated.

"Frank, get into the plane and pull it over into the middle of the landing strip so we can see everything. I don't like being so close to the ranch house."

The engines turned over. Jake kept his hand resting on the butt of his gun while Frank taxied the Cessna 180 over to the center of the runway. He turned off the magnetos and they listened as the engine's roar diminished to silence.

"Let's get out of the plane, Jake. It's too damn hot in here."

"If you'd seen what I just saw, you wouldn't want to get out."

Jake explained what he found in detail, and Frank began to sweat profusely. It was hot, but he suspected the perspiration rolling down Frank was not just from the heat.

## CHAPTER TWENTY ONE

"Claire said they would be here in an hour and a half. Well, I've got five hours of fuel, and I think I'd feel a lot better passing time circlin' up in the sky."

"Do it!" Jake exclaimed. "The Forest Service will definitely reimburse you."

Frank taxied to one end of the field and turned facing into the wind. He pulled the throttle all the way open and began picking up speed. At seventy miles per hour, he would pull the Cessna off the ground with full flaps. Faster and faster the plane raced until they were up in the air, soaring over the ranch house.

Frank looked back at the ranch and thought he saw a huge black bear at the southern end of the runway. His conscious mind registered it as a bear, but he felt cold fingers massage the back of his scalp. He had only seen it for an instant but felt something tugging at his narrow view of reality. Something about the bear was wrong.

• • •

Bobby watched the shadows creep closer to camp. The sun sank lower on the mountains behind them, causing a dark line to visibly move from the cliff towards the water. He had a dreadful feeling—knowing night was coming. It was relentless; an unalterable fact, that it would soon render them a small island of firelight in a vast sea of darkness.

*God, we're vulnerable,* he thought. Last week he had worried about money, drunk drivers, criminals, all the petty day-to-day anxieties that plague twenty-first century human experience. This evening, he worried about a hellish predator that murdered people as if they were insects. Like ancient peoples, even though we're civilized, we still find ourselves prey to the night hunter.

"Time to draw for shifts," Jerry said as he held out his "Aussie" hat to him. Bobby drew a piece of paper with a two on it. That meant he had the second shift from 1:00 to 4:00 am. Jerry ambled around until everyone had drawn his or her respective times. Abby, Beth, Suzi, and Linda had drawn the first shift; Bobby, Jerry, Scott, and Jacques had the second, while Plato, and Jim got the third. A second drawing was held to see which two people would have to double up on the third shift. Bobby and Beth were the unlucky winners.

*Thank God I'm not rowing tomorrow,* he thought, although his concern raced ahead to the rapids in the Impassable Canyon, some of the most challenging on the entire trip. Abby would be calling the shots. It would be okay. And she would probably get more sleep.

Bobby moved his chair closer and closer to the river to stay in the sunlight, finally giving up when the shadow passed into the water. He carried his chair back up to the fire and placed it next to Jerry's.

"You ever notice how personal hygiene is the first thing to go to hell in a crisis?" Bobby asked after looking him over for a moment.

"Yeah, as a matter of fact, I'm surprised you're not drawing flies."

"I only brought it up because I thought I smelled the outhouse, and the wind was blowing from your direction," Bobby retorted.

"Well that may be, but you smell like you've been bobbing for cat turds in a litter box," Jerry blasted back.

"You win, asshole, I can't top that."

"You can't? Shit, you must be sick or something cause you're usually the grossest sumbitch in the world. Just look at you."

They both laughed, and it quickly became contagious. One by one, they all began laughing. After a few minutes, the outburst started to die down. Bobby could just tell that everyone felt better, even though nothing in the situation had changed.

*That's it,* Bobby thought. *Laughter makes us feel better. Where there's laughter, there's hope.*

Though totally spent, he felt better somehow, though he couldn't understand how he continued to move around.

He sat in the sand next to Phydeaux and scratched behind her ear. He then searched and found the trigger spot on her back. Scratching it caused her to pound the ground involuntarily with her rear leg.

He was petting her and telling her what a good dog she was, when Jacques returned from the kitchen box.

"You know, if it wasn't for Phydeaux, we'd probably still be at Pistol Creek in the same condition as those people at the camp today," Bobby said.

"Yeah, she's definitely worth her weight in gold on this trip. I think I'll keep her," Jacques said with obvious pride.

"I'm going to get me a good ol' dog when I get back home. I haven't had a dog in over seven years." He fell silent in his memories. For a moment he thought he might start crying, but the feeling passed. "I got real close to one special dog. Then, when he was thirteen, his arthritis had gotten so bad I had to put him to sleep. Worst day of my life, this trip not included of course.

"Anyway, I didn't think I'd ever be able to have another dog, but now I

## CHAPTER TWENTY ONE

believe I'm ready. Phydeaux reminds me of all that's noble and good in dogs. Besides, she's one hell of a monster alarm." He shook her face with his hands.

He started to get up, but Phydeaux jumped on him knocking him over. She licked his face. They wrestled, though Bobby had no idea where his energy came from.

He looked up to see Jacques chuckling at him. Laughter sounded so good. Once again, Bobby realized that in the darkest hours, laughter was a most necessary element for survival.

*This would surely qualify,* he thought.

Jim walked over, and helped Bobby up.

"That plane's been flying around somewhere upstream for over an hour now. I wonder if it's Search and Rescue," he said.

"God, I hope so, but there aren't any landing strips this far down. I don't think there's even a chance of them getting us out of here tonight," Bobby replied.

Darkness finally encroached into the canyon.

# 22

### REINFORCEMENTS

"Frank, this is Sheriff Bonham, come in, over."

"Hello Sheriff, we're sure glad to hear your voice. What's your twenty, over."

"We'll be landing at the ranch in about fifteen minutes. Is Jake Ellison handy?"

"Ten-four—just a second."

Frank handed the microphone to Jake.

"This is Jake."

"Say over," Frank instructed.

"Over," he said.

"Jake, Claire told me that you went inside and found our suspicions to be correct. What did you see?"

"Sheriff, I can't tell you what I saw over the radio, but it's as bad as it can be. It's so bad that I wish I didn't have to go back…uh, over."

"Well, you'll have to go back in so you can show me everything that you touched. Then, when the boys from Boise get over here they can print you so as to not mix you up as a possible suspect. Anyway, we'll see you in a few minutes, and then we'll talk. Over and out."

Frank and Jake circled once and headed back into the wind. Bringing the plane in with a slight bounce, Frank taxied up to the end of the field nearest the house and pulled off the runway.

Jake looked at the ranch house as if it were haunted. He dreaded going back in no matter how many people went with him. Evil emanations reached all the way from the house to the plane, where they stirred his spinal fluids, and squeezed his bulging bladder. Even in the heat he shook from the chill.

It wasn't long before he heard the hum of an engine.

"Sounds like a Lycoming—Cherokee 140 B—must be Charlie's plane." Frank informed him. Then he saw the older aircraft as it made its final approach. It barely cleared the trees at the far end but landed smooth as glass.

Jake knew the other pilot, and Frank was right: it was Charlie Simpson. A flyer every bit as good as Frank and happened to be his main competitor. Both men came from a totally different breed of pilots. They landed in places that a British Harrier would have trouble landing and flew in weather when most people wouldn't even go outside—constantly putting themselves in harm's way.

*Well, it looks as if Mr. Harm has already been here*, Jake thought.

From beside Frank's Cessna, Jake watched the men exit the aircraft. John Bonham, Earl Bohannan, and Joe Bob Everett were all big men. Amazing that Charlie managed to squeeze them into the four-seater and still found enough elbowroom to actually fly the plane.

Jake Ellison had always felt tall at six feet, but these men looked huge even to him. Sheriff Bonham stood six-foot-three, and 240 pounds, hard as a bowling ball, and he appeared to have only a trunk and a head. No neck.

Earl Bohannan passed six-foot-two and a good 220 pounds, but he wasn't fat. Jake figured he still could move rattlesnake-quick whenever the need arose. A person who seldom overlooked anything, the chief deputy was cunning and headed what was known as the Major Crimes Division of the sheriff's department.

Since the budget cuts, the sheriff's office no longer separated murder from rape, or robbery from narcotics. Any heavy felony got dumped into Earl's lap to solve, and from what Jake had heard, he was usually successful.

Last, but definitely not least, came Joe Bob Everett. Resembling a polar bear, he stood six-foot-six, weighed about 265 pounds, and had a physique comparable to the Incredible Hulk. Jake knew it was not wise to anger Joe Bob. He'd watched the big deputy beat five loggers half to death in a Challis bar one night. Within a few minutes, three of the loggers awaited ambulance transport to the Salmon emergency clinic. The other two needed intensive care—the type only available in Boise.

"Sheriff, I'm glad you're here. I've never seen anything like this. You're not going to believe it," Jake said, surprised by how calm he sounded.

John Bonham stopped walking, turned his head and spat brown mucilage on the ground beside him. "Sun's already below the rim; I s'pose we'd better

## CHAPTER TWENTY TWO

get to the house and have a look before the lab boys get here." He turned to his deputies, but mainly looked at Joe Bob. "Now I don't want y'all to touch nothin'. Understand?" the sheriff asked in a commanding tone.

"Yeah sheriff," Joe Bob answered.

Earl nodded.

The closer to the house they came, the faster Jake's heart beat. "I don't want to go back in, John."

"Well, technically this is your jurisdiction, so I'm afraid you'll have to, Jake. I'm here at the request of the Forest Service, and you're the district ranger—you need to be present on the scene. Besides, like I said, I need to know everything you touched while you was in there."

"That's easy, I didn't touch anything," Jake returned.

"Jake, for Christ's sake, you're a grown man. Now, pull yourself together, and let's go take a look at what you said you saw."

Jake shuddered involuntarily as the two big deputies looked on. He wasn't so scared now. Instead he felt sick at the thought of seeing the body again and smelling the stench of the kitchen. He could see his reaction hadn't been lost on Earl Bohannan.

*Earl's the only one with sense enough to be scared.*

After a moment of silence, Jake spoke, "Okay John, it's getting dark, and I don't suppose we'll be leaving for a while, so I guess we have to go in. But just for the record, our jurisdictions overlap here, so don't pull that shit on me; I know better."

"Jake, I'm just trying to get you to help. You're all right now that we're here. You and ol' Frank can leave right after the SCI-Unit gets through with you. They might need some blood and hair samples from you to make their job a little easier, but after that you're free to leave if you want," the sheriff said as he motioned toward the ranch house. He craned his neck to spit once again, then pulled a large wad of chewing tobacco out of his jaw and threw it toward the airstrip.

The house looked dark and forbidding. The light in the kitchen still shone from Jake's earlier visit, but it filtered to a dull glow in the windows of the house, giving the appearance of sinister eyes watching their approach.

Jake thought about flying out at night. He didn't like flying over the mountains during the day, but at night, he really hated the thought.

This night, however, he would be more than happy to go. In fact, since the sheriff had mentioned that he could leave as soon as the state cops were through with him, he felt anxiety release its gut-wrenching grip. The crime team would be coming real soon, he thought, as he walked toward the house. They would ask him some questions, fingerprint him, and then he and old Frank would be on their way back to Challis. In fact, if they got back early enough, he planned to go to the Crazy Horse Lounge, and get as close to "brain damaged" as he could in whatever amount of time the bar remained open.

Twilight's last gleaming had acquiesced to night, with a faint glow along the ridge remaining as the only evidence that a day had been. They walked toward the house, leaving Frank and Charlie by their planes.

The front door beckoned—still open from Jake's earlier, rapid departure—and darkness already filled the interior of the room. Pools of shadow concealed the dusky concession area.

The sheriff drew his service revolver, turned on his flashlight, and slowly entered. He moved the beam around the room until he found a switch to his right. He pushed it up, and light filled the spaces around him. The room looked deserted, so he motioned for the others to follow him. They all walked in—Jake Ellison last.

"I think there's something behind the concession counter that you should see," Jake warned. "It's real bad."

Earl Bohannan had seen many bad things in his twenty-five years of law enforcement. Most of the bad things had been at car wrecks, shootings, cattle mutilations, or the finding of the occasional decomposed body, but what he saw behind the bar soared to the top of his bad things list.

Walking to the end of the counter, he noted a helmet on the floor faced away from him. He couldn't see the face, but he saw the glistening white of a vertebrae, barely visible, sticking out from under the helmet and knew what it held.

"Holy shit!" he gasped. At first he couldn't make his feet move. He took a deep breath and exhaled as he walked forward. Because it might contain evidence, he didn't want to touch it, so turning it around was out of the question. Still, he did want to get a closer look. The helmet faced into a corner, so Earl got on his knees and peered around it at an angle.

The sheriff and Joe Bob had walked to the end of the counter behind him and watched.

"God Almighty! How the hell could anybody do this?" he asked in revulsion. He stood and backed away, then turned to the others.

"John, what could someone use to twist a head off a body?"

# CHAPTER TWENTY TWO

"That's got a head in it?"

"That and part of a neck," Earl replied. "The spine looks like a screw tip. I've never seen anything like it. Somebody twisted this fucking head off a body."

"There's more in the kitchen," Jake told him as he turned away from the counter and pretended to study the beer clock on the opposite wall.

Everybody left the concession area and conducted a room-to-room search, together. Their investigation revealed nothing, until they reached the dining area.

Earl took notice of the pipe lying next to the door; there were marks on them where they had been crushed. He noted that they appeared to be the same width as the doorjamb but didn't know what significance that might have, so he filed it away for future reference.

Upon entering the dining hall, he noticed the overturned tables and broken chairs. Joe Bob flipped the light switch, and the room ignited with an eerie ambience.

The lawmen had all smelled blood on numerous occasions. The coppery smell had faded, but its mix with decomposing flesh had gotten stronger in the stifling heat, leaving little doubt that at least some carnage remained to be discovered close by.

The big lawmen walked three abreast to the kitchen doors as Jake trailed. Earl entered first and was immediately assaulted by sights, sounds, and smells.

The drone they had thought to be the generator turned out to be flies buzzing by the hundreds. They covered their mouths and noses with their hands as they beheld the grisly scene. Vomit mixed with rotting flesh formed a vile gas that turned every stomach in the room.

*Investigation called off due to nausea*, Earl thought to himself.

"My God in heaven!" Joe Bob shouted as he rested his hand on his revolver.

"I never saw one person with so much blood in them," John said.

"Somebody cleaned and gutted him like a god dam deer," Joe Bob said, sounding incredulous.

Earl walked back toward them and said, "John, there's another one in the closet. It's a woman, I think. Somebody went out of the way to make it hard to tell. She's been cleaned and gutted just like this one."

The closeness of the kitchen made it hard for them all to see. But Earl could tell—the sheriff saw. "What the hell happened here? Why would somebody mutilate people this way?" he asked. He found this frighteningly similar to the White River killings of the Britton family. Now it did affect their jurisdiction, and John would have to find the killer or killers to get re-elected.

"By God, I'll get these punks," John said.

Earl knew John Bonham had the habit of always thinking in political terms. John was a good politician, and a reasonably good lawman, but he wasn't a detective. Joe Bob wasn't really a detective either. He just happened to be the biggest, meanest lawman in the State of Idaho. He was mainly along for intimidation.

Earl figured himself to be the only true detective in the bunch. He absorbed crime scenes like an amoeba. At the present he examined what appeared to be bloody dots on the floor of the kitchen.

The dots led out into the dining room toward the door where the PVC pipe had been cracked, but tapered off into nothingness about halfway across the dining area. They looked like strangely shaped platters, and had unusual configurations that resembled old-style football cleats. In places, they appeared to have slid severely scratching the wood.

A logical explanation for all these clues existed, though he couldn't make sense of them yet. They would fall into place—they always did.

He continued searching the kitchen and the storeroom for evidence. *Anything.* He wanted to collar this one fast.

In all his years of law enforcement, he'd never seen a killer as brutal as this one. He also saw the similarity between this and the White River killings. The entire Brittain family had been torn to shreds in much the same way according to a friend with the White River Sheriff's office. He thought of the children that had been killed and mutilated, and he felt his own anger rising. If they did catch up to the killer—or killers—first, he would look the other way while Joe Bob administered a little wild-west justice. Knowing Joe Bob, he figured that it would mean blowing their legs off at the knees with a twelve-gauge shotgun and leaving them to bleed to death in the mountains.

Earl had never considered summarily executing a perpetrator, but then again, he'd never seen anything near this level of violence exhibited by one before. And, with the courts of today…who knows what would happen? Shyster lawyers could get guilty people off. Might even get this guy off.

The thought of shotgun executions reminded him of his own shotgun lying in the back seat of the Cherokee. "Hey John, I think we should get the shotguns," Earl suggested. "It's apparent that whoever did this is crazy. A pistol won't always stop a crazy, but a blast of buckshot will."

"Yeah, I think you got something there. Besides, we still have to check the outbuildings. We might ought to bring Frank and Charlie inside while we're at it; they'd be safer with us, and none of us knows how to fly a plane."

## CHAPTER TWENTY TWO

"Good point," Earl replied.

"Plus, we still don't know how many of them we're dealing with. Could be that a group of river runners took LSD, or angel dust and went over the edge." John pulled a wad of Bull-O-the-Woods out of a small sack and shoved it into his jaw. "You're right about one thing, nobody in their right mind could have done this. Let's go get those shotguns," the sheriff said. "There's not a whole lot else we can do but wait for the state and the feds to get here and take over." They walked back the way they had come.

As Earl led the way out of the ranch house, he noticed the air seemed to lighten. It had been oppressively heavy inside. Outside, it was a summer night with a gentle, cool breeze blowing out of the south. The moon wouldn't be up for sometime yet, which made the Victor Ranch appear as dark as indigo. He observed stars but little else. The only other things he spotted were the two glowing embers over by the planes—the fire on the ends of Charlie and Frank's cigarettes.

They continued walking to the airstrip. The closer they got, the more Earl sensed that something was wrong. The night had become totally quiet except for the sound of their footsteps, which seemed to echo off an invisible wall somewhere in the nearby darkness.

*That's what's wrong.* Charlie and Frank were talkers. Earl began wondering why he couldn't hear the hills and valleys of their conversation. It wasn't probable that the two wouldn't be lying to each other and talking shop.

He squinted his eyes to try to focus on the planes. Then he noticed that the cigarettes didn't really look like cigarettes. Instead, they looked like someone had taken a pumpkin, and carved out only the eyes to make an unfinished jack-o-lantern. *What an imagination.*

When they were less than 100 feet away, he called out:

"Charlie!"

No answer.

"Frank!"

No answer.

After a few seconds, the cigarettes vanished into thin air. They just winked out of existence.

"CHARLIE! The sheriff shouted.

No answer.

"I don't like this," he said as he drew his pistol.

Joe Bob, Earl, and Jake did likewise. The holster snaps and metal against leather sounded loud in the otherwise silent darkness.

"They were there smoking a minute ago, I saw them," Joe Bob said.

"Frank doesn't smoke," Jake informed him.

"What the hell were those two glowing things then?" Joe Bob asked rather confused.

"Good question," Earl replied.

They continued their approach with caution. When they arrived at the planes, Charlie and Frank weren't there. They found no evidence of a struggle; they were just gone.

"Frank did this to me earlier," Jake told them. "He was off in the bushes taking a crap."

"Joe Bob, get our shotguns out of the plane, and let's have a look around—together. Earl, see if you can raise Salmon on the radio. I want to know how long before the cavalry gets here. Then we're going to find our pilots, and if they're trying to be funny, they won't think it's funny when I get through with em'. No sir, I "guaran-goddam-tee" you they won't be laughing."

...

The group's four women had managed to draw the first shift by coincidence. The fire blazed and reflected off the cliff wall and trees surrounding the camp. The women sat together in lawn chairs facing out in four different directions but soon changed to walking sentry-duty in order to stay alert.

After the moon came up, the canyon took on an entirely different facade. It gave off just enough light to create images in the mind. Abby walked the riverside of the camp when movement on the water brought her to a halt. Suzi came up behind her.

"What the hell is that?" she asked.

"Shine the Maglite on it and we'll see," Abby said.

Suzi ran to the table and returned with the flashlight. She turned it on, and the beam cut through the air like a ray gun.

It illuminated an empty raft drifting slowly by, still hidden in the shadows of the opposite cliff. A moment later another floated by, followed by another, and another, until over a dozen had floated past. It felt like watching a ghost parade. Beth and Linda looked on in fascination but kept a nervous watch on the camp in case the rafts were a diversion.

"More than likely the owners are the dead folks we've been passing for the last few days," Suzi said grimly. Eerie sight, seeing them all drift by silent… empty…dead."

## CHAPTER TWENTY TWO

A red raft that looked exactly like the one Abby had rowed up to Indian Creek drifted past. Then a familiar yellow kayak floated by, and Suzi recognized the markings. They had left it up on the bank below Marble Creek.

*Someone put it back in the river, but why? And who?* She wondered.

The sentries became much more alert after the passage of the phantom rafts. Suzi believed the boats were harbingers of something else approaching, something not as benign as empty rafts.

*Something that I injured*, She thought as cold ghost fingers played arpeggios up and down her spine.

Five minutes passed when Abby thought she heard a noise upriver. She noticed Phydeaux looking upstream with her ears standing at attention. The dog growled low in her throat. All four women stopped marching and turned their attention to the river. Phydeaux barked and tugged at her rope. Abby heard a sound similar to the "hee haw" of a rap singer coming from upstream. There were great gasps, countered by loud splashing as the unseen intruder came closer.

"Help me!" someone begged from the darkness.

Several flashlights panned the river. Suddenly, a dark shape sliced across the water and aimed at the shore with considerable speed. It sliced the water so quickly, that it literally skidded up onto the sand beach.

It was a dark, blue kayak; the man inside it looked totally spent, and terrified. He appeared to be in his early twenties, average height and weight, with red hair and freckles.

Standing next to Abby, Suzi had been holding the pistol very steady with her finger on the trigger since the shadow first appeared. She let out a long moan as she lowered the weapon. Beth and Linda ran over to the man and helped him out of the kayak.

He sobbed uncontrollably, and they held him as he staggered to their campfire. Part of it surely had to be the relief at having found other living, human beings, Abby thought; the other part sounded like a dark, gut-wrenching sadness that expanded from within him, begging to be set free.

Phydeaux's barking awakened everyone in camp including Bobby. Activity bustled all around the camp.

Plato poured a glass of Stoli's, then hurried to the man and offered it to him. The man took it and gulped it down, not realizing it was vodka until he exhaled and tasted the alcohol.

"Water," he gasped, holding his throat.

Jerry handed him a canteen, which he emptied in less than thirty seconds. He put it down, as his wild eyes scanned the faces around him.

"It's all right now," Bobby assured him, knowing that "all right" was a temporary condition at best, and subject to rapid deterioration.

"When you can, tell us what happened," Abby said soothingly.

The young man looked up at her, then at Bobby.

"Do you know? Do you know it's out there?" he asked looking at Bobby like a man pleading for someone to acknowledge his sanity.

For a moment, Bobby took him to mean: "it's out there—right now—just outside the firelight." He gripped his K-Bar and looked around nervously for a few seconds until he realized that the man meant it was out there—somewhere.

Bobby suspected that if he had been alone like this poor guy, he wouldn't have looked, or acted nearly as rational. The only comfort he'd had the last few days had been from the company of his friends. "Yes, we know. Can you talk yet?"

The man hung his head and cried again-a heart-rending wail, followed by more uncontrolled weeping.

Phydeaux, who hadn't trusted the intruder at first, made her way next to him. She pushed her nose under his arm trying to comfort him. She whined and stuck her cold nose into the young kayaker's ear, on his neck, in his face, until he was finally brought out of his despair. He began gently scratching the side of her head. The others watched in silence as Phydeaux worked dog magic on the man. At long last, his crying abated to the point where he could speak.

"My name is Daniel—Daniel Webb. My group was camped at Hospital Bar. Last night, about three hours after the storm hit, something attacked our camp, something big—REAL big, and faster than anything I've ever seen. Three people went down before we even knew anything was wrong. It moved through our camp and didn't make a sound. Not a single sound. Killed four more over at the hot springs on the south end of the camp. I could hear them screaming…." He began crying again, but regained his self control much faster as he returned to his story. "My brother and I each grabbed an oar and ran for some big boulders behind the camp. I set the oar against it and shinnied up it until I got on top of the rock.

# CHAPTER TWENTY TWO

"My brother did the same thing, but he wasn't fast enough. The monster went for him before he reached the top. It picked up the oar with him on it and slammed him into the rock." Daniel tightened visibly. Bending at the waist, he began rocking slowly back and forth. Tears flowed down his freckled cheeks.

He looked at Abby. "It picked him up and tore him open—just like you'd tear and peel an orange. Bit a big chunk out of his insides." He sobbed and had trouble speaking. Bobby found his own eyes clouding at the man's loss. Daniel rubbed his eyes and took a deep breath before continuing.

"It was dark, but I could still see it in the moonlight. It ran back to camp and dropped Jonah, my brother, in the dirt to die. Then it finished off the rest of the group in one shot. They tried to escape in the rafts. I don't know how it killed them, but I could hear their screams cut off, one by one. The silence got to me a lot worse 'cause I knew it would come back for me. Then I saw its eyes—Jesus God." He shuddered. Jerry handed him a second canteen, and he drank several small sips before continuing. "It covered 100 yards of rough terrain in about six seconds. I could see it building up speed to jump up onto the rock with me, so I took the oar and held it like a lance. I almost dropped it when it got within twenty yards cause I could see it. Most horrible thing I ever saw.

"When it jumped, I finally came to my senses, and held up the oar. I jammed it right in the throat. It almost knocked me off the other side of the rock, but I stayed on. It put me flat on my back, and I had the breath knocked out of me, but I stayed on that rock. At first I figured I must have killed it judging from the impact, and the fact that I'd caught it so square.

"I peeked over the edge, and saw it rolling on the ground. I think I hurt it pretty bad though, 'cause I could see it thrashing around holding its neck. But it still didn't make a sound. That's what scared me the most—not one sound."

Daniel fell silent for a moment, and Bobby listened for the night noises. He heard an owl hoot from upriver and figured they were safe for the moment. The young kayaker drank from the canteen again, and then he went on.

"It ran toward the river, and I couldn't see it anymore. Spent the rest of the night on that rock." Daniel shivered as he recalled, "It got really cold and I was scared—more scared than I've ever been in my life—" He stopped abruptly. "Jonah's really dead. He was my twin brother; we grew up together—but—I don't feel anything. I should be feeling something—we did everything together—now, I'll never see him again." Again Daniel held himself and rocked back and forth.

*We're losing him*, Bobby thought.

"Daniel, what else happened? You said it was cold," Bobby said, encouraging him to continue.

Daniel seemed puzzled for a moment but then remembered where he was, what he was doing, and continued his story.

"I stayed awake all night watching the river from that rock thinking it would come back for me. The worst part was after the moon went down and it got dark again." Daniel put his face into his hands and rubbed.

Bobby remembered watching that same moonset. He and Jim had been drinking hot coffee while standing close to the fire for warmth. Bobby's respect for Daniel's survival ability went up another notch. No matter how bad off you think you are, somebody else has it worse, he thought as the young man continued.

"Later, I saw something big and dark moving through camp and figured my time had come. Turned out to be a bear. I heard it rummaging around in the coolers. Scared me at first, but I got to where I was glad it was there. It must have eaten until it made itself sick on cookies and candy, 'cause I heard it puke. It left just before dawn. I saw its shape wandering up the bank. Never thought I'd be sorry to see a bear leave, but I was. Somehow, it being there made me feel safe at least. Like it was my ally or something.

"A while after it left, I heard a noise above me on the rocks; turned out to be a small herd of mountain goats. They stayed until dawn.

"Once the sun cleared the ridge, I saw all the bodies. It hadn't been so bad in the dark, but in the sunlight…" Daniel took another pull on the canteen and wiped his mouth on his paddle jacket sleeve. He looked at Bobby and said, "I knew I had to get off of the rock, and that was the hardest part. As fast as that thing moved, I wouldn't have stood a chance if it had still been hiding, waiting for me. So I stayed on the rock until about 10:00 o'clock this morning—or was it yesterday?

"Then, I finally put the oar over the side, and slid down. I ran to my stuff and gathered up my wet suit, lifejacket, paddle, and a garbage bag. I filled it with what food I could find that the bear hadn't spoiled and threw it into my kayak. I got in and hauled ass. Figured I'd have to send the police back for Jonah's body. There's no way I could have brought him out," he said looking at Bobby for confirmation that he had done nothing wrong. Bobby shook his head and put his hand on Daniel's shoulder. He remembered similar guilt feelings about Gretta. Daniel continued his story.

"I paddled fast, so it would have to hit a moving target. About an hour

## CHAPTER TWENTY TWO

downstream, I came to a big waterfall and ran it without scouting. Nasty hole caught me and rolled me over a few times, but I managed to get back up and escape out the end of it. From there, I fought like crazy to get to the Victor Ranch. I figured they could help me. It took about an hour of constant paddling to get there."

Everyone remained quiet as Daniel spoke. It reminded Bobby of telling scary stories around a campfire when he was young. Only this time, the bogeyman was not make-believe, and he wasn't nearly so far away.

"When I arrived, I could see the ranch-house path from upstream. But when I got closer, I saw that it was there," Daniel said.

"You saw it in daylight?" Bobby asked in astonishment.

"Yes, I saw it—in daylight," Daniel replied with a shudder.

"What did it look like?" Abby wanted to know.

Daniel fell silent for a moment. Then he answered. "It had eyes that made me want to crap my pants—and it was big too—real big, with claws that looked like they could tear a Mac Truck apart. Its hide looked like the darkest shade of black I've ever seen. Almost like watching a cartoon of something from Jurassic Park only in real life. And teeth—but thank God I didn't get close enough to see them too good. It might have had a tail, but I'm not sure. Anyway, I saw it on the beach smelling around like a dog trying to pick up a scent."

Bobby realized that it was probably on the exact spot where they had been only a few hours before, and he wondered if it was his scent the thing trailed.

"It looked up; then I knew it saw me," Daniel said. "Locked those eyes on me, and for a minute, I couldn't move. I just floated, paddle in my hand, scared half to death—frozen solid."

Bobby sat, spellbound. Daniel had come as close as he had—maybe even closer-and lived. Only this kid had actually seen it in sunlight. He admired the young man for having survived when so many others hadn't.

"It walked along beside me on the riverbank. When I finally snapped out of it and paddled like hell to get away, it followed me. It ran along the banks, over rocks, through bushes—I couldn't lose it. It would disappear around rocks, but then reappear traveling over terrain a deer couldn't cover. I paddled as fast as I could, but it kept up with me. After paddling all morning, I thought my arms were going to fall off, but it's amazing what you can do when your life's at stake."

"Tell me about it," Bobby said remembering his Olympic record swim at Aparejo Point. "What happened next?"

"I finally got ahead of it when the left bank turned into a cliff. I thought I'd won, but it jumped into the water and swam almost as fast as it had run. Just like a submarine.

"It swam around the cliff and got out of the water again. It seemed to be a little faster on the land and started closing the gap. The river made a sweeping left turn around a bar, which gave it the advantage. It ran across the bar, cutting my lead to less than thirty feet. Then, thank God, the river turned back to the right, and the left side became impassable. It jumped back into the water and swam after me again. I paddled even harder and faster than I had before. I didn't look back because I could sense it right behind me. I knew if I dropped one stroke, it would close on me, so I kept paddling until my arms finally gave out. I kept getting this terrible feeling that it would never give up 'cause I'd hit it in the neck with the oar."

"You're in good company," Suzi said.

He looked up at her puzzled and tried to smile but fell short. He turned back to Bobby and went on. "Finally, I looked back, and it wasn't there anymore. So I floated on, resting my arms and watching for it. About four or five miles below the ranch, I saw some rafts, so I pulled over to get help. I was going to warn them, but they didn't need it; it had been there already. Dead people in the same condition as the ones at my camp were everywhere."

Bobby affirmed. "We saw them too."

Plato and Bobby filled Daniel in on their own experiences, while the rest of the group either went back to bed, or guard duty. Daniel listened to their story with equal interest and cringed when they told of the findings at the ranch and the attack at Sheep Creek. Phydeaux remained next to him, and he seemed to take extra comfort in her attention.

"We've never seen it all at once, how big did it look to you?" Bobby asked.

"It was about eight or nine feet tall when it stood, but mostly it crouched. Its body vaguely resembled a human's, but it wasn't anything close to human. More like your worst nightmare taken to the limit."

*You've actually seen my worst nightmare*, Bobby thought.

"It looked like if you touched its skin it would be slick. But like I said before, the one thing that stood out most were its eyes. Like looking at death himself. When it looked at me, I wanted to run, but I froze. I couldn't move; I can't explain why. I was just scared so bad that I couldn't do shit." Daniel looked up at the sky full of stars.

"I can't figure out why my twin brother is dead, and I'm still alive," he said.

## CHAPTER TWENTY TWO

With all their years of studying philosophy, neither Plato nor Bobby had an answer.

Bobby poked the fire with a stick and thought for a moment. The kid must be relieved to find there were indeed others who had been in the wake of the beast, and survived. Now the kid knew he wasn't crazy—at least no more than us.

Bobby figured that silence would be Daniel's worst enemy, so he encouraged him to continue from the point where he had left off.

Again, Daniel started slowly: "Anyway, I couldn't rest there with the dead, so I got back in my yak and took off thinking that it was under the surface of the water, waiting for me." He paused and drew a deep breath. "I wish I'd taken a map or a guidebook, 'cause I never knew where I was.

"I paddled a few more miles until I came to another campsite. No one was there, so I pulled over. I'd just missed a nice spot on the left, and I was thankful to find this one on the right. There was a class-one rapid, just to the left of a boulder bar that looked too deep for the thing to walk across, but too swift and shallow for it to really swim, so I figured it might be safer than some of the other places—at least if it was still on the left side of the river."

"You just described Woolard Creek Camp," Jacques informed him. "That's about where you'd have been according to your calculations."

"Well, it was a nice place to rest, but I was too nervous to sleep. So I just relaxed my muscles, and tried to loosen up. I must have rested a good while, 'cause the sun moved enough to lengthen the shadows across the camp. I couldn't really rest much, since I had to keep an eye on the river the whole time I was there; then I hid my kayak in the bushes so it wouldn't give me away.

"Later, I heard an airplane and figured it was going to the ranch, but I knew it wouldn't do me any good. I couldn't go back that way. It was between me and there. Besides, the contour of the land made hiking back out of the question anyway, so I figured the river was my only way out. Thought I might be the only one left alive on the entire Middle Fork, so I was determined to either paddle until I found someone or reached the confluence.

"I found someone: a guy in a cataraft. I saw his boat on the right and pulled over expecting to find more dead bodies. I was close. He was in bad shape. He got slashed deep in his stomach, and his guts protruded through the wound. He was hurt bad, so I stayed with him. Stayed with him until he died, just after sunset. Decided right then and there, that I was going to travel all night if I had too. I got back into my boat and paddled like hell, running rapids in the dark, until I got here. That's it," he said as he searched each face as if to see if his account had been believed.

Daniel thought for a moment, and sighed. "That's all I know about it. My arms are probably too sore to lift it, but I sure could use a cup of coffee if you have enough," he said as he leaned back against a cooler. He had tired of talking.

Bobby felt drained by Daniel's story, and he didn't feel like getting up to get him the coffee. He was relieved when he heard Beth say, "I'll get it." She stood up, and walked to the stove, poured a cup and brought it back to him. "I'd give that a few minutes to cool. It's camp-coffee—pretty strong," she said as she handed the cup to him. She returned to the table to pour one of her own.

"I thought I'd been through a lot," Bobby heard Beth say to Abby. "I'd be crazy if I'd gone through what he went through." She walked back to the perimeter, and resumed her guard. The night's still young, he thought.

Bobby walked over and hugged Beth. "This is the last night, Beth. By this time tomorrow night, you'll be on your way out of here…going home. Only twenty hours, and twenty-four miles separate us from the cars. We're going to make it." Of course he knew the main obstacle wasn't the distance, the time, or even the rapids.

# 23

## THE LOFT

*I'm screwed*, Jake thought. An unseen hand had subverted his plans for an early departure.

It had become obvious the pilots had disappeared—vanished into thin air. The other three men looked as spooked as he felt, a condition Joe Bob hadn't experienced since puberty, Jake would bet.

Earl reached Salmon on the radio and learned that the State Criminal Investigation Unit wouldn't arrive until after midnight. The feds wouldn't make it until morning. They were on their own.

Since the search around the planes hadn't yielded any clues as to the whereabouts of the pilots, the sheriff announced plans to search the rest of the ranch. Jake took note of a barn, equipment shed, and two storage sheds.

The thought of staying at the ranch scored lowest on his list. His heart pounded in his chest, and if he hadn't been in such great shape, he would have thought he was on the verge of a heart attack. *Just indigestion.* Taking a deep breath, he let the air out of his nose and tried to stop his hand from shaking. *What the hell am I doing here?* He asked himself—not for the last time.

With shotgun in hand, John Bonham led the way to the barn. Jake tried to stay in the center of the men as they walked across the open ground. He longed for the sound of an approaching aircraft. That would mean reinforcements, and, that he could leave.

The sheriff opened the big double doors and walked into the barn. From just inside, he shined his flashlight into all the visible areas. The musty smell of ancient horse manure still hung in the air; it mixed with an underlying odor that wasn't strong enough to draw a comment, but nevertheless caused all faces to grimace slightly. Jake didn't like it.

He knew there hadn't been horses at the ranch since the new owners had taken over, but other than that the barn looked exactly the same as it had the last time he'd been here the year before. Hay covered the entire floor, and the vague shapes of various horse tools still hung on the walls. Something about going inside the barn repelled him, but being left alone outside in the darkness, repelled him even more. He followed John inside.

Jake couldn't see into several of the stalls, or into the loft. The lawmen entered the barn with extreme caution, each with one hand holding flashlights, the other clutching a shotgun. Having neither a shotgun nor a flashlight, Jake stayed close to Earl. His hands, both of them, remained glued to the big .44 magnum revolver.

Dusty air made the beams of light clearly visible. Nothing moved except the dust floating through the dank air.

"Joe Bob, you look up in the hayloft; Earl, you and Jake take the stalls, while I look in the supply closets," Sheriff Bonham gave the commands, turned and walked toward the supply closets.

As Joe Bob climbed the ladder to the loft, he heard the movements of the men below. It was hard climbing with the shotgun and flashlight, but both were non-expendable items in his humble opinion. The climb was slow and tedious, but at last he reached the trapdoor and pushed on it—something heavy laid on top. He pushed harder and the weight yielded. Whatever had been on top slid off behind the raised hatch. He stuck his head into the loft and was met by a pair of cold, gleaming yellow eyes. He couldn't see what they belonged to, and he felt fear invade his bowels. The eyes reflected back from four feet off the loft floor. He stood transfixed on the ladder, unable to speak or move. The eyes regarded him as if he had interrupted something. Finally his paralysis broke, and he brought the shotgun and the light to bear on the owner of those eyes. The creature turned to the side, and it was then Joe Bob got a view of the loft denizen.

A huge rat sat atop three stacked bales of hay, chewing on something that resembled raw beef. Joe Bob hated rats. Pushing the safety off, he leveled the end bead on it and pulled the trigger. Twelve thirty-caliber slugs erupted from the end of the barrel. Seven found their target, turning the rat into a flying chunk of dead gristle, blood, and bone. The shotgun's roar was so loud it

# CHAPTER TWENTY THREE

seemed to actually explode inside his head. Ringing filled his ears drowning out all other sounds. Now besides being in the dark, he was temporarily deaf as well.

"Joe Bob! What is it?" the sheriff's voice demanded.

Earl and Jake put their backs to the wall across from the stalls.

After a tense minute, the shock began wearing off, and minimal hearing returned.

"Joe Bob, what were you shooting at?" the sheriff demanded.

"A rat! A big, fucking rat," Joe Bob answered.

"You shot a rat? God dammit Joe Bob, you ain't got the sense God gave a salted slug."

Joe Bob would allow no one but John Bonham to talk to him in such a manner, even then he ignored the reproach.

"John, there's something else up here. The rat was chewing on something. Let me check it out, and I'll be right down."

Joe Bob climbed up the rest of the way into the loft and shined his light on the meat the deceased rat had been nibbling on. As the big deputy came closer to the object, goose bumps formed all over his body. His thoughts searched through file cabinets of memories, like trying to solve a what's-wrong-with-this-picture game. When the correct file had been pulled, and the meat recognized for what it truly was, Joe Bob got sick. He put his hand over his mouth as if that would stop the flood from gushing out his throat. He gagged several times, but the only thing to come up was stomach acid and bile. The meat on the hay was a human hand covered with blood—fresh blood.

There was something worse nagging at Joe Bob's psyche. The little clerk ran down the corridors in his memory again, until it pulled another file. He was afraid to look in it this time because the implications were too terrifying.

The hand was covered in blood, but the shape of the wings on the ring situated on the third finger of the severed hand left no doubt that it was Charlie's aviator ring; which meant this was Charlie's hand. Suddenly, he found himself less sick and more afraid.

Then, another electrifying thought stabbed into Joe Bob's mind. *What if I looked behind the trap door?* Something had been on top of it, and he'd forgotten it when he saw the rat. Now, he was ready to climb down the ladder, but that would mean going by the trap door. Slowly he moved his light to the hinged, wooden drop. *The weight on the trap door could have been Charlie*, he thought—*or somebody else.*

"John! Earl! I think you'd better come up here—HURRY!"

Earl had never heard fear in Joe Bob's voice before that moment. It sent frosty waves through his bladder, and his skin erupted in small bumps. He walked to the ladder right behind John, and the two men ascended the rungs, leaving Jake alone on the dirt floor of the barn. He didn't appear happy about it either.

After John reached the square portal to the loft, Earl remained on the ladder and stuck his head through; he saw Joe Bob with his back against the hayloft wall, shaking, standing at the midway point between John and the grisly remnant of the pilot.

"John, that's Charlie's hand. Look at the ring," Joe Bob said with a shaky voice.

It was unthinkable that Joe Bob was scared, but it was obvious he was. The sheriff scowled at him as he walked over to the hand.

"It's Charlie's ring all right. I noticed it on the flight to the ranch," the sheriff said. "Mother fucker!"

"Who's doing this?" He turned and looked down to Earl, and then up to Joe Bob.

"John, you're missing the point here," Earl said. "The main thing to think about right now, is that Charlie, and probably Frank, were killed in the fifteen minutes we were inside the ranch. The fucker that killed them is still here!"

Earl climbed into the loft and examined the dreadful discovery. He took special notice of the manner in which the wrist had been severed. It appeared to have been cut by a knife or hatchet on top and ripped raggedly along the bottom. The bone was splintered and jagged. "How the hell was this done?" he asked looking up at John.

"Ain't adding up," John stated.

"There's something behind that trap door. I pushed it off when I came up," Joe Bob said as he pointed his light at it.

Earl turned and added his flashlight beam to the rectangular wooden cover. He had a good idea what was behind the trap door and didn't want to look. For the first time in his career, he wanted to walk away, and leave the investigation to the state boys; of course he was unable to do so. Detectives investigate—*it's what we do*, and Earl Bohannan considered himself a good detective. He walked slowly to the trap door, set his shotgun down and drew his side arm, just in case Charlie wasn't behind the hatch. Carefully, he pulled

## CHAPTER TWENTY THREE

it forward. It wasn't Charlie. It wasn't Frank either. The mutilated body of a German Shepherd lay twisted in the hay.

"God almighty! None of this is making sense," Earl said as he let out his breath and faced the sheriff. "We need a SWAT team here—now!"

"Hey, get down here quick!" came a terrified cry from beneath the loft. "Somebody's outside the barn." Earl looked over the edge and saw Jake with his back to the ladder; the big Ruger shook in his hands. It was cocked and pointed toward the open barn doors. The sheriff ran past Earl and climbed down the ladder; Joe Bob followed suit. But Earl stayed to observe the mangled carcass of the dog.

The dog's teeth were covered with a substance that appeared to be either oil or tar. *The same stuff that was on the knife in the kitchen of the ranch house*, he thought. He wanted to touch it and check its texture, but its repellant stench changed his mind.

*What the hell?*

"Earl, we're going over to the main house—come on down here," the sheriff said. "I think we'll wait for the others to get here before we start looking around again. Besides, at least there's lights on over there."

"I'm coming," he said as he began his descent.

When he was a third of the way to the bottom, he looked up to notice something he hadn't seen on the way up. The edge of the loft was only two feet from the hatch. By leaning out, Earl could look up from underneath. Several new indentations had been pressed into the wood. There were four holes in the side, and two holes underneath the end beam. All stood out since the wood inside the holes shined like yellow pine, as opposed to the weathered surface into which they had been pressed. They were spaced evenly, four feet apart, and looked to penetrate about an inch into the beam. It looked as if some tool had exerted tremendous force on the wood, causing it to crack around the holes.

*Like a countersink.*

Other thoughts continued to trouble him. How did the dog get up in the loft? If the dog had been lying on top of the door, how did the killer get down? The door had to have been shut, and then the dead dog laid on top of it.

"A twenty-foot drop to the earthen floor of the barn?" He asked to no one. *Too high for a man to jump*, he thought. Interesting.

Why would someone jump when they could climb down the ladder? Or maybe they used a tool to hang from the beam.

A tool that clamped into the wood like...claws? He pulled a small notebook from his jacket and wrote the unusual data and his thoughts into it.

After the sheriff yelled at him for taking too long, Earl climbed down to the ground and joined the others.

The men all checked their weapons to make sure they were cocked, with chambered rounds and safeties off, before they exited through the barn door.

Jake Ellison trembled. He heard the conversation in the loft and noted the fear in Joe Bob's voice. He had never been this close to a killer before and already knew he didn't like the experience.

The men made their exit the way lawmen entered a warehouse when they knew a burglar was still inside. Earl watched their backs, while John and Joe Bob looked ahead and to the sides. Jake looked everywhere.

At last they reached the house.

After everyone was inside, Jake said, "I need a drink. I don't think getting a few beers out of the cooler will hurt the investigation, but it sure will help my nerves." He went over to the beer box and opened it, careful to avoid the helmet. The sheriff didn't object, so Jake took out a bottle of Corona and drank it down in several big gulps. After finishing the first, he opened another and began sipping on it.

They sat in the concession room occasionally talking but mainly they sat listening. They trained shotguns on both the entry door, and the door leading to the other rooms. If anyone came in uninvited, the welcome would be deafening.

After a while, something unexpected happened. The lights faded and went out, leaving the four men in total darkness. Three flashlights came on almost at once, making the room an unearthly setting of moving shadows.

"What the hell is going on?" Jake cried.

"Sssssshhh!" Earl commanded. "Be quiet, everybody. I heard something."

They all listened. The room was as quiet as a funeral home at midnight.

*Crreeeeaaaak.*

"What was that?" Joe Bob wondered aloud.

"Ssssshh," Earl repeated.

Something moved inside the ranch house. The floor settled under enormous weight. Jake thought the sound came from the dining room.

A glass shattered.

"The dining area…definitely," Earl said.

"Somebody turned off the generator, and they're in here with us."

"OHGODOHJESUS!! Jake cried. Joe Bob put a hand over his mouth. It covered most of his face.

"Quiet, dammit, Jake," the big deputy whispered.

# CHAPTER TWENTY THREE

For a while, all was silent. Then, a creak sounded from the front porch.

"Whoever you are, this is the sheriff—open the door, and come in with your hands up!"

It's usually the other way around, Jake thought.

• • •

Bobby dreamed that Abby kissed him gently on the lips. She kissed him again, a little harder. Then she planted a deep kiss on him that brought him to life.

His eyes opened wide with surprise.

*This is real.*

It took him a few seconds to realize what was happening. When he did, he reached up and wrapped his arms around her, putting gentle pressure on her back, pulling her down on top of him. Bobby returned it passionately with a deep kiss of his own. She moaned softly, as her body responded. He wanted her as much as she wanted him, and their passion increased until it was cooled by Beth's taking notice.

"Are you guys going to sell tickets?" she asked, trying to be funny.

Abby jumped off Bobby and attempted to regain her composure. She turned back to him, "I just came to get you up," she said.

"Well, you certainly did that," he replied.

Beth laughed at her. Bobby saw Abby flash her an expression, and it did a remarkable job. Beth's laughter changed to a chortle. Abby turned back to Bobby. He smiled his best rogue's smile, and opened his sleeping bag to invite her in.

A small chuckle betrayed her.

"It's time to get the rest of you up—it's your turn on guard duty," she said, still trying to stifle a laugh. She looked around to make sure no one other than Beth was watching and kissed Bobby one last time.

She stood and walked back to the fire.

"Hey boy, get your lazy ass out of bed and come on," Jacques chided. "Your coffee's gettin' cold."

Jacques gave Phydeaux some slack; she dashed to Bobby and licked him up and down, until he was laughing in fits and gasps.

"Okay! Okay! Pull her back, dammit, I'm getting up," Bobby gasped through his laughter.

The second shift at Elk Bar began in higher spirits. Phydeaux wasn't apprehensive, and Daniel added his company to the group. He seemed dead tired, glad to be alive, and anything but sleepy. The night was lit by a half moon. It waned toward the new moon, and the effect of its reduced illumination created shadowy mirages across the far end of the beach.

What light it offered formed images on the rock face of the cliff that bordered the far side of the river. Bobby stood, coffee cup in hand, squinting his eyes, trying to see if one of the images might not be an illusion.

He sometimes perceived the slightest motion, but his flashlight always dispelled his fears. The movement would be a bush or plant, blown by a spectral breeze.

The claustrophobic feeling of being in such a remote and isolated canyon gave him the jitters. He knew they were buried in a deep gorge, with a small wooded beach as their only home for this longest night. There were no trails out from Elk Bar. Nowhere to run.

The boats had been pulled up into camp where they could be watched since the thought of swimming out was not a scenario to anyone's liking.

To pass time, the five men discussed their theories about the creature's existence. Where did it come from? Why did it disembowel people? Why had it chosen the Middle Fork of the Salmon to wreak havoc? *Why now?*

# 24

### THE CARNIVAL

"Don't shoot! It's me...Frank."
"Frank! Jesus Lord Almighty!" Joe Bob shouted.
"Praise God!" Jake acclaimed sounding like a tent-show evangelist. His ticket out had returned. The front door opened and Frank stumbled inside. He was out of breath, and as white as a sheet. It was quite obvious that he had come close to ending up like Charlie. His eyes bugged out like a cartoon character in a haunted house. The darkness, broken by flashlight beams, made him appear unworldly. Though shaken, he began to explain:

"I swear this is true. I swear it to God O'mighty!" He bent at the waist and put his hands on his knees. He breathed a ragged breath, coughed, and looked up. "Charlie and me was standin' over by the planes when he decides to go over and piss on a pecker-pole pine." He sucked in another uneven breath and leaned back against the door. "'Piss here' I says to him. 'Naw,' he says. We might be there for a while, and he don't want to be smellin' u-reen' all night. So he goes over to the tree and unzips his britches. Ain't forty feet away from me, and I can see him 'cause he was wearin a white T-shirt. Then I hear'd him gasp. Just floated up into the air about ten feet off the damn ground, biggest nigger I ever seen holdin' him by the neck."

"What?" Earl asked.

"And he must have been naked, cause he was the blackest sumbitch I ever seen all the way to the ground."

A noise from the other end of the ranch house caused everyone to fall silent for a moment. All guns pointed toward the door leading to the hall.

"Just settling," Joe Bob said nervously.

"Get back to your story, Frank," the sheriff said.

"Awright." He looked directly at Jake. "Charlie's feet hung about four or five feet off the ground. I mean this sumbitch gave a whole new meaning to the word big. Charlie kept a gaspin for air, kickin, and tryin to get a'loose. Hittin this bastard right in the face, but he grabbed Charlie's arm and broke it like a matchstick. I heared it snap. Swear to God."

"He broke his arm?" Earl asked.

"Shore did."

"Did he say anything to Charlie?"

"This guy he didn't say nothin'. Not a damn thang. Charlie kept a tryin to scream, but the nigger had him by the throat. All he got out was a few gurgles. I yelled, but ch'all didn't hear me. Figured I couldn't run this a'way, 'cause the sumbitch was tween me and here, so I turned and high-tailed it towards the other end of the strip fast as I could 'til I reached the markers. About sixty feet from the woods, I turned to take another look. That's when I seen him comin' for me, covering that airstrip in half the time it took me to go the same distance. For a big sumbitch, he really moved. Lucky for me, I found a tree I could climb and shinnied right up it. An oak. I went up as high as I could and then jumped over into the next tree. I hid up there for a while, 'cause I could hear him movin' down below. Caught a glimpse of him through the branches."

"What'd he look like?" Earl asked.

"It was dark, so I could barely see him. But he was carryin Charlie under his arm like he didn't weigh nothing. After he give up lookin' for me I seen him one last time. A tunnel down through the leaves let me look to right where he stopped, and I got a real good view at him. Couldn't make out no details, but he put Charlie down and sniffed the ground like a dog. Then he looked up right at me. I thought he seen me, but I guess he didn't. I seen him though. He had eyes like evil, devil's eyes that glowed in the dark. Man, when he looked at me I just about messed my britches. I thought he could see me, but thank the Lord he didn't. He grabbed up Charlie, and run off."

"Did Charlie do anything? Say anything?" Joe Bob asked.

"Charlie wasn't sayin' a damn thang." Frank took a minute to catch his breath after talking. Jake watched the other men looking at each other with raised eyebrows—as if Frank were lost in another bullshitting round with one of his pilot competitors. Jake found himself having a hard time believing it.

He glanced over at the poor pilot and realized fear actually radiated from the man.

## CHAPTER TWENTY FOUR

*Frank believes.*

Usually, he would have figured Frank to be a gullible believer of the supermarket tabloids, but not tonight. Something authentic ran through his story.

Jake wouldn't have thought he could ever been more terrified after the incidents the day had already delivered. But he was. The part about the eyes and sniffing like a dog did him in. He fought the urge to go to the men's room. Seemed like the beer had traveled faster than usual.

"Go on—what else," Earl coached.

"He run off. Headin' this way from where I was, so I stayed up in that tree for a long while—up till I heard a gunshot, sounded like it came from over at the barn. I figured y'all killed the sumbitch, so I climbed down and headed back here. Stayed low—kept my eyes open. Just walked up when you yelled at me, Sheriff."

"Frank, let me be sure I got all this straight. You saw some alleged eight-foot, naked negro perpetrator beatin' up on Charlie after we went inside the main house. Then he carried Charlie under his arm like a football while he runs for a touchdown at the other end of the airstrip chasing you. You climbed a tree, and this guy gets on his hands and knees and starts smelling around like a dog, and he had devil eyes that glowed in the dark. Is that about it?" John asked.

"That's right...what? You don't believe me?"

"Earl, how long were we in the house?"

"No more than twenty minutes," Earl replied.

"That ain't much time for this guy to kill Charlie and run—"

"What? Do you know he's dead?" Frank asked.

"We found part of him in the hayloft—his hand," Joe Bob snarled.

"Yeah, but we don't know that he's dead, based on that," Earl said.

"Right," Joe Bob said, "I forgot—he's probably doing fine—his Goddam hand was ripped off, but he's fine—shit."

"No, he's probably dead, but probable, and certain aren't the same thing, Joe Bob. You know that," Earl said. He looked back at the pilot. "But, if Frank's story is true, that means the killer was close by when we went to the planes."

Jake remembered glowing lights that looked like cigarettes next to the planes, and a shiver rolled through him.

"The killer went to the barn while we were there calling dispatch," Earl said. Jake began quietly shaking.

"Where the hell is the rest of Charlie?" Joe Bob asked.

"I'm sure he'll turn up," John said. "Right now I think we'd better just sit tight until the reinforcements arrive. I don't feel like looking around no more until they're here. Thinkin' about somebody being at the barn while we were at the planes is starting to make me edgy. Don't sound like this guy could be human. As big and fast as you say he was, I'd bet it's a goddam grizzly bear on the loose. They're fast and strong."

"It wasn't no goddam grizzly bear," Frank protested.

"Well, I'm just glad you're okay, Frank. Maybe the others will be here shortly, and we can leave," Jake said. Hope had returned with his pilot.

"Don't count on that now. They'll want to talk to Frank for a while."

*Screwed again*, Jake thought.

"That's a pretty wild story—you sure that's the way it happened, Frank?" Earl asked.

"As God is my witness, and may He strike me dead right now if I'm not telling the truth, that's the way it happened."

Jake had been thinking of his own salvation, when another thought slid into his mind.

"There are people all up and down this river. What if this isn't confined just to this ranch?" Two flashlights stunned his eyes. He put his hand up and flinched, before they shined up to the ceiling.

"Sorry," Joe Bob said simultaneously with the sheriff.

Jake focused past the purple dot. "There could be as many as 300 people on the river at a given time. Granted, they're spread over 100 miles, but that still puts quite a few within reach. Maybe this guy, or these guys decide to hit boaters. They could wait, flag them over, and do them in right there. We could have people dead that we don't even know about yet," Jake said, hoping it wasn't true.

"There's a cheery thought. I guess we should find a way to warn them," said the sheriff.

"How do you propose to do that?" Earl asked. "We don't even have any idea where the folks who run this ranch are."

"We know where two of them are," Joe Bob said.

"Well I damn sure don't feel like going back out to the planes, but if that's the only way, then we gotta do it," John Bonham stated flatly.

"We could use the radio in the dining area if we can get the generator working," Jake suggested.

"Well, I'd rather go back to the planes myself," Earl said. "I know that somebody was back in there a while ago. Somebody big enough to creak the

## CHAPTER TWENTY FOUR

hardwood floor pretty damn loud."

"I didn't even make the floor creak, and I'm pretty sizeable myself," Joe Bob added.

"You all heard it, too," Earl said.

"I heard it," the sheriff said as he gripped his shotgun slightly tighter and looked at the door that led to the rest of the house.

"Yeah, me too," Jake concurred.

At that moment, the twin engines of an airplane sang from the outside sky.

"They're here…praise Jesus," Frank said.

They all bolted for the door. Being policemen, John and Joe Bob stopped, opened the door slowly, shotguns in one hand, and flashlights in the other. They walked single file onto the porch and visually searched the area. When they felt satisfied that no threat was present, they walked into the yard toward the airstrip.

"Man, that's gonna be tricky. I hope they got a damn good pilot. Landing on an unlit airstrip at night ain't something a pilot does many times during a career. Hell, it's like tryin' to set down on a damn aircraft carrier," Frank said as he searched the sky for a plane.

"There's two of them up there…yeah, I can see another set of running lights over there," Jake said as he pointed to the east. He felt a small trickle of relief flow down his backbone—mixed with cold sweat. Maybe he could leave after all. The taste of a cold gin and tonic called out to him from The Crazy Horse.

The lawmen shined their lights up at the circling aircraft as they approached the airfield. Frank ran to his plane and opened the Cessna's door; he turned on the radio.

"Hello, state police?" Frank gave them a moment to respond. "This is the Victor Ranch…come back, over." After a few more seconds of silence came the reply.

"Hello Victor Ranch, this is Lieutenant Adam Spalding with the Idaho State Criminal Investigation Unit. My pilot wants to know where the hell we set this thing down, over."

Earl spoke to John. "I'll be dipped in shit. Spalding came himself."

"Lieutenant Spalding, this is Frank Wright. Can your pilot hear me? Over."

"Yes I can hear you, Frank. This is Walter Red Elk. Tell me where I can find the boundary markers for our approach, over."

"Roger, Walter. The tree line on the north is where you make your approach. You're heading south, alongside the river. Soon as you clear the trees, drop down and level off. We'll get the planes facing that way, and turn on the landing lights. Hopefully, that'll be enough to get you down, over."

"I got you, Frank, thanks. I'll call the other pilot and pass it along to her in case she wasn't listening, over and out."

"An Injun and a woman pilot, what'll they think of next?" Frank said to Jake as he re-hooked the microphone.

Frank had Joe Bob and Jake physically turn the Cherokee around facing across the field. Then he started his Cessna, turned on his landing lights, and taxied over to the riverside of the strip.

"At least they'll be able to see this end of the field," Joe Bob said. Jake hoped so.

When the planes had safely landed, three men climbed out of a Beechcraft.

"Forensics and CSI guys," Earl told him.

Then three more detectives exited from a Cessna 172.

"Oh shit—Ernst Zumwalt. God, I hate that son-of-a-bitch," Earl said as he spit and walked away with a scowl. One of the new men glared back at him, and Jake figured he knew which one Earl meant.

• • •

The second shift at Elk Bar neared an end, and there had been no attack. In fact, Bobby thought, it seemed as if it had all been a bad dream. The insects played their night music, while birds sang rich flute-like melodies for a late summer's night.

Phydeaux occasionally drifted off to sleep, but the sentries promptly awakened her. After the third time, she began to express that she was getting angry. Jerry even tried to get her to drink coffee, without success.

Daniel suggested that since he was going to be awake anyway, Bobby should try to get some rest. Normally he would have protested, but he was too tired to even do that. Thanking Daniel, he went to his sleeping bag. He had to double up on the final shift, and he knew he wouldn't last that long if he didn't sleep. Crawling into his bag and snuggling into the goose down, he fell fast asleep one minute after his head hit the pillow....

## CHAPTER TWENTY FOUR

...A beautiful day, and he drifted on a river. The sky appeared so blue it looked almost purple. The scenery was truly inspiring, with snow-covered mountains in the distance, and colorful trees lining both banks. Rowing his raft down an endless series of non-threatening class-three rapids, the sound of the river filled his ears, along with the cry of an osprey. He absorbed every sensation as if it were real.

This dream had none of the oppressive qualities of his nightmares. This dream felt good, and happy. He could feel warm wind caressing his face, tempering the splashes of cool water that doused him at every wave. After a while the rapids tapered off into calm, moving water. He had forgotten the real problems of the outside world and just floated.

The trees thinned out, and he noticed a large flat area on the right side of the river. As he neared a break in the trees, he could clearly see a country fair in progress.

Bobby pulled his raft over and climbed out. He wanted to go to the fair, and like a child he found himself walking into its midst. Cotton candy and overcooked hot dog smells filled the air, and he gawked at the wonders of the carnival. Carnies hawked their wares or games while the flow of people walked endlessly by.

He wandered onto the midway and saw the freak show tents. Barkers called for people to pay admission to see the two-headed mule or the snake-man.

Then, everything faded away except for one concession: a stage constructed in front of a large tent. The picture on the canvas sign next to the tent chilled Bobby's innards. A barker on the stage called out to him in a sing-song rhythm: "The ancient Sheepeater Indians of what is today known as Idaho valued their dogs highly. Dogs warned of approaching enemies, especially one particular enemy familiar to their valley.

"This creature crossed from Russia eons before our ancestors discovered the wheel. No one has ever seen it and lived—before now. But you have the opportunity. Come see the legendary Hidebehind, bane of the Northwood loggers, the dreaded Basilisk of ancient Greece who could turn people to stone with a single glance. Come see the world's most fearsome creature. Yes sir, the most deadly beast to ever stalk our planet is waiting just inside this tent, and it won't cost you a penny." The barker pointed at Bobby. "See the dreaded soul-eater, the Wendigo, the creature that has remained hidden throughout recorded history. Step right up. It's alive, guaranteed to be real, and it's waiting for you *inside*."

The picture of the beast on the canvas sign terrified him, mainly because it looked like the thing he'd seen in his dreams, under the water, and through the bushes at Pistol Creek, but also, because it seemed to stare directly at him.

Equally terrifying was the visage of the barker: a zombie version of Pat. He wore a straw hat and a striped sports suit, but his flesh had taken a pasty-white color, and bruises lined his face. His eyelids were gone, as was his right cheek. He looked much worse than his incarnation in the previous nightmare, as if he were degenerating into something sinister and malicious. He continued to pitch to a paralyzed Bobby Aldrich.

A slick arm slipped under Bobby's elbow, the way a woman might cozy up on a second date. He turned his head with much effort and saw Gretta. Her very dead face smiled through cataract eyes and grinned through skeletal teeth.

"Hi, Bobby," the corpse said in a harsh, raspy voice.

Bobby stood mouth agape. A man's voice spoke from behind him.

"I'm glad we found you again," The Judge said as he walked into Bobby's field of vision.

"We thought we'd lost you," Bonnie said as she appeared to his left.

Bobby tried to scream, but he couldn't utter a sound.

"Listen Bobby, we haven't got much time. It's come for you. This is it. You can be resourceful, or you can join the carnival with us," Bonnie warned.

"You'll need luck, Bobby…lots of luck, so say your prayers. It wants you… it wants to keep you at the carnival," Gretta cautioned.

"Countless others met it unprepared; now they're here. We weren't, and here we are. Be prepared, Bobby…be prepared," the Judge advised. "You have to be able to see."

Gretta spoke. "It's close…very close. It can even see you sleeping right now. You're the one it wants, because you know it." Her voice mellowed. "Lots of people are psychic, Bobby. Hundreds saw the same visions you saw. The projected fears of dying people broadcast in the last few seconds of their lives. But you're the first psychic that's come close to it in the outside world. You've seen it since you were a child, and it's seen you. It knows you, Bobby, and more than any of the others, it wants you." Gretta's voice echoed down his mental mineshaft. "It wants *youuuuuuuuuuuuuuuuuuuuuuuu*."

Bobby tried to turn away from the dreadful tent but instead began slowly floating toward it. He drifted across the midway, up onto the stage, where the "Pat-zombie" handed him a ticket as he went into the open tent door.

"Enjoy the show," Pat said softly.

It was dark inside, and the tent, like his childhood closet, took on strange

## CHAPTER TWENTY FOUR

dimensions. The door behind him vanished leaving him in total darkness. He felt himself moving through the astral void at tremendous speed, and in the distance he could see a pinpoint of light. His cosmic velocity continued to increase as he followed a silver thread from his navel. He flew down the thread toward the distant point of light. The closer he got to it, the more familiar the light became, until he finally recognized it. He slowed as he approached the opening.

Firelight played on the cliff wall behind the campsite of Elk Bar. He floated for a few seconds above the scene and watched Daniel scratching behind the ear of his newfound friend, Phydeaux. He saw where Abby and the others lay sleeping, while Jerry, Jacques, and Scott kept a close watch.

Bobby observed his own body, as he tossed and turned from within the nightmare below. The thread connected to his navel. He wanted to float down the silver thread and rejoin his body but instead a force pulled him away.

His field of vision moved up the cliff behind camp. Upon reaching the top of the precipice, he found himself staring at a black canvas, the darkness nearly total. The moon didn't make it to the ground under the tall Ponderosa pines, but still he stared into the night. "You have to be able to see," the Judge's voice reminded him.

He started fading from the dream. In fact, the darkness had just about claimed him, when suddenly, two burning eyes flashed open less than three feet in front of him. Shocked by their unexpected manifestation, he froze and watched.

They seemed to float in space in a discorporeal state as they moved closer to him and looked down. The hate burned as the eyes focused on their intended victim. For a moment, Bobby felt relieved that the eyes weren't looking at him anymore. Then, he realized they were. They were looking directly at the figure in his sleeping bag below, and their intent was clear: *murder*.

He wanted to wake up but found himself unable to do anything and more afraid than he had been the day of the twister, in all the nightmares in his life. Now, more than anything he just wanted to escape. Maybe it wasn't so bad at the carnival.

The thought of actually facing the beast seemed remote. Impossible even. To fight he would have to be able to move. To move he would have to want to, and he didn't. He just wanted to close his eyes and let what ever happened, happen.

*What about the others.*

If he didn't overcome his fear, Abby, Jerry and the others would be forced to die because of him. But what if he did take action, and it was the wrong action—like on the Klamath. Would he let that mistake dominate the rest of his life? If he didn't answer that question, the rest of his life wouldn't last long enough to matter. The answer slammed into him like a fist. He already owed for Gretta. For Gary. For Bonnie and The Judge. For Pat. He had promised to even the score. And he remembered what succumbing to fear had done to his childhood. Bobby knew how to do one thing better than all others. The Marines and Sensei Tao had trained him. Bobby knew how to fight. Summoning the remainder of his courage, he faced the demon.

He regained the use of his astral limbs and floated forward by exerting will. Playing it by ear, the way he had done with the Marines so many years before; he kicked at the beast. His foot passed right through it as if he were a ghost.

The shadow creature must have perceived something, however; it moved back from the edge for a moment and showed its teeth. He knew this wasn't just the product of a child's nightmare, this was a real-live killing machine, which somehow managed to find a gate from hell that had been accidentally left open and had made its way into our world. Bobby spoke to it with a shaky voice.

"If you don't behave, you'll be asked to leave, asshole. I think it's only fair to tell you that I know karate." Bobby back-fisted its temple and heel-palmed its face.

Apparently the beast couldn't feel the attack. It didn't flinch. However it did seem to hear Bobby's words. It looked warily around. Unfortunately, it didn't understand English, but it must have known where the words came from. It moved to the edge of the cliff and looked straight down at Bobby's body, sleeping below.

Perched on the edge of the precipice, it readied itself for a jump to the biggest pine tree in the middle of their camp. Bobby saw that from there it could drop down into their midst and pounce before anyone knew what was happening.

*I have to wake up. I've got to wake up now! Please God!*

He could still see the beast crouching, waiting for the most opportune moment to leap across to the tree. Still, he couldn't wake up.

His only hope would be to push it off the cliff somehow. His time ran out—the beast tensed to spring. Bobby ran at the creature, passed right through it and fell towards earth as he screamed,

"NNNNOOOOOOOOOOOOO!"

He saw his sleeping bag coming closer as he fell towards it, finally slamming into his own body with psychic impact.

## CHAPTER TWENTY FOUR

His cry awakened everyone in camp, including Phydeaux. Bobby sprang up and scanned the top of the cliff for eyes. He knew they were there, but he couldn't see them. He pulled the K-bar and gripped it by the blade—ready to throw.

"What is it?" Jerry asked with the big handgun pointing up into the night.

"It's here! I dreamed—it's up there about to pounce down on us! It's there!"

"You scared the Be-Jesus out of me," Jacques said with relief. "A dream."

"This dream wasn't like any I've ever had before. I'm telling you I was up there. I could see this camp. It's up there right now," he said pointing to the spot where he'd just been.

Phydeaux growled, and every eye in camp turned toward her. Sniffing the air, she growled again. She seemed unsure as she searched the top of the cliff, until her gaze stopped on the precise spot Bobby had jumped from in his dream. Everyone looked wide-awake now.

It was 4:00 a.m., and the shift change wouldn't be necessary; none of them would sleep again.

# 25

## THE CAVALRY

While the newcomers from the SCI-Unit looked around for themselves, Earl sat at a table with John and Joe Bob. The pilots, Janet Wilson and Walter Red Elk sat with Jake Ellison across from them. The three lawmen spoke quietly.

"What do you think that noise was a while ago?" Joe Bob asked the sheriff.

"I think somebody was in here and went out through that broken window," John replied.

"I agree," Earl said. He thought for a moment and turned to John. "Frank's story, the dog, Charlie's hand, the cigarettes up by the planes, the sounds, and the way the bodies were desecrated all seems crazy. I know they fit, but I'll be damned if I can see how. Those dots on the kitchen floor, and that ooze on the knife don't make any sense either. It looks like somebody was tap dancing with football cleats on, and opened a stinky can of thirty-weight with a butcher knife."

Earl looked at the window, then at the door: "I do have one idea though," he said as he walked over to the hallway door and called to Harold, one of the forensic men.

"Have you already dusted these pipes?" he asked.

"Yeah, but don't pick them up. There's a positive set of prints on several of them, and I haven't transferred them yet."

"How about if I stick something in the end so I don't have to touch them?"

"Okay, but be careful. You heard Spalding," Harold said.

Earl went to one of the closets and returned with a broom. He inserted the handle into the end of the pipe, picked it up, and held it across the door. The marks on the pipe corresponded with the exact width of the doorframe.

"Interesting," he said. Earl noted the shelf on the left and the loop handle on the right side of the door. He gently placed the crushed pipe back on the shelf, picked up one that hadn't been crushed, placed one end through the loop, and pushed the pipe over until the end slid home onto the shelf.

"Looks like someone got locked in. What do you think?" Harold asked.

"Could be," Earl replied. "One thing, though, the windows can't be locked from the outside. Even if they could, they're easy to break. That, in fact is what happened to that window in there. It was broken from the inside out. Somebody went out that way."

"Hell, it wouldn't take no time at all to break out that window," Joe Bob said.

"Right, but the thing that puzzles me is that anyone with half a brain would expect that. That leads me to believe that one of two things may have happened: First, our perp has the mentality of a low-grade moron and locked somebody in, or somebody tried to lock in the bad guy and bought themselves a little time to escape. If I had to choose between the two, I'd choose the latter."

"Sounds good," Joe Bob said.

Earl said, "Well, whoever this guy is, he's strong enough to crush PVC pipe. I think he tried to pull the door off the hinges too. Look, they're bent. That took a hell of a lot of force to do that. Not that hard to kick a door off the hinges, but did you ever try to pull one off?"

"Not lately," Joe Bob answered.

"Anyway, the way I see it, our killer is trying to pull the door in, while somebody gets a little more time to escape—hopefully. The perp then shatters the window and gains egress."

"Boy you've got one hell of an imagination, Colombo," a voice berated from behind them. It was the voice of Ernst Zumwalt. "Leave it to the great Earl Bohannan to solve the crime at the scene."

"Don't let your ego get in the way and you might actually learn something at a crime scene, Dipshit." Earl fired back. "Look, why don't you go make some coffee, watch Harold dust for prints, or something. When we find somebody alive, you can interrogate him. How about that?" Earl said. His muscles tensed and his blood pressure felt like it had doubled within a few seconds.

"Don't forget, Bohannan, we're in charge now. If you find something, you tell the lieutenant, understand?" Ernst ordered instead of asked.

## CHAPTER TWENTY FIVE

"Leave us alone, asshole, or you're gonna piss me off." Joe Bob said. He bolted up and gave Ernst a look that conveyed the danger in doing something so foolish as "pissing him off."

Ernst quickly found a different place to investigate.

"Someday that guy's gonna go a little too far, and I'm gonna shove his head up his ass like a suppository," Joe Bob said as Ernst walked away.

"He's a legend in his own mind," Earl joked, feeling his muscles relax as soon as Zumwalt was out of sight.

Harold laughed. "Spalding didn't want to bring him, but he was one of the only detectives in the station who was available when the call came in. I'll ask the lieutenant to keep him away from you. He sure can be a pain in the ass," Harold said as he turned back to his fingerprinting.

Joe Bob followed Earl to the broken window. Earl shined his light outside and Joe Bob did the same.

"That's funny, there's no heavy object laying around out there. Seems like the guy would have thrown something heavy through it to break it. Then again, why didn't he just open it and climb out?" Earl asked.

"Maybe he's as stupid as Zumwalt," Joe Bob replied.

"I hope so, 'cause then he'll leave lots of clues."

# 26

## FALSE HOPES

Ernst Zumwalt loved power. Being a cop gave him the sort of power he craved. He liked playing "good cop-bad cop" because he always got to be the bad cop. Easy for him, since he used other's fears and had the habit of always assuming people guilty until proven innocent.

When Lieutenant Spalding asked him to accompany the chopper pilot to look for boaters down river, he heard "suspects" instead, and figured he had been given the most important job in the entire investigation. But he sometimes wondered if he were being sent just to get him out of the way.

*Naw! Couldn't be.*

His pilot, a man called Raymond—a small bearded man with sandy blonde hair down to his shoulders, waited for him.

*A goddam hippie pilot,* Ernst thought as he boarded the helicopter, scowling at the man as if he too were a suspect.

An hour after daybreak they took off from the Victor Ranch. It wasn't long before they came upon the butchered bodies at Cold Springs Camp.

"Shit! Put down so I can take a look," Ernst demanded.

Since the hippie pilot hadn't left the chopper, even at the ranch, he hadn't yet seen any carnage. He had probably sensed something terrible had happened at the ranch for county, state, and federal agencies to be working together, but until that moment he hadn't seen how bad it really was. Bodies posed twisted in the dirt while buzzards fed on their eyes and tongues. It faired too much for the hippie. Luckily, the Scorpion 'copter didn't have doors. A round bubble of plexi-glass with two open side portals made it easy for the pilot to vomit out his side without much trouble.

*Pussy*, Ernst thought to himself. The small helicopter touched down; he unclasped his seatbelt and climbed out of the chopper and waited for the rotors to stop.

The air hung heavy with the smell of blood and death. Flies, ants, and other insect scavengers covered the putrefying bodies. The numerous vultures didn't appear to be concerned with Ernst's proximity. He threw a rock at one and missed. The vulture moved slightly, like a boxer slipping a punch, and the rock whizzed impotently by it.

They didn't take him seriously, until he drew his service revolver and shot one in the neck, blowing its head off. His side arm, a Smith and Wesson model 28, .357 magnum, had a report loud enough to scare most of the birds into nearby trees. Taking aim at a buzzard in the closest tree, he center-shot it off the limb. They retreated farther. He followed and killed one more before they left the ground and began circling again.

"Hey man, they're only doing their job," Raymond shouted.

"Shut up, pussy. You're just along for the transportation. Don't forget it." Ernst growled as he looked at the delicate pilot with his "try-me" expression. He held his gun in a threatening manner, and gave a heavier, older version of Deniro in "Taxi Driver," looking as if he were about to say: "*You talking to me?*" He liked that scene and practiced it at home in front of his mirror.

The hippie pilot learned quickly that Ernst Zumwalt wasn't going to become an animal rights activist in the near future. Ernst guessed he decided to take his advice to remain quiet. The boy shut up. *At least he's smart enough to know who not to fuck with.*

Ernst walked around the campsite looking for clues. They lay about everywhere, but he discounted almost all of them. One however, he saw very clearly: the imprint of a sandal close to the shore, and no body lying nearby. It looked fresher than all the others. Ernst reasoned that it belonged to the killer; he filed it away. The ball of the foot had worn smooth while the rest looked rough.

He noticed the dots in the sand. For a moment he thought about them. Since they didn't make sense, he chose to remember the footprint instead. He wiped sweat from his forehead. *Today's gonna be a "testicle scorcher."* Probably up around 95 degrees by 3:00 o'clock. This place would stink even worse by the time forensics got here. He was glad he didn't have to spend much time at this one.

He had seen a few murder scenes before, and he'd been the first on the scene of many auto fatalities when he'd worked patrol in Bozeman, but this took the

## CHAPTER TWENTY SIX

record. It could be the worst multiple murder in Idaho's history. Even better, it could make him a hero if he happened to be the cop who solved it. That would shut up that college boy, Earl Bohannan. *Hell, I might even run for sheriff in White River against old do-gooder,* Ed Rawlins. He pictured the footprint in his mind and smiled.

After Ernst felt satisfied that he had been at the scene long enough to appear detective-like, he returned to the helicopter, having stayed a few minutes longer just to make the hippie pilot a little more uncomfortable.

"What the hell happened here?" Raymond asked. His voice filled with revulsion and fear.

"What the hell does it look like, peckerhead? Somebody killed over a dozen people and chopped them up. Now get us out of here before he comes back for you," Ernst ordered.

Raymond sat with the controls in his hands, but he didn't move. His mind still worked as if to digest the inhuman violence of the horrible place. He shook his head and pulled his attention back to Ernst's last command and obeyed.

He restarted the rotors. The chopper rose slowly, and they resumed the search. Ernst radioed back and gave Spalding the bad news: the killing wasn't confined to the ranch.

• • •

Bobby sipped coffee with Abby and Jerry at one of the camp tables. The sun bleached the mountain peaks behind them, but it hadn't quite reached the camp. The Coleman stove hummed as it warmed a second pot of "cowboy" coffee. Hardly anyone spoke above a whisper. The air hung heavy and still, and noise seemed to carry much farther than usual. Bobby figured he could have heard a twig snap 100 yards away. A few birds sang upriver, but they were too far away for him to identify them. Their songs made him feel a little more at ease, but he wished they'd fly closer so he could really relax.

Jacques and Plato walked up. "I'm still trying to figure out what happened last night. You mind telling us about this dream again, Bobby?" Jacques asked.

Though he wanted to forget about it, he went into even greater detail, including the astral projection, and this time it was clear that the others chose to believe he had been the recipient of a vision. Phydeaux had all but confirmed it.

After Bobby concluded, everyone sat quietly until Jacques made a suggestion: "Let's fire up those steaks for breakfast, and whatever else we've got to carry us through the rest of the day, since we won't be stopping for lunch. We'll need our strength to sustain us for twenty-four miles of class three/class four whitewater. Jacques sat down rubbing his belly and smiling with a big cigar clamped in his teeth.

Jerry, Bobby, Abby, and Beth made breakfast while everyone else kept watch. In no time they served it up. Bobby swore he had never tasted a meal so delicious, even better than the breakfast at Marble Creek.

Phydeaux made out like a bandit. Several steaks were left over, since the people they had been intended for wouldn't be claiming them—another sad reminder.

"Put your dirty dishes in the pickle barrel. We'll wash them at home," Jacques said.

The sound of the word "home" had never sounded so sweet to Bobby. The mood at Elk Bar again neared optimism, since there'd been no attack the night before. The thought that they might actually make it off the river alive, began rooting into his mind. Striking camp with an economy of motion, they prepared to leave.

Bobby watched Jim topping off the air in the raft's tubes with the foot-pump, while Jerry loaded and strapped down gear. They finished the task in record time. Just when they were about to launch, Scott shouted, "Hold on. Be quiet, I hear something."

Everyone fell silent. Bobby expected something to come out of the water, or lunge from the woods, but instead he heard the sound of an approaching helicopter.

"Yes! It's about time!" Jim shouted as the helicopter approached.

The rotors sounded like someone beating a drum inside Bobby's head. It reminded him of war. Worse, it brought back the memory of his last helicopter ride with the dead boy on the Klamath; he was glad to see it anyway. At last help had come.

The chopper gently touched down on the spot where the rafts had been pulled the previous evening. Sand flew everywhere, but they all ran toward it anyway—ignoring the sting. The first contact they'd had with the outside world in almost a week, and everyone was elated. Jim and Linda held each other, Suzi and Beth jumped up and down as they ran closer, until Jacques pointed up at the blades and ran a finger across his throat. They smiled and bent down as they ran in. A tornado of pine needles and sand whirled about, biting his skin, but Bobby didn't care. It gave him an excuse for the tears in his eyes.

"Thank God you're here. Can you get us out?" Beth pleaded. "Is there room for at least a few of us?"

# CHAPTER TWENTY SIX

"We aren't a rescue mission, lady," the man replied harshly. He looked around from face to face, obviously hostile. "Tell me, why is it that everyone else on this river is dead, and you all somehow miraculously survived?"

"Because we have a dog, asshole," Jacques blurted out as he made his way through the group. "Who the hell are you anyway?"

"I am Detective Ernst Zumwalt from the Idaho State Criminal Investigation Team…homicide division," he said as he produced his shield.

"Well Detective Ernst Zumwalt, we've lost five of our party in the last five days. These pretty ladies here lost three of their group, and this gentleman lost eleven. He's the only survivor. The goddam thing even killed his twin brother, so don't act like we made it unscathed. We've lived in terror for the past four nights and five days, so please, lighten up on the third degree," Jacques requested with his refined manner.

"What do you mean—goddam thing'?" Ernst asked.

Bobby walked up to the belligerent detective.

"Look, we've been through an ordeal—"

"What do you mean goddam thing?" Ernst repeated turning his gaze on Bobby.

"There is *something* out there. It kills. It's faster than a mountain lion, and it never makes a sound. What else do you want to know?" Bobby asked, angered by the man's unfriendly manner. "Look detective, we'll answer any questions you have, but please make arrangements to get us out of here. We're in danger. Every minute we stay on this river we're in more danger. I know this sounds hard to believe, but it's true. There's something out there deadlier than anything you can even imagine, so please call in another chopper, one that's big enough for all of us."

The man stood glowering at him. He stood a little shorter than Bobby, but appeared to outweigh him by a good thirty pounds, all in his gut. His face looked as if it hadn't cracked a smile in years. Bobby turned to walk away before he lost his temper with the cop and did something he might regret later.

"Hold it right there! I saw that same footprint in the sand at a crime scene upriver. Why don't you explain why it was there," the detective bellowed.

Bobby spun around and saw the man's hand resting on the butt of his revolver. He slowly walked back and got in his face.

"The reason it was there, was because I was there. We went in because we heard shots the night before. We figured, correctly, that they might have a gun. When we found them, they sure didn't need it anymore. They were already dead before we got there."

Zumwalt began to back away from Bobby toward the helicopter.

Seeing Beth talking to the pilot, Bobby moved closer. The detective walked around to the passenger side.

"Get this thing ready to take off," Zumwalt ordered.

When the pilot ignored the order, Bobby moved next to Beth so he could listen.

"There aren't anymore helicopters in the area. The soonest we could round up a chopper big enough to take all of you out would be tomorrow morning," the pilot told them. "There aren't any more landing strips on the river. You'll either have to wait here or go ahead and leave by boat. It's your choice," he explained.

"Get this thing ready to take off, asshole. I'm not going to tell you again," Zumwalt yelled.

"Hey pal, I'm not staying on this river another night, no fucking way," Jim said as he walked up.

"Me either," Scott agreed from behind him.

"I'm not staying," Suzi said.

"Listen!" Zumwalt shouted. "It don't make a shit to me if you all swim out, or stay here, but there will be police units waiting for you at the confluence, so if you do float out don't try to pass them. I'd like to have a few words with each of you." He looked at Bobby, then at Jacques. "I'll see you later," he said as he boarded the helicopter and fastened his seatbelt.

Beth grabbed the frame, stood on the landing rails and refused to budge. "Please take me. I'll just hold on. You won't have to worry about me," she begged. Bobby knew exactly how she felt. He certainly didn't want to stay another minute. Here set their means to escape. It made sense that the cops should get at least a few of them out.

"Take off, asshole. Quit fooling around with that bitch and get us out of here."

Looking at the detective, the pilot flatly said, "No."

Bobby gasped when Detective Zumwalt drew his gun and put it to the pilot's temple. "I said get us out of here."

This time the pilot obeyed. Bobby heard him throttle up. He watched Beth nervously. She clung tight. The helicopter rose up into the air and was slightly thrown off balance by her weight on the side rail.

"Beth!" Bobby and Jim yelled in unison as they ran to the river's edge. The chopper quickly rose to about thirty feet over the water. Before they could do anything, Zumwalt kicked Beth in the stomach, knocking her off the rail.

# CHAPTER TWENTY SIX

Tumbling end over end—down toward the water, she landed flat; she slammed into the river with a loud pop and disappeared under the surface.

Beth felt the sharp intrusion into her abdomen. Her breath shot out of her like when her older brother used to punch her in the stomach. After tumbling several times, she hit flat on her back. The shock of the impact knocked her senseless. She sank deeper and deeper until her ears hurt from the depth and the cold. Her body tingled in the frigid darkness, and all she wanted to do was sleep away the pain; then she came to.

*I'm going to drown.* Her arms folded around her aching belly in a protective fashion. Her lungs and back burned. She wished she could have taken in air before she sank. Now she had no buoyancy, and the current rapidly pulled her downstream. Another thought released her arms from their involuntary tuck position.

*What if it's under the water. It could be coming for me right now.* Straightening her body, she began taking baby strokes. What would Abby tell me to do? Disoriented in the dark water, she wasn't sure which way was up. She felt the direction of the current, trusted her intuition and swam with all her remaining energy. She broke the surface far below the point of impact and gasped for air-already dangerously close to missing the bottom of the beach. If she did, a rapid waited just below the corner. Little hope remained for her survival unless she made the shore. But her muscles, already sluggish from the glacial-cold water, refused to help.

Then it grabbed her from behind and she panicked. It was waiting for her after all. Too weak to scream or fight back, a moment passed before she realized that it wasn't the beast that had her, but a human being—Daniel.

He pulled her to shore as the others ran up. She hung limp as death but managed a weak smile of thanks.

"Are you okay?" Abby asked as she put her arm around her.

She couldn't speak, but held a "thumbs up" to show that she was indeed okay, before she hugged her throbbing midriff.

Jim looked downstream. The chopper had already moved out of sight, but his gaze traced the sky where it had been only seconds before.

"What a fucking rat that guy is," he said.

"That guy wins the flaming asshole prize of all time," Linda added. "He thinks we did all this? Damn him!"

Jacques turned and looked back up the beach toward his raft. He motioned for them to make their way back toward the boats and addressed the group as they walked.

"Well ladies, gentlemen, I for one, think the time for departure has arrived. Whoever he is, he certainly seems intent on rubbing salt in our wounds. Though we might be able to have his job for what he did to Beth."

Abby said, "I'll have a lot more than just his job."

Jacques pulled the cigar out of his mouth. "Right now, we've got more important things to get past. I'll lead today. Up until now, the river has been child's play. Today, however, we'll encounter ten major rapids. We won't have the luxury of stopping to scout them because of the risk factor involved in doing so, but if God's willing, and the creek don't rise, we'll be out of here by this evening. What say we get the fuck outta Dodge? Pardon my French again, ladies," Jacques concluded as he took his oars in hand.

• • •

Ernst called the ranch from the helicopter and informed The Lieutenant that they had discovered one group of people still alive, camped at Elk Bar, and that he considered them the prime suspects in the case. Lt. Spalding told him they would be intercepted at the confluence, and he was to continue his search for more survivors.

Ernst felt proud of himself. While the others were at the ranch digging through bullshit, he was doing real police-work: finding the killers. He smiled until he found Raymond looking at him. He changed his expression to a sneer in less than a second. He liked the effect it had on a spineless sissy like this hippie. The pilot's head snapped back the other way. *I've still got it.*

He didn't see anything unusual until they came upon another grisly scene at Otter Bar, eleven miles down river. They circled but didn't land. Zumwalt took the opportunity to shoot at another buzzard. This time from above.

After circling the camp for a few minutes, Ernst signaled the pilot to leave. "Go on," he ordered.

Raymond pulled the chopper up and away from the camp.

Three miles further down the canyon, Raymond pointed at something below them. "What do you make of that?" He asked.

Ernst had been lost in the reverie of preparing to interrogate the two men who had angered him when the pilot's interruption brought him back. "Go down, we'll take a look," Ernst replied.

Raymond lowered the Scorpion down into the canyon. He leveled off at

## CHAPTER TWENTY SIX

fifteen feet from the water's surface. Below and ahead of them lay a rapid with three channels formed by two huge "house-rocks." Wrapped around each of the two monstrous boulders were several empty rafts-a dozen more rafts floated in a pool above the rapid.

"Looks like somebody's building a damn out of boats. If the rest of those rafts in the pool wedge in there, it could choke up the whole river. Maybe we should go back and warn those folks," Raymond said.

"Maybe you should shut up, and leave the thinking to me. I've got a job to do. If I finish and there's enough time, we might go back and warn them."

Ernst looked out his side of the helicopter and saw several kayaks placed on top of some rocks on the right side of the river. He was wondering how they had come to be placed on the rocks when he felt and heard a loud "thump." The aircraft listed to the pilot's side.

"Aaarrrgggghhh!!!" Raymond screamed.

A huge black shape ripped the pilot's seatbelt out of the floor, and lifted him out of the seat as the helicopter fell several feet in elevation.

Ernst saw it but had no idea what "it" was. It pulled a screaming Raymond through the open portal of the helicopter.

Standing on the side rails, it crouched low apparently to avoid the rotor. The chopper listed a second time causing the huge black beast to fall, taking Raymond with it into the water.

Ernst Zumwalt screamed in terror. The helicopter spun out of control. He tried to grab the stick and imitate what he had seen the pilot do, but it only caused the chopper to climb and spin. The final result: he hit the rocks even harder. The Scorpion crashed into the left wall right at the river's edge. A boulder intruded into the open portal and shattered Ernst's right knee before the helicopter slid into the current. He cried out his agony as the river poured into the cockpit.

Ernst took a deep breath, and then the water inundated him. By the time he'd unfastened his seatbelt, the chopper had been pulled downstream and a few feet away from the bank. The current grabbed the bubble and pulled it toward the left chute of the rapid.

With effort, Ernst managed to exit the cockpit and break the surface. He took another gulp of air and spotted a large rock just off the right bank, slightly above the unusual barrier. Even he knew the probable death he would face if he went under the rafts. With both arms and his one good leg he swam for the rock.

The cold water acted as an anesthetic to his injury. He couldn't move his leg, but at least the pain was more bearable in the icy water. He swam across the eddy-line behind the rock and submerged for a few seconds, but then the eddy pulled him to the backside of the boulder. Climbing up onto it, crying out in pain with each movement, he watched helplessly as the current sucked the Scorpion into the left opening, where it wedged between the cliff wall and the first huge boulder on the left. The angle and depth at which it was lodged formed a massive white wave, made even bigger when moments later one of the rafts broke free of the pool and floated down to wrap against the chopper's frame.

No sign of Raymond. Even through his pain-saturated mind, it dawned on him that he was totally alone, miles away from help, with no one coming for hours. Worse yet, maybe he wasn't alone. Something had pulled the pilot out of the chopper. *Something that looked and smelled like hell.* Panic seized him, and he reached for his holster. He let out a breath with a long sigh when he discovered his gun still in it.

His mind raced through countless thoughts. He remembered Jacques' and Bobby's story and wondered if he might have been a little hasty in passing sentence on them.

*What the hell am I dealing with?* He asked himself. *A serial killer wearing a snake hide?* He'd been alone for about ten minutes without any sign of Raymond or the black thing when he had a third realization. In his hurry to leave the ranch he had left his speed loaders in his travel bag, and he had wasted four of his six bullets shooting buzzards.

Laying on the rock in agonizing pain, Ernst Zumwalt had to admit he was truly scared—scared to death.

# 27

### ENDGAME

Ernst Zumwalt felt the hot flare of pain erupt every time he tried to move, as if someone had surgically opened up his knee, placed a red-hot coal inside it and sewed it back up. When he heard something and looked behind him, the pain felt like an auger bit had drilled into his knee in search of the buried coal, and then fanned the ember to a white heat. He tried not to move.

He heard a splash, then water dripping on rocks.

"I'm a police officer!" he shouted to the unseen suspect. "Show yourself."

No response

"I have a gun," he threatened.

No response.

He would have dismissed the whole thing as a hallucination except for the pain. A hallucination wouldn't have been capable of ripping Raymond right out of the chopper. He wouldn't be trapped on a rock in the middle of nowhere with a broken leg if it had been a hallucination. However demented this perpetrator was, he was real.

Rolling over, Ernst screamed from the bite of the sharp bone moving against torn tissue and pulsing nerves. He faced the direction of the sound, but nothing was there. He cocked the big revolver and waited.

He had only two bullets left. They were both hot-loaded, soft-nose bullets that would make a small entrance wound and a large exit hole. Having only two bullets meant he would have to let whoever it was get close before he fired. In fact, he would have to let the killer get right on top of him.

He turned facing down river. Although he didn't hear a sound, all of a sudden, Ernst knew something was behind him. He felt torn between turning slowly and spinning lightning fast. While he decided, the sun passed behind a cloud…a strange-shaped cloud…a cloud that only covered the large rock he was on.

Spinning around, he saw a back-lit shadow of monstrous proportions standing above him on the small cliff. Even though a fresh wave of pain tore through his knee, he raised the revolver and fired. But the shadow moved back over the edge of the cliff too quickly. He missed.

Now one bullet remained. He couldn't believe he had missed from less than twenty feet. Rated in the top five marksmen in the entire state police department, at that distance he seldom missed targets the size of a bird. Next time, he would wait until the assailant was in the air before he fired. For the psycho to get to him, he would have to jump to the rock. *Just try it, and I'll center-shoot your ass-eyes into the drink.*

Ernst watched as more rafts floated out of the pool, into the current and added their mass to the growing dam.

*He's waiting me out*, he thought. Ernst watched as the shadow threw several kayaks over the cliff. The perpetrator's purpose finally dawned on him: The guy was building a trap for the boaters he'd questioned earlier, the only ones left alive. Ernst also realized that the very boaters he had accused this morning were his best hope of survival this afternoon. He couldn't swim with a broken leg. Planes might locate him, but they couldn't get him out; it would take some time for a rescue helicopter to be called in.

Then, Ernst realized why the murderer had chosen this particular spot to build a trap. By the time the oarsmen saw the dam, it would be too late to pull over. Even if a boat reached this side of the river, there was no way out. Small, steep cliffs bordered both banks. It looked like the Elk Bar suspects were either doomed to drown, or they would have to face the "shadow man" up on the cliff.

He hoped the dark costume slowed the guy down in the water. If it didn't, a bad situation would become even worse.

Within moments his focus had shifted from a well-ordered police investigation to a phantasm where he fought for his life.

Ernst blinked away drops of sweat. The sun beat down and burned his skin. He'd been right about the day: It was a scorcher.

• • •

## CHAPTER TWENTY SEVEN

The rapids were continuous, and the closer they got to the take-out, the more hope filled Bobby's soul. There hadn't been an attack at Elk Bar and it appeared they would make it.

They felt optimistic until they reached Otter Bar. Bobby stared at scavengers cleaning up carrion. The group slowly passed in silence. Before he rounded the corner below the camp, Bobby turned to look back and saw another reaper-like corpse lying in the sand, pointing with an outstretched finger toward the confluence.

*Hopefully, you're not a harbinger.* He stared at it as if he thought it might come to life and raise its head to smile at them, but as they floated by, the corpse disappeared behind a grove of trees without moving.

Rubber Rapid wasn't nearly as big as he'd expected; Hancock Rapid had been trickier. It had required a series of strong pulls to miss a rock known as the "Sharks Fin"-a particularly nasty looking axe-blade. Cliffs bordered the coming rapids on both sides, making the river seem less than "user friendly." Now he understood why they called this the Impassable Canyon.

Bobby looked ahead to see Jacques and Phydeaux leading the way. He glanced back to check on the others. Plato and Scott followed, and then Jim and Linda. He saw Daniel paddle his kayak along side Jim's boat. Unlike Pat, Daniel would not ride in a raft. He said he preferred the speed and mobility his kayak offered. It had saved him once, he said, and he figured to stay with a winner.

Last of all, he caught a glimpse of Jerry and Suzi in the sweep boat, not the most popular position in the caravan, since his own boat had been stripped of its floor and passenger while running sweep.

The group had just finished a major rapid called The Devil's Tooth, when Bobby rounded a sharp bend in the river.

"What the hell? I've never seen anything like that before," he said from 100 yards above the entrance to House Rock Rapid. He beheld the curious, colorful, makeshift dam ahead. Wrapped boats had effectively blocked all three of the narrow channels. Luckily, they remained in the calm pool above the rapid and Abby held against the current. Bobby studied the extraordinary scene.

The Quinn Guide recommended the slot on the left, but the author had never seen the huge standing wave formed by a helicopter wedged at its entrance. A raft had wrapped onto the frame of the submerged Scorpion, making the water bulge as if a giant rock were buried just under the surface. A kayak, pinned by the sheer force of the water, held against a vertical cornice on the cliffside and a cleft in the house rock. An impasse. Any attempt to run the left channel would most likely result in a flip, a broken neck, or both.

Then Bobby saw the belligerent detective from Elk Bar, sitting on a rock forty feet below Jacques, waving his arms frantically and screaming to be heard over the raging rapid just below him.

"What is that guy doing here? Where's the pilot?"

"I don't see anyone else," Abby said.

It was clear that the detective desperately needed rescue—Bobby could see blood soaking his trousers from a wound on the man's right knee. They were close enough that he heard Jacques yelling to Phydeaux.

"Something's wrong, girl, watch out!"

"Watch out" sent Phydeaux to attention and she ran to the front of the raft. Bobby knew that an eddy would exist behind the rock, and he knew what Jacques intended to do. He planned to cross the eddyline at a ninety-degree angle and pull up behind it. Hopefully, the eddy would be strong enough to hold the boat while he helped the man in. Even if Jacques made the eddy and rescued the detective, it would be little more than a temporary fix. There didn't appear to be a way around it.

Jacques had set up for the entry when something rose out of the eddy and onto the rock behind Ernst Zumwalt: a hideously huge, black shadow. Bobby flinched backwards and held his arms up in an automatic defensive reaction.

Phydeaux went crazy, barking at it. Jacques froze for a few seconds. Regaining his ability to function, he flexed the oars against the current. He held even with the pull.

"Oh God…he can't hold there for long," Abby said softly.

Soon Jacques would tire and drift towards the rock. Already he'd been caught by the gravity of the right channel and would have to pass right by the deadly menace. Bobby figured Jacques would give the river a fight—if he got the chance.

Bobby saw it clearly, in this world, for the first time. It was more dreadful than anything he had ever dreamed in his nightmares. Fear won again. All his promises to get even flew away like scared birds. He couldn't face this thing. Panic seized him like a vise. He felt more helpless than he had on the Klamath.

No one else could speak; they just stared in awe.

# CHAPTER TWENTY SEVEN

The beast was huge: over eight-feet tall. Bobby estimated it to weigh 400 pounds. Darker than ebony, it appeared to absorb any light that came in contact with it. Eyes the color of hot lava focused on the marooned man. Its bipedal body bore its only resemblance to humans. It had feet shaped like paddle blades, with six nasty-looking claws on each foot facing downward like spikes.

*That's how it swims so fast*, he thought. Its arms and legs were long and muscular, reptilian in appearance. *That's how it runs so fast.* It was thick through the torso, and its head sat on wide shoulders. Jaws flared behind the ears to accommodate an enormous mouth, which housed what looked like dozens of long, sharp, yellow teeth. The hand-like appendages had two claw-like fingers, with an opposing thumb-claw. They looked hard and sharp.

After the shock of first seeing the creature had worn off a little, Bobby understood the chilling importance of what was happening. The enemy no longer attempted to conceal its self.

*This is it*, he thought, as he watched Jacques being helplessly pulled by the current toward the rock.

# 28

### NOTHING TO *FEAR*, BUT *FEAR ITSELF*

To Bobby's horror the creature grabbed the detective by the neck with its left claw and lifted him off the ground. It held him up above its own head and examined the man for a moment. The top of the detective's head hovered ten feet over the rock; his feet kicked and dangled.

The beast's other claw jabbed into his abdomen, disappeared into the cavity and dug around inside the wound. The detective's eyes opened wide, and his face changed to a mask of anguish. The thing appeared to study his expression. It then turned its head and gazed at Bobby, as if it wanted to show him a preview of coming attractions. It rammed its claws up into the cavity, grabbed the beating heart, and ripped it out. Zumwalt's eyes remained open for a few more seconds as the enemy ate it in front of him.

Bobby sat in shock and thought that some part of the man had been aware of what the thing had eaten. After swallowing the heart, it stuck its face into the opening and cleaned out the cavity like a child sucking down spaghetti. It then threw the shell of Ernst Zumwalt all the way over into the left channel, where it was entrapped by an exposed section of the helicopter's frame. The white foaming reversal wave turned bright red for several seconds before gradually returning to white.

Blood and tissue dripped from the cavernous mouth of the massive beast as Jacques looked on, terrified. Phydeaux barked madly from the front of the boat. She sensed the fear increasing in her beloved master. The boat slipped within five feet of the rock when the beast turned its attention to the dog.

Bobby shouted, "No!" but Phydeaux jumped from the unsteady boat. She lost her footing, and almost ended up in the river, but scuttled up the slanted rock and dodged the enemy's first swing.

"No, Phydeaux!" Bobby felt powerless watching the dog dodge the thrusts of the enemy. "God, please help her."

"Oh God!" Abby cried out.

It grabbed at the dog, and for a second after it attacked, it was open; Phydeaux went in. She lunged for the place where genitalia should have been and sank her fangs into hard flesh. The stench filled her nostrils immediately, as she shook her head from side to side, ripping the wounds savagely, in much the same manner as a shark shaking a tuna, or a pit bull shaking a cat.

The enemy, enraged by the pain, reached down and grabbed her through her shoulder, causing her to yelp, which forced her to release her jaws. In reaction to its pain, the beast flung Phydeaux into the makeshift dam. She bounced off a raft tube and rebounded halfway to the rock. She cried out, then went under.

*No!* Bobby could barely see through his tears. It wasn't fair. She had warned them—had saved them. What justice was there in the world? Hate and pain filled his heart, and for the first time since he was a child, he gave up all hope.

Jacques grabbed his spear and launched it at the enemy. It hit the shoulder, but only sank in two inches. The spears had been designed for impaling, not throwing. The weight wasn't heavy enough as a missile. He searched for something more effective as his boat perched on the front of the rock. Pulling the spare oar out of the straps, he jumped to the front of the boat. He had taped a kitchen knife to the end, so he quickly removed the safety cover, and turned to face the creature. Instead of swinging the oar, he jabbed.

His first jab caught the enemy in the mid-section; the blade sunk in to the hilt. Bobby thought for a moment that he might have killed it. Jacques turned the oar trying to sink the spear deeper. Then he pulled it out and stumbled to find better footing. The creature doubled over for an instant, but when Jacques tried to strike a second time, it seized the oar and used it as a lever. The blade of the oar was under Jacques' right shoulder, and his arms were locked around the shaft

With a powerful thrust, the beast catapulted him into the air in the same flight path as Phydeaux only higher. He landed on the house rock inside the

## CHAPTER TWENTY EIGHT

right channel. He hit flat on his back, bounced once, and fell into the rapid on the other side of the dam. Bobby saw his blood splash all over the rock.

His raft pulled back into the current and fed into the right channel, where it wrapped against the rock, adding one more layer to the neoprene/Hypalon dam. The creature turned back toward Bobby.

It looked like it was about to dive into the water and come after him when a white blur attacked it from behind. "Phydeaux!" Abby shouted. It was. Somehow the dog had survived and managed to swim back to the rock.

*Her lifejacket*, Bobby thought. The eddy had pulled her back.

She bit hard into the thing's calf and shook it, as if she might actually kill it. As if she knew the beast had killed her master, and she intended to get revenge.

Bobby wished he had enough courage to dive in and go to help her, but he didn't. He watched helplessly as the monster grabbed Phydeaux through the same wound and flung her again—much harder. She flew through the air for several seconds before a solid impact with the cliff wall seventy-five feet away. She hit with a sickening "thud" and dropped into the river.

Bobby's heart sank. Phydeaux and Jacques had been disposed of so quickly. Jacques had been like a favorite uncle, but Phydeaux's demise crushed him almost as bad. He had grown to love the dog in a very short time, and it broke his heart. Having watched the courageous fight Jacques had waged against the thing, without causing it to even slow down, he wondered if it could be defeated.

He also knew that the enemy wanted him most of all. He could sense it. He had known this beast. For decades he had been connected to it in some horrible way…a way that put him at the top of its list.

The motion of the raft brought Bobby back. He assessed the situation and realized that Abby had chosen to take them into a probable death from drowning, as opposed to a certain death at the hands of the dark enemy. She ferried across toward river left, where the helicopter created a giant reversal wave. That would have been bad enough, but a kayak had pinned in the worst spot possible. Even if they gained enough forward power to blast through the wave, which was doubtful, the kayak formed a barrier that would force the front of the raft under its hull. It looked hopeless, unless they could somehow jump at the same instant and clear the obstacle the kayak presented. Otherwise they would be re-circulated into the keeper hole time and time again, beaten to death while they drowned.

But Abby had a different idea in mind. She pulled hard as they back-paddled against the force of the river's increasing velocity. She told him she planned to hit the rock with the nose and swing the rear end of the raft around so as to enter the gate sideways. She had them crouch on the left side of the boat. When the boat hit the reversal wave, they would automatically be on the high side; when the left tube reached its apex, they would be in position to dive over the pinned kayak to the open current below. It was a long shot, but it was their only shot.

As they neared the rock, Bobby stared up at the monster. Its gaze followed him. Mocked him.

Then an idea popped into his head from out of nowhere. He made a quick mental measurement. The distance between the moving raft and the beast was well beyond Bobby's effective knife-throwing range, but he suspected this might be his last chance to even things up in case he died in the oncoming torrent. In an unsteady, moving raft, he held little hope for his accuracy. He couldn't effectively predict how many turns the heavy Bowie-knife would make. The distance to the enemy made such an attempt seem foolish, but the knife pulled his hand down like a magnet.

Standing, he braced his left foot under the right tube....

...The entrance was fifteen feet away.

He braced his right foot under the thwart....

...Ten feet.

"Hold me, Beth!" he ordered; she immediately complied by grabbing around his waist.

...The entrance was only five feet away.

The beast temporarily turned its gaze on Jim and Linda as they cleared the corner above.

Bobby took the knife in his right hand with the blade facing outward from his palm. He inhaled and took the knife back like a baseball pitcher, and let out a loud "KEEEAAAA" as he launched it, aimed for the center of the thing's chest.

He had thrown the knife hard in as gradual a rotation as he could manage; it appeared to be traveling in slow motion as it cleared the distance between man and monster.

At that moment the raft impacted the rock causing him to fall onto the floor. He never saw the result of his throw.

Up until now, the creature had been silent. From the bottom of the boat, Bobby heard a growing sound, even above the noise of the rapids.

# CHAPTER TWENTY EIGHT

As they entered the gate, Abby saw the beast crying out in pain, the handle of Bobby's K-Bar sticking out of its left eye.

The thing grabbed at the handle as it continued issuing an unearthly scream. It pulled the knife out of the dead runny hole. The remaining orb burned to a bright yellow, before fading to crimson red. It threw the knife back at Bobby. The blade struck the cliff wall as the raft passed through the gate and fell impotently onto the seat next to Abby, covered with a vile ichor. Knowing she only had a second to discard it before she was into the hole, she grasped it with her left hand. The handle radiated heat, and the ooze stunk like buzzard offal, but she quickly tossed it into the river, wiped her left hand on her shorts, and re-gripped the oar. The boat swung into the wave sideways.

"JUMP! NOW!" she shouted, as she climbed the rising tube.

Beth jumped to the left side of the raft. Bobby barely recovered enough to climb the "high side." The three jumped as the big blue raft climbed to a sixty-degree angle. The boat flipped just after they jumped, but all three had been off balance when they leaped from the boat, and as a consequence, they didn't clear the kayak. They landed on top of it and were pulled down into the "suckhole."

Inescapable. Battered like straws in a hurricane—trashed over and over again with little hope of rescue, they re-circulated back into the slot. The raft spun in the hole with them. They bumped it several times. Bobby came up under the raft and couldn't get air. The boat flipped, and he managed a quick gasp before he went under again.

The raft was eventually buffeted against the cliff wall and caught by a powerful lateral wave. It plastered to the cliff like wallpaper. Beth came up in front of him and managed to gulp a breath of foamy whitewater, then went back under. Bobby felt his knee strike something with great force, and his left leg went numb down to his foot. He reached for Abby before she was violently pulled down into the dark water. She surfaced near the top of the wave, where she was then pulled under again and again.

Beth came up unconscious, and Bobby knew it had been her head that hit his knee. Her limp body made a trip back into the hole, only to emerge on the reversal and be pulled back in. The fourth time she was sucked back into the hole, her life jacket caught the downstream jet above the trough, and she disappeared under the surface.

Bobby witnessed it and screamed, "Swim for the tongue!" He yelled again when he saw Abby pulled toward the hole. "If we hit the tongue, it'll pull us under the reversal!"

She hadn't heard but a few key words in Bobby's instructions; she had been sucked under. But she had heard the word "tongue." She came up and saw Bobby actively swimming for the mound of water upstream of the hole. At the second he crossed the trough, he went limp and disappeared under the surface. Abby did the same; a moment later she felt the current grab her like a rag doll and pull her deep under the turbulence.

A rock slammed into her thigh. Another grazed her head, knocking her senseless for a moment, but Abby kept tucked as tight as possible. Finally, she came up in a slow moving pool just below the rapid. Taking several deep breaths of cool, aerated air, she looked for Bobby and Beth.

Bobby swam for the right bank of the river with Beth under his arm. They were thirty feet downstream of the makeshift dam. He still heard the outcry from the wounded creature over the rapid's roar. Luckily, he didn't see it. He pulled Beth's lax body up onto the rocks. He panted and his heart raced, but he focused on giving her CPR. *Check for her pulse.* At first, his own throbbing vessels interfered with his being able to find one, but eventually he located a faint beat in her carotid artery. He placed his mouth on hers and filled her with the contents of his lungs. Eleven more times he repeated the procedure before Beth responded.

As Abby swam up and dragged herself out of the river, Beth began coughing and vomiting water. Gushing like a fountain for almost ten seconds, before going into a violent coughing fit, she seemed to be coming around so Bobby turned to Abby.

"Are you okay?" he asked.

She too panted like a dog, but she managed a "yes" between gasps.

"Take care of her, Abby. I'm going back to see if I can help," he said as he bent at the waist and tried to catch his own breath. He had no idea how he could help the others, but he knew he had to try; something compelled him to confront the monster again. He had to go back upstream. Someone always had to go upstream, the kid from the Klamath reminded him.

He slowly climbed the rocks to the shelf above, and stumbled back up-river toward the barrier.

# 29

## GOODBYES

Jim and Linda saw what Bobby, Abby, and Beth couldn't see-the rage of the enemy. The beast screamed its pain at the world, covering its eye with a claw and writhing all over the rock. They had witnessed Bobby hitting it with the knife, as had Jerry and Plato who had rounded the corner just ahead of them. It was clear that if Bobby somehow survived the fury of the hydraulic "washing machine," the vengeful monster would almost certainly kill him for this. *Like Pat.*

Jim opted for the same route Abby had chosen. He hadn't seen the outcome of her descent, but it would have to be better than becoming the object of the thing's attention. While the beast still wailed and held its eye, Jim intended to take advantage of that distraction. "Linda, paddle hard forward," he ordered. They sat in the rear of the raft's center section with gear stored behind them in back, leaving the front of the raft empty and light.

"When we get to the top of the wave, try to jump up onto the bridged kayak. Then, we can pull the raft over it," he shouted.

"Okay," Linda yelled back.

Their red Riken raft floated into the chute, down into the hole, and rose onto the reversal wave. The bow of Jim's boat went up but not as far as he had hoped. They jumped to the front tube and grabbed across the kayak's bottom. Pulling himself out of the raft and up onto the submerged kayak, he held on tightly to the perimeter line. Linda tried to imitate him, but the shell had been cracked by the forces already exerted on it. The kayak sagged for a second before breaking in two pieces, sending them back into the violent hole.

Jim clung desperately to the rope, as he and the boat were washed back into the artificial "keeper," but Linda had been separated from the raft and was being "maytagged" in the most vicious part of the hydraulic. The jagged halves of the kayak swirled in the white turbulence, threatening to bite her with their "ripsaw" teeth.

Jim pulled himself into the raft and grabbed a paddle from the foam nearby, when he saw Linda recycled into the slot five feet to the left of the boat. He took his paddle and held the T-bar handle out to her. She grabbed it, and he pulled her to the tube. A second later he landed her inside the boat. "Thanks," she said catching her breath. Jim felt proud; he could always count on her. Springing onto the rear tube, he locked his feet under the thwart of the spinning raft.

Using his paddle as a rudder, he kept the boat from turning sideways in the hole. *Surfing the meanest hole on the Middle Fork of the Salmon without the benefit of a crew.*

"Find your paddle—we've got to get out of here!"

Linda tried for it, but it was being recycled just like she had been. The elusive paddle made two trips just out of her reach before she finally snatched it and took her place on the side opposite Jim.

"Forward!" he yelled, and Linda dug-faster and deeper, but the wave proved too powerful. He was about to yell "Harder" when he realized she was already giving it all she had. The left channel was effectively closed by their presence; they would need to find another means of escaping the huge hydraulic hole.

Jerry saw Jim and Linda in the left channel's monstrous reversal. The right channel would be asking for evisceration by the angry beast. It looked as if Plato and Scott had decided to try to squeeze through the middle chute instead. Rafts encroached on both sides of the entry, leaving only about three feet between the left and right side of the gate, but Plato's boat measured six feet wide.

Plato pulled on the oars to buy more time, as Scott removed his rescue knife and braced for impact. Apparently, he planned to puncture the tubes on the rafts as they entered the gate. The resulting deflation might allow their raft to pass through without adding to the barrier. *If it works for them, we'll try that way.*

Until that moment, the enemy had been oblivious to anything other than its pain. It then focused its eye on Scott and stopped screeching. It crouched

## CHAPTER TWENTY NINE

twenty feet away, still on the rock where Jacques and Phydeaux had been killed, when Scott and Plato passed it. They had been concentrating on not being wedged into the narrow opening and couldn't see it coming.

Jerry watched, terrified, as the black phantom leaped eight feet up, and ten feet over to a rock bordering the right channel. He yelled at them, but the "railroad train" rumble of the water was too loud. They didn't hear his warning. Displaying incomparable agility, the creature sprang up onto the rock. Jerry could see that it stood poised directly above Scott and Plato.

Scott jabbed the knife into the first tube. It issued a loud POP, and a gush of air. He quickly moved to the opposite side and stabbed another tube. BAM. The rafts had wrapped several deep, so he kept stabbing one after another. BAM-POP-BOOM.

The raft wedged in tightly, and a wave came over the rear tube. Plato jumped forward to prevent it from being pulled under. The 600 pounds of gear in the back compartment did not jump, however, and the rear of the boat was pulled under anyway.

Luckily, Gary's kayak prevented it from flipping them over backwards. Ironic, Jerry thought, as if Gary had reached out of a watery grave and lent a helping hand. The rear compartment sank a foot or less before it came to a halt on the pinned kayak. The raft angled up causing both men to climb to the front—which was now the top—and grab hold.

Scott was too busy and couldn't see the sleek, black arm as it reached down from the top of the rock. Plato ducked, and shouted "LOOKOUT!" just as the claw snagged the rear of Scott's lifejacket. "Oh Jesus, No!" Jerry yelled. Suzi whimpered. The beast lifted Scott up as if he were nearly weightless. Kicking and slashing with the knife, Scott cut the arm that held him. A black oily substance washed across his right wrist.

Jerry watched helplessly while Scott tried to stab his knife into its other eye, but the beast cautiously held him just out of reach and studied him, as if oblivious to his onslaught.

Scott swung with all his might, sinking the needle-sharp blade through the creature's upper arm. "That's it, kill the son-of-a-bitch," Jerry shouted, even though his words dissipated in the river's rumble. The thing reacted with the speed of a striking viper, cutting the top of Scott's arm, snapping the bone and ripping the flesh off to the elbow with its scissor-like claws.

"Oh God!" Jerry shrieked. Suzi moaned as she backed into the center compartment with him. They were only fifty feet away from the same fate. For a moment, he sat numbed, and then he remembered.

Scott screamed as his hand, still gripping the knife, fell into the water. The enemy fixed him with its remaining eye and glared. Taking its free claw, it stuck two fingers into his eyes—facing palm up. The opposing thumb-claw went into the indentation at the back of his head. It closed its fist. The two fingers sank into flesh, where they joined the hand as the thumb-claw penetrated the rear of the skull causing Scott to go limp. It kept squeezing until the head crushed like a soda can, then it tossed him over the edge of the rock.

The beast looked down and searched for Plato who was no longer there. Standing erect, it scanned the river below the dam with its good eye, then turned upstream. At that instant there was a sharp report, and its left knee exploded in pain. Seconds later, there was another shot followed by an explosion in its right knee. It fell off the rock and landed in the boat precisely on top of Scott's dead body. It writhed in agony. All its rage temporarily focused on Scott's carcass. It threw his body into the rock, point-blank, where it bounced into the raging current and vanished.

*Time for the final exam,* Jerry thought. All those tests in high school had been forced on him. He didn't mind the work, but he had hated the pressure. This went beyond the limit a normal mind should have to cope with. The biggest sliver of terror that had ever stabbed his soul was the sharp fear that he might miss with all three bullets. As badly as his hand shook, that seemed a probability.

"Hold us in this eddy, Suzi." Jerry traded places with her. The eddy might hold the raft for a moment, but it wouldn't for long—not without help. He had to act quickly or lose what might be the last opportunity.

She struggled at the oars trying to hold them in the eddy behind the same rock where the creature had killed the detective. Jerry sighted in on its kneecaps from twenty-five feet away. The end of the pistol moved with a palsied rhythm. *Oh God…please.* He cocked back the hammer and tried to focus through the tears. The indecision hung around him like smoke. *Do it!*

He watched it murder Scott and his vision instantly cleared. His hands suddenly steadied on the grip, and he pulled the trigger. The minimal recoil made him wonder if the shell had been a dud. He aimed again. Once more the report came to his ears—much less than he expected.

He had found it almost as hard as trying to shoot from horseback, but providence rode with him, and both bullets struck home. *If it can't run or swim, it can't come after us any more.* He had aimed for its knees. But it was still

# CHAPTER TWENTY NINE

alive, and it looked angrier than anything he had ever seen. He hadn't acted fast enough to save Scott. He knew that realization would set in later. For now, he had to think. *Only one bullet left.* The final exam wasn't over. If a knife in the eye only slowed it down, he wondered what a .38 caliber round in the chest would do? He hoped much more.

The beast became a "whir" of motion, enraged to the point that it began slashing everything within reach. Jerry watched it crush coolers, slash foam seats to ribbons, and split open dry bags depositing clothing all over the boat. Within seconds the gear turned into confetti.

Then, it stopped its frenzy with a terrifying suddenness and looked for the source of its pain. As Jerry took aim, its single eye found him. The palsy returned.

Bobby ran on the cliff above. He was out of breath, and his side burned as if hot lead filled his spleen, but he could now see the entire play of events from his new vantage point. He saw it turn its gaze to Jerry. In an attempt to distract it, he picked up a large rock and threw it. The rock missed by several feet. Jerry and Suzi were less than twenty feet from Plato's raft. They held in the eddy, but what if it could still manage to swim somehow? He threw another rock. This one hit it in the left shoulder and got its attention. He saw it was torn between killing Jerry or coming after him. Bobby launched another grenade-sized rock at it.

His earlier knife-shot had hit the beast at an angle. It had entered the eye, and exited through the place that corresponded with a human's temple. This rock hit the knife's exit wound, and Bobby got its undivided attention.

*You ask for this*, he thought...*what now?*

The beast let out another piercing wail as it tried to stand on shattered legs. It screamed its hatred at him. He brought pain, the likes of which it had never known existed. Worse than the pain, he had brought something intolerable. For the first time in the creature's existence, it felt fear, the same kind of fear it caused in its victims. It had fed on that fear for centuries, but now fear—its own fear—fed on it.

If it didn't kill the man, it would lose something beyond value: its invisible identity. This man had not only seen Itself, this man knew Itself.

It had to stop all these people, but it had to kill the dreamer first.

Jerry hopped out of the boat and up onto the rock, while Suzi held the raft in the eddy by back-rowing. He hoped to get a steadier shot from the boulder. The beast kept trying to climb up on the side of the big rock it had just fallen from but couldn't stand—the wounded knees must have been too painful. *Thank God.* Still, it tried harder as it again screamed its hate.

Jerry couldn't fire the last bullet until it faced him squarely. *I've got to quit shaking.* He wanted a "dead center" shot this time.

"OH GOD!" Suzi cried. One of the oars slipped out of the oarlock, and the raft drifted out of the eddy. She scrambled to place the oar back into the lock but couldn't manage to get the narrow part of the oar into it first. Drifting toward the dam and the horrible thing waiting below, she floated directly into Jerry's line of fire.

"GET DOWN SUZI! GET ON THE FLOOR!" he shouted.

She kept trying to get the oar back into the lock.

"GET DOWN!" he screamed again.

In a state of panic, Suzi began throwing things at the approaching monster: The troublesome oar; the creature batted it aside; The water jug; it caught it and threw it back at her.

She ducked the jug and fell to the bottom of the boat where she cringed as she saw its hideous form grinning at her—showing dreadful teeth, which "clacked" loudly as it slammed its mouth shut. Any second, she knew it would grab the front of the boat and climb in with her.

She tried to curl up under the seat, but a thwart lived up to its name and thwarted her escape.

A huge black shape crawled up onto the slashed pile of cargo in the rear compartment of Plato's raft. Grabbing the perimeter line on the front of Jerry's boat, it pulled itself up onto the tube. Suzi shook with violent spasms as it eyed her. It reached for her just as another rock hit it in the neck. Half standing in spite of the pain, it aimed its burning, Cyclops' glare on whoever threw it.

"OVER HERE, ASSHOLE!" Jerry's voice screamed above the rapid.

The enemy turned its attention back to Suzi, as if it planned to kill her first, and then go after the two men. It reached for her, and was only inches from closing around her throat, when an unseen hand pushed it back.

The .38 special slug hit it in the center of the chest. It slipped off the tube and vanished under the water.

## CHAPTER TWENTY NINE

Ever since he had been knocked out of the raft by Scott's body, Plato had been holding onto the bowline from under the front tube of his boat…hiding. He felt something slick brush against his leg. A second later the dreadful monster popped up only five feet below him. It held onto the same bow rope. Reaching up with newfound strength, Plato grabbed the nearest D-ring. He tried to pull himself up but he was too tired and the current too strong. He grabbed the perimeter line with his other hand and began pulling himself back an inch at a time.

Bobby was relieved to see Plato emerge from under the boat, but the look on his face told him that the bullet hadn't finished the job. He ran upstream a few yards and gained a better view.

The monster pulled itself closer to Plato. It was losing strength fast but not fast enough. It reached with its other claw and came within two feet of him. Plato grabbed the next D-ring and pulled himself away. They hung like that for a minute…motionless.

Then Bobby saw a way. The idea came into his mind as if God had hammered it in with a sixteen-pound psychic sledge. He saw a means to defeat the enemy, and he didn't like it. *Ironic. So simple.* He wasn't so tired to not feel fear. He trembled with fear. But if he didn't act immediately, he would again bear the responsibility for more deaths. That would haunt him for the rest of his life.

Just like the first time he had climbed into a raft or stepped into the ring for his first fight, Bobby squared off against his old enemy, fear. Knowing full well this next action might cost him his life, he backed up, took a breath, and ran toward the precipice. He jumped off the cliff, sailing through the air for what seemed to be an impossibly long time, his heart pounding with dread. He hit the water upstream of Jerry's boat without too much pain.

The frigid water had drained him before, but this time it woke him up. Bubbles rose all around him in the darkness. The dread erupted into a prayer and he surfaced along side the raft. Bobby grabbed for the perimeter line but missed the first attempt and was almost pulled under Plato's boat-within reach of the monster's claws. His second attempt snagged the line, and he pulled himself partially onto the tube. *I can't do it.* Now too exhausted, he could go no further. His breath wouldn't come. *No use.*

Suzi screamed when his hand came over the tube, but when she realized it wasn't a claw, she crawled out from under the seat and pulled him into the boat. He could barely stand but somehow managed with her help. Taking the remaining oar out of the oarlock, he handed it to her. "You've got…to help me…got an idea," he told her through his gasps. "Come with me."

He crawled to the front of Jerry's boat, then carefully onto Plato's shredded cargo hold. Suzi followed. They made their way to the front of the raft where they found themselves only four feet from a nightmare visage.

Bobby opened Plato's throw bag, and the rope came out in a lump on the floor. He tangled it into a wad, until it was thoroughly messed up, and he turned back toward the beast. The kid on the Klamath had shown him a way out. He threw the mass of ropes into the creature's face. It entangled the beast's neck and arms.

"Hit it in the head—make it let go of the bow-line," he shouted.

Suzi hesitated. Dare she hurt this monster again?

"Come on—hit it!"

She took the oar and began jabbing the black beast in the face. Even with all the wounds it had sustained, it found the strength to go into a fury. She jabbed again, and it chomped off the end of the oar blade. She hit it in the neck with the jagged remnant of the oar, but it clung tenaciously to the rope and began to pull itself inexorably towards her.

Bobby changed tactics. He took his clip-lock knife and reached over the bow of the raft. The razor-sharp blade cut through part of the rope, but before Bobby cut the last quarter inch of the line, he looked into the blazing eye of the beast.

He saw the monster in his childhood closet and thought of his friends: Gretta, Pat, The Judge, Bonnie, Scott, Jacques, and faithful Phydeaux whom he would never see again; he saw venomous hate and murder that had tracked him through hundreds of miles of bad dreams. He knew what would happen when he cut the rope, and he savored the last few seconds.

…Bobby swung his knife in a powerful arc, cutting the remainder of the rope.

"TRY THAT ON, MOTHERFUCKER!" he shouted just when the monster lunged at him and slashed.

The claw tore through his lifejacket as the monster fell into the water. It fought the tangled ropes as Bobby moved quickly. Powered by adrenalin, he grabbed the carabineer clip on the loose end of the rope and slammed it home

# CHAPTER TWENTY NINE

against the D-ring on the front of Jacques' wrapped boat. Seconds later, the line pulled tight, creating a huge, "rooster-tail" wave.

By entangling it in a rope attached to a fixed object, it should drown. The river exerted tons of force per square foot, making it an impossible adversary—even for such a formidable creature.

Bobby fought back jagged laughter as he hugged Suzi.

The nightmare had finally ended. Bobby sent a silent thanks to the boy on the Klamath.

Euphoric, Bobby stood next to Suzi; they held each other and began laughing.

"Help!" came from under the boat.

Looking at each other, they both exclaimed, "Plato!"

Bobby reached down and grabbed the right shoulder of his lifejacket, Suzi grabbed the left, and they pulled him in with the same technique used to land a large sturgeon.

Plato fell onto the floor of his Maravia, totally exhausted.

"Thanks," he choked out.

Jerry swam up and climbed in to be with them.

"We got that son-of-a-bitch," he said with tears flooding from his eyes. "We got it."

They held each other and cried shamelessly. What had seemed like hours of battle had in reality been less than fifteen minutes from the time Jacques had rounded the corner until the present. A lifetime for some, for others the end of a lifetime.

They gazed at the huge watery fan at the end of the rope. Water shot twenty to thirty feet into the air and looked as if someone were holding a ski rope behind a boat and had refused to let go after they had fallen face down. Someone big and dark.

• • •

Jim and Linda, still trapped in the hole, neared exhaustion. A miracle mixed with good boat handling had kept them in the twelve-foot raft. They had surfed the hole for a long time, almost too long. The current continuously tried to turn the raft sideways, but Jim didn't allow that to happen. He had been stuck in some of the meanest holes on the Cheat, the Gauley, and the

New Rivers back in West Virginia. He'd had lots of practice in Sweet's Falls, Big Nasty, and Recyclotron—this wasn't much worse. He knew that eventually the boat would fill with water; it was close to it now. "Not much longer," he shouted to Linda. The raft inched into the slot, and they took on another thirty-plus gallons. They bumped six more times before finally being "submarined" under the huge reversal wave. Before they were inundated, Jim shouted, "Hang on to something!"

Linda looked desperately but couldn't find anything to grab. The raft went through the wave backwards and spun. She felt the pull of her lifejacket lifting her out of the boat, when her knee brushed one of the dry bags in the rear compartment of the raft. Grabbing a cam strap, she hung on for her life. When the Riken resurfaced, it resembled a bathtub more than a boat. Water ran out over the tubes.

As they rounded the rock, Jim saw the strange wave with a rope leading back towards the dam. The end of it was attached to one of the wrapped boats, which flexed back and forth from the strain on its other end. He caught sight of Bobby and Jerry frantically waving their arms, motioning them to the left, away from the plume of water fifteen feet off the right bank.

The current seemed determined to take them back toward it. Jim fought the heavy boat to a forty-five-degree angle facing river left, as he and Linda dug for all they were worth. The water seemed more like thick molasses, and the raft literally weighed a ton.

Jim sat on the right side of the boat and stared at the huge dark shape at the head of the plume. He knew it would not be in their best interest to come close to the top of the spray; he knew what was under the surface, and he couldn't quite believe what must be true: *It's dead.* As he watched it coming closer, the weight of the boat pulled him within six feet of the wave, but he found strength to avoid it. The raft passed through the fountain, but missed the object, that had created it. As the raft emerged on the other side of the spray, they both turned to look upstream. He read the relief in Bobby's face, and it told him that things were going to be all right again. He looked over at Linda but it was hard to see through the tears in his eyes.

Linda grabbed the bail-bucket and began the arduous task of emptying the hundreds of gallons of water from the raft. Jim glimpsed Abby and Beth on the right bank. He wanted to pull over and rest more than anything, but he was unable to control the heavy-laden boat. He and Linda were swept around the corner into the waiting rapids.

# 30

## CONFLUENCE

"Do you think it's dead?" Suzi asked Bobby.

"It's got to be," he replied. "It's been stabbed, shot three times, and drowned." He shuddered at what felt like emanations of hate radiating from under the wave and half expected to see the water start boiling at any moment.

*It's got to be dead—got to be.*

Together they pulled Jerry's boat over Plato's and through the opening as Daniel stood on the cliff wall above them. Jerry threw a rope bag to him and he pulled them down to where Abby and Beth waited on a rock. Beth's color reminded Bobby of mayonnaise left out of the cooler too long. She still coughed but seemed to be all right otherwise.

Bobby rolled over the tube and fell into the shallow water, totally spent. He floated in his lifejacket next to the boat until Abby grabbed the collar of his vest and pulled him to the bank. He managed to stand for a moment on shaky legs, before he collapsed onto the rocks. Abby wrapped her arms around him and wept openly. This time, Bobby was too tired to cry. He told himself there would be plenty of time for tears in the days ahead.

"I'm glad you're safe," she said.

"So am I," he answered through a weak smile. "I guess you better plan on showing me Portland now."

"My pleasure." She kissed his cheek tenderly.

Daniel walked up re-stuffing the throw bag.

"Is it finished?" he asked.

*Why is everybody asking me?* Bobby wondered. He thought for a moment before answering.

"I think so. I think it's over," he answered.

Daniel looked back at the plume, and a tear trickled down his cheek. Bobby thought of Daniel's twin brother. *Time won't heal all wounds.*

"We're all going to have to pile into this boat unless somebody wants to walk back up and swim out to the dam," Jerry advised. No one volunteered, so they all agreed to squeeze into Jerry's raft and to send someone back for the remainder of their equipment at an unspecified future date.

Plato stood on the shore, staring at Jacques' boat. Bobby reflected how he and Jacques had been friends for twenty years. He had also stood by helplessly and watched while Scott had been lifted to his doom.

Bobby released Abby from his embrace, held her hand, and stood facing up-river. So many deaths. Moments ago, he'd felt the greatest relief he had known in years, but suddenly his heart sank. He hadn't seen what happened to Scott, but he had witnessed Jacques' and Phydeaux's downfall. Phydeaux had saved all of them. She had given her life trying to defend her master. You couldn't ask for more from a dog. He felt the tears coming sooner than he had expected.

Even though he hadn't known him that long, Bobby thought of Jacques with bitter sadness, Jacques who carried the heaviest load, who performed his one-man vignettes to entertain those around him, who always smiled with a cigar clamped between his teeth.

*If only he hadn't tried to rescue that asshole. He and Phydeaux would still be alive.* However, Bobby knew that way of thinking didn't hold water. If events had changed, it might have come after them in the river, or from the rock next to the left channel. It might have killed them all. He couldn't succumb to second-guessing how it might have been, had things turned out differently.

Then he remembered Craig Redmond on the Klamath. For the first time he felt sorrow rather than guilt. Bobby realized he had finally thought of him by his name instead of "the kid." In fact, the memory of his body hanging on the rope at Hell's Corner had been the revelation that had saved them. And for the first time he realized he wasn't responsible for everything bad that happened in the world. Though for days, the haunting thought that he had somehow drawn his childhood fears into the real world had plagued him.

*No more.*

Looking downstream, he saw the river relentlessly pulled toward sea level. Fate seemed to be just like a river, with branches and channels that mindlessly cut through human canyons. Just as the river never jammed logs in order to

## CHAPTER THIRTY

kill unwary boaters, life held no ill will towards human existence. Fate merely swept people along the currents of their own choices. True, bad things did happen to good people, but from that day forward, Bobby promised himself he would only take his share of the responsibility for them. His shaking muscles interrupted his train of thought and he staggered to a nearby rock to sit down before he fell.

Exhaustion had taken its toll on everyone else too. Sleep depravation and the adrenalin overdose had caught up to him at the same moment everyone else stopped talking.

Although less than two miles from the confluence with the Main Salmon, they might as well have been 200. They sat nearly motionless in a collective daze.

Abby stirred first and began rounding the others up to leave. She managed to help the remaining survivors into the raft. It was crowded, but they found room. They took one last look at the rooster-tail wave before they rounded the corner to search for Jim and Linda.

About a mile downstream, they caught sight of a large house-sized rock on the right side of the river. As they approached, Jim and Linda paddled his small Campways out from behind it. Bobby glanced from Jim's grim expression to the front section of his boat. *Jacques' and Phydeaux's bodies.* Jacques lay on his back, knees over the tube with Phydeaux next to him.

Bobby's eyes watered up. With his throat constricting, he looked at Phydeaux's face. Her head hung limply over Jacques' side. Something about the way she guarded her master, even in death, broke his heart. Then, one of her eyes opened and looked at him, followed by a listless wag of her tail.

"Phydeaux!" Bobby cried with joy. "There is a God!" He wanted to jump across to the other boat and hug the dog, but she didn't look like she would survive it.

"Oh my God," Abby cried. "What a good girl. How on earth?" Tears of joy streamed from her green eyes. In fact, everybody wept.

Several voices called to Phydeaux all at once. Her tail attempted two more sluggish wags. She tried to lift her head, but cried out in pain. *She's got to hurt all over*, Bobby thought. "The life jacket with the bear patches must have padded the impact," he said. Bobby winced at the sight of a broken rear leg, and three nasty wounds in her shoulder where she had been stabbed by the rending claws of the beast. She tried to move into her original position and cried out again.

"Be still, Phydeaux," Jacques groaned. Looking up at Bobby and Abby, he tried to force a smile.

"We thought you were dead," Abby said.

"I'm not?"

"Jacques—thank God. How bad is it?" Bobby asked.

"I've had worse, I just can't remember which past life it was in."

"Jacques!" Plato exclaimed. "I'm so glad—I...I...," he wrestled his emotions, but he finally managed to speak. "Does this mean that poker is still on for Friday?" Tears spilled from his eyes.

"Sure, amigo..." Jacques grimaced and took a moment fighting down a wave of fresh pain. "But, you'll have to come to the Intensive Care Casino if you want to play with me."

"We found them floating around in this eddy," Jim said. "Phydeaux had just about slipped out of her lifejacket. She had her nose up like a snorkel but was practically submerged. Jacques was out cold, but his type-5 vest kept him floating on his back. I guess he and Phydeaux went through Jump Off Joe and Goat Creek Rapids while they were unconscious. Truth is stranger than fiction, huh?"

"Could we please go now?" Jacques asked. "Phydeaux and I need a hospital, and I want to get away from that thing back there.

Bobby was about to assure him that the creature was, in fact, dead this time, when his mind filled with the dreaded image of the plume once again. He floated toward it as if he were there, as if he were in one of his nightmares, but he could still hear the voices around him. The plume drew him closer. He visualized the spray thrown off by the spinning weight at the head of the wave. In an instant, the fan of water abated, leaving the frayed end of a rope dancing on the surface, and a large shadow sinking deep into the pool below where the wave had been. Bobby shook off the apparition, but it left him trembling.

"What's wrong?" Abby asked.

Cold dread filled his spine, and he felt as if his gut had been torn out. "I don't know if anything's wrong," he said trying to steady his hands. "I just had a vision of the rope breaking, and the thing sinking under the water. It might not be anything, but after the last few days, I'd like to get out of here."

Everyone looked back upstream nervously.

"It's dead," Abby reassured him.

"It's been tight-lined for almost 20 minutes," Suzi pointed out. "We know it's an air-breather 'cause we heard it suck wind after it killed Pat."

"Yeah, but it had been under water a long time before it sucked wind," Bobby reminded her. "Let's get a move on and keep our eyes open just in case."

# CHAPTER THIRTY

Jerry and Jim both called "forward paddle," and once again the boats moved downstream toward the confluence. Cache Bar, the first take-out, lay just below that point. Their cars, however, were parked at Corn Creek, four miles farther down.

Less than a quarter of a mile above the juncture with the Main Salmon, a slanted rock barely broke the surface about 30 feet off the right bank. On the rock lay a body that resembled Raymond, the helicopter pilot from Elk Bar.

They shouted at him. Bobby felt relieved when the man raised his head warily. Seeing them, he tried to lift his arms to wave but couldn't. He appeared white as though completely drained of blood, and he shivered even in the ninety-degree heat. Bobby recognized it as first-stage hypothermia, or shock from injuries. His teeth sounded like someone typing in rhythm on an old Smith Corona Standard.

"Can you talk?" Daniel asked as he pulled up next to the rock.

Raymond couldn't answer.

"Get him off that rock and into my boat. He's in shock. I can't take time to treat him now. We'll have to make for Cache Bar and treat him there," Jim said.

Jim and Jerry lifted Raymond into the rear of Jim's boat. Breaking an ironclad rule to never tie anyone to a boat, they strapped him on with cam straps. Otherwise he might have fallen back into the water without a lifejacket.

Twenty minutes after they joined the Main Salmon, Bobby saw a flurry of activity on the right bank: county sheriff's patrol cars, along with state police, and unmarked but obviously government-issue sedans.

The boat landing was easily recognizable from the river. Several deputies waved them over to the ramp. Two men, standing taller than the rest walked down to the river's edge to meet them. Both men were dressed casually, with their badges prominently displayed on the left side of their work shirts. The bigger one wore a cowboy hat. They watched silently as Bobby and Abby pulled the raft up onto the shore.

"We're sure glad to see you," Bobby said to the smaller of the two men.

"I'll bet you are. I'm Chief Deputy Earl Bohannan, and this is Deputy Joe Bob Everett." He noticed Jacques and Phydeaux, and then he recognized Raymond. "We'll get medical help for everyone who's injured. Then if you're up to it, we'd like to ask you some questions."

"Please make sure there's a good vet available," Bobby said. "That dog has made some life-long friends on this trip…she saved our lives."

Earl looked at the dog and smiled. "We'll see that she gets top priority," he assured him.

"Doc Blackman lives in Salmon," Joe Bob advised. "He's as good a vet as there is in the State of Idaho. I'll have the paramedics take your dog there when they drop these gentlemen off at the clinic. It's not a hospital, but they can fix most things, if their injuries aren't critical."

Jacques, Raymond, and Phydeaux were carefully loaded into a police car and sped toward Salmon, miles away.

• • •

Earl liked the trip leader, Bobby Aldrich. Shortly after the introductions, he could tell that nobody in his group was a killer. They were victims of the same evil force that had ripped through the Victor Ranch. He had been close to that killer, and he couldn't wait to begin debriefing the survivors in hopes that they would be able to tell him who was responsible.

One of the women, a small dark-haired woman, named Beth, demanded to be taken away from the river. For now the landing area would have to serve as a base of operations. When one of the officers told her she would be questioned here, she went wild. She screamed for a helicopter. Several officers tried to explain that there weren't that many helicopters within hundreds of miles, and that for security reasons, they all had to stay here. There were two travel trailers and a small Winnebago that had been brought in to accommodate them, and dozens of armed officers, but even with her safety assured, she fell to her knees and begged them: a pitiful sight. Her fear was the most real Earl had ever seen on a human face. The officers led her away, while a taller, more confident woman walked along side trying to soothe her.

*Jesus H. Christ.*

Earl accompanied Bobby to the small R.V., and a nice one at that. "This is going to be your home for the night. Why don't you clean up a little, rest, and then I'll come back later and we'll talk, all right?"

"You're not taking us to a police station?"

"No, the entire area is quarantined until tomorrow at the earliest. That's why everything has been brought here." The detective was aware of the group's exhausted state. He tried to be courteous and patient with them, even though it was hard to restrain his curiosity. He watched as deputies led the others to the trailers to get some rest.

## CHAPTER THIRTY

Two hours later, Earl found Bobby standing in the doorway of the Winnebago, staring at the river. The man looked half dead. His hair stood in all directions, and even his beard appeared to have grown just since he'd been there. "I need to ask you some questions," Earl said.

Bobby stretched, then walked back inside and put on his Parker Guitars T-shirt. Earl motioned for him to sit in the breakfast nook; he did. The detective went to the refrigerator, took out two Dr. Peppers, and returned to the table. He offered one to Bobby, which he gratefully accepted. Earl took a small tape recorder from his jacket pocket and turned it on.

"I'm interviewing witness, Bobby Aldrich, at Cache Bar. Testing." He began the first interview:

"Please state your name for the record."

"Robert T. Aldrich."

"Are you giving this information under duress?"

"No."

"You are not a suspect, Bobby. That's why I haven't read you your rights. I just want to ask you some questions that hopefully will help us find whoever was responsible for all the killings. Were you the ones who placed the Mayday call from the Victor Ranch?"

"Yeah, actually Jacques did…but how did you know? We never reached anyone."

"You're wrong there. A little boy just east of the mountains picked up your call, but he didn't get to the unit in time to catch you. That's when we went into motion." Earl leaned back and took a long sip from the bottle. Setting it on the table he continued: "Now Bobby, I'd like for you to start at the beginning and tell me everything you can remember about what happened."

The younger man talked for almost two hours. Earl noted his struggle to keep things in chronological order, often getting off track and having to retrace his mental steps. Sometimes he stopped, choking back tears, but Bobby eventually got to the part where they arrived at the boat landing.

Earl listened with an occasional nod of the head, or an affirmative word, but the story was fantastic. Over the years he'd questioned hundreds of suspects, and thousands of witnesses, and he'd developed a sense of knowing when he was being lied to. He knew instinctively that the man believed what he was saying. He wasn't lying. Earl felt more certain than if he'd hooked him up to a polygraph. Recognizing the fatigue factor, he thanked Bobby and told him he was free to try to get some sleep.

Earl felt eager to meet with Joe Bob and several other investigators to compare notes. He started to leave when he turned back to face Bobby. "I find what you told me hard to swallow, but I think you're telling me what you believe is the truth. I sure hope you're mistaken though, 'cause if you're not, I'd have to change my belief system, and I don't want to do that. I don't want to believe in monsters—we have enough monsters walking around inside human bodies. But if your beast is real, then we have to realize that we don't know everything, and that's hard to do in this day and age—to admit that something like this could exist and we wouldn't even know it."

"I know it exists, I know it's real, and I know I had to change my belief systems or more than likely I'd be dead right now," Bobby said. "I'm going to keep hoping that the one we killed is the only one in existence, but I think that's unlikely, don't you? We might be sharing the planet with a new life form that doesn't have a very high opinion of us except as a snack."

"I pray you're wrong," Earl said as he turned to leave.

"Oh, would you mind doing me a favor?" Bobby asked.

"What's that?"

"Would you mind having somebody call my folks and tell them that I'm okay? I'd hate for them to be watching the news and hear about all this—they're not too thrilled with my profession already."

"I'll see to it…we'll talk again in the morning. Good night."

It was still light outside when the detective left for the meeting.

Earl met with Lt. Spalding and a group of officers in a large motor home. The entire group of rafters had been questioned. Their stories matched without exception. The officers, however, could not believe that a monster really existed. That part, they figured, had to be some sort of group hallucination.

It was one matter to have this kind of mass murderer on the loose and another to have no suspects. Earl hoped a human suspect would turn up soon, not only to relieve the heat, which would be substantial in the light of the present body count—71 dead—but also to relieve his worry that something might exist outside of what he knew to be real; that thought scared him worse.

•••

"It's not looking good," Joe Bob said. He and Earl stood by the county "paddy-wagon" and scanned the mountains to the south. "John's really on the rag about this. He's organizing a posse to go back into the canyon. He's even called in the National Guard. The Governor's really pissed off. Sam Baker, that Oregon Supreme Court Justice, was one of his closest friends. They were

## CHAPTER THIRTY

fly-fishing buddies, and he's hot to find whoever did it and nail their ass to the wall."

"What if something like what they described really does exist?" Earl asked. "It might be a little hard to nail an ass like that to the wall. Frank reported what he saw, and nobody believed him, yet it sounds remarkably similar to what Aldrich described to me. Now we've got ten witnesses whose stories all fit together like a glove saying that some eight-foot reptilian monster killed 18 of their people, and God knows how many more along the river that haven't even been found yet. That killing in White River is identical to the ones at the ranch, and Moody said the FBI thinks that M.O. goes back 25 years or more. I'll tell you, Joe Bob, if what they told us is true, I hope these guys are right about them killing it, cause the thought of something like that on the loose makes me consider giving up police work."

"Then I've got some more bad news for you," Joe Bob said. "The first helicopter arrived late this afternoon and went up to the sight where the rafts were all clogged up. They landed nearby and looked around. Everything matched up with these people's story, except that whatever had been on the end of the rope was gone."

Earl looked out the window of the motor home. The mountains loomed above the evening shadows. He felt the chill of the coming night, and for the first time since the early morning hours, he felt afraid.

# 31

## TORNADO WARNING

**B**obby jumped from sleep. He heard something that brought him back from the deep, and he was suddenly wide-awake. He listened for anything that might reveal what his subconscious had heard, and where the sound had come from. Another noise confirmed its location.

*Something's outside the R.V.*

It came to a stop below his window. For a moment he lay motionless on the bed listening. Something brushed against the side of the Winnebago, and then a soft *TAP TAP* came from the window.

He wanted to look, but the fear of seeing a one-eyed nightmare leering back at him froze him as still as death.

*TAP TAP TAP*

He searched for his clip-lock knife. *Oh shit! The police took it.*

*TAP TAP TAP*—harder this time. Sweat dripped from his brow. He backed away from the window.

"Bobby? Are you there?" It was Abigail's voice. He let out the breath he had held and opened the curtains. He pointed to the front door and put on his cut-offs as he went to open it.

He found Abby and Beth looking around as if they thought they might have been followed. "Come in. Sure beats sleeping on a tarp in a big pile, and there's no guard duty," he said as they entered.

Abby went to the booth and sat, as did Beth. They weren't smiling.

"They don't believe us," Abby said. She didn't appear worried as much as she seemed disturbed.

"I know, but would you believe our story if you hadn't been there yourself?"

"Probably not, but I still don't like the insinuation that we're not telling them everything," she said. "I'm a prosecutor, for Christ's sake."

"I want to go home," Beth moaned. "I just want to go back to Portland and forget all of this."

"I don't think we'll ever be able to forget," Bobby said. "I think this is going to haunt us for the rest of our lives. It's like we survived the Jim Jones massacre in Guiana—even if we can forget it from time to time, somebody will always be there to remind us."

Bobby talked with them for a while, until exhaustion caught up to him, and his head began to nod. They had all been running on fumes for the last two days, and the time to pay seemed to be at hand.

He went to the bathroom and came back to find them both leaving. Beth exaggerated a yawn as she and Abby stood and walked to the door.

"Where are you going?" he asked.

"I'm going to see Beth back to the trailer we're sharing with Suzi, then I'd like to come back and discuss something with you."

Bobby wondered what that might be, but they were out the door before he could ask.

A short while later, he heard a knock on the door just before Abby let herself back in. "God, it's scary outside—even with cops everywhere," she said as she walked up to him.

Bobby searched for words but heard himself speaking before he found them: "You could stay here if you want—then you wouldn't have to walk back. I mean…." The words died in his throat.

Abby smiled at him. It was the same smile she'd gifted to him the first time he'd seen her below Pistol Creek Rapids. "There's only one bed…is that a proposition, Mr. Aldrich?"

Bobby swallowed, but his mouth had suddenly gone dry. Even after a week on the river, Abby looked better than a hot fudge sundae. "I…I…just want your company." His knees shook as he glanced at the bed. Abby followed with her eyes.

"I think you're scared," she said as she walked past him and sat on the edge of the bed. She gently patted the mattress next to her.

"Me? No way."

Abby said, "I want to be close to you. I want you to hold me."

"I want that, too."

They undressed, folded the covers back, and slipped under the cool sheets

## CHAPTER THIRTY ONE

together. Bobby felt the heat from Abby's legs as she spooned back against him. He had left the bathroom light on, and it gently filtered into the camper. She looked incredibly beautiful in its soft light.

It seemed almost strange not to be listening for the tinkle and rattle of the perimeter line. The comfort of the bed lulled him.

She turned to face him. "How about a goodnight kiss?" She said.

Touching the side of her face with his fingers, he kissed her cheek, he kissed her ear, her forehead, her neck, and then he kissed her lips. She leaned closer and passionately returned his kiss. Her emerald green eyes focused somewhere far away and then slowly closed. He felt her hand caressing his shoulder, his chest, his stomach. Being intoxicated on exhaustion made his skin hypersensitive to each of her movements.

He wanted so very much to give her pleasure, to share himself with her. The same electricity that pulsed through his fingers the first time he'd touched her now ran the length of his body at all points of contact. *Thank God we both survived.* After the incident on the Klamath, he didn't think he would ever know happiness again, but here he was—with the most beautiful woman he had ever seen.

As their hands explored each other's bodies, he watched her expressions of pleasure, and listened to her soft moaning. It aroused him more than anything he could remember.

He nibbled softly on her earlobe, as his hand moved slowly between her legs and pressed gently. He brushed his lips along her neck, then down kissing her breasts. As his fingers teased and played lovingly into her warm wetness, she sighed and moved her hips in rhythm to his hand. Her expression bordered between ecstasy and pain. She gasped, letting out a low, sensual moan and arched her back, reaching out and pulling him even closer.

Bobby eased on top and slowly pushed his hardness inside her. Surprised by his sudden entry, she gasped as he penetrated deeper into her. She shuddered.

The murder of his friends had carved a cavern of pain inside his heart, but her love filled it to overflowing. It was as if some primal force invaded his senses and demanded, "Life!"

Their bodies melded together as waves of ecstasy overtook them. Bobby groaned with each thrust. He kissed Abby wet and deep, and it took him over the edge. At the apogee of his climax, Abby started her second. Shuddering for what seemed an eternity at the height of its intensity, they both began crying, racking sobs, as they held onto each other desperately and tried to drain every bit of pleasure that could be taken from the moment. It was as though all the tension of the past week was being released through the exquisite sensations in their bodies.

They held each other for a long time and continued to cry quietly. It was the deepest emotional experience he had ever shared with another human being; he didn't want it to ever end.

Bobby looked into her eyes, and through the tears, he understood that this was the beginning of something special for both of them, an ironic gift from the monster.

After a few moments of silence, he was the first to speak.

"So what do you think? Am I still invited to Portland?" he asked as he brushed hair out of her face."

"You can move to Portland if you want to," she replied. "Then we could do this every day."

"Every day? I was thinking more like twice a day."

"Twice a day on weekdays maybe, but weekends at least four times a day."

"Do you think we might actually find time to eat?" he asked.

The next morning they were all questioned again. The interviews took over four hours this time, and it was conducted jointly, by the FBI and the Idaho SCI-Unit. While the interrogation proceeded, computers accessed every known piece of information on each survivor. The law enforcement people checked DMV records, criminal records, wants and warrants, and local police information thoroughly. When it was ascertained that no more information could be added, they were again released. At 3:30 p.m., Earl and Joe Bob came into Bobby's borrowed R.V.

"We found your rafts and equipment. After we finish looking them over, they'll be released to you," Joe Bob promised. "Unfortunately, we found no other survivors."

"You know Bobby, nothing about this case stacks up unless what you told us is true. Then it all makes sense. The feds analyzed that black crap on the knife at the ranch. I overheard them say nothing like it exists, scientifically. But it's not enough to change the way this is going to be handled. The official line is going to be either that a group of Satan worshippers, or some terrorists went on a rampage. But I want you to know that's not my position. I never thought I'd believe in the boogey man, but no human did this. I think the Sheriff and Spalding know it too; they just don't want the press to sink their teeth into them, which brings up another point. Over 200 reporters and relatives are be-

## CHAPTER THIRTY ONE

ing held back below Shoup, about 30 miles up the road. They're going to want to ask you a bunch of questions once you go by. You can tell them the truth, or you can tell 'em what we're going to. It's up to you. But if y'all tell them what you told me, you'll probably find the supermarket tabloids with your pictures on the front, and a headline reading: 'Bigfoot Lives says survivor of whitewater hell,' or 'Aliens exist—I've seen them—admits Oregon river guide.' Now I don't know you very well, but my guess is that you wouldn't want to see yourself on the rack every time you go down to buy milk. Not to mention having the Area 51 crowd camped out on your front porch."

Bobby thought for a moment. He had forgotten about the news potential and possible hysteria a story like this could generate.

"I sure as hell don't want to end up on a tabloid. I want to leave this behind me the fastest, easiest way I can. I just want to get back to my life. Is there any way to get by them?"

"Sooner or later, you're going to have to answer their questions or they'll hound you to death. Think it over; we'll be letting you all go in about an hour." There was a knock on the door. Joe Bob let Abby and Beth in—they sat at the table.

Earl said, "We located the dam yesterday, but the rope had been frayed loose by the weight. We'll send divers down to try to recover the bodies of your friends. If we find them, we'll have the local police in their respective communities notify the next of kin. We'll be taking you to your cars in about an hour, so hang on a little longer. The state boys are looking through your rafting stuff right now, and as soon as they're through, you can go." He turned to leave, but Abby stood up and blocked his exit from the trailer.

"I want to know if you believe us," she demanded. She hadn't been privy to Bobby and Earl's conversation. Bobby sensed that she placed a great weight on speaking the truth and being believed.

"I don't think you're lying, Ms. Jones. I think that something strange and terrible came here, and I think it came through White River on its way. There's no way to prove it, 'cause there wasn't anything on the end of that rope; we're still looking for whatever it was. But I'll tell you this—I hope you were right about having killed it—I really hope you're right. If it's still alive, this could be only the beginning. Even worse, there could be more of these things. I sure don't like that thought—excuse me," he said as he slipped by her and walked outside, followed by Joe Bob.

Bobby rode to Corn Creek in the front seat of the cruiser with Earl, while Beth, Abby and Plato rode in the back. Joe Bob took the rest in a van.

Corn Creek depressed Bobby. Dozens of cars waited for drivers who would never come to claim them. Daniel's brother's car was there as was Gretta's van.

"Good luck, folks. It won't be easy forgetting about this, but try to put it behind you. Here's my card if you remember anything important. Otherwise, goodbye," Earl said handing Bobby the card.

"Thanks, detective. Good luck to you, too." Bobby watched as the police car and van drove off into the distance; a smoke screen of dust followed them like a vapor trail.

Jim suggested they all hurry and drive back to Cache Bar to pick up the boats on the way to Salmon. He and Linda needed to be in Boise by the next morning to catch a plane, and it was still an eight-hour drive.

Bobby reached up under the wheel-well of the van and located the magnet-box that held Gretta's spare key. He felt strange about getting into the van. Not only were a number of Gretta's things inside, but it was the first time he and Abby were going to be separated. He felt scared that somehow their bond might be broken. The magic might fade away. He turned, looking for her and saw Daniel crying openly, sitting on the ground. He walked over to him and knelt down.

"Are you going to make it, Daniel?"

"It's just hard to leave. Jonah's spirit is out there somewhere. I may never be this close to him again," he said through his sobs. "I feel bad—what with leaving him here."

Bobby gently grabbed his arm and helped him up. They locked hands to elbows and Daniel thanked him for being there. Bobby told him to look him up if he was ever in Oregon. Daniel opened the car door and climbed into the driver's seat; he left his kayak behind. He told Bobby that he planned to drive back to Montana, but he would never kayak again. He said goodbye and drove away.

They loaded the boats onto the trailer. Suzi rode with Jerry. Bobby took Jim and Linda in the van, Abby took Beth in her Suburban, and Plato drove Jacques' pick-up truck.

As they passed the confluence, Bobby noticed two empty police cruisers with doors open, and no officers nearby.

"Should we stop?" Linda asked.

# CHAPTER THIRTY ONE

He drove on without speaking. At this point he would stop for nothing, but he watched the cars disappear in the dust from the rear-view mirror, and he was momentarily filled with a sense of unease. He left the Middle Fork of the Salmon for the last time.

The roadblock in Shoup allowed them to pass without incident. However, several press cars followed them all the way to Salmon.

When the group arrived at the clinic, Jacques and Phydeaux looked to be in better spirits. Both wore bandages on various parts of their diverse anatomies and casts on limbs, but they looked willing and able to travel.

The press caught up to them just as they exited the small clinic, and it proved to be almost as much of an ordeal as Earl had warned. After a considerable battle, they managed to get to the cars and escape without revealing the truth. They stuck to the story that an unseen killer had been on the rampage. It wasn't a lie it was just a half-truth.

The drive to Boise gave Bobby an opportunity to think. Most of that time he tried to keep the gruesome memories of the past week out of his mind by thinking of Abby. They spoke very little, as night descended across the lonely Idaho highway.

Late that evening, Bobby dropped Jim and Linda at a Holiday Inn in Boise. A warm, night breeze rustled gently against his clothes, and an occasional car broke the otherwise silent parting.

"Stay cool, Bobby," Jim said. "Next time let's do an easy river, like the Zambezi or the Yangtze, okay?"

"I'll start working on the permits," Bobby replied, but the humor fell short even for him.

He kissed Linda on the cheek and hugged Jim, then watched as they carried their dry bags into the lobby of the motel.

*It's really over now*, he thought. He didn't know when he would see Jim and Linda again, but what saddened him most was that he didn't think they would ever share another river adventure together.

*Next week it will all be a memory*, he thought as he climbed back into the car and drove away alone. The drive home in Gretta's van proved to be the loneliest in his life.

Bobby and the rest of his friends returned to Oregon, where they tried to get on with their lives. He sub-contracted guides to run all of his trips on the McKenzie, while Jerry continued making frames and trailers, but neither of them got back on the river. He did get to see Portland. In fact, he drove up every Friday night and stayed until Sunday evening. He and Abby talked of getting married the following June. Amazingly the nightmares left him alone for the first time since childhood.

The bodies of the dead were eventually found, and the story was the biggest crime news since Ted Bundy's killing spree. The police blamed an unidentified satanic cult for the massacre, and the killers were still at large according to the reports. After a while, the coverage tapered off, and reporters quit coming around.

Ten months to the day, after the showdown at House Rock Rapids, Bobby and Abby went on a picnic in a beautiful park just south of Eugene to celebrate Abby's victory. Ernie Butters had been sentenced to death by injection and had lost his first appeal.

They hiked up Spencer's Butte to a lush green meadow, and laid out a tablecloth on the ground. It offered solitude and scenery. He sat in the grass and watched the puffy white clouds change shape on the dark blue canvas, while Abby fed him slices of apple.

The sky became more and more cloudy, until the air grew thick and sticky. It rapidly changed from a peaceful day in May, to a threatening, menacing afternoon. Dark cumulus clouds took shape over nearby Creswell and boiled as they approached. A line of wall clouds descended right before their eyes. Funnels dropped halfway to earth and receded back into the clouds.

*This can't be happening here; this is Oregon, not Texas.*

He looked up to see a massive cyclone lowering from the wall cloud. Trees, dirt, and debris immediately exploded into the sky as it touched down. He estimated the twister to be a quarter of a mile across at the ground. It appeared to be standing still.

Bobby grabbed Abigail by the hand and turned to run back down the trail, when he noticed the deathly quiet. He tried to run, but his feet stuck like magnets to metal ground. The daylight quickly faded into night. He turned his gaze back toward the path and again tried to raise his feet—without success.

He focused his every effort on moving away from the tornado. He grabbed

# CHAPTER THIRTY ONE

a nearby bush and tried to pull himself free of the powerful hold. He pulled harder, but couldn't move. Looking ahead, he saw another bush that stood between them and a two-foot deep trench where he perceived they would be safe. He fell on his stomach and tried to crawl—dragging Abby by her wrist. The wind blew with freight-train ferocity, but only the dreadful silence filled his ears. The bush ahead of him…rattled.

If he could crawl against the force that held him, he and Abby could make it to the safety of the ditch behind it. He strained and gained six inches. He strained again and gained six more. It was slow going, but he could see a light. *Funny.* He looked up and did see a light shining from deep in the same bush he was striving toward. It was a familiar amber-color.

Looking over his shoulder he saw the twister almost upon them. He glanced back at the bush. With suddenness, faster than his eye could focus, the bush was moved aside; the silent enemy charged—sending its message through the ether, directly to the center of Bobby's brain.

"AAAAAHHHHHHHHH!" he screamed as he sat up and frantically surveyed the meadow where he had dozed.

"What is it?" cried a startled Abby.

Bobby sat up, looked at the sunny afternoon, the wildflowers, and shivered. He knew the meaning of the dream.

"It's alive, Abby…It's still alive."

*The End*